Magna Carta

Book 4
in the
Border Knight Series

By
Griff Hosker

Magna Carta

Published by Sword Books Ltd 2018

SWORD BOOKS

Copyright © Griff Hosker First Edition

The author has asserted their moral right under the Copyright, Designs and Patents Act, 1988, to be identified as the author of this work.

All Rights reserved. No part of this publication may be reproduced, copied, stored in a retrieval system, or transmitted, in any form or by any means, without the prior written consent of the copyright holder, nor be otherwise circulated in any form of binding or cover other than that in which it is published and without a similar condition being imposed on the subsequent purchaser.
A CIP catalogue record for this title is available from the British Library.

Dedicated to Isabelle May Hosker, my first granddaughter!

Contents

Magna Carta 1
Prologue 4
Chapter 1 6
The Boar Hunt 6
Chapter 2 22
Border bandit 22
Chapter 3 43
Squire's quest 43
Chapter 4 57
Welsh war 57
Chapter 5 71
The brink of disaster 71
Chapter 6 89
The Durham solution 89
Chapter 7 101
Fighting for the Scots 101
Chapter 8 119
Traitor's fate 119
Chapter 9 133
The peaceful year 133
Chapter 10 141
Civil War 141
Chapter 11 159
Magna Carta 159
Chapter 12 174
The King comes North 174
Chapter 13 189
French Invasion 189
Chapter 14 207
The King is dead! 207
Chapter 15 229
The Battle of Lincoln 229
Epilogue 242
The End 243
Glossary 244
Historical Notes 245
Other books by Griff Hosker 256

Prologue

King John had lost Normandy. The Empire which the two King Henrys had built was gone. My great grandfather and grandfather had led men to help secure that land for King John's father, King Henry, and in a few short years, his son had lost it. All the men who had died in those wars had died in vain. Had they not gone to war in Normandy how many of them would have returned home to England to father sons who might now be tilling fields? We owed a duty to our king. Kings owed a duty to the people they ruled. King John did not seem to see that.

We had secured our northern borders. King John had not lost the north. He had made a good attempt to do so but thanks to the men I led, the knights of the north and of my valley, we had trounced King William at the Battle of Norham. The punitive reparations would keep him quiet for a little while. That did not mean we could relax our vigilance. There were still border raiders. Some were just brigands and bandits who thought to take from those who worked but others were more organised. Knights led men to terrorise and to take cattle. They crossed the wall and came south to take that which the farmers in the borderlands could not hold on to. It did not help that there was no Bishop of Durham. Philip of Poitou had died. As the Pope had excommunicated King John and there was an interdict on the clergy of England no replacement could be appointed. We were in limbo. Aimeric of Chartres, Philip of Poitou's nephew had taken the opportunity to take over the reins of the Palatinate. He held Durham until a new appointment could be made. We did not like each other. I did not trust him and he resented the fact that I had the authority to command him. I was lucky that the knights of Durham preferred me and were loyal to the Earl of Cleveland. Knights like David of Stanhope and Stephen of Spennymoor would keep a wary eye on Aimeric.

The one good thing which had come from the King's visit was that I now had my title returned to me and I had been given permission to build a wall around my hall. I was not allowed to build a keep and so I used strong towers and a good barbican to keep my family safe. My castle was a bastion against enemies from the north. In the year since the war, I had been able to give my attention to my valley and my family. I was enjoying the longest period of peace ever. From the time of the Battle of Arsuf to the Battle of Norham I had been fighting one enemy or another. The year of peace had allowed me to spend time with my wife and family. I had ridden my lands and visited my people. I had ensured that the lords who owed me fealty were also as secure as I was. We had peace but it would not last.

King John had had to travel to Ireland. There the barons had risen in revolt. I had not been asked to follow him. Had he done so I would have declined. I was needed in the north. There were elements in the north who were unhappy about King John and they murmured rebellion. They did not do so in my presence. I did not like King John however his son was but a child. Until he grew we could not replace the tyrannical King John. We had had one period of anarchy in this land and the war had lasted for eighteen years. I would not, willingly, help to begin another. I also knew why the northern barons were unhappy. They were in debt to the King. They owed him money. King John was a greedy king and they knew that he would seek to have the money he had loaned them paid back. Rebellion was a cheaper way of avoiding payment.

War would come. I might be caught in the middle of it and so, unlike many of the lords and barons in the heartland of England, I had retained all of the men at arms and archers who had fought the Scots. More, I had trained and recruited new ones. It was not an army I commanded but I led enough men to deter any foes, foreign or domestic. I had a fine line to tread between rebellion and loyalty. My family had always served the rightful King of England but King John was pushing that loyalty to the limits.

Magna Carta

Chapter 1
The Boar Hunt

My Aunt Ruth, who now lived with us, had seemed to become younger as the years went on. She had lived alone for so many years and I was her only family. Our letters, when I was in exile, had brought us close but it was since I had become lord of Stockton that she had become rejuvenated. Perhaps that was my children. I had four. Alfred, Rebekah, Isabelle and another son William who was now almost a year old. To my aunt, this was a joy. Her husband, Sir Ralph, had been killed a few years after she had married. She had lost one child and never had another. My family became the family she never had and she spent as much time as my wife would allow with them.

She came to me one evening after the children had been put to bed and my wife was telling the girls a story. "You know, Thomas, that I count myself the luckiest woman alive. I lost the only man I thought I could ever love and had given up on having my own family. Then you returned from the Holy Land and Sir William found me. He was a fine man. When you brought your family here then my world was complete. It was as near as I would get to a family of my own. I get to see bairns growing and developing into fine young people."

"You complete our world."

She smiled, "You are kind." She hesitated as though she was about to step over some invisible boundary into my privacy. "You have done well in the wars and brought in ransom but this castle costs coin to run. You are generous to your people and do not overtax them. Know you that I have a great deal of money. Sir William was not poor and I have been frugal. I know that our family lost much when King John came to the throne and I have ensured that we are prepared should the worst happen in the future."

I looked around. Although I trusted all of my servants if one of King John's spies heard my aunt he might deem it to be treasonous. "Do not fret, Aunt, I have also hidden coin. We will not have to be wanderers again."

She nodded, "Then you should know where my treasure is hidden, should ... well, I am no longer young." I was about to speak and she held up her hand. "I am not a fool. God has taken everyone that I love save you and your family. One day he will take me." She handed me a parchment. "William and I buried the chests so that King John's tax collectors would not get all that we had saved. Here is the map. You could dig it up now for I will no longer need it but it is hidden and it is safe."

I took it. "Thank you but I pray we shall not need it."

"As do I but..." she patted my hand and then stared into the fire. She was remembering. We sat in silence until the memories had been burned away by the fire. She stood and kissed me on the forehead. "May God watch over you, Thomas."

Alfred was now old enough to be interested in all things military. That was not a surprise. He lived in a castle that was filled with warriors. My men trained every day and Alfred had grown up with the sound of clashing steel and neighing horses. Rebekah had seen other young boys begin to train as squires. After Aunt Ruth had retired she joined me.

"Alfred, tonight, was asking when he could ride behind you with hauberk and helmet, shield and sword."

Alfred had been with me when I had gone to war. Petr was my squire but Alfred had come to watch the horses. He now had a taste for it. I had been a squire when I had been younger than Alfred. It was natural that he should wish to emulate his father. He was the eldest. I nodded, "I know. He has been asking me for some time." I smiled, "It is to be expected. He came with us on the last campaign. He was not a squire then but he was close to combat and he watched the others. He coped well. I think he could train to be a squire."

"We agreed that he was too young to train as a squire. The world is more dangerous now."

"I told him that."

"And you told him that it was my decision." I nodded. She shook her head. "You are a brave man, Thomas; the world knows that yet you fear to tell a boy no and you put it upon my shoulders."

She was right but, in my heart, I wanted my son to ride behind me. My men would watch out for him. We would see that he came to no harm. "I know that you do not wish him to go to war yet. I respect those views. Yet he will become a knight one day and that means that he must train as a squire first. You cannot change that. You have your own view and I respect it."

"But you do not agree with me." I said nothing. Whatever I said I would be in the wrong. "He has barely seen ten summers. Give him to me until he is twelve and then he can train. He is still my child."

She was making a mistake for all that Alfred had done last time was fetch food and groom horses. A servant could have done the same. He needed training but I conceded defeat. There was no war in the offing. "I will."

"Then you will tell him!" I nodded.

I was not looking forward to that conversation. It would not be helped by the fact that the sons of my archers and men at arms who were the same age and younger than Alfred were already training. You could not begin training an archer's body soon enough. My archers and men at arms also saw this as a way of giving their sons discipline. Training all day kept them out of mischief. It also made for good warriors.

I went out to the inner ward and climbed the steps to the fighting platform. The sun was just setting in the west and we always had good sunsets at this time of year. I walked around my walls, looking first into my town and then, as I passed through the gateway, to the well of St. John. As I had expected some of my men at arms were gathered there. It was a place of peace and many believed that it was special. All that I knew was that they gathered there each night and talked.

"Pleasant evening, lord."

I looked up as Henry Youngblood, who was captain of the guard that night, spoke. "Aye, it is Henry and all the better for the peace." I gestured to James Broadsword, Richard Red Leg and the others who were chatting at the well. "It is good to see old warriors such as James enjoying the peace of their later years."

Henry laughed, "If there was war, lord, then James would be the first with a sharpened sword. He is a warrior through and through."

"Aye well, the King is in Ireland. The Scots are quiet and we can enjoy the valley. There is no war for the present. How are your sons?"

"Tom and Sam are both getting to an age where they need something to occupy them. My wife is pulling her hair out. They climb everywhere and know how to find trouble even when there is none to be found!"

I laughed. "I am lucky! My Aunt keeps a close eye on Alfred and William is too small yet."

"Alfred will be a fine warrior, lord. He has the build and I have seen him ride. It comes naturally to him. He and his pony are often to be seen riding with Tam Hawker. The two of them love ferreting around in the woods. He has skills with a sword too. My men now say that they no longer take it easy with him. They are watching for his tricks."

I nodded, Tam was more than a hawker, he was my gamekeeper. However, his hawks, or rather my hawks, were his pride and joy. I had allowed Alfred to ride with him as a way of keeping him out of trouble while giving him skills that would be useful when he became a man. I knew that Alfred would still have pursuits to occupy him but he would be upset when I told him that he would not be beginning his training as a squire. I had made no promises but there had been an understanding. "Well, I will bid you goodnight and hope you have a peaceful watch."

"Thanks to your other lords we will be the last to discover trouble."

As I made my way back to my hall I knew that he was right. We had a ring of fortified halls and castles to the northeast and west. My men kept a good watch. Life was good.

The next morning, I braced myself for a confrontation with Alfred. My own mother had understood that I would go to war. She had thought she would have many more sons and daughters. She was fated to have just the one; me. My wife was more fortunate we had four.

I watched Alfred take his sword and hurry towards the outer ward to practise with the other squires and boys. Petr, my squire and Ridley the Giant's son, was supervising them. He was bigger and taller than all of them. My hauberk barely fitted him. He was a good teacher and he played no favourites. I watched as he organised the boys into pairs and handed out the wooden swords they used to practise with. Alfred was desperate to use the real sword he carried at his waist whenever he could. Petr knew the capabilities of each of the boys and youths because he paired them in order of ability rather than size.

I watched as Alfred sparred with Brian, the son of Padraig the Wanderer. It soon became obvious that while Brian was bigger, Alfred had far more skill. Without being cruel or patronising, he played with Brian. I could see that he would be able to defeat him any time he chose. It was almost as though he heard my thoughts, or, perhaps he caught a glimpse of me for he quickly beat Brian's guard and had his wooden sword at his opponent's throat in a blur of wood.

I clapped, "Well done you two. Come, Alfred, I need to have a word with you."

As we wandered away from the others he asked, nervously, "This was not because I finished him quickly is it, lord?"

"No, although I will have to speak with Petr. It is not fair on Brian to be toyed with like that. You need a better opponent."

He nodded, "And that can only be Petr."

It was confidence and not arrogance that made him speak thus. "You have skills."

"I will need them if I am to be a squire."

He had led me to the very point I wished to make, "And that will not be for a couple of years."

He stopped and stared at me. "But I am ready now. I came with you and the King to Norham! I did not disappoint you, did I?"

"No, but then you were little more than a servant. Had you come close to combat then you would not have been ready. Spend more time training. It may be less. Just until you have seen twelve summers. You cannot have too much preparation to be a knight."

"But I am ready now! I can ride, use a sword and lance! I train each day with the other squires and men at arms."

I made my voice steelier. "You are ready when I say that you are ready. You can continue to train with Petr. When you are a couple of years older then you will have even more skills."

He stared at me. It was as though he was trying to read my thoughts. "This is my mother's wish is it not?"

My slight hesitation gave him the lie, "It matters not. Besides, there is no war."

"Then if there is no war I cannot be in danger so I could become a squire. Or is it that you do not wish me to be your squire."

I held his shoulders, "That is not the reason." I needed something to make up for this. I felt guilty. I could not help it and I felt disloyal to my wife. I tried to be a good father and husband but it was all too easy to make mistakes. I was surer in battle! "I will tell you what. My knights and I have not hunted for a while. I will see Tam the Hawker and he can find us some animals. You will be with my knights and their squires."

"Yet I will not be a squire. I will be the earl's son clinging on to his surcoat."

I shook my head, "It is a chance to prove that you are the equal of the other squires but, if you are not confident…"

"I will do it! I will show my mother that I am almost a man!" He strode back with me to the castle keeping pace with me. He was showing me that he was becoming a man. As we went in I knew that King John was the way he was because his father had not spent as much time with him nor had his mother. He had grown up influenced by those who were not his family. I would not make that mistake. I was a father and knew my responsibilities.

It was typical of my wife that I could not do right for doing wrong. When I told her she was not happy, as I hoped she might be, she erupted! "A hunt! That is more dangerous than war! Animals do not play by any rules!"

I sighed, "Tam will be with him and you allow Tam to take him riding. What is the difference?"

Mollified she nodded. "I suppose I will have this with William too?"

I grinned, "Probably and more for he will see his big brother training with me. It is all your fault; you married a knight!"

She laughed, "That was a wise decision. Would that I could wave a wand and make this land peaceful so that my men would not need to risk their lives."

When I spoke with Tam he told me of two places where we might hunt. "In the woods between the two becks at Hartburn is a large family of wild pigs. They have been unsettling Tom the Pig's animals and damaging his fences. They need culling. If we can kill the old boar the others may move off. There is another large colony to the west of Elton. They may go there."

"Wild boar can be dangerous. And the other?"

"Between Hartburn and Yarm, there is a large herd of deer. They would be easier…. And safer." I nodded. I was about to say we would hunt the deer when Tam scratched his beard and said, "If it is young master Alfred you worry about do not. He is the best rider in your castle and has a good eye. I have watched him throw a spear. He rarely misses and he never falls from a horse."

"But a wild boar, Tam!"

"When he becomes a warrior, he will have to fight a more dangerous foe, a man. Until he has sunk a spear into flesh then he can never be a warrior. Forgive me being blunt, lord, but when you were young did you find it easy to sink a spear into a man's flesh?"

He was right and I knew it. "You would watch over him in the hunt?"

"As though he was my own, lord."

"Then we hunt the boar."

I sent word to my knights that there would be a hunt on the day before the next market. I knew that many of my lord's wives liked to visit the market. This would be an opportunity for them to do so and it might put me in my wife's good favours once more. She missed the company of other ladies.

Sir Edward, Sir William and Sir Fótr all said that they would like to hunt. That was a good number. Sir Ralph of Whorlton declined. He would have had the furthest to travel and his wife was with child again. Tam suggested taking half a dozen archers with us and I agreed. They had sharp eyes and even sharper senses. I had Mordaf and Gruffyd, my two Welsh archers as well as Dick One Arrow and Cedric Warbow who would come as escorts and to lead the horses which would, hopefully, carry back the carcasses of the animals.

Although we often hunted wild boar on foot it was more dangerous. The greatest danger in hunting them from horseback was to the rider's mount. I would take Skuld. She was the cleverest horse I had and appeared to have senses which were almost supernatural. She was, however, getting old and I would not take her to war again. I enjoyed hunting from the back of a horse but Alfred had never done this and so I spent the afternoon, the day before we hunted, showing him what he needed to do. I took the two boar spears.

"See, Alfred, they are different from a normal spear. This is a bar just behind the head. That prevents the spear from penetrating too deeply. Unless we are very lucky or highly skilled then it will take more than one spear to kill a boar. You will have to lean from your saddle. Tam tells me that you can do this."

He nodded, "Aye father."

"But you will not be riding your pony. It is too small. Alan, the horse master, has chosen you a small palfrey which he thinks you can ride. Come let us ride to the common and see how you get on with each other."

My son nodded and we headed to the stable. The union of a rider and his horse was a special one. The best pairings became one. That was so with Skuld and me, Flame and me. I could ride both with just my knees and the weight of my body. Alan brought out the horse. Star was a good-looking horse. That did not always mean that it would be a good one but it boded well. She nuzzled her head against Alfred and I knew that all would be well. If a horse shied from a new rider then it was to be avoided. A knight did not need a fearful horse. He needed a brave horse that would die for him. My father's, Storm Bringer, had died for him at the Battle of Arsuf.

I mounted Skuld and watched Alfred as he mounted his horse for the first time. I smiled at Alan, "I think this horse has a new master, Alan."

"Aye lord. I have been watching Master Alfred with the pony, Goldie, I knew he would be ready for a horse and prepared this one. She is a good one. Star still has a little growing in her. She will last him for three or four years."

My son looked at me. The look meant nothing to Alan but I knew that he was asking me if he would be a squire then.

As we rode through the gates I watched my son as he assessed his new horse. He did not waste time, as many might, waving to others to show them that he had something new. He wanted the best out of Star. The common had some of the animals from those who lived in the town. It was grazing for Stockton. There were, perhaps, a dozen cows, and goats there. There was no pen and no wooden wall. The animals were all tethered and so I led Alfred to the north side of the common. The woods were close to the edge along that side for the land fell away to the river. It would do.

I am not certain if mine was the best way to teach but it was my own and I was used to it. I showed Alfred what he had to do. I used a rogue weedy shrub that had grown just five paces from the wood. "This is the boar. When you ride you need to keep your horse as far away from the boar as possible. They have tusks that can rip out the guts of your horse. Star is smaller than Skuld and in even more danger than most horses. It means you have to lean out to the side when you ride. I will show you." I had the advantage that Skuld had done this before. As I leaned out she reacted by shifting her weight to the left. I raised my arm and thrust the spear into the bush. "You do not throw! The boar spear does not fly as well as an ordinary spear."

He nodded but I saw the nervousness in his eyes. He would want to impress me.

"You try."

He did better than I had expected and managed to lean out but the spear missed the bush by a whole pace. Alfred was disappointed.

I nodded, "Good."

"Good? But I missed!"

"Had you struck the bush the first time then it would have been remarkable and more than a little lucky. This way you will practise until you get it right. It will take the rest of the afternoon. Remember Alfred, this is a skill you can take to the battlefield." He looked at me. "When you chase men on foot you have to lean from the saddle. You do not throw your spear for then it is lost. You have to learn to thrust. This is training for war as well as the hunt."

Once he realised that he became focussed. Later, as we headed back, walking and leading our horses for Star was tired, Alfred was smiling. He had hit the bush on the last five passes. "You are ready but I will still have Tam riding behind you as well as two archers."

"I am not a baby!"

"No but you are a novice and none of us would risk your mother's wrath if aught happened to you. This is as close as I can take you to train for war. It is not a game. You are not sparring with Brian. Here the boar will try to kill you and your horse if he can." I saw my son look at his new horse. Already he was fond of it. "Horses die in war, Alfred, and in the hunt. For a knight, it is a fact of life. Remember that."

The hunt would change my son but that couple of hours on the common saw the change from the child to the man.

My knights and their families arrived in the early morning on the day of the hunt. Some had left home before dawn. We were already dressed for the hunt. We wore long leather boots and leather jerkins which covered our bodies and our knees. Our arms had forearm protectors. We would be riding through bushes and shrubs which would tear cloth to pieces. We also wore gauntlets. Boar hunting was a dangerous pastime. If Alfred had had his way we would have been hunting by dawn. The squires of my knights led the horses they would use for the hunt. While my wife greeted the ladies and their children we gathered in the stables. Sir Edward knew them as well as any. His father, Edgar had been one of my grandfather's scouts and Edward had been brought up here. He ruffled Alfred's hair, much to my son's annoyance.

"So young Master Alfred, today you ride on your first hunt! You will enjoy this."

"Did you enjoy your first hunt, Uncle?" My children all called Edward uncle for he was as close to an uncle as they were likely to have. He was now a grey beard.

He grinned, "My first hunt I was younger than you and on foot. Nor did I have a boar spear. I had a dagger for I was with my father and uncle, my namesake, Edward. As I recall I was a year or two younger than you." Alfred flashed me an irritated look. "We were beating. It was in the woods south of the river by Thornaby. Aye. It was a day much as this one."

Sir William said, "Then we are in the hands of an expert. I confess, Sir Edward that I have rarely hunted the wild boar and I have never killed one."

"Nor me." Fótr had not been born in England. He came from Sweden. I was not even certain they had boars there.

"Then you will have to watch Sir Edward and me. We hunt them because they are hurting our people. Normally we might spare most of the herd but not today. Kill as many as you can and, hopefully, the others will move away from men." I smiled, "And if we are successful then we eat well! There is nothing finer than wild boar!"

Tam led us towards the Oxbridge. We passed the farm there. Ralph of the Oxbridge waved as we passed. "You hunt the wild boar, my lord?"

I nodded, "We do and we blood young Alfred."

"Then you do us a favour, lord. They have been eating my crops. The clay here makes it hard enough to grow them as it is."

"God willing, we will end the threat."

The land dropped through scrubby bushes to the green beck. We would follow it to the place where it was joined by the muddy beck. I suspect the old people who had lived here when the Romans came had different names but my folk had named them thus and they stuck. We had to climb a little for the stream had made a deep cut. It was there that we tied the horses that would, hopefully, carry home our dead boar.

The damp boggy woodland which lay just four hundred paces ahead was perfect for wild boar. Had they stayed there then we might have only taken a couple but we now had more farms close by. Tom the Pig provided the town with ham in the winter. If these boars continued to prosper then my folk would have less to eat. Before we rode off we looked to Tam. He seemed to sniff the air. Shaking his head, he said, "The wind is behind us. They will smell us. We will have to take a detour."

We headed along the greenway to the lonesome house. A family had lived here in the time of my great grandfather. A

Scottish raid had taken the wife and the children. When their father returned from fighting for the Warlord he hanged himself. Men said that it was haunted and none would live there. Once we had passed the house, I smiled as I saw some of the squires clutch their crosses. Then we headed up the ridge which led through the woods. It brought us out at Tom the Pig's farm.

He came out to speak with us, "Thank you for doing this, Sir William. These boars are a menace and they are damnably dangerous."

"It is Sir Thomas who leads this hunt. I am sorry that you have lost some of your pigs."

He nodded, "The buggers get the scent of the boar and off they go! Still, my lord, not as bad as a Scottish raid. You can't eat Scotsmen!"

We headed off across the small field he tilled for his vegetables. I could see that the boar had eaten everything. We were now silent and rode in a long line with Tam at the fore. Once he scented the boars he would signal and drop back behind me to protect Alfred. I too was as nervous as some of the others for I had not hunted boar for some time. The boars liked to forage around the roots of the oak trees which grew so well in the wood. They grew best close to the green beck. Tam held up his arm. The beasts were close. I could not hear them but a sudden gust of wind brought their stink to me. One reason why hunting was such good training for battle was that men had to look for signals and to act as one while fighting for themselves. As Tam moved backwards I raised my boar spear.

Edward and I were in the centre of the line with William and Fótr at our sides. Our squires were behind as were the Tomas brothers. Our squires carried a supply of spare spears. We were entering a tangle of bushes and small trees. Once the herd heard our noise then they would flee and we would have to react quickly. The secret was to get as close to them as we could. Skuld was a marvellous horse. She picked her way delicately through the undergrowth. Her ears moved constantly and she sniffed the air. It was like riding a good hunting dog. We did not use dogs. They barked and could get too excited. Most dogs were too brave for their own good and I had seen too many good dogs eviscerated by a boar's tusks!

I spied a sow. She was a fat one. I raised my spear and Skuld stepped a little closer. I was almost within striking distance when Fótr's horse stepped on an old branch and it cracked. It was then I spied the old tusker who ruled this herd. He was less than ten paces from me and his beady little eyes swivelled in my direction. I saw the scars on his back. They were the marks of spears as well as tusks. This one was a survivor. He chose me as his target.

He turned and came at me so quickly that I barely had time to react. It was Skuld who saved me. She reared and spun as he came for her. I stood in the stirrups and found myself above the beast. He was fast for an old one and, even as his head turned to rip the guts from my horse I had thrust down to a point at the base of his neck where his spine met his skull. Sometimes you aim for such a place and miss by the width of a little finger. In that case, the beast is just hurt. I was lucky. I found the exact spot I was aiming for. My spear drove down and the life went from the ancient boar.

As I was turning to reach for the spear proffered by Petr, the sow I had spotted ran at me. It was Alfred and Tam who saved me. She would not have killed me but a gored leg would have weakened me as a warrior. Alfred's spear struck first and he rammed it in her side. She squealed and turned on him. As she did so she exposed the back of her neck to Tam. He struck. Not as clean a blow as mine it nonetheless slowed her. Dick One Arrow and Cedric Warbow sent two arrows in to her at point-blank range and she died.

The woods were filled with the sound of fleeing, squealing boars and horses and riders crashing through the thin branches of small trees and bushes. Petr handed me a second spear and I whirled Skuld to follow the others down the valley. This was easier for they were on the run. If they turned they would face two or three spears. Mordaf and Gruffyd were using short hunting bows and they were using them from the back of their horses. Their arrows would not kill. They would wound and slow. I heard the splash of water as some boars crossed the beck and began to clamber up the slope on the opposite side. That suited me for the wood went, with just one break for the road, to the woods at Elton. They could go there with my blessing.

We stopped at the edge of the stream and hunted the few that remained. I turned to see that all of my men had survived as had their horses. Fótr's horse had a long wound along her flank. It would need stitching. I was not certain if he was more upset about his horse or the fact that he had alerted the boars to our presence. None of us mentioned it. Tam estimated that at least two young boars had escaped along with five sows and five young ones. They would join the Elton herd. We had killed the old boar, three sows, three young pigs, two boars and a sow and seven suckling pigs. While my archers went for the horses Tam and I lifted one of the young pigs onto the back of his horse and we took it to Tom the Pig. He had not expected the gift. A wild pig was a treat.

"Thank you, lord! I will say a prayer for you and your family on Sunday!"

"Thank you, Tom."

By the time we had reached our men they had gutted the boars and sows and they were already on the horses. We walked our animals back for we had to use two of the archers' horses too. Tam carried the offal in a sack he had brought for just such a purpose. When we passed Ralph of Oxbridge Tam gave him a heart and the liver and kidneys from two of the animals. I gave him a suckling pig. We had more than enough.

Fótr went with Tam once we reached our castle. He needed his horse healing. I sent one of the sows for my men at arms and a young sow and two suckling pigs for my archers. They had earned it. Geoffrey had servants ready to take away the other carcasses. Nothing would be wasted. The skins would be taken and cured. The meat would be butchered. The best cuts would be cooked for the feast. The cook would make other cuts into a stew while the rest would be preserved. The hooves would be rendered down. They made a good glue and the bones would be made available to those in the town. They would enrich stews and soups. Our butchers always left plenty of meat on them.

As Alfred and I walked to my hall he said, "I see what you meant, father. When that sow turned on you I did not have time to think. My spear did not penetrate as far as it should. If that had been a man then I would have been dead."

"I thank you and Tam. As the old warriors would say, 'I owe you a life'."

He smiled and shook his head, "You gave me life, father, you owe me nothing."

I nodded, "You managed to kill the suckling pigs easier."

"I made certain that I struck hard and true. They died quickly."

My wife, Lady Margaret appeared in the door. She had Isabelle in her arms. My youngest daughter was now at the age when she recognised and reacted to me. She giggled. My wife pulled her away from me. "Do not touch her. I can smell the blood on you from here. Bathe first." She glanced down at Alfred. It might have appeared a casual look but I knew she was checking to see if he was whole.

"Our son is fine and he acquitted himself well today."

"Good. Had he not then you would have been as well to spend the night in the woods." She was a protective mother!

After we had cleaned ourselves we dressed and went to my hall where Geoffrey had some chilled wine for us. It had been a warm day and now, as the afternoon sun began to slip into the west it was the perfect drink. The other squires and knights were there.

"How is your horse, Fótr?"

"Tam says that she will heal but she will need to stay here for a month or two."

"I have room in my stable. You have other horses?"

"Thanks to the Scots I have many."

I was lucky in the men I led. All were like family to me. Apart from Aunt Ruth, I had no other. We got on well. I had eaten in some halls, like those in Sweden and the Holy Land where you could not enjoy the food for you were too busy wondering who was plotting against you. We just got on. It helped that Aunt Ruth presided over the diner like a matriarch. All deferred to her. She was the arbiter of disputes. Edward, in particular, regarded her as a surrogate mother. It was she who had sent him to me in Sweden and she had given him her manor of Wulfestun. For his part, he fretted and fussed over her. He was attentive to her every wish. When the meat she was cutting looked tough it was

Edward summoned a servant to have it replaced with some of the fillet. I found myself wishing that this could never end.

It was Sir William who brought me back to earth. "Sir Thomas, I had visitors last week. They were priests on their way to Durham."

"They called at Hartburn and not Stockton?"

"Do not be offended, lord. It was market day and they feared that the road would be thronged. They took the back road which passed the old residence of the bishop."

Mollified I nodded, "What did you learn?" I noticed that Edward and Fótr were now paying close attention.

"Robert Fitzwalter is stirring up the barons again."

That could affect us. One of his distant cousins was Sir Hugh Fitzwaller. Sir Ralph had married his daughter.

"He is always stirring up trouble."

"Aye lord, but this time, on the orders of the King He sent his half-brother William Longespée, the Earl of Salisbury. he was summoned to the tower. Fitzwalter has fled to Normandy where he raised the standard of rebellion there."

"And the King?"

"On his way back from Ireland."

I nodded, "Then it seems our peaceful life is about to end."

The table had gone quiet and my wife said, "Why? The Baron has fled."

"He has many friends in England. They will see this as more evidence of the tyranny of King John." I saw my wife's hand go to her mouth.

Aunt Ruth said, "If my nephew cannot speak openly in these walls then it is a sad day. Besides, when a King acts like a tyrant it is up to all good men to say so!"

Chapter 2
Border bandit

My son accepted the fact that he had almost two years to wait to become a squire. It had been the hunt that had shown him his limitations rather than my wife's words. He had seen how hard it was to kill an animal. Had it not been threatening my life I am not even sure that he would have stabbed it with as much force as he mustered. With that problem temporarily solved I was able to concentrate on the running of my manor. I made sure that I regularly visited York to speak with the Archbishop, Geoffrey. I had helped him on more than one occasion and he trusted me. Since Philip of Poitou's death, I had been the lord he could rely upon to keep a watch on the Palatinate. I was no fool; I knew that he wished the new Bishop to be one of his priests. The men who ruled the church sought power just as much as kings and barons. I also helped to ensure that the roads leading to the north were guarded. He and the High Sheriff did not get along. As he was King John's half-brother, the Archbishop was a friend in case I needed a counsellor with the King's ear. Like all of the clergy in England, he was suffering because of the interdict and his excommunication. Money was in short supply.

I was visiting York with Petr, Alfred and four of my men at arms. It was November. I could buy gifts for my wife and Aunt Ruth. We had had a good year and my coffers were full. One advantage of my friendship with the Archbishop was the accommodation he offered us. We stayed in his palace. I had not warned him of my impending arrival but his captain of the guard admitted me to his hall directly we arrived. His steward, who was also a priest took Petr, Alfred and me to our chamber. The men at arms would be housed in the guard room. They did not mind. They could enjoy the pleasures of the Saddle Inn. The whores there were clean and the prices reasonable. There had been much competition to accompany me on this trip to York.

"His Grace has some business to deal with. I am sorry for the delay, lord, but I have no doubt that he will have you dine with him. Until then please use any of the chapels or cloisters for contemplation."

Magna Carta

He did not know me. I could not sit and contemplate. When we had changed I led Petr and Alfred to walk through the narrow streets close by the cathedral. Known as the Shambles they were a warren of little streets and alleys. I would not wish either my son or squire to venture there alone but my surcoat was known and it would take a brave man to risk the wrath of the Earl of Cleveland. The two of them were both intrigued and terrified in equal measure by what they saw as we walked from the cathedral to the river. I was recognised by men who had fought alongside me and others knew my story. The hero of Arsuf was a song sung by troubadours throughout the length and breadth of England. Most of them were an exaggeration. I had learned long ago that no matter what I said they preferred the heroic version of the troubadour.

I used the walk as an opportunity to look at the stalls which sold goods I could not buy in Stockton. I would return in daylight, for the short days meant that dusk was upon us. The goods on sale were also the poorer ones. The better buys were to be had early in the day. You came at this time to buy a bargain. If you wanted quality then you came in the morning. I wanted quality. There was an inn by the river. It was not the Saddle. That was in the Shambles. This one had a view over the river and was frequented by those with Viking blood. I chose it because I thought it might help Petr think of the land of his mother's birth. They also served fine beer. The Vikings brewed the best ale. All of my men said so. I think my men at arms might have chosen this inn but for the fact that they knew that it might lead to fights and a Viking fight ended in death more often than not.

Alfred took it all in with wide eyes. He was drinking strong beer. I knew his mother would not approve but Petr and I could watch him. He was fascinated by the tattoos some of the warriors had on their faces. Most had plaited beards and moustaches. I saw one with bones in the ends. It may have been animal bones but it impressed Alfred. As we headed back, through the dark and chilly streets he asked Petr, "Why did your father leave your mother's homeland, Petr?"

"He followed your father. He was not born in Sweden but my mother was. She loved her homeland but she said it is a cold place. The knights there are poorer than the knights here. My parents are content here." He smiled, "In Sweden, I would not have the chance to become a knight."

"Are you a Viking?"

Waving his arm around the men he laughed, "At best half-Viking. My father is big enough to have been a Viking hero. These are not real Vikings; at least not most of them. A real Viking spends most of his time at sea. He seeks adventure. My mother told me of men who sailed beyond the western seas."

"Did they not fall off the end of the world?"

"Who knows? They never returned but if you found a land beyond the Western Sea why would you return? I know that there are men who sailed further west than Miklagård is to the east and they found a land there without a single person. The world is wider than we know, Alfred."

The Archbishop sent word to us, when we arrived back at his palace, that he would dine with us but it would be just a small affair. His servant said that there would be fewer than twelve people in attendance there. That was unusual.

I saw that he had reserved a seat next to him. On the other side of me was a man who was obviously neither warrior nor priest. He had the corpulent look of a merchant. As we entered I said, "Petr, watch Alfred. It seems we will not be seated together."

"Aye lord."

Petr knew how to drink little and to keep his eyes and ears open. He would ensure that Alfred did the same.

"Sir Thomas, this is an unexpected pleasure."

"Thank you, Your Grace."

"Let us dispense with these titles. I am Geoffrey and you are Thomas. We are, after all, old friends."

I immediately became suspicious. He was being effusively friendly. We were not old friends. I had done him some favours and he knew I was a bastion to the north that was as far as it went. He wanted something from me. I would drink sparingly.

He waved over his steward, "You may begin to serve now. We are all here."

I said, "I am sorry you waited for us. We were not told of a time."

He shook his head, "This is my fault. When I heard that you were here I altered our dining arrangements. The men around this table were specially selected."

The word conspiracy flashed across my mind. I recognised a couple of the men at the table. The Chancellor of York was there as was his Dean, the leading canon and the captain of his guards. The merchant and the man next to him I did not recognise. When we had been in the town I had heard rumours of a rift between King John and his half-brother. I had dismissed them as idle gossip. Perhaps they were not just rumours. My visit to York suddenly seemed like a bad idea.

The conversation centred on the food. The Archbishop of York kept a good table. He had been Chancellor of England under his father, King Henry, and a good Chancellor knew how to accrue coin. The Archbishop was rich. We had just finished the roast pike when the Archbishop broached the subject which was the reason for the small gathering.

"How remiss of me. I have failed to introduce you to the guest seated next to you. Sir Thomas, Earl of Cleveland, this is Godfrey of Beverley."

I turned. The merchant looked older than me but, on closer inspection, I could see that he was not. The fat had hidden his age. The man smiled at me. His hands were adorned with rings and, around his neck hung a seal of office. I did not recognise it. He smiled, "This is an honour, Earl. We have all heard of your exploits; even in Beverley."

I hated having to make conversation with those I did not know. I had grown up in a world of war. It had only been for a brief time in La Flèche and since I had come to Stockton that my wife had forced me to speak to those who were not warriors. I was uncomfortable and did not enjoy it. At least in my castle, my wife would arrange the seats so that I could speak with other knights.

"And what is it that you do, Godfrey of Beverley?"

"I trade in sheep and horses." He held up his seal. "King John has graciously given me the right to trade with Flanders and the Baltic." He turned to the man next to him. He was an older man. He was older than I was. He had the gnarled hands of a farmer. He was in direct contrast to the merchant and they made an incongruous pair. "This is my elder brother, Ranulf. He has a farm at Matfen, north of the Roman wall."

I suddenly became intrigued. There was a tale here. Why did the two brothers live so far from each other? What was Ranulf of Matfen doing in York?

The Archbishop spoke, "Godfrey came, with his brother, to speak to me several days ago. As I am due to return to Normandy in a day or so this has proved inconvenient for me. I believe that you were sent here by God."

I had been intrigued and now I was confused. What had this to do with me? "Sent by God?"

Ranulf spoke. I was aware that the conversation in the room had died. I now saw the reason for the intimate gathering. The Archbishop could trust all of the people in the room. "My lord, I came to the Archbishop for I need help." His voice was distinctly from the north. He sounded different from his brother. "A month since, when I was at the market in Hexham selling some sheep, my farm was raided by Scots from across the border. There is a lord in Hawick." He shook his head. "He is no lord! He is a bandit that the King of Scotland sanctions. Alexander of Hawick is an evil and venal man. He took my wife and two daughters, Sarah and Maud. He murdered my men and took their families too. He sent a demand for ransom. He knows that my brother is rich."

Godfrey spread his jewelled hands. "And I would pay the ransom but my coin is all tied up at the moment. Come January and I will have the coin which the Scot demands." He shook his head, "I have no children. My wife died. Sarah and Maud are the nearest I will ever have to my own children. Believe me, Sir Thomas, if I had the gold then I would pay it."

I was still confused. This had nothing to do with me. "What about the Sheriff of Newcastle?" I did not like the man and he had tried to have me killed but he was the law in that part of the land.

The Archbishop shook his head, "Ranulf appealed to him but he said that as they were across the border he would not risk the peace,"

I felt myself becoming angry, "That man did little to help us win the peace that we won. It is the Scots who have broken the peace by raiding across the border!"

The Archbishop smiled, "See, Godfrey, I told you that Sir Thomas had been sent by God."

"What have I got to do with this?"

"Thomas, the world knows you to be a true knight. You do the right thing even if it means exile. You do not bow the knee to tyrants and you do not allow the innocent to suffer at the hands of evil men. You tried to save Prince Arthur and his sister. It was not you who failed them it was others. We would have you go across the border and bring back the three women and the rest of the captives."

I was stunned. I looked down the table and saw my son and squire's faces. Their expressions were those of pride and not shock. "Let the Scot know that you cannot pay yet."

Ranulf said, "Lord, I did that. He said he did not believe us. He said that we were delaying. He sent the head of one of the boys he had taken as proof that he meant what he said. If the ransom is not paid by the second week of December then he will give my daughters to his men to be used."

There was a pause to allow that to sink in and then Godfrey said, "And the ransom would be higher. I cannot allow my nieces to suffer. Sir Thomas, the money means nothing! I will pay the ransom to you if you can fetch back my brother's family."

I shook my head, "If I took the ransom then that would make me no better than this Alexander of Hawick." I turned to the Archbishop, "Geoffrey, York is rich. Use the money from the See. Godfrey will pay it back in January."

"I would that I could but York is not as rich as you might think. King John has taxed us harshly this year and I am leaving for Normandy at the end of the week. I fear, my lord, that if you do not rescue them then two young women and countless others will have their lives ruined."

I pushed away the beef. It tasted sour in my mouth. They were taking advantage of me. I knew that. Despite what the Archbishop had said I knew that he could have found the money from somewhere. I looked over to Alfred. My wife had almost been abducted. I had been sent to rescue her and that had turned out well. I had failed to save Prince Arthur and his sister was now incarcerated in one of King John's castles. Perhaps the Archbishop was right. Perhaps I had been sent here by God. I saw Petr looking at me. His mother's people believed in three spirits who determined men's fate. They spun and they wove. I did not believe it but this seemed to me to be fated.

I turned to Ranulf. The Archbishop and Godfrey of Beverley were immaterial. "Ranulf, how old are your daughters?"

He beamed, "You will save them?"

I shook my head, "Answer my questions for I am not yet decided."

"Sarah is twelve and Maud is sixteen. Maud would have been wed already but the man to whom she was promised died in the battle against King William of Scotland."

That was another reason I would accept the task. One of the men who had fought for me had died. Maud's life had almost been ruined. If I sat and did nothing I could not sleep at night. Had I not come to York I would have been blissfully unaware of their plight. This was like the box of Pandora. It had been opened. The carrot was out of the ground.

"And this Alexander of Hawick, does he have a castle?"

"He has a fortified hall with a tower. The men he has are all bandits. They raid both sides of the border. The land between the wall and Scotland is a wasteland. Will you help me, lord?"

I looked around at the expectant faces. I did not want to do this but I knew that I had to. Being a knight had responsibilities and this was one of them. "I will, Ranulf, but I will need you to come with me. I know not the land and your family do not know me."

"Lord, I am no coward. This is my family. Without them, I am nothing and my life is nothing." He glanced at his brother, "You need not fear for me. I know how to use a sword."

Smiles replaced the looks of apprehension. The Archbishop put his hand on mine, "You will not regret this, Thomas."

"I hope not for I have lost enough men already. They are as valuable to me as your coin is to you, Geoffrey."

The Archbishop lowered his voice, "Do not think badly of me, Thomas. I have a document written for you. It may help should you incur the King's wrath." He saw the look on my face and he smiled, "Sometimes doing the right thing is the wrong thing to do. Let us say that what little I can do I will. The document will be ready for you when you leave." I did not understand his enigmatic epigram. It did not matter. I had a quest.

I was aware that my shopping expedition would have to wait. We would have to ride back to Stockton on the morrow. Godfrey spent the rest of the meal saying how he would repay me. I saw, in Ranulf's eyes that he knew the real reason I was doing this and it had nought to do with gold or silver.

Eventually, I asked, "How much is this ransom?"

"A thousand pounds of silver."

My mouth must have dropped open for I saw the Archbishop smile. "But King John only asked for ten thousand pounds of gold in reparations from King William."

Ranulf nodded, "The Scots have been doing this along the border since the war ended. It has never been as much as this but others have had family members ransomed for five hundred pounds of silver. However, this is the furthest south they have ventured." He shook his head, "I should have taken my family with me then I would not have lost them nor the eight men who died defending them."

"No, brother, it is my fault." Godfrey of Beverley turned to me. "I visited a year since. I confess that I took servants and fine horses. All saw how rich I was. I was vain and I have been punished by God. I told all of my riches. I was boasting."

"And thus, are sins punished." The Archbishop had the last word.

When we retired to our quarters it was Alfred who was full of questions. Petr silenced him. "Alfred your father has much to ponder. He has to decide which men to take and how he can safely extract the three women and more from a tower. It will not be easy."

He was right. I could not simply turn up with my retinue and demand their return. Alexander of Hawick would hold up in his tower. I needed to devise some means of luring the lord from his tower and hall. Only then could I risk attacking. The sixty miles from York to Stockton would be the time to rigorously question Ranulf. We needed to strike sooner rather than later. This bandit would be warier the closer it came to the second week of December. I needed to get home and leave immediately. I had a night and a day to plan this raid.

    We were up early. This was a church and the priests had been up since the middle of the night, praying. The Archbishop and his chancellor were waiting for me in the refectory. Before I had even eaten the Archbishop handed me two parchments. "This first is the document I promised you last night. It grants you the revenue from the lands around Northallerton." I looked up at him. He nodded, "It may help you to protect the Baron there. I know his affiliations and family ties. Besides, the coin will help when King John sends his taxmen. In addition, it is a buffer to your lands from the south." He handed me the other piece of parchment. "This one is my written orders to cross the border and rescue the hostages. I do not think the King would worry about this but you have other enemies, do you not? The Sheriff's hands will be tied by this parchment." The Chancellor handed him a purse. "I cannot pay the ransom but I can give you this. It is a hundred crowns. I would not have you risk your horses and men without recompense."

    I took the purse simply because I would be able to give the coins to my men. They would be risking their lives for my honour rather than my life and it was only fair that they should reap the benefit.

    I never saw the Archbishop again. He left for Normandy and died a year or so later. Due to the interdict, no Archbishop could be appointed and the land grant was invaluable. King John took the revenue from the See to finance his wars. That was in the future. As we rode north I concentrated on the matter in hand. I learned that Alexander of Hawick had many manors around the border. He had half a dozen disreputable knights who followed his banner and fifty or so bandits who posed as men at arms. In a straight battle, I would easily win. This would not be a straightforward battle.

    By the time we approached the village of Appleton, south of Yarm, I had formulated my plan. It would be too late to leave by the time we reached Stockton and I would have to send riders for the men who would accompany me. I sent Richard Red Leg ahead to warn my wife of our guest and then to ride to Fótr's hall. I would need just one knight. This would need archers and my doughty men at arms.

As we crossed on the ferry Alfred said, "This is not war. Can I come with you?"

I shook my head. "This is more dangerous than war. In war there are rules. Squires are not deliberately attacked. These are bandits and brigands. A wild pig is more civilised than these. You have another year, at least, to serve before you can become my squire. Use it to develop those skills you will need. Can you play a rote yet?" He shook his head. "Sing a ballad?"

"Father, these are not knightly attributes. It is horsemanship and swordsmanship I need."

I laughed, "To be a knight you need other skills. I have never needed to play a rote or sing a ballad since Arsuf but, before then, I had to learn. Use the time now rather than when you are a squire. It has to be endured. You are lucky that you can read and write. You have three languages and that helps."

Petr nodded, "I still need all of those skills, Alfred. I may never become a knight for some of them seem beyond my grasp. Listen to your father. Use the year well."

When my wife met Ranulf she smiled and made him welcome but when he was taken to his chamber she said, "What does this mean, husband?"

I sighed, "It means I ride north on the morrow." I told her all.

She shook her head and, smiling, kissed me. "You are a good man and a true knight. You cannot leave those girls with such a man as you describe but you will take care, will you not? This valley needs the Earl of Cleveland just as much as that family."

I went directly to my warrior hall. David of Wales lived there. I sent Petr to fetch his father. He lived in a small farmhouse to the east of the Oxbridge. While we awaited him, I told David about our problem. He nodded, "This will not be easy, lord. Bandits who live in woods can be overwhelmed but with a tower, these will be like trapped rats and they will fight hard. It is not the numbers we need. It is a good plan."

"And I hope I have one. We will wait until Ridley comes before we speak of it. Which men will you take?"

He knew his archers well and he knew those who served Sir Fótr. We made a list of thirty archers we would take. When he arrived, Ridley knew of the task. I saw from his face that this father of seven needed no inducement to rescue two girls.

"How many men will we need, Ridley?"

"We need enough to overcome and then subdue them, lord but not so many that they will hear of our coming. If you take Sir Fótr's men then twenty should suffice."

"Good," I told them of my plan and then went back to my hall.

Sir Fótr arrived halfway through our meal. "I came as soon as Richard Red Leg spoke to me. I am here to serve you, lord."

"This is not war, Fótr. You can say no if you choose."

He smiled. "I am a bachelor knight. I have no one to worry about at home. I just have my squire, John. If I fell then you would appoint another knight. It is good."

When I had explained my plan to him he returned to his hall. We would ride to Norton before heading north. My horse master, Alan, chose good horses which could cope with the rough terrain we would encounter. I took Skuld with me. She was getting old and I feared this would be one of the last times she went to war. Too old to breed I would retire her to my fields. She had earned the right.

We headed north quickly and made Matfen an hour after dark. It was the advantage of travelling with so few men. The men at arms and archers made do with Ranulf's barn and we stayed in the house. Ranulf had four men left to him. They had been with him at the market. Their women had been taken but they were not for ransom. The four were desperate to come with us and rescue their own wives from captivity. They would be enduring a form of slavery. They would be kept by the bandits to be used when they chose. They were keen to leave. They would be our scouts.

We went over our plans. Northwest of Hawick lay the small village of Denum. It was where the brigands kept their animals. It had a small unfortified hall and there were ten men at arms who watched the animals. The men whose wives had been taken believed that their women had been taken there. Ridley the Giant would take two of the Matfen men, six archers and fifteen men at arms. They would capture the hall and drive the animals south. Ridley would ensure that at least one man survived the attack to take the word back to Alexander of Hawick. I counted on the bandit knight chasing after English raiders. When he did so then we would assault the hall and the tower. It was not a perfect plan but we all agreed that it had the greatest chance of success. As it was just five miles from the tower it would allow Ridley and his men to rejoin us before Alexander of Hawick reached Denum.

We had forty miles to ride and in the short days of early winter, we would have to travel mainly in the dark. That suited us for we would be hidden by darkness. One of the scouts, Rafe, knew of a place we could camp. As we headed north-west, before dawn had broken, the weather turned. Flecks of snow fell with sleet and rain. It made for uncomfortable riding but it would hide us. As what passed for the day progressed the snow gradually replaced the sleet. By the time we reached the deserted huts in the middle of the forest, there was a layer of white all around us. We would be hidden.

The huts had belonged to English folk who had been driven from their homes by the constant raids from Scotland. The walls stood and most had part of their roof remaining. By using cloaks, we were able to stay dry. We would be just five miles from Hawick. I had the men repair the huts as best they could and then I had them put logs down between the houses. It gave protection and I had plans for the future.

That night, as we ate our frugal meal I spoke to Ridley and his men. "Take the animals and drive them south. If you are pursued then abandon the animals and get here quickly. I do not wish you and your men to be risked. Besides, I will need you to fight this Alexander. We can always collect the animals later on. The priority will be the captured women." Ranulf, along with other farmers, had had many cattle stolen. If we were able we would return them but I wasn't hopeful.

We rode through virgin snow. It was a danger I had not anticipated. The Scots would be able to follow us. We could do little about the weather. It would slow up the brigands when they rode to Denum but, equally, it would slow up Ridley and his men as they tried to get to us quickly. They could not come the direct route. They would have to come in a loop.

After we parted from Ridley we took the path along Siltrig Water; the small stream which led to Hawick. The blizzard which had begun in the middle of the night still raged. It would keep people indoors. We could ride in the icy water and hide our tracks. Ridley would not have that luxury. I followed Egbert and his brother Ethelbert. When their families had been taken they had scouted out this stream and discovered it was the best way to reach the town. The stream joined the river which flowed northeast and eventually joined the Tweed not far from Jedburgh. The hall and tower lay at the confluence of the stream and the river.

Any man we met would now be an enemy. Our archers followed the two scouts with bows at the ready. They did not have great range loosing from the back of a horse but they were accurate and would be able to silence any Scot who threatened to give us away. The snow had abated but the wind still blew flurries in our faces. Even the Scottish dogs which might have given away our position were indoors and silent.

We stopped in a stand of trees some four hundred paces from the tower. Egbert stopped us before we could be seen and we dismounted. Our horses had had a hard ride and needed rest. I wriggled my way to the eaves and peered at the tower. There were sentries on the top. It had one door which was reached by a ladder. That meant the women and the warriors would be in the fortified hall. That too was accessed by a single door. The difference was that this one had stone steps leading to it. While we waited I watched and saw half a dozen warriors emerge, go to the side of the tower and make water. The sentries bantered with them. The wind prevented me from hearing them but it boded well for it showed that they did not expect danger. On the far side of the hall, closer to the river were the houses and farms which made up Hawick. I saw smoke spiralling from them as they kept warm inside their homes. Leaving Will son of Robin to watch I returned to the others. I took the bread and ham from Petr.

"They look relaxed. My plan should still work. David, have four archers watching the tower. They cannot climb into it quickly. We stop any who flee there. We will burn any out if there is time. Fótr, we will lead the rest of the men for the hall. There is but one door in and out. With the rest of our archers to give us cover we should be able to break in. That is not the hard part. That will come when we try to escape. We fall back to the place we camped last night and there we will give them battle. Ranulf you and your men will have to protect your people. We can fight the bandits but not defend the women at the same time."

"Fear not, lord, once we get them back we will stop them taking them again."

We sat to wait. Until Ridley struck we could do nothing. Will had just been relieved when one of his reliefs, John the Archer, ran up to us. "Lord, a rider has just ridden in from the northeast."

Leaving the rest to prepare Fótr and I ran to the eaves. Would the Scots take the bait? We knew from Ranulf and his men the rough numbers who would oppose us. If the majority left then we might succeed. If not then it could be bloody. The rider had left his horse outside and run into the hall. That meant they did not keep a good watch from the hall; just the tower. My archers could give us time to get closer to the hall before the alarm was given. Suddenly the door of the hall burst open and the warriors ran to something I had not seen from my vantage point. There was a door in the side leading to stables that lay before the hall. They wasted time clearing the snow to allow them in.

It was then I saw Alexander of Hawick. He was a huge man. He shouted and bawled at his men. He wore a short hauberk. His arming hood hung down and he held his helmet in his hand. It was an old fashioned one with a nasal and strengtheners over the crown. His sword was a long one. I had seen them before. They were called a hand and a half sword. Most men would need two hands to wield one but some men, large men with big hands and arms like oak saplings could use just one hand.

It took time to get the horses saddled and brought up from their stables. That gave Ridley and his men more time to escape from Denum. Once the horses were out they were mounted. When sixty men mounted and left I knew that Ranulf had underestimated the numbers we faced. It might have been deliberate but I preferred honesty. I would still have come. I saw eight men return into the hall. I did not know how many were in the tower.

Fótr and I returned to the others. "They have taken the bait. I counted at least eight men who remain in the hall and there are an unknown number of them in the tower. David, clear the tower. The rest, we ride for the hall and gain entry. Fótr, you saw where the stables were, have your men secure that. It may be there is another entrance into the hall from there."

"Aye lord."

"If we are to succeed then we cannot waste one moment. Be swift and be ruthless. These are bandits!"

After donning my helmet, I mounted Skuld. David's archers had already run back to the edge of the woods. They would go on foot to get as close as they could to the tower. Four hundred paces put the men in the tower beyond their range. My shield hung by my leg. I drew my sword and spurred my mount. The going, through the virgin snow, was not as quick as I would have liked. I knew that the snow on the ground around the hall had been flattened by the riders already. That still lay one hundred paces from us. We were spotted. One of the sentries sent an arrow towards us. It fell short and then when Cedric Warbow's arrow struck him he fell from the tower. Three other men appeared and shouted. The wind and the height of the tower prevented the words from carrying and another sentry fell. By that time, I was close enough to the hall and I leapt from Skuld. She would not wander.

I ran to the steps. Out of the corner of my eye, I saw Fótr lead his men to the stables. Behind me, in the tower, I heard the clash of steel. The door of the hall opened when I was just three steps from it. The Scot who emerged was armed but he looked towards my men and not down the steps. It proved to be a fatal mistake. I rammed my sword through him and, pushing his body to the ground, ran in.

After the snow bright ground outside the interior was Stygian and that nearly cost me my life. A spear was rammed at me. I saw it at the last moment and turned. After ripping my surcoat it rasped against my mail. I brought my sword diagonally across the Scot's neck. My sword sawed across his naked neck. It was a mortal wound. As my eyes adjusted I saw that this was an old-fashioned hall. There were no rooms. It was like a Swedish long house. Women screamed and, in the light of the fire in the centre, I saw twelve warriors grab their weapons and run at me. Luckily, I was not alone. My men had joined me.

We were wearing mail and they were not. We were ready for combat and they were just keeping warm. On their side, they knew the layout of their hall. I was wearing gauntlets and when the first Scot raised his sword to slash down at me I blocked it with my glove and swung my sword into his side. I pushed him to the side. One Scot jumped up on to a table with the intention of leaping down on me. I held up my sword and he impaled himself as he jumped.

The sudden appearance of Fótr and his men ended all resistance. There were just the dead, women and children left. I took off my helmet. "Ranulf, have you found your people?"

His voice came from the dark, "Aye lord, and others beside!"

"Then take them back to the trees. We will have to ride double. The rest of you, flee now for we will burn this hall!"

There were screams and cries as they realised they were losing their home. They would find shelter in the village. When I stepped outside the brightness of the snow almost blinded me. Fótr joined me, "We found six horses. We may not have to ride double."

"Good. Henry Youngblood, fire the hall. David of Wales fire the tower!" I wanted to draw Alexander and his men back from Denum. The more of my men we had in the forest the better chance we had of success.

"Aye lord." I saw that Ranulf and his family were huddled together. Egbert and Ethelred had some women with them. At least one was of their family.

"Put the large captives on the six horses Sir Fótr found. The rest will ride double. Ranulf, there will be time for reunions in Matfen. Move your people out and get them to the village!"

"Aye lord, and thank you!"

"Thank me when we are out of this with your family safe. Until then we take nothing for granted."

I mounted Skuld and turned to see palls of smoke rising in the sky. It had been more than an hour since Alexander of Hawick had ridden to Denum. By now he would have reached it and realised that Ridley and his raiders had fled. Would he follow their trail or head back to his town? Not knowing the man, I could not predict what he would do. I just had to stick to my plan.

"Fótr, take your men and ride as quickly as you can to the village. Improve the defences."

"Aye lord."

I waited for my men at arms and archers before I left. Until we were reunited with Ridley then we risked failure for there were at least sixty bandits who would be trying to get at us. The trail back was much easier for it was now trampled by our horses. I was aware that time was passing. Fótr would be at the village already but the women who were riding the horses were struggling. It could not be helped.

We were at the point where we had parted from Ridley when Mordaf ap Tomas shouted, "Lord, I see Ridley the Giant through the trees."

"David of Wales, take your archers back to the village quickly and prepare our defence. I will wait for Ridley."

"Aye lord."

If my archers and Fótr were there then we could defend the logs and wrecked huts. I saw that Ridley and his men were driving cattle and they each had a woman or a child on their horses. He saw my face and said, "I know that I have disobeyed you, lord but the cattle shifted the snow and made it easier for us. We found twelve captives in the village."

"Any sign of pursuit?"

"I have my archers behind us and they have not seen any."

"Then move back to our camp and we will follow."

I had just twelve men at arms with me. We watched the sorry convoy of cattle and captives as they headed the last mile to the place we would defend. I was about to give the order to move when Henry Youngblood shouted, "Scots, my lord!"

I turned and saw movement in the distance. I decided to take a chance. Our cloaks were light in colour and the light was fading. We might be hidden if we did not move. "Hide near a tree. When they come close we attack quickly and then retire to the others."

None questioned my judgement and all obeyed. I was lucky. I had a huge fir tree before me. The snow made it even bigger I slid my sword from my scabbard and listened. I heard horses and Scottish voices.

"Lord, I have their trail."

"And I!"

"Then there are two bands. This is not a little raid! I want their leader a prisoner when we catch them. I will roast him alive!"

The first two voices had been closer to me. Their lord sounded further away. They were scouts and we would take those. I could hear their horses as they stepped into the soft snow. I heard their breath and those of their riders. It was Henry who drew first blood. I heard the sound of a sword and then there was a scream. I spurred Skuld and the Scot suddenly saw me to his left. I stood in the stirrups and brought down my sword upon his head.

"Ambush!"

"Fall back!" I saw as I pointed my sword that my men had slain or wounded six. The rest were thirty paces from us and the dead men and horses were between us and Alexander of Hawick. We galloped through the trees with the warband in hot pursuit. We had a mile to travel and we covered the ground quickly. We knew where we were going and the Scots did not. Their leader had them in a line to stop us escaping. It allowed us to build up a lead which I had no intention of losing. David of Wales had left a gap for us to use and we charged through it. The Scots were just forty paces behind us. As we did I heard the bows of my archers as they sent arrow after arrow into the charging Scots. I dismounted and slapped Skuld. I drew my dagger and ran to the logs.

The gap still remained but Ridley the Giant was already there. Swinging his two-handed sword, he hacked through the chest of the leading horse. The rider was thrown and landed two paces from me. I was not sure if he was dead or alive. I made certain that he was dead and then I joined Ridley. It was our archers who won the battle for us. The Scots wore no mail and my archers' arrows could penetrate any protection a warrior might wear, even mail.

As darkness descended I heard Alexander of Hawick shout, "Fall back and reform!"

While my men rebuilt the log barrier I turned, "Did we lose any men?"

Ridley said, "Two of mine were wounded that is all."

"We stay here this night. One man in two will keep watch. Fótr, relieve me in a couple of hours."

"Aye lord."

I took off my helmet and handed it to Petr. "I will get us some food, lord." We had left food there when we had gone to raid Hawick. It would be cold but still welcome.

As if reading my thoughts Gruffyd ap Tomas shouted, "I will get a fire going, lord. There are bairns here who are freezing. The Scots know where we are."

I saw that we had men who were watching the trees. I sheathed my sword and walked over to Ranulf and his family. His wife dropped to her knees and began kissing my hand. "Lord, you are a saint!"

"Rise, gammer, it was the Christian thing to do." I looked at the two girls. The elder and her father had their arms around the younger one who was sobbing. "How are the girls?"

The elder one said, "Sarah is still upset. One of the men you slew in the hall had promised to take her while his lord was away. Had you not come…"

I nodded, "We will keep you safe now. My men will watch over you."

Ranulf nodded, "Thank you, lord. All that they say of you is true. It was lucky you were in York."

"Aye, it was." As I went back to the log barricade I wondered at that. Would the captives have been rescued? It was unlikely. If we had had a Sheriff upon whom the people could rely or a Bishop then perhaps but we now had lords in the north who served themselves. We had peace but the people did not enjoy that peace. I was too far away to be an influence. Perhaps some higher force had been at work and sent me to York. As I watched, into the night, I wondered what the effect of the captivity would be on the two girls.

My reverie was interrupted when David of Wales gave a low whistle. There was danger. I drew a sword and dagger and I waited. I felt Petr step closer to me to watch my back. I could hear his breathing. Stillness was a weapon in the dark of night. Shadows showed more clearly against the white snow. All of my sentries knew how to use swords and we still had mail. Even so, the Scottish killer who crept close to me was almost upon before me I knew he was there. It was his smell which alerted me. He stank of rancid grease and dung. Almost without thinking I whipped my sword across and down. I was rewarded by the crunch of metal on bone as my sword drove into his skull.

This was bandit work and any other men at arms and archers might have been at a disadvantage but mine were well trained. More than that they had all fought in wars covering many countries and there was no trick that was new to them. The cries and groans of the dying were all that we heard.

A Scottish voice said, quietly, "Are they dead yet?"

He was answered with a slit throat as one of my archers ended another killer's life. David of Wales shouted, "Your killers are dead, Scotsmen. Shall we come for you?"

We heard scampering as the ones we had not slain fled. We were vigilant and they did not like that. We had been saved by mail. Their blades had edges and not points. They were useless against mail.

Fótr appeared at my side, "Lord?"

"I am awake. Get some sleep, take Petr with you."

I would sleep when I reached Stockton. Excitement coursed through my veins. If I laid down then sleep would not come. My men had a fire going and they had food cooking all night. I walked to the fire to warm myself not long before dawn. To my surprise, I saw that Fótr and Petr had not gone to bed. They were talking with Sarah and Maud. My knight and squire had their cloaks around the shoulders of the two girls and they were tucked against the wall of a hut. I did not disturb them. They were young and the two girls were smiling. Sarah had been tearful when last I had seen her. Whatever Petr had said to her had made her stop crying. I took a bowl of the stew back to the barrier. Ridley the Giant had relieved Henry Youngblood.

"You can sleep, lord. I will watch but I do not think that they will try and attack again."

"I know, Ridley, but I cannot sleep. Besides your son is becoming close to one of the captives, Sarah."

He smiled, "She is pretty. He has his father's eye for a fair woman, lord. Perhaps this is meant to be. If they choose each other then she will be safer in Stockton than here and my son needs to spill his seed."

It was not the way my wife would have spoken but Ridley was a plain-speaking warrior and he was right. Petr was old enough to be wed. Many lords did not allow their squires to marry. I was not so precious. If this was a true joining of spirits then I would not stand in their way. Perhaps Fótr was close to ending his days as a bachelor knight.

As dawn broke it became obvious that the Scots had departed. I sent my men into the forest to collect anything of value and to make certain that they had gone. We collected little of value. The treasure had been the captives. We had recaptured all of the Matfen folk and ten others besides. We would return them to their families. As we headed south, through an icy, white world, I felt content. In the grand scheme of things, this meant little. If King John or the Sheriff of Newcastle knew then they would barely register the fact. To me, it was the most important thing I had done in a while. When it became obvious that Fótr had overcome his infatuation with Eleanor, Fair Maid of Brittany, then I knew that I had been meant to visit with the Archbishop. Our meeting had been his last act. It seemed fitting that two young lives had been saved and four young people found happiness. I was content.

Chapter 3
Squire's quest

The winter was a harsh one. The snows we had encountered close to the border had encroached south. It seemed to stop at the Tees but that did not help us. We had barely made it home before another round of blizzards and winter storms struck. Movement was almost impossible. We were well prepared in the valley. I had made certain that my reeves had organised the farmers well and we had food stored. It was the animals who were in the greatest danger. I authorised the use of oats and barley for feed. We slaughtered some of the older cows and we prayed for the snow to stop. It did, on St. Stephen's Day. My men at arms and archers took the opportunity to clear some of the snow from the common so that our horses could graze and exercise. Fishermen took to their boats to reap some of the bounty from the river. It was a pause in winter's war. When a truce came we used it well. I rode, with Petr as far as the Oxbridge to make certain that none had perished during the storms. All were well. When we went to church, we thanked God that none had been taken by the cold.

As was typical of our valley the storms ceased and was followed by a week of ice and freezing temperatures. Aunt Ruth felt it more than most. She was old. We ensured that the fires in the castle were kept lit. We had wood that we had copsed in the autumn. Alfred and the squires went with Petr to cut down more firewood from the woods. We were using our store up quickly and the newly cut wood would need to dry out. My son was growing. He understood the need to do things which were not knightly. Petr had told him of the scenes we had seen in Hawick. He saw that there were knights who were not honourable. We had not managed to slay Alexander of Hawick and he would rear his head again. Beasts like Alexander had the knack of surviving however it would take him time to replace the many men we had killed. With twenty of his horses captured he would not be as mobile as he had once been.

Fótr and Petr both came to see me a month after we had rescued the captives. Petr had visited with Fótr on more than one occasion. It was no surprise. They had been squires together and had much in common. Fótr and Petr's mother shared a language and a heritage. Fótr spoke first, "Lord, we would ask you permission to ride to Matfen when the roads are clear."

"That may not be for some time. The thaw is many moons away."

My knight nodded, "Aye lord, and that is why we ask permission now. As soon as the roads are passable we would venture north."

I nodded. I knew the reason but I had to ask, "And why do you wish to return to Matfen? It is a long way just to see the new grass grow."

"Lord, know that I only saw Maud briefly; I spent barely three days in her company but I know that she is the one who will be my bride. I thought I loved Eleanor Fair Maid of Brittany but I see now that was infatuation."

"And this is different? How do you know?" I remembered the half heart that the royal captive had given to Fótr when he had been my squire.

"I am older and this time Maud has shown me that she returns my love."

"In three days you know this?"

"As I recall, lord, you and Lady Margaret knew in an even shorter time and in similar circumstances."

I nodded he was right. "And you, Petr, are your reasons the same?"

"Sarah is young, lord, I know that but she is older than the bride that King John took. She was frightened and fey. That night when I put my cloak and arms around her she took comfort in my presence. When we parted at her father's farm she was tearful."

"They are not grounds for marriage, Petr and besides, you are a squire. You cannot marry. You either become a knight or leave my service."

"I know, lord. I would be a knight but if I was not able to do so then I would leave your service." He shook his head, "However reluctantly that might be. That is the strength of my feeling lord. My father was a man at arms and I would serve you in that capacity if I had to."

I knew then that this was more than just an infatuation. "And your purpose in riding to Matfen is?"

Fótr said, "I go to ask for Maud's hand and Petr asks for Sarah to live with his mother in their home until his position and situation are resolved." He smiled, "I think this would suit your son, lord for it would allow him to become your squire and it would fit in with lady Margaret's wish for him to wait another year to begin training."

Petr nodded, "It is, lord, as my mother might say, *wyrd*."

"That is not Christian, Petr, but I can see it in these events. And would you become a knight?"

"I did not think I wished to be a knight, lord. Learning to write, speak languages were bad enough but with fingers like these the playing of the rote would seem impossible."

I knew what he meant. The rote had but four strings yet they were so close together as to make its use a precise art. I had not picked one up since before Arsuf and I am not certain that I would have been knighted if the playing of the rote had been a requirement. However, the fact that he was willing to learn showed the depth of feeling. "I daresay that my son will help you. Especially as this might hasten his progression to squire. You have my permission but that also depends upon Ranulf. He may not wish to lose his daughters."

Fótr nodded, "Aye lord. This is not a foregone conclusion. We both know that. This is our quest. We have both prayed to God. If Maud's father rejects my suit then I know that I am not worthy and I will endeavour to become a better knight."

When I told my wife, she was not surprised. "There are few girls in Stockton whom they could court. From what you say although their father is a farmer his family have connections. This Godfrey of Beverley has the ear of the Archbishop. I just worry about the two girls. They had to endure the privations of bandits. Do we know what happened to them while they were captives?"

I knew what my wife meant and I could not answer her truthfully although I had an idea, however unpalatable that might be. "Petr and Fótr will know more than we do. Let us not make up a story. They have to wait until the snow has gone and then speak with Ranulf. Petr will be training hard to become a knight.

He has all the martial skills he needs. Alfred can help him with the rest."

My wife suddenly realised the implications of this course of action. "Our son still has a year before he can train as a squire."

I nodded, "And this would not mean he would be my squire. Surely you do not think that teaching languages, reading and the playing of the rote are dangerous?" I smiled as I said it.

My wife shook her head, "Thomas of Stockton, you are devious! I pity your foes for you have a mind like a steel trap. I would not put it past you to have created this situation!"

"Then you give me more credit than I deserve. I knew nothing about this."

It was February before the two of them and Fótr's squire, John, were able to travel. I sent two men at arms with them and my wife sent gifts for the family. In the weeks since I had told her of their plans, she had mellowed. Our son had shown that he was growing for he became Petr's teacher and he was a good one. Aunt Ruth helped and Isabelle and William were included in the reading and writing lessons. For my Aunt, this was a joy unbounded. A wedding was the one thing missing in her life and to have two in the castle would make it complete.

The thaw meant we had news from the south. I heard about the death of the Archbishop. We heard that the King was back in England and scouring the land of those barons who had opposed him in Ireland. King John was not one to forgive and forget. He bore a grudge and I feared for my land. My great grandfather had lived through one civil war. A second one had cost us, Normandy. I prayed that we would not have a third. Ralph of Whorlton sent me the news that he now had a son but his wife's father was not well. Thanks to the Archbishop's gift Northallerton paid homage to me. That would create a problem. Sir Hugh had no sons. Legally the manor should pass to his nearest relative, his daughter but would this be viewed with suspicion by my enemies? Sir Ralph was my knight. I would wrestle with that problem when it became necessary. There was also good news. Godfrey of Beverley sent a gift of two war horses and two palfreys.

The three were away for half a month. As we approached the spring equinox, when the days and nights were the same length, I wondered at the delay. Alfred was even more worried and he took to watching from the north gate. It was he who spied them as they arrived. Their faces told me that they had been successful. I did not need to ask a question for Alfred raced down, "Well?"

Fótr looked at me and I nodded. "The girls' father agreed to our proposals. Their mother was happy that they would be married to two lords and safe from the raiding Scots in Stockton castle. With your permission, lord, we have agreed to a summer wedding on the longest day. That will give Petr the opportunity to continue studying to be a knight. Sarah will stay with Petr's family until then." He paused, "I know that I have a fine church, lord but I would be honoured if I could be married in the Warlord's church."

"Of course. You had better tell your parents, Petr." He nodded and ran off. "I will speak to Father Abelard for you, Fótr. You will have much to do in your hall." He cocked a quizzical eye at me. "Your home is the home of a bachelor. It has been many years since a woman looked at the hall. In your place, I would ask Lady Margaret to ride with you and advise you. Ladies do not suffer the same conditions that we warriors find acceptable."

He nodded, "Thank you, lord."

When they had gone Alfred could not wait to ask me, "Well, father, does this mean I train as a knight? Can I be your new squire."

"Petr is not a knight yet. He has much to do. When he has passed all of his tests, held his vigil, received his spurs and been dubbed then and only then will you be able to begin as my squire." He nodded, "And you must have seen twelve summers." His face fell. He would have to wait beyond the date of the marriage of Fótr and Maud. I did not think that Petr would have mastered reading and writing by then.

I think that Alfred realised it too for he nodded. "Then I still have much to do to ensure that Petr is schooled. This is harder than I thought."

For me this was unexpected. Having to teach Petr had brought out different qualities in Alfred. He would be a much better squire and knight for the experience.

I also found that the proposed marriages pleased my wife. She was fond of Fótr. He had lost his family in Sweden and we had taken him on. He had been part of my retinue when we had rescued her from those who wished her harm. He had fought for her when little more than a boy. Marguerite had come with us from Sweden and as Petr's mother made Petr almost an honorary nephew to my wife. The hug she gave me showed me how much she approved. I do not think she had thought it all through. She saw two weddings. She saw the opportunity to furnish a hall. She did not see her son beginning his training to be a squire and, ultimately, a knight.

Petr began to pester me. He wanted to be tested on those skills he knew he would need to pass the test of knighthood. He rode at the targets. He managed to do so, using just his knees. He fought Henry Youngblood on foot and won. He recited the vows he would take. He even managed to play the rote and sing a ballad. It was not very good but it did not have to be. It just had to be sung.

"You realise that you have to sing before ladies?"

He nodded, "I know. Could it be before Lady Margaret, your Aunt Ruth and my mother first? That would give me confidence."

I smiled, "We could wait until Maud and Sarah arrive for the wedding."

"No lord, that would be a disaster."

"Then practise. You have a month. I hold a feast for my knights to honour the dead of Stockton. You can do it then."

He agreed. The feast had been begun in the Warlord's time. Initially, it had been to remember Sir Wulfric and Sir Richard but, over the years it had been to remember all the dead warriors who had died for Stockton. When I had been in the Holy Land and Sweden, not to mention Anjou, the celebration had been in abeyance. Since we had returned we had ensured that we remembered the dead for we now had dead of our own to recall.

As we prepared we heard news from the south that King John had exiled more barons who had opposed his will. The Irish barons had been quashed and some had had estates in England confiscated in reparation for their rebellion. The King was warning all knights of the folly of insurrection. I did not like

King John but, since the war against William of Scotland, he had left me and my lands free from his tyranny. We paid our taxes and they were too high. That was a small price to pay to be out of his eye. I think that we were too far north for him to worry too much about us.

Sir Richard de Percy visited with me. He brought other barons from his lands which lay both to the north and south of mine. We had fought together against William of Scotland. He was a knight whom I could trust. I would stand in a shield wall with Richard de Percy. He was an honourable knight. He was, however, also a rebel. He had lost two manors as a result of King John and he was bitter. He did not like King John and unlike some others was active and vociferous in his opposition.

As soon as his banner was sighted my wife became worried, "Thomas, Sir Richard is a dangerous man."

"He is a good knight and we stood together to fight the Scots."

"That I do not doubt but King John has spies everywhere. You risk all by allowing him here."

"And can I refuse him? You are condemning him out of hand. He is a friend, he is a neighbour and he visits with me."

I could see the worry on her face but she nodded. She would have to trust me and my judgement.

He swept an arm around my inner bailey and my newly constructed walls. He had a military eye and I saw him appraising its qualities for both attack and defence. "This is a fine castle. You managed to persuade the King to allow you to build walls then?" I nodded, "But not a keep." He shook his head. "You are a bastion against the Scots. Bamburgh is the King's castle and it has a keep. Why cannot yours have one too?"

"I am content. We have made the walls thick. They cannot be mined for there is water around them. My hall is more comfortable than a keep. Besides I have the best of men to defend my walls."

"Aye. I envy you your archers and men at arms. They seem to flock to you. I would I had men like that."

"What brings you and your fellows here? Had I known we could have hunted."

He lowered his voice, "My visit is not about a trivial matter. Thomas, I come here because I know that you are of the same mind as me. You do not trust the King nor do you like him."

"However, he is my liege lord. I may not like him and I do not have to trust him. He is my King and I will not be a traitor."

"Are you not a traitor to your country?"

"Those knights who rebelled in Anjou and Normandy, were they patriots? Many had estates in England too. I gave mine up for I have honour. Have they honour? Do not ask me to get into bed with fellows like that."

"Thomas, we do not speak war. We speak negotiation. We ask no man to fight King John. If we can gather enough of the great barons of the country to meet with the King we can ask him to grant us rights. And you are one of the great barons."

I was intrigued, "Rights?"

"We seek a council of barons who would be there to ensure that the King behaves in a fair way. He has taken land from men he does not like. That is not right. We wish him to obey the laws of the land."

"He is King."

"And as King, he should obey the same laws as we do. If I took your land you would appeal to the courts."

"But we cannot do that with a King."

"Not yet but with a Council of Barons there would be men who could arbitrate."

"It sounds fair but why should the King allow such a document to be created? What does he gain?"

"It is not about what he gains. It is about what he loses. The treaty and the document are the conciliatory approaches. If he does not choose to agree then we withdraw our support for him. We stop paying taxes. We refuse to serve the forty days we are required. If the King will not support us then we refuse to fight for him."

"But you would not fight against him?"

There was a slight hesitation and then he said, "No, we would not bear arms against our King."

I did not believe him but I do not think he lied to me. He meant what he said. He would not bear arms but if the King appeared at his castle with an army then he would fight. I nodded, "I beg you not to mention this again while you are here. I need time to think on this."

"Then you are with us?"

My voice became harsh, "Do not try to put words into my mouth. I said that I will need to think on this and I shall. Now come, everyone will think that we do conspire!"

Sir Richard kept silent about our talk. He entertained the table with anecdotes about life further north. I knew that he had come to secure my support and my answer had given him just enough encouragement. What his visit did tell me was that this conspiracy was still in its early stages. The exile of Fitzwalter had damaged the barons. He was their leader. Would Sir Richard assume his mantle?

When Sir Richard and his party left for Topcliffe I was relieved. He would call in at York and I knew, even though he had said nothing, that he would try to strengthen the support for the barons. Perhaps I was a coward. I put the conspiracy to the back of my mind. I had a squire to knight and two marriages to oversee.

The remembrance feast was an opportunity for all of the knights of the valley to gather. The exception was Sir Ralph. His father in law was at death's door. The priests had administered the last rites but the old knight hung on. Sir Ralph was missed, as was his wife and children, but we had enough knights with their families to do honour to the dead. It was not a maudlin feast. There was singing and there was gaiety but that came after we prayed to God and then bowed our heads. We remained silent as we remembered those who had fallen. For me, that was my father. For Aunt Ruth it was her brother and her father. Each remembered someone who had died. In the warrior hall, the men at arms and archers would be doing the same. We were all brothers in arms.

Before the celebration could really begin, poor Petr had to endure the performance on the rote. He had already done so for his mother, Aunt Ruth and my wife. They had all been supportive and his mother had cried tears of joy. This was his real test. He had to sing before knights and their ladies. They were, however, all friends.

I knew he was nervous but Alfred and he had worked on a short song. It had the beauty of being an English translation of an eastern song and so easier for him to learn. There was silence as he began.

I wonder what was the place where I was last night,
All around me were half-slaughtered victims of love, tossing about in agony.
There was a nymph-like beloved with cypress-like form and tulip-like face,
Ruthlessly playing havoc with the hearts of the lovers.

He finished. He had made a few wrong notes on the rote but he had sung it perfectly. There was silence and then my hall erupted in a cacophony of cheers and applause. Petr was popular. Even before he had been my squire he had come to war with his father Ridley the Giant. He had endeared himself to all by his willingness to do anything that was asked of him.

I smiled, "Petr, you have passed that test."

We both knew that just two remained: the master of languages and reading and writing. Alfred had ensured that those tests were easily passed! He did so flawlessly before my knights and they applauded him. The ordeal over I saw him, and my son visibly relax. For Alfred, this was one step closer to his dream.

I was seated next to Sir William of Hartburn. He had drunk well and, while he was not drunk, he was in a good mood. "Thank you again, lord, for inviting me here. La Lude was a place I loved but I could not be lord there under a French King."

"Is it any better here, William? We both know that King John is not the best of kings." I did not want to embroil William in the conspiracy but I needed to know his views.

"You are right but you will not allow him to be a tyrant." He smiled, "The Bishop of Durham learned that!"

"Then you are happy here?"

"Hartburn is not La Lude but I like it. I have begun to clear that wood where we were hunting wild boar. Stephen the shipwright has bought the timber from me already. He will use the oak and sycamore for his ships. The rest he will sell to Thomas the timber merchant. I have had all the branches which would make good arrows sold to Harry the Fletcher. It is good wood. Now that the soil has warmed my men at arms and archers will compete to see who can remove the stumps the quickest. David and Andrew, Tom the Pig's sons have asked me if they could have some land to farm for beans and oats." He shrugged, "It is not grapes nor is it wheat but I am content. I do not bow the knee to a French King."

I sat back and enjoyed the feast. We were relaxed and we remembered well. More than that, we were of one mind. We would not serve a French master. We would not rebel against the King. The Warlord had served his grandfather and his father. Along with his grandmother, he had saved England from Stephen of Blois. I had to believe that blood would out.

The wedding came hard upon the feast. This time we had invited those from further afield. De Percy, de Vesci and the Sheriff were all invited. Only de Percy attended. Sir Ralph and his wife attended. Sir Hugh had died. Once the wedding was over I would use the power given to me by the Archbishop and award Northallerton to Sir Ralph. Sir Petr would have a manor, Whorlton, when he became a knight.

Petr had worked hard. He had a purpose and he stood his vigil just two nights before the date of the wedding. Father Michael could not marry him on the same day as Fótr; he had banns to read but three weeks after he would be wed. It would be a smaller ceremony without the lords of the north but none the worse for that. My men at arms would all attend with their families for Petr was one of them.

My hall was filled as was my guest hall. The inns of Stockton did a roaring trade. Lords brought their ladies, their servants and some men at arms. The burghers of Stockton made much coin. Godfrey of Beverley came. He sought an audience with me.

"Lord, you did all that I asked and more. For my nieces to be married to two of your knights is a dream. I would offer you coin but I know that will you refuse it. You are unusual, not to say unique. I can think of no other knight who would refuse a king's ransom and do that for which the ransom was intended. Know you that I have money for both my nieces. Their husbands shall want for nothing."

I shook his hand, "You are an honourable man. You do what you do for family and that is the most important thing you can do."

I had many lords at the wedding. I could not enjoy Fótr's happiness as much as I would have wished. I was aware that Sir Richard Percy had words he wished to say to me. There were other lords I had invited who were also keen to garner my favour. I was now Earl of Cleveland. Gone were the days when I was a simple sword for hire. There was an expectation now.

What I did do was to speak with Sir Ralph. I would not burden him with such a large manor as Northallerton without speaking to him. Sir William of La Lude had been more than happy with the tiny manor of Hartburn. Perhaps Sir Ralph would feel the same. As the other guests arrived I took Sir Ralph to one side. I led him by my river. At this time of year, it was beautiful. Herons patrolled the water and trout jumped. The water was as still as an ice flow. We walked down the path which led from my quay to the marshes where migrating birds nested in summer.

"I am sorry for your loss."

"He lived a good life. It was never glorious but he was a happy man. His friendship with you meant more to him than anything. He regaled every dinner with tales of you in Arsuf, Sweden, Anjou. He had never been at any of those places but he knew your story. He was happy in his later years and that is all a man can ask."

"You have grown wise."

He laughed, "Four children will do that."

"And your father?"

"He died six months since. I should have told you but with Sir Hugh…"

"Do not apologise. I am sorry. You have lost two fathers."

"I lost my father long ago. I know not why he did not return with us."

I did but I could not mention it for I had been sworn to secrecy by his father. I changed the subject. "And now I have an offer to make to you."

"Aye lord."

"Know you that the Archbishop of York gave me the fealty of Northallerton and the manors thereabouts?"

"I did not, lord."

"Well, it is true. Ralph, we are alone and you can refuse if you wish. I would offer you the manor of Northallerton."

His mouth opened and closed. He looked at the river. A seal had raised its head and then disappeared. "Can I do it, lord? It is an important manor."

"Oh, you can do it but the question is do you want to? Whorlton is small and it is comfortable. Northallerton means you have to be polite to men you do not like. You will have merchants who wish you to help them. Farmers will come to you with their problems. There is no pressure here. There are others I can appoint but I know you, Ralph. You are a good knight and Northallerton will be better for your lordship."

He nodded, "If you think I can do it then that is good enough but Whorlton, it is a good manor and I like the people there. Who would be lord of the manor?"

"I have not asked him but I thought to offer it to Sir Peter."

"Sir Peter? I know not him?"

I laughed, "Aye you do. It is Petr. Father Abelard has told me that when he is knighted he needs a Christian name. To us, he will still be Petr."

"Then I am happy but why did Sir Fótr not need a Christian name?"

I put my finger to my lips and said, "He should but the priest in Anjou did not know that. This is his wedding day. Do not spoil it!"

I was happy when all of my guests left. I liked an empty castle. My Aunt, in contrast, was as happy as a spring lamb. She had spent too many years isolated in the north. Now she saw the rebirth of Stockton. As the last guest left she took my arm. "Thomas, I loved my brother but he made the mistake of following a king who did not deserve that attention and devotion. I know that you will not make that mistake. I have sat, for three days, listening to the men you invited to the wedding. You are a man of power yet you do not know it. Even the King fears you." I stopped walking and she nodded. "It is true. Sir Richard Percy seeks you as an ally for he knows that you are one of the few men whom John fears. I am proud of you. My brother," she crossed herself, "is in heaven and he is telling all that he has a son who is the true heir of the Warlord!"

Her words meant more to me than any title or plaudit from one of my peers.

I knighted Sir Peter, as he became, in my hall. There were a handful of knights there but his mother and father were there. Ridley the Giant was a great warrior but I watched tears course down his cheeks as his son became a knight. He would have to call him sir yet I knew that he did not begrudge the title.

Ranulf and his family, Godrey included, stayed for the second wedding. This one was different. It was one of the men at arms, James Broadsword who explained it to me. "Lord, this is like a wedding from my youth. We are common folk. Lords and ladies might look down on us but this, to me, is as grand as Sir Fótr's. Is that sacrilegious?"

"No James, it is honest and I too am pleased that my hall is filled with archers and men at arms. Without them, I would be nothing."

Chapter 4
Welsh war

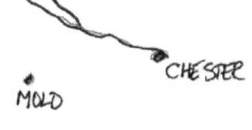

*MOLD CHESTER

*WRECSAM

*SHREWSBURY

6 miles

I had to ride with Sir Peter to Northallerton. It was one thing to tell Sir Ralph that this was his new manor and domain but it was not as simple as that. There were the legal niceties. There were no other heirs and claimants but there would be those who did not approve of my action. They would be local men who sought more coin and more power. By coming with my men at arms and banners flying we told them that any opposition to Sir Ralph would be dealt with by me. My part in the battle of Alnwick and Norham had been noted. There was no trouble. It took a week to complete the formalities. There was no new Archbishop yet; the papal interdict forbade any official appointments. The See was still administered by the dean and canons and thanks to the letter of authority from Archbishop Geoffrey all went through seamlessly. My newly knighted squire used some of Godfrey of Beverley's dowry to buy some gifts for his young wife. He would move to Whorlton but there was no hurry. Sir Ralph had left archers and men at arms there to guard the small castle. Sarah still needed time to fully recover from her ordeal and Aunt Ruth and my wife, not to mention Marguerite were helping the shy young woman become more confident.

As harvest time approached my people entered the busiest time of year. The blizzards of the last winter had warned of what nature could do and nothing was left to chance. Trees were copsed for firewood. Animals were carefully watched. Birds were chased away from ripening crops. Fish were caught and dried then either salted or pickled. Game was hunted to cull the older animals and ensure that the rest survived.

It was in the middle of such frenetic activity that William Marshal arrived. He was now old and he looked weary. He had served the Kings of England for many years and he was well over sixty years old. His arrival meant only one thing. The King either wished to punish me for something I had done or he needed something from me. The old Earl Marshal arrived with a small escort of his own household knights. He was the last link to my great grandfather. My great grandfather had been the first Earl Marshal and the role had been defined by the Warlord of the North. William Marshal was also old fashioned and did things properly. He had a gift for my wife. It was some Flemish lace. He greeted Aunt Ruth with warmth and affection. He had served with her brother in the Holy Land. He did not rush into the purpose for his visit. Instead, he walked my walls commenting on the new features I had added. It was as we stood on the river wall watching a heron hunt fish that he came to the point.

"King John requires you and your knights for forty days service." He said it flatly. It was a duty I owed the King. Others like de Percy and de Vesci might refuse but I would not.

"And Scotland?"

He smiled, "William will not venture south again and your treatment of Alexander of Hawick has set a precedent. The Scots now know that their raids will be punished and punished harshly. Your raid was not sanctioned but as it was approved by the church it has put you in the King's favour."

"Then the knights of Northumberland will be with us and the knights of the Palatinate?"

"You will lead the knights of the Palatinate. I go there when I have spoken to you. As for the knights of Northumberland... let us just say that there is a problem there but King John will deal with them when he has solved the problem of Wales."

I was surprised, "Then we travel to Wales? It will have to be a short campaign for it will take a week to reach Wales and a week to return."

William shook his head, "Your forty days begins when you reach Chester."

There were no sentries close by us. My men were discreet. They had ensured that we could speak without anyone listening. "My lord, you owe me this, at least. What is the reason the knights of Northumberland do not obey the orders of the King and yet I must?"

He looked at me and his eyes were sad. "Thomas, the knights of Northumberland will be punished. King John does not suffer such public humiliation. His face is as stone at the moment but once we have quashed the marcher lords and the Welsh with whom they have allied then they will be dealt with. You have land and you have loyal knights. You would not have them lose their manors, would you?" He must have seen the flash of anger in my eyes for he shook his head, "I do not threaten you. The King does not threaten you for you will obey, we both know that. I am merely telling you the consequences of opposing King John."

I nodded. He was right. The King had the right but he did not have the right to use such draconian punishments. Was Richard de Percy, right? Would a conspiracy of barons be able to modify the King's actions? I was a warrior and not a plotter.

"The King now has a son. Henry of Winchester is already four years old and a healthy child. He has a second son, Richard, who is a healthy two-year-old. We will not have to seek an heir to the throne." The old marshal was telling me that there was hope beyond King John. "I am getting too old for war, Thomas, but like your great grandfather, I cannot retire. However, the King has asked me to watch over young Henry. Know you that I will make certain that he becomes a good King!"

His words were laden with hidden meaning. King John was a bad King of England but we had hope for the future. I took heart from his words.

At the feast my wife hurriedly had prepared, William was gracious. Alfred assaulted him with questions. I saw the look of worry on my wife's face. Alfred would now be my squire and rather than a period of peace in which he could be trained safely we would now be warring against the Welsh. Her son would be in danger.

"Is it the north of Wales or the south in which we will fight, Earl Marshal?"

"It will be in the heartland of Wales. You do not want to fight in North Wales, Master Alfred. They have mountains there. The Welsh are masters of ambush and their archers the equal of your father's.

Petr, now Sir Peter, asked, "I heard that the King had married his daughter Joan to the Welsh King, Llewelyn. Does this not make him family?"

"You are astute, Sir Peter. The King thought it would. Joan is not legitimate and so has less power attached to her. It seems that the bargain was one-sided and the Welsh King has ambitions. Welsh marcher lords have stirred up the Welsh to want even more power than they enjoy."

King Henry had given the marcher lords more independence to ensure that the Welsh were kept behind their mountains. It seemed to me that their change in attitude was as a direct consequence of King John's policy.

William Marshal left the next day. "When I have sent you the knights of the Palatinate you will leave for Chester. There, Ranulf de Blondeville, Earl of Chester will lead you and your men along with those of Chester and Lancashire, to sweep down to Shrewsbury. There King John will have the rest of our forces. I will be with the King. God speed, Sir Thomas," he leaned down, "be of good heart. There is light behind this cloud which hangs over us."

"You will not return with us?"

He shook his head, "I must speak with the Sheriff and then I take ship and sail south. Fear not I will be with you but I have much to do for our King."

We also had much to do. I sent riders to warn my knights and to summon them to Thornaby for the muster. Wales was many leagues hence and we would need tents. We would not be campaigning in winter but autumn was the time of rains and unpredictable weather. Alfred needed equipping as a squire. He would not be fighting. His role would be as my servant but he required protection. Petr's old hauberk was too big but we still had Sir Fótr's and that would have to do. We had the local smith make him a helmet. It was a simple one with a nasal. That would be all that he would need. He had a sword already. Unlike me, he would only need one horse. He would take Star. The two were now as one. I would not be taking Skuld to war. She was getting too old. I took Flame, my warhorse and Alan, the horse master had a palfrey of the same blood as Skuld. Scean was a lovely natured beast. She was not as good as Skuld but no horse could be. She was, however, the same colour and temperament. The bigger difference was her size. She was closer to a warhorse in height and would bear me, even with mail.

It was Petr who had the most difficult of tasks. He had to leave his young wife and ride to Whorlton to bring his new men to the muster. His squire was his younger brother, Henry. He had seen thirteen summers, the same as Sarah and this would be his first foray into the world of war. His mother fretted and, in a perfect world, we would have had time to prepare him. His father, Ridley, would be with us and he would make sure that his third son was trained as we rode.

James Broadsword would watch my castle. I did not take all of my men. It was my knights who owed service to the King. I left more than half of my men at arms in my castle. Sir Edward, Sir William and Sir Fótr would do the same. William Marshal was right, the Scots would not break their treaty, at least not for a while, but Alexander of Hawick had given us a warning of what individuals might attempt.

Baron David of Stanhope led the men of Durham. I would be leading sixty knights of the Palatinate. Thanks to the experience of fighting alongside me the men of Durham now had more archers but, like me, they had left half of their men at home. Harvest time was approaching and the land needed protection. We crossed the river on the last day of August and joined the men of Northallerton, Whorlton, Normanby, Yarm and Thornaby. I had eighty knights, a hundred men at arms and a hundred archers. With twenty servants and our horse herd, we were spread out for a good half-mile along the road. We headed west for, as it was still fine weather we would cross the Pennines by Skipton and head down past Clitheroe to Chester. That way we had castles where we could stay. There would be six castles, one for each day of our journey.

The long ride allowed me to get to know some of the new knights from Durham. My reputation was such that more knights were willing to ride to war than hitherto. Stephen of Spennymoor told me that Aimeric of Chartres still obstructed me whenever he could. He was one person who benefitted from the papal interdict. From what David of Stanhope told me he was defrauding the Palatinate at every turn. There was no one to monitor him. I thought of a way as we left the high, barren ground which divided England in two and dropped to the fertile farmland of Lancashire. I would mention it to King John. If there was money to be taken from Durham then he would have it rather than the nephew of the Bishop of Durham. Once a new Bishop of Durham was appointed then Aimeric would not be a problem.

There was a huge camp outside Chester but as I counted the banners I saw that they had only a few knights more than I did. As the leader of this battle of knights, I was accommodated in the castle and I dined with Ranulf de Blondeville. He had been married, albeit briefly, to Constance, Duchess of Brittany. The marriage had been dissolved when she had deserted him. King John had been suspicious of the Earl of Chester and had had estates confiscated. They had been returned to the Earl and he made certain that he obeyed every order of King John.

He knew of me but we had never met. His step-son had been Arthur and it had been Ranulf's association with Arthur which had resulted in his lost estates. It gave us something in common. We had both been fond of young Arthur.

"This is the first opportunity I have had to thank you, Earl, for what you did for Arthur and Eleanor. They were used as pawns in the great game of thrones. I was saddened by Arthur's death."

"For my part, I was angered. He was murdered and his murderer never brought to book!"

He looked up at me, "There are some men who are above the law and we can do little about it." We both knew, or suspected, that King John himself had been the murderer.

I remained silent. He was now close to the King and I would need to watch what I said. I did not want to be entrapped.

Ranulf de Blondeville was a clever man. He changed the subject. He knew the reason for my reticence. "There are many knights who have found excuses not to obey the call to arms. It is a mistake on their part for King John has a long memory and an even longer arm. I am pleased that you are here. Know that although the King has put me in command I know that your experience is greater than mine. If I make a mistake I pray that you tell me before men die."

I was relieved. I had now grown used to command. "Thank you. Will we have battles to fight before we reach Shrewsbury?"

"We have to pass through the land of King Llewelyn. He will contest our passage."

"You have scouts?"

"I have the men of Denbigh. Their lord, Baron Jocelyn, is young but he has good men who serve him. His archers are good and his men at arms know their business. He is not at the muster. He and his men are waiting for us at the head of the Clwyd Valley. They will be our scouts."

"And mounted men?"

He had noticed that all of mine were mounted, even the archers, "Only our knights, squires and half of our men at arms are mounted. The rest are foot."

As I retired that night I felt better. The Earl appeared to be willing to listen and he had at least one good knight. I had served with worse.

We headed towards the border the next day. After crossing the Dee, we were in the borderlands. Ostensibly English, it was like the land around Hawick. It was contested by both sides. I had suggested to the Earl that my archers and those of my battle form the scouts until we reach Sir Jocelyn. He acceded to my request. We could have taken a more direct route but King John wished us to draw some of the men of Gwynedd towards us. If we could weaken the enemy before we joined the main army then King John had more chance of winning. It made sense. We rode for Mold.

Sir Jocelyn was not as young as Ranulf de Blondeville had intimated but he had the look of a border knight. His horse looked to be hardworking and his men wore a variety of armour. Some wore mail while others just had a metal-studded leather jerkin. His archers had war bows and looked like Mordaf and Gruffyd, two of my Welsh archers. They were broad and stocky.

He nodded to me but reported, as was right and proper, to his liege lord, "My lord, there were men watching this road. They are dead but when we scouted ahead we found that they have a large number of men at Wrecsam. There were too many for us to shift."

The Earl of Chester looked at me, "It is a much-contested place. Sometimes the Welsh hold it and at others we do. This is one reason for this campaign. I had thought to have a chevauchée. This will do as well. The Welsh have held it for the last five years. They have a castle but no town wall."

He was seeking advice. I asked him, "How would you do this?"

"Surround the town and then use our men on foot to assault it under cover of our archers. The castle would be hard to take!"

"We do not need the castle. We need to reduce the town and destroy the warriors. I would suggest that we ride there with all our mounted men. Those on foot can follow and guard the baggage. This way we can eat Welsh food this night."

The Earl looked surprised, "You are confident that we can reduce this town?"

"If what you say is true then I believe so. The houses will be made of wood?"

He nodded, "As is the castle."

"Wood burns." It was as simple as that. If the Welsh expected a ponderous approach they were in for a surprise. I wanted to ride in at the charge. I waved over David of Wales. "We attack Wrecsam. The Earl's archers appear to know their business. Ride with them. Harass the Welsh archers. They are the danger."

"Aye lord." I turned to Alfred. "I will ride Scean. You stay with the baggage and Flame."

"What if you need a spare spear, lord?"

I smiled, "I will not and the other squires will be with you. This will not be your first battle." Our war horses were too valuable to risk and our squires would be best employed guarding them and our baggage.

We spurred our horses down the road. I rode behind the Earl of Chester and his household knights. I rode with Sir Edward, Sir William, Sir Ralph, Sir Fótr and Sir Peter. The rest of my knights followed me. A knight always fought better with men he knew and trusted. The knights of Durham rode at the rear. The knights of Chester and Lancashire followed us. If the Welsh were expecting us to come and surround them then they would have sent men for help. Even as we rode south I expected men to be coming from the hills to the west. Speed was our best weapon.

The archers and men at arms had not bothered with the road. They had ridden across fields. I smiled as I saw only men at arms to our flanks. David of Wales did not suffer fools gladly. He would have hurried and harried the archers of Chester. By now they would have dismounted and their arrows would be falling upon the Welsh who were awaiting our ponderous approach. Ahead of me the Earl of Chester began to slow as we passed the farms which lay outside the burgh.

"Do not slow! If you have not the heart to attack the Welsh then let through those that do!"

The insult worked and the Earl and his oathsworn spurred their horses. As we neared the town we came upon the town common. I pulled Scean's reins to the left and spurred her. I led my knights to ride parallel to the Earl of Chester. We now had a body of twenty knights. As we passed the Earl I shouted, "Form line!" I pulled up my shield and hefted my spear.

I could see, ahead of me, that the Welsh had not expected this attack. Bodies littered the ground before their houses. They had not brought their archers forward. We were faced by a few knights but mainly men at arms. They expected us to slow and to stop but we did not. Lowering my spear, we charged into the Welsh knights and their retinues. They were not ready. They met us when they were not moving. I pulled back my arm and punched at the Welsh knight with the green dragon on his shield. It was not the cleanest of strikes for the common was not flat. I hit him in the right shoulder. My spear felled him from his saddle and he toppled to the ground. My knights knew their business. Ralph was probably the least experienced for Whorlton had been at peace but even he killed with his first strike. We were not in the business of ransom.

When the men around the standard, both knights and men at arms fell, we were through their best. They had many more men but they were on foot and they were preparing to face a static line. We tore into them. Those, like Edward who had lost their spears, used swords to lay about them. My spear was still whole and my second victim was a mailed man at arms whose spear wavered up and down. Mine did not and it struck him in the chest. This time the spearhead broke and I let go of the now useless shaft.

Drawing my sword, I leaned to the right, relying on my shield to protect my left side. I swung in a wide arc. The Welsh spearman thrust up at me but he mistimed his strike. It was easy to do at a fast-moving target. My blade could not miss and I took his head. It flew into the air and was carried towards the Welsh fyrd who awaited us. I was aware of William and Petr close behind me. They were slaughtering all who came within the range of their swords. Then the men ahead of us broke and raced for the safety and security of the town and the wooden castle. We followed them into the streets. Had they not panicked then they might have darted into the houses where they would have been safe but mailed horsemen drove sense from their minds and they sought the security of the castle. Leaning to the left and the right we slew fleeing Welshmen. Many were saved by the sheer numbers we had to kill. I reined in when I saw the castle ahead. They would have crossbows as well as bows and Scean was too valuable to risk.

"Hold here!" A Welshman suddenly ran from his house screaming. He was wielding a wood axe. I wheeled Scean and as her flailing hooves made the Welshman flinch I hacked down through his shoulder. The axe fell and the man screamed this time in pain and not in anger. His lifeblood was already pumping away. My men at arms and the Earl of Chester had now caught up with us.

"Henry Youngblood, take our men around the castle and see what there is on the other side."

The Earl reined in, "That was a wild ride!"

"But they are now trapped in the castle. I would suggest we take what food and booty there is to be had and then fire the town."

"There may be women and children in the castle."

"There probably will be but we shall be gone and if they cannot douse the flames they can leave. If we leave the town behind us, Earl, then we will have to fight our way if we are to pass it when we return home. Make it a blackened piece of earth. When we win this war, you can rebuild it."

"You fight a hard war in the north."

"We have learned how to make our enemies fear us."

We camped outside the town and watched it burn. The fire did not spread to the castle. They used their water to soak the walls. Our archers sent arrows within to hamper them. Wrecsam as a stronghold was lost to the Welsh. I had lost no men but the Earl of Chester had. His men had not been as experienced as mine. They had been too slow and needed orders. Mine did not. We ate well and listened to the efforts of the garrison to contain the fire. They won but they would be in no condition to do anything else. When we left the next day, there would be no one to attack us.

We were four miles from Wrecsam when we spied danger. Sir Jocelyn's scouts reported large numbers of men to the west of us as we headed south to Shrewsbury. The Earl of Chester nodded. "These are the men who were summoned to come to the aid of Wrecsam. Now that they see it burned they know not what to do." I could hear the question behind his words. He wanted advice. This was not my border war. I kept the northern march safe. This was his land. He looked at Sir Jocelyn.

The younger knight knew what to do. "Earl, we should chase them hence. They have numbers and that is all. They are the archers and hill farmers. I have fought them many times. In their rocky passes, they are hard to shift but here they are in the open."

I nodded, "Sir Jocelyn is right. The King would rather we arrived late but having destroyed the Welsh of the north than arrive in time and leave those who might reinforce their king."

With two of us sharing the same opinion he nodded. "Sir Roger, have your knights stay with the baggage, the squires and the men on foot. Dafydd of Ruthin, take our archers and those of the Earl of Cleveland. Harass the Welsh."

Although it meant having one in four of the archers holding horses the use of mounted archers meant we could close quickly with the elusive Welshmen who were prone to take cover whenever possible.

He turned to me. "I will take the left; you and the knights of Durham take the right. This way we can use a pincer movement." He was learning and growing in confidence.

Once again Alfred was relegated to the baggage and I could see the disappointment on his face as he passed me my spear and led Flame to the baggage. He had thought a squire's life to be glorious. It was not. Most of the time it was almost menial work. So far, he had not needed to even carry my standard. It remained furled in the wagon with our spare weapons, tents and blankets.

I held the spear aloft and point it north. My knights formed a line with our men at arms behind us. Spurring Scean we galloped forward. The ground was dry and our hooves thundered. Had the Earl not sent the archers ahead then the thunder of the hooves would have sent the Welsh running. They could not run so long as our archers were engaged in a duel with their own. Their bows sent arrows at archers protected by leather while their farmers and their men at arms sheltered behind shields.

I saw that there were just ten banners. That meant that ten knights had led their men from their rocky homes. They would have expected to fall upon us as we besieged their town. Had I been their leader then I would have fled. This would not end well for them. Some of the farmers took to their heels and simply ran from the battlefield. They had not expected this. The Welsh archers switched their arrows to our lines of horsemen. It meant that more of their bowmen fell. They were skilled and horses and knights fell. However, as we closed with them so our archers were able to move towards the static Welsh line and cause even more causalities.

As we had to negotiate our archers we were unable to maintain a solid line. That mattered not for we attacked men without mail. I chose, not an easy target, like a farmer with no mail. I rode directly at the knight with the nasal helmet. He rode at me. He had a warhorse. A warhorse is the best animal in a mounted battle but to be most effective it needs to have speed. Then it is unstoppable. The Welshman was not moving fast enough and I was. I switched Scean from the Welshman's left to his right. My horse was nimble and responded instantly to my knees and the reins. I pulled back my right arm and punched with my spear. His spear was on the wrong side of his horse and I struck him in the chest. It was a hard blow and the head broke from the shaft. He tumbled from his horse and I drew my sword. I saw a figure run to the knight. I was about to strike when I saw that it was his squire. I raised my sword and galloped after the fleeing men at arms. I left those on foot for the men at arms who followed us.

Scean's hooves ate up the ground. The man at arms I pursued kept looking over his shoulder. He should have been trying to evade me. Turning around merely slowed him. Had he leaned forward over his horse's mane he would have been able to travel faster. I was able to switch Scean from side to side without losing speed. I drew closer and closer as the Welshman tried to anticipate my moves. Using my spurs, I moved Scean closer with one last burst of speed and brought my sword across the back of the man at arms. He threw his arms in the air and fell from his saddle. One foot was caught in the stirrup and his horse stopped.

Reining Scean in I held up my sword to stop those behind me. The last couple of horsemen would escape us and we did not need to damage our horses too much.

Dismounting I sheathed my sword and went to the horse and took the other foot from the stirrup. The bloody corpse fell to the ground. I grabbed the reins and began to walk back to our baggage. I saw wounded men being despatched. None had surrendered. More than half had escaped us but they, like the men of Wrecsam were no longer a threat. Two knights only had escaped.

I passed the squire who knelt by the lord I had slain. He stood defiantly with his dagger in his hand, "I will not surrender!"

I heard Sir Edward, behind me laugh, "Cheeky little Welshman, isn't he?"

"Aye and brave. I do not ask surrender, son, take your lord's body and his horse and go home. Today is not your day to die." He could not believe his fortune and he hefted his dead knight onto the saddle. I watched as he led him west.

Edward said, "It is a fine horse, better than that sumpter you lead, lord."

I shook my head, "There will be a widow who has lost her husband. She can sell the horse. There will be others for us to take. These are just hill farmers. The real warriors we shall meet further south."

After collecting and tending to our wounded and dead as well as taking the horses and mail from the dead we only made a few more miles before we had to camp again. Alfred could not understand it.

"We are supposed to be at Shrewsbury! Will the King not be angry at the delay?"

"He may be but he gave the Earl of Chester the task of scouring these lands so that one of our flanks was secure. Unless you are a hawk flying above the land then you cannot know what lies around the corner. Our scouts have done well. We have defeated two bands of enemies and lost but a few men. All of this is good. This is warfare, Alfred. It is not as it is written in the books you have studied. They were written after the battle when the winner could take credit for that which was accidental. You and I live in the real world. We fight the men who stand before us." I pointed west. "Today there was a lord who died. I killed him and his squire defended his body. That was me at Arsuf and it could be you tomorrow. I live because King Richard brought his men to my aid. The squire lived because I remembered Arsuf. Your story is not yet written. Do not hasten the day that you draw your sword in anger. Watch how men fight and learn."

He nodded. He was beginning to learn.

Chapter 5
The brink of disaster

We only had twenty miles to travel the next day and there we saw the encampment of King John. It was not as large as I might have expected. I recognised many of the banners but there were others, I had assumed would be there that, were missing. One of the heralds who met us directed us to a field which would be our camp. Leaving Edward to organise it I walked the camp seeking William Marshal. I wondered if he would be with the King. He was not. I found him at his tent, with his younger son Richard.

The old marshal looked pleased to see me. "Did you have trouble? Richard, get the servant to fetch wine for the Earl."

I sat on the chair his squire found for me. I told him of Wrecsam and then the battle afterwards. "That flank is safe but the army we join does not seem as large as I expected."

"Many lords have chosen to ignore the command to muster and others pleaded excuses which were pathetic falsehoods." He shook his head and, lowering his voice said, "Do they not know this King of England? He has some of the traits of Henry and Richard but..." He waved a hand as though to shoo a fly away. "No matter. I am old and weary. I have but a few years to endure this world."

The wine came. It was good but not as good as that from my vines in La Flèche. Those days were gone, never to return. "Where are the Welsh?"

He drank some of the wine and, pointing west, said, "They are gathered at Welshpool. It is fifteen miles west of here and the Welsh King has the mountains at his back. There are many marcher lords who have joined with him as well as the other kings of Wales. I fear that the marcher lords have just created a new problem for us. Before now we could set the Welsh off against each other. If they all follow Llewelyn then we have a problem. The last thing we need is a single Welsh King."

"And where is the King?"

"He has ridden with some of his advisers. They are scouting out the Welsh."

"And you are not with them?"

"I am a relic of the past. I served King Henry and King Richard. King John suffers me."

I shook my head in disbelief. William Marshal had served England faithfully and there was no more loyal knight. He was now discarded. Had this been the fate of my great grandfather? Would it be mine? I needed to look at my world. I needed to speak with Aunt Ruth. In a world of shifting quicksand Aunt Ruth was a rock on whom I could depend for truth and wisdom.

When the King returned, just before sunset, I was summoned along with the Earl of Chester to a council of war. Surprisingly the King began with praise. "The Earl of Chester and Cleveland have managed to quash the threat of a flank attack from the north and that has enabled me to plan a battle which will bring victory. I am grateful to the two earls."

I saw the Earl of Chester preening himself. I was more cautious. King John would be equally critical if we made a mistake.

"Tomorrow we march to Welshpool. Although the rebellious lords and the Welsh kings outnumber us we have superiority in knights. I will use that superiority to sweep them from the field."

From what I knew of the Welsh that was a mistake. Their strength lay in the bow.

"I will command the centre. The Earl of Chester will command the right flank and the Earl of Cleveland the left. My aim is quite simple. We will initiate a charge by heavy horse and simply drive the Welsh from the land they presently occupy."

There were cheers from those lords he had taken with him to scout out the field. Only William Marshal and I were silent. His plan was a recipe for disaster. That evening as my knights and I sat around our fire our squires prepared for the battle. Alfred would be needed. He would have to follow me with spears and Scean. Sir Peter stood, even though the rest of us had not finished eating. "I will go and make certain that Henry knows his business. This will be his first battle."

As he left Sir Fótr laughed, "He will go and check on Alfred more like. I know your son is worried that he does something wrong. I think this campaign is showing Alfred of your worth, lord. When other captains defer to you then it brings home your standing."

"I like not this order of battle for the morrow." They looked at me expectantly. "It will take the morning to reach the battle. We will be spotted from miles away for Welshpool has elevation. They can prepare the battlefield. The King intends to deploy into battle lines as soon as we are there. That allows the Welsh King and his allies to counter us. Do not forget that he has marcher lords with him. They know King John. They know how King John will fight. We need surprise."

"You would fight the battle differently?"

"Aye Ralph. I would camp first and fortify our camp. I would send archers and horsemen around his flank to make a surprise attack on his rear. The King is right we are outnumbered but we have superior men. We use that superiority to strike at the ordinary men. King John's problem is that he wishes to cow the enemy and intimidate his barons. I am a warrior who just likes to win battles." I stood. "I will go and speak with the Earl Marshal. He might be the voice of reason the King listens to."

The earl was sat with two of his sons, William and Richard. He gave me a wan smile as I approached, "See, William, I told you that the Earl would be along."

His sons nodded and stood, "We will ensure that you can speak in private."

The Earl's fire was close to the King's. The two brothers and their men at arms stood twixt the two camps and talked loudly. They would ensure that we were not overheard. I sat next to the Earl. "I know what you will say Thomas and I agree. I am sat alone around my fire because the King has dismissed me. He wants men around him who say yes to his plans and assure him that we will overcome our enemies."

"Then at least ask him to speak with the Welsh King and rebels before we attack."

He looked at me curiously, "Why? This is not like you Thomas."

"It will give us the chance to prepare defences. If we march at the speed of those on foot then it will be afternoon when we arrive. If we can delay the attack then the baggage can be enclosed and protected. We can rest our horses too. I know the knights will ride on fresh war horses but what of the men at arms? Their horses will be barely able to manage one charge.

Finally, they are in the west. We will be able to attack from the east and as the battle progresses we will, increasingly, be in darkness."

The Earl nodded, "Sound ideas all. I will ride with the King tomorrow. I will not tell him that it was your suggestion. He still does not like you but he respects you as a warrior. Perhaps he will listen. You have a good mind for war. The north is lucky to have you."

I stood, "And this is not the north, is it, Earl?"

He shook his head, "We do not have the luxury of choosing our battles, Thomas. When this is over you will return north. All will be well. I envy you your lair. Mine is in Pembroke. I rarely get to visit there and now I would have to fight the Welsh and the Marcher Lords to reach it!"

When we left the next day, we were in the middle of the column. Alfred rode next to me leading Flame and the captured sumpter. "I know not why we lead this horse, father. It is not a warhorse."

I nodded, "But it is a horse. Who knows when we might need it. When I was in the Holy Land there were many times when such a horse would have been invaluable. Besides, it carries the spears, helmet and shield. Scean will be fresher. Before the battle is fought and won I may need her fresh legs."

As we neared the battlefield my heart sank. King Llewelyn was no fool. He had his camp and battle lines arrayed behind the River Severn. I knew that here it would not be very wide; perhaps twenty paces but it would still break up our attack and mean that we would not be able to approach at the charge. It would be a walk at best. That would negate the advantage we held.

Edward saw the problem too. "A frontal charge would be madness, lord."

"And yet that is what we do. David of Wales."

My captain of archers rode up and joined us as we descended towards the river. "Lord?"

I pointed to a small wood that ran along the other side of the river of the Welsh side. It looked to be half a mile or so from the Welsh camp. "Send Mordaf and Gruffyd to that wood yonder. Have them ride well to the south before they turn and ford the

Severn. I would know if we can hide archers there. If we can then take all of my archers with you. You will be our guardian angel to stop this battle ending badly for us."

"Aye lord." He turned to give his orders to two of our Welshmen. If the Welsh occupied the woods then the two of them might be able to bluff their way out of it.

"Just our archers?"

"Yes, Edward. We will need the archers of the Palatinate to counter the Welsh ones."

The King halted us four hundred paces from the river. It was the first sensible decision he had made. We had all been given our orders and when his horn sounded we began to prepare for battle. Our archers tethered their horses close to the baggage and formed a line closer to the river. If the King noticed that my valley archers remained mounted he said nothing. The men at arms were prepared and they formed a line behind the dismounted archers. I handed Scean's reins to Alfred and went to the sumpter to fetch my shield and helmet. That done I was about to take a spear when Richard Marshal rode up. "Earl, the King would have you join him. He goes to speak with the Welsh." He smiled, "My father persuaded him."

As I mounted Flame I said to Edward, "Have the men cut some stakes and place them before our camp. If we have to fall back then we will have somewhere to defend." We did not have long but any defence was better than none.

"Aye lord."

It would be a small group of knights who would ride to meet on the sand spit in the centre of the river. The King, William Marshal, the Earl of Chester, William Longespée, the Earl of Salisbury and myself. His half-brother, William Longespée, carried the standard. We said nothing as we rode to the narrow river. To meet us were the Kings of Gwynedd, Deheubarth. and Powys. As well as four marcher lords. I recognised the livery of one of them. It was one of the de Ferrers family. I had met and slain members of that family in the Holy Land and Anjou. I had no doubt that I would be recognised. I did not know the lord who bore the distinctive shield. I knew that he would make for me once the battle began.

As we waited for the kings and rebels to descend into the river I prayed that the King would change his mind about fighting the battle he had planned. Already the sun had shifted. We had, perhaps four or five hours of daylight left.

Llewelyn, later to be called the Great was in the ascendancy. King John would allow him to become a greater king than the one who met us. The other Welsh kings were minor in comparison. Had the marcher lords not been present then I believe that the King's plan might have worked for, as we waited for the discussions to begin I saw that the Welsh knights were wearing old mail and none had the full-face helmets which we wore. Their horses were palfreys and not war horses. The marcher lords, in contrast, were armed and mounted as we were. The combination of those knights and the Welsh archers was a lethal one.

King Llewelyn spoke and that told me that the others deferred to him. "Why have you come here to Wales? Are you here to make war on us? If so then the crows will feast on your men and horses."

"King Llewelyn. you are married to my daughter and for that reason, I am in a forgiving frame of mind and will overlook the effrontery of this display before me." He jabbed his right hand at the marcher lords. "I see before me rebels and it is they who are the cause of my presence. Hand them over to me and we shall retire." He saw de Ferrers for the first time. "Godfrey de Ferrers, you are an ungrateful cur! I have given your family estates and bestowed coin upon you and this is how you repay me?"

De Ferrers laughed, "You have lost the right to rule just as you have lost Normandy. If you want us, John Lackland, then come and get us! You may have brought your northern hunting dogs but they will avail you nothing."

King Llewelyn shook his head, "Peace de Ferrers. Kings are talking!"

I took heart from the fact that de Ferrers coloured. He was not happy to be spoken to like that.

William Marshal spoke, "Can we not end this amicably? No one wants bloodshed here."

King Llewelyn nodded, "You are well respected here, Earl Marshal, but it has gone beyond talking. This will be settled by arms. It is right that it is fought here on this river which is the mightiest in this land. The ancient ones worshipped it as the Sabrina. Do your worst, King John. God is on our side and the land will protect us too!" He turned his horse and led the others back up the bank.

As we turned and rode back William Marshal said, "Will you not reconsider your plan, Your Majesty? When we charge the river will slow us down and then their archers will have free rein."

The King shook his head, "The only thing which changes is that we walk our horses to the river and our archers and those on foot will line it. My standard will signal the advance to the river. When we have crossed the river and arrayed, I will sound the horn three times. Then we will charge!"

The Earl Marshal looked at me and I shrugged. The die was cast but I had my own plan to avoid disaster for those whom de Ferrers had called the hunting dogs of the north. I would save as many of my men and those of the Palatinate as I could.

When I reached my men, I saw that David of Wales and the valley archers were not there. That meant they had been able to hide in the woods. I could rely on David of Wales. It would not win the battle for us but it might save some of the men at arms and knights who would charge into the Welsh arrows.

"Henry Youngblood, I want a ditch digging here. When we advance you and the men at arms are to provide protection for the archers by the river. The ditch and the stakes will be our last defence."

"It will not be a deep ditch, lord."

"I know but it must be there to slow up the enemy."

"Aye lord."

"Alfred, summon David of Stanhope. Edward, have my valley knights gather." When they arrived, I explained the plan. "I think that this attack is doomed to failure but we must prosecute our part. I believe that the King will order a withdrawal. I have my men at arms preparing a shallow ditch. It might help. The archers and men at arms of the Palatinate will guard the river bank." I shook my head, "It is the knights who will suffer this day," I looked at Alfred, "and, I fear, our squires."

I mounted and turned to Alfred. "I will not need Scean. If I lose Flame then I will make my way back to our lines. If my horse is lost you must get back to our men at arms."

"I will not leave you. Besides, I carry the standard. If I ride back then your knights will follow."

I gave him a steely stare, "Precisely! You are my squire and you will obey me. If you do not then you will no longer be my squire. Understood?"

"Yes, lord."

I donned my helmet and took the spear. My knights joined me. The Welsh and the rebels were singing and banging their shields. They were confident. King John's standard was lowered and I shouted, "Forward."

I saw that the men who faced me were a mixture of the men of Powys and rebels. De Ferrers had chosen to face me. There was a shield wall of men at arms backed by archers. I could not help glancing to the woods which lay just one hundred and twenty paces from our left flank. I could not see my archers and I was looking for them. Protected by the river their arrows would slow down any pursuit. The water came up to my thighs as we forded the river. Poor Alfred had to endure water up to his waist. This was not the best preparation for a first combat.

I had Sir Edward on one side of me and Sir William on the other. My other valley knights were to my right and the knights of the Palatinate to my left. William Marshal and his household knights were further to our right. That gave me hope. My other hope was the sun. it would be in our eyes, which never helped, but we would be looking down and the fading light behind us would, increasingly, make it harder for their archers and easier for ours. Perhaps I was clutching at straws but I had learned that, in warfare, the margins between victory and defeat could be narrow indeed.

The King was in the front rank but I knew that as soon as we charged his household knights would form up before him. We would not risk a king. In truth, he would be safe enough anyway. A captured king was more valuable than a dead one. Young Henry Winchester was safe in Windsor castle. If the King died we had a new one in waiting!

The three horns sounded. We had three hundred paces to travel. For two hundred of those paces, we would be within range of their arrows. We would be travelling slowly. I had heard of some knights who had armoured their horses. I knew that I might have to consider it. I waved my spear and the knights of the north rode to battle. I did not think that we would all return. With archers facing us, there was a temptation to ride faster but that would have been a mistake. The Welsh shield wall was a loose one. If we could hit them at the charge then we would sweep through them and disorder their archers. The flaw I saw in the Welsh plan was that they were relying upon their horsemen counter charging us and that would necessitate them riding through their own men.

I held my shield before me to my left. That way Flame was afforded some protection for his head. I would rely on the strength and integrity of my mail and my helmet. The Welsh had good bows, good bowmen but they used the barbed arrow. Our horses could be hurt but only a knight with a poorly made helmet would suffer too much damage.

The arrows began to fall. The first few fell short and the second was long. It allowed us to get up to the canter. I glanced to my right and saw that our centre, led by the King was ahead of us. Their line was not as tight but they would hit the spearmen soon. An arrow struck my helmet. It made my ears ring but my padded hood and arming cap prevented any damage. Two arrows struck the cantle on my saddle and three more hit my chausses. They were targeting me. We were one hundred paces from them when I lowered my spear. To my left, I was aware of a horse tumbling and throwing its rider. To my right, there was the clash of steel on wood as our centre hit the Welshmen of Gwynedd. We had a continuous line still and I saw a couple of the Welsh spearmen wavering. Their archers were bravely sending arrow after arrow towards us but soon they would be trampled beneath our horses' hooves unless they ran.

Twenty paces from the Welsh line I spurred Flame. An arrow had nicked his side and he was angry. His mouth was open and his teeth were already seeking a target. As I pulled back my spear the Welshman who faced me thought better of it and he ran. I brought my spear forward and hit the surprised archer he had exposed by his flight, in the chest. There was a loud crack on either side of me as spears hit shields, helmets and bodies. I was desperate to look right and see how the King fared but that would have been disastrous. I pulled back my arms and skewered a fleeing archer in the back.

I heard a horn and, looking ahead saw that the line of rebel and Welsh horsemen were readying for a charge. My knights were still with me and were almost in a solid line. I gambled. "Alfred, signal the charge!" He lowered the standard to face the enemy. Not all of my knights would see it. That did not matter. Enough would and they would know that we followed through with our charge. If I had had two squires then the second would have had a horn.

De Ferrers rode for me. He had a lance and he had a good warhorse. He was eager for vengeance. He was too eager for the knights around him were echeloned back. Godfrey de Ferrers had the best horse and he was waiting for no man.

I sacrificed the length of strike for accuracy by choosing a spear. De Ferrer's lance wavered up and down as he rode over the rough ground. He would hit me first and I would have to take the hit and hope it was not a mortal one. I shortened my grip so that only half of the spear stuck out before me. It would have looked suicidal to the rebel knight who charged me. I had allowed him to approach from my right where I had no shield. That meant he had no shield either. He had done this before for he stood in his stirrups to add power to the blow. He rammed it at me. As luck would have it although he aimed at my middle the ground made it rise up and catch my helmet a glancing blow. Splinters shattered. Some came through the holes in my helmet but, mercifully, they missed my eyes. I had to strike almost blindly but when I rammed forward I was rewarded by the rasp of the spear on mail and then, as he began to pass me, his momentum drove my spear into his middle and finally tore it from my grasp. He tried to stay in the saddle but I knew it would be in vain.

I had no time to take a spear from Alfred. Instead, I drew my sword. De Ferrers' charge meant I was through their horsemen. I was facing their fyrd. I felt reckless for I had done that which I thought impossible, I had broken through their knights. I spurred

Flame. By now he had the joy of battle in him. He reared as I spurred him. That must have terrified the fyrd for they turned and fled. With my household knights and their squires, we drove deep into the heart of pig farmers, yeomen and villeins. Our horses did most of the work for us and I only had to lay out two men with the flat of my sword. Then I heard King John's horn. We were in retreat.

I was close enough to my knights and squires to shout to them, "Fall back! We have done enough!"

I saw blood spattered surcoats. I saw a couple of squires nursing wounds but we were alive. I turned and we headed back. David of Stanhope and Stephen of Spennymoor had held the charge of the knights but they were hard-pressed. We did not charge we almost walked into the rear of the line of knights from Powys. The shock of our sudden attack made them wheel away and I shouted, "Knights of the Palatinate, we have done enough! Fall back."

Our attack had made the enemy fall away but seeing us flee they turned to charge after us. Our horses were spent. Edward and I were at the rear. I glanced over my shoulder and saw twenty knights almost upon us. Behind them were fifty more. When David of Wales unleashed his arrow storm it came like a bolt of lightning on a summer's day. Our arrows were not hunting arrows, they were knight killers. As Edward and I descended to the water the sun began to set behind the Welsh hills and the men of Powys died. By the time we had scrambled up the other bank, it was over. The men who had chased us were heading back to their own lines with arrows still finding men and our warriors were all chanting. The King and the Earl of Chester might have suffered a defeat but we had not. We had been a heartbeat away from their baggage. I would take that as a victory!

The knights of Durham had suffered. They had lost squires and knights but those who had followed King John and the Earl of Chester had lost more. My archers had been our saviours. I was summoned after dark to the King's tent. I saw that he had suffered a wound as had William Marshal. The King glowered at me, "How is it, Earl, that you always survive these battles and other, worthier knights do not? I have lost household knights whom I value."

I forced myself to remain calm, "I would say luck, Majesty, save that most of my men survive too. Perhaps they are better trained."

He waved an irritated hand as though to dismiss me. "We shall need you and your luck in the morning. I suspect the Welsh will take advantage of this setback and attack us."

I was going to speak but thought better of it. William Marshal spoke for me as he had had the same idea. "Lord, let them attack. They will have the same problem that we had. They have the river to cross and our horses have made the bank both slippery and harder to climb. We cannot win this battle but we can ensure that we do not lose. Dismount our knights and have them fight on foot."

I saw the King chew his lip. His half-brother, the Earl of Salisbury was the deciding factor, "If our archers can do what Cleveland's men did then we can make them bleed before they even get to the river."

The King agreed. By the time I reached the camp Flame's wounds had been seen to and Alfred had already sharpened my sword. I said, "You did well today, Alfred. You followed orders. Did you have to use a weapon?"

He nodded, "I used your spare spears and thrust them into the men who were fleeing. I could not hold on to them, lord and I lost them."

"Then that is a small price to pay. Tomorrow you will be mounted and holding my banner. Make sure you wear your arming cap and helmet. Use your shield. Sitting on a horse you will be a target."

"We just wait for them to attack us?"

"We just wait. Now fetch food. I am hungry."

I joined my knights sitting around the fire. "Sir Fótr, Sir Ralph, how are your squires?"

"Happy that they have survived the battle and that they have a wound which they can show."

Sir Ralph nodded his agreement, "They were bloody rather than damaging. They may both be stiff tomorrow but by then we will be heading home will we not, lord?"

I shook my head, "We stand and wait for them to attack. If they do then we have a chance of getting home unscathed. If we flee we will be chased and harried all the way to Oxford and beyond."

Gilles brought Sir Edward some food. He sniffed at it then said, "If they attack then we can hold them. I counted twenty dead knights yesterday including de Ferrers. They have plenty of men left but the ones who fought us broke. When they come they will be worried."

Sir Peter said, "Then all is well?"

Edward shook his head, "There will be precious little booty and treasure."

Sir William laughed, "You have followed Sir Thomas too long. There will be other wars and other battles. We are alive, Edward."

Sir William said, "And we still have our honour."

"My men kept a good watch. They had benefitted from the late battle for they had slipped over the river and taken the valuables from the dead rebel and Welsh knights. They also found four horses wandering, riderless." We had fought enough wars and battles to know how to make the most of the aftermath.

Ridley the Giant woke me before dawn. I looked around, "Alfred?"

My sergeant at arms grinned, "He was grooming the horses after you retired, lord. I thought to let him sleep. There will be little for him to do this morning."

"The enemy, are they awake?"

He nodded, "The night sentries heard them well before dawn. They are planning an attack. I heard them moving their horses. We have time, lord. Henry Youngblood has horsemeat cooking. Those small Welsh horses make good eating... if there is nothing better to hand." He turned to go, "I have had Master Alfred's horse saddled for him."

My men were resourceful. "Thank you, Ridley."

"My sons have told me how hard it is to be a squire."

When I heard the Welsh horns I woke Alfred. "Come, dress. Soon the battle will commence."

The Welsh horns were to order the enemy into their positions. All of the men on the left flank were already in position. Some of those in the centre were a little tardy but as we did not need horses it was of little matter. After Alfred had made water he ran to me with my shield.

"Go and eat something. Your horse is saddled. I will call you if they come earlier than we expect." I carried my helmet and slung my shield over my left shoulder. Our spears were already rammed into the soft earth where we would fight. My knights were already there. Edward had a war axe. He grinned wolfishly at me. "A horse might charge you, even with a spear sticking from it but I have yet to see one charge with no head!" I had seen Edward wield an axe before. It was a frightening sight for he had long arms and a broad body. He could almost have the same reach as with a spear.

Alfred arrived with my standard before the Welsh had begun their advance. Some of the King's men were still hurrying into their positions but we were ready. Unlike the Welsh wall of the previous day, ours was a true shield wall. We had a solid wall of shields and, behind us, our men at arms had their shields pushed into our backs. Their spears were ready to be thrust over our shoulders. Also, unlike the Welsh, we stood close by the river bank. We were far enough away from the slippery, muddy morass. We had solid footing. My men had laid the ashes from the fires there so that we had grip. I was not sure that the other two battles had done the same. I could not think for all of them.

The rebel knights and the knights of Powys rode in a long line backed by men at arms. The knights from the other two kingdoms were dismounted and they followed. Before all of them came the archers and, bringing up the rear were the fyrd. David led my archers to stand on the edge of the river bank. There was a deadly duel between both sets of archers. Amazingly I saw archers release and then watched the flight of an incoming arrow so that they could avoid it. The rate at which they could send their arrows was slower. More importantly, it allowed their horsemen to close with the river without suffering too many casualties. There were only fifty or so knights and they came not in a straight line but as individuals. That way they could avoid the archers.

As soon as the knights facing us dropped into the river I shouted, "David of Wales, withdraw." Our archers were vulnerable to an attack from horsemen. I would not risk them. Our shields were already locked. I saw the triumph on the faces of those knights with open helmets turn to horror as their horses struggled to get up the bank. During the night our men had used it to make water and to relieve their bowels. The bank was like a cesspit. As horses' heads appeared our spears swords and axes harvested a bloody crop. Knights fell into the water. Some drowned. Others tried to scramble up the bank.

All the time their archers were sending arrows into our lines. David of Wales' men returned the compliment and the Welsh archers were thinned. Our arrows did more damage. All the while the men at arms and dismounted knights lumbered towards us. I knew from our crossing that only the tallest of knights would cross successfully. I wondered what their kings thought would happen.

William shouted, "Lord, the Welsh are making inroads into the King's position."

It was obvious to me that their mounted horsemen had managed to distract the King's men and they had a foothold on the bank of the river. His men had failed to make it wetter and it was not as slippery. We could do nothing. We were pinned by the advancing men on foot. I saw that these had ladders with them to help them scale the bank. This would be a hard-fought battle. Archers had been hit. Although none had been killed there were still a couple with wounds. The Welsh who came across used shields to protect themselves. Even so, warriors died. As they scrambled to the top we awaited them. The ground was even more slippery now for horses had tried to clamber up and failed. As the first warriors ran at us they slipped. I speared one who lay on the ground before me. He wriggled like a fish and, as I pulled out the spear, he slipped back to the river and his body knocked more men from the ladder. As the river filled with dead, dying and wounded men so some used their comrades to make a bridge. Others were drowned as mailed warriors stepped onto them.

I still had my spear and with my long reach, I found I was able to punch the spearhead at their faces as they came up the ladder. It is a strange thing but when you poke something at a man he jerks his head back. It is self-preservation. Normally that would save him but when he was clinging to a ladder and top-heavy with a helmet and mail, he cannot keep his balance. After I dealt with four in this way the fifth reached up and grabbed my spear. He still fell backwards but he took the spear with him.

Men were now fighting all along the line. Most had to face men who had managed to make the top. Without my spear, I had no way to keep the Welsh at bay and I drew my sword. Two men managed to make their way towards me. They had a strange gait with feet wide apart but it seemed to be effective. Neither had mail. Both had swords and shields. They were not knights and looked to be the men at arms of an impoverished knight. My eye took in that their swords were old and slightly pitted. We were no longer a solid wall of shields and I had room to move. I stepped forward on my left leg and punched with my shield into the face of the one to my left. At the same time, I swung my sword in an arc. The man on my right had a helmet but no mail hood. My sword struck flesh and ripped open his neck. As his blood sprayed the other Welshman I continued my swing and my sword hacked into his side. Both men fell backwards and rolled into the river.

Alfred shouted, "Lord, they are winning in the centre!"

"Then let us end this. Men of the North, push them back into the river!"

We all roared and either punched or stabbed at the same time. It took the Welsh by surprise and we hit them hard. They tumbled and fell into the body choked river. The current was taking them downstream.

"David of Wales fetch up your archers! Squires and men at arms, support the archers! Stop the Welsh from crossing here." As our archers passed through I shouted, "Knights, form a wedge behind me. We go to the aid of our King!" It was a rough wedge and lacked the order I really wished but it would have to do. I intended to drive up through the rebels who had surrounded the King and William Marshal. My archers could stop any more men crossing behind us. "March!"

The first men we came upon were either wounded or stragglers by themselves. Those that were able, jumped back into the river and the others were slain. Their cries alerted their fellows to the danger and some of the rebels turned. William and

Edward flanked me and both of them knew their business. Their shields guarded me and our three swords, backed by the rest of my knights carved a bloody path through the rebels. We could have stopped then for we had achieved our objective. Men could not fight on two flanks at once and the ones who could, slid out so that the press was not as tight as it had been.

William Marshal was an old warhorse and he shouted, "King John and St. George! For England!" With his sons and oathsworn beside him, he pushed towards the river.

I shouted, "Turn them!" By the simple expedient of turning to our left, we were still protected by our shields while we were also able to swing our swords. As the rebels found the slippery top of the bank so their armour made them slip and topple into the water. These were knights. All of them had hauberks. Few managed to scramble to the other side. With the defeat of the rebels and the men of Powys, King Llewelyn had no choice. He sounded the retreat. They were beaten.

The rest of the English archers made their retreat difficult and almost as many men died trying to get back to their camp as had died in the fight by the King's camp. We reformed our lines and waited for a second attack but none materialized. A truce was arranged so that the wounded of both sides could be recovered. David of Wales and Ridley the Giant slipped downstream to take the mail and swords from the knights who had been swept closer to the sea. They found them on sand spits and rocks.

The truce was extended and once again we met with Llewelyn on the spit of sand. This time there were no rebels. It was just the Welsh kings. I saw Llewelyn apprising me. He nodded, "You deserve your reputation, Sir Thomas! We might have defeated your King had you not done that which you did in the two battles. I respect you but do not take offence if I say that I hope you stay by the northern border from now on."

I smiled and saw the Earl Marshal smiling too, "I serve my king and go where he commands."

In contrast, King John was not smiling. This was the third time I had saved him and he did not like it. "King Llewelyn, as you are married to my daughter I will forgive this action but from this day the border with Wales is this river over which we fought."

The three kings looked at each other and nodded, "Agreed."

"However, I cannot forgive the rebels. I demand that you cease to support them."

"Demand?"

The King coloured and then nodded, "You are right. I request that you cease to support them."

"Then I agree."

And with that, the Welsh war was over. Of course, we had to march south to take the manors of the rebels. King John gave the best to his supporters but he also rewarded the men who had fought with me and we needed wagons to take back our booty. We headed north and I was relieved that I would not have to go to any of my ladies and tell them that their husbands and sons were dead. We had all survived and I thanked God.

Chapter 6
The Durham solution

We also had news relating to the Palatinate. It had ever been a thorn in my side. Philip of Poitou had been all too brief interlude of stability. King John had appointed Richard Poore as Bishop of Durham but the appointment had been quashed by Pope Innocent. However, John de Gray was a churchman who was also a powerful man. More importantly, he was close to the King having loaned him money before now. When I told the King, while he dealt with the marcher manors, of Philip de Poitou's nephew he became incensed and promised to send John de Gray's nephew, Richard to oversee the financial side of the Palatinate. He wanted his money! Until he arrived then I was given the power to remove Aimeric of Chartres from power.

The long journey home allowed me to speak with David of Stanhope and the other senior barons. Alfred listened attentively. His time in Wales had shown him that there was more to being a knight than riding a warhorse and wielding a sword. The Durham knights identified the men who might cause trouble when I tried to remove Aimeric. The fact that they were not with the rest of the Durham knights was evidence enough of their feelings. Richard de Gray could deal with the coin, he was said to be gifted in that area, but when it came to military solutions then that would be my task.

When we reached Piercebridge Sir Ralph took his leave of us and headed back to Northallerton. His appointment was confirmed by King John. His brave action in the battle of Welshpool had made it impossible to do other. Sir Peter would join him at Whorlton when he had collected his wife from Stockton. He was ready to be lord of the manor. I knew that his mother would find it hard to be parted from her son and his new family but knights did not have the luxury to pick and choose their manors.

Once we had crossed the Tees, David of Stanhope led the men of Durham home and we had the last leg of our journey to Stockton ahead of us. I watched Alfred looking on our valley with new eyes. He had been to the western border of England

and seen that we were lucky to live where we did. Here we had one enemy, Scotland. In Wales, there were three kingdoms as well as many rebel lords. Perhaps my wife had been right to wait until he had seen more than twelve summers before allowing him to train. He had had to grow up and take responsibility for himself. He had helped to train Petr to become Sir Peter. Now he could concentrate on the knightly skills of war and with peace on the border that might be a less dangerous process.

Arriving in Stockton I was dismayed to see that my Aunt Ruth was not there to greet me. My wife saw the look on my face, "Do not worry, husband. It is a winter chill. She had one before and she can recover. Sarah and our daughters have been caring for her." She looked at Alfred, "I am more concerned to see if our son has all of his limbs!"

Alfred grinned. I saw that he was now a head taller than his mother. "Our father kept me safe from harm. I felt guilty that others were enduring wounds and I was able to watch from safety." It was not a lie but it was far from the truth. He was becoming a man and learning that you did not worry women unnecessarily. When he had sat on his horse behind me at the Severn he had been hit by many arrows. Luckily, he took them on his shield and others struck his cantle. One even hit the standard. We would have to find a new staff for it.

After changing from my riding clothes and briefly washing I went to my aunt's room. Sarah was there. She now looked like a woman. When we had found her with the other captives she had been thin with haunted eyes. Marguerite's food had put meat on her bones and the safety of Stockton's walls had helped her lose her fear of men and Scots in particular. "Thank you for caring for my aunt, Lady Sarah. Your husband is here and now you can leave for your new home at Whorlton."

Her eyes lit up, "Thank you, lord." She paused. "He is not hurt?"

"He is too good a knight for that!"

She was an innocent and fey young woman. He reached up and impulsively kissed my cheek. I knew of many lords who would have taken offence but not me. I was delighted. Petr had worked wonders with her.

Magna Carta

She left us and Aunt Ruth held up her hand. "Petr has a good one there! I hope he appreciates her!"

"And how are you, Aunt?"

"These winter chills are becoming annoying! Everyone fusses around me as though I am an invalid! It is good that you are back and, I take it, with success?"

I sat on the edge of the bed. My aunt was not like other women. Her husband had been taken when she was young and she had taken a keen interest in war. She would have made a good warrior for she had a sharp and perceptive mind. I told her all. I saw her nodding at the decisions I made. I omitted my reckless charge into the fyrd. That might have incurred the wrath of my wife. When I had finished she said, "This King is incompetent! He will not need you again?"

I shrugged, "I know not but he has had the forty days required of me this year. We are safe until next year. He has many enemies. The knights who rebelled had been his close allies at one time. I fear that the French may seize the opportunity to exploit this disunity."

"Invade?"

"King Philip is ambitious and he has bested King John at every turn. There are English rebels at his court and they are in touch with those in England." I shook my head, "When I hear grumbling knights who seek to seduce me to the side of the rebels I think that they are fostering the cause of France. De Percy has the best idea. If we can curb the King's power legally then we will have a better kingdom."

She squeezed my hand, "Tread carefully, Thomas, there is a fine line between Baron de Percy and Fitzwalter."

"I know, Aunt Ruth, and I have too much to lose here to risk all. I am a patriot and I will defend my land. King John is a bad king but he is of the blood of King Henry. Our family has sacrificed too much for me to abandon him."

We had two months to await the arrival of de Gray. His arrival coincided with the onset of winter. He arrived in one of the last ships before the river froze up. His family had estates in Norfolk and the voyage was easier than braving winter roads. He came with a retinue. William Marshal had told me that the de Grays were rich. Any family which could afford to loan money to a king knew how to make coin. Although Richard was a competent young man I did not like him. He was not a likeable man. He was arrogant and he was fussy. He did not like the north of England.

As soon as I greeted him in my hall his words rankled immediately, "I pity you, Earl. You live in a dreary, cold and windswept land! I can see why there is no Bishop here. Even if the Pope sanctioned one it would take a fool to take on the task."

I struggled to keep my voice calm, "And yet you chose to come here. Is that not a contradiction?"

He gave me a knowing smile, "King John wishes it and my uncle knows how to please our liege lord. Besides, it will not be for long. My uncle assures me that a delegation of bishops is even now on their way to Rome to persuade the Pope to revoke his interdict and restore the rights of the church to England."

"Persuade?"

"The Pope always needs coin. The interdict will be revoked and the money that I can save from Durham will pay for the persuasion of the Pope. When Richard Poore is appointed he will find a secure and stable palatinate; financially stable that is. I understand the other matters are in your hands?"

His self-confidence was infuriating in one so young. "Quite so."

My wife and steward, Geoffrey approached, "We have a guest hall for you and your people. I hope that you will be comfortable there during your short stay."

"I doubt it. I cannot see anything in the north which will make me comfortable. So long as you have a fire and a plentiful supply of wood to burn then I will be happy."

Geoffrey, my steward looked appalled but he had served Aunt Ruth in difficult times and he took charge, "If you would follow me, my lord."

When he had gone my wife, who was normally pleasant about everyone said, "I am sorry, husband, but the sooner that man is in Durham and away from us the better. I have spoken but a dozen words with him and already I do not like him."

I laughed, "I had to endure a great deal longer. He is lucky to be walking for he insulted Stockton!"

I would have to escort him to Durham. Aimeric would not relinquish power easily. I would take Sir William, Sir Fótr and Sir Edward with me as well as my men at arms and archers. Aimeric had had enough run-ins with us and would know the worth of my men. We left the next morning and, as the snow was falling, I told my wife that we would stay a couple of days in Durham. The last thing I needed was for something to happen to the King's man. I would have to ensure that the garrison were loyal, not to Aimeric but the Palatinate.

We had gained horses from the Welsh foray and although they were not as good for war as the ones we had they were more than adequate for the retinue of de Gray. Alfred had grown into his role as a squire. He did not wait to be asked which horse I would take; he knew. Scean was saddled and ready for me. I had servants to prepare my clothes but it was Alfred who had my weapons ready for me. He did not bother with my shield and helmet. If we needed those then I would have lost my grip on Durham. Although James, my servant, had a cloak for me, when I reached the portico which built to allow us to mount when it was inclement, Alfred had the cloak with the sealskin cape around the shoulders. It would keep me dry. I also smiled when I saw that he had loaded the sumpter we had captured from the Welsh, with our baggage. We had named him Bounty. On the ride back from Wales Alfred had found that the horse, contrary to his first impressions, was intelligent and hard working.

As we mounted I smiled. De Gray and his men had thin cloaks. They would be soaked before we reach Thorpe! By the time we reached Durham, he would be thoroughly miserable. It might make him move more quickly. The ride which in summer would take just a few hours might now take almost all day for the snow had begun to fall. Until it settled it would make the cobbled Roman roads slippery.

Even though we were at peace I still had two of David's archers as scouts. They rode ahead of us. Our guests rode huddled together behind my knights and me. It gave me the chance to talk to Edward and the others about Durham. "I do not expect Aimeric to be happy about this turn of events but I hope that he will not be so foolish as to try to use force against us. De Gray is the King's representative."

Fótr knew the dead bishop's nephew as well as any, "Lord, he has much to lose. He has a palace in Durham and a lodge in Auckland. He has servants and power. He has men to protect him. Why should he give all that up?"

Edward answered with a snort, "Because he is merely a caretaker, a temporary steward. He will have coin secreted away and he will use that."

I shook my head, "King John does not wish him to benefit from his time in Durham. David of Stanhope and the knights of Durham told the King just what he was like. Richard de Gray has orders to allow him to leave with that which he brought. He will not go quietly into the night. We have to ensure that he does not use violence. I have already instructed Ridley and David of Wales to neutralize the guards."

Fótr was persistent, "And if he does not let us in?"

"Then we will not need to worry about him making trouble for I have orders to execute him if he resists. King John was most insistent that Aimeric should pay for his abuse of power."

Edward and William gave me an incredulous look. I shrugged, "Do as I say, not do as I do, seems to be his creed!"

I had deliberately not warned Aimeric of our arrival. Despite our mutual distaste, he allowed me entry to his castle, palace and church. His sentries were polite. "Bad night to be out, my lord."

"Needs must. It is Ralph is it not?"

The man swelled up as I remembered his name. It was only because he had been unpleasant to me once. "Yes, my lord."

"We will be staying the night. You can bar the gate when we are through."

"Yes lord."

I saw the question in his eyes. It mattered not. When we had spoken to Aimeric Henry Youngblood and four of my men would take over the duties of sentinel until I made the garrison swear allegiance to me and Richard de Gray. I would take no chances. As we dismounted I could not help smiling for Richard de Gray was blue with the cold and was shaking so much that speech was impossible. I waved Ridley the Giant forward and spoke quietly to him, "Guard Lord Richard de Gray, Ridley. I am not certain that his presence will be welcomed."

"Aye lord." He walked over and helped the young man down. "You are here now, my lord. There will be a fire inside I have no doubt."

De Gray looked up at the gentle giant beside him. Even had he been capable of speech I am not certain he would have found the words to answer.

After sending Padraig the Wanderer and my men at arms to the warrior hall, I waved to David of Wales and he led his men to the stables. The men at arms of my knights headed for the preceptory and church. They were there to protect the priests.

It was the steward of the hall who greeted me when I banged on the door. "My lord, we are not expecting guests I am not certain…"

I pushed the door open, "This is not a social visit. I come on the King's orders. You now have a new master." I leaned and said quietly so that only he could hear, "Steward, the days of Aimeric are over. Remember that if you value your position."

His eyes flickered to the right as he considered warning Aimeric. Then self-preservation took over. He nodded, "Of course, Earl. I am a loyal subject of the crown and the Bishop of Durham."

It had been some time since I had been in Durham. Philip of Poitou had been alive the last time I had walked the corridors. As I headed for the hall I heard unseemly laughter and the sound of women. This was a religious establishment of men. When I threw open the door I saw that Aimeric and his close associates, none of them priests, were having a feast. The women who were there were doxies and whores. Some looked to be younger than Sarah. The opening of the double doors and the draught of cold had an immediate and sobering effect.

Aimeric stood and shouted, "Earl, this is most unseemly. Do you not warn a man of a visit? We are celebrating!"

"I can see that." I had the parchment which I had taken from Richard de Gray's chilled hands. "This is from the King. You are dismissed from your post and another is appointed."

It was as though someone had slapped his face. His mouth dropped open and his eyes widened. "The King cannot do that. The Pope has an interdict! There can be no new bishop."

I smiled, as my men filtered into the hall. I saw some of Aimeric's cronies, realising that their time was up fingering their weapons. "The new Bishop is in Rome. Perhaps even now Richard Poore is heading here to take up his role as Prince Bishop. The appointment I speak of is Lord Richard de Gray." I waved my arm and de Gray stepped forward with his shadow, Ridley the Giant, behind. "He is here to examine the finances of the Palatinate to discover why the revenue the King should enjoy has diminished since the death of the last Bishop of Durham."

Bloodshed might have been avoided but for two things: Aimeric did not accept defeat gracefully and the men he had used to secure his position were not willing to lose the life they had come to enjoy. I did not know any of the mailed and armed men in the room but they were obviously mercenaries who knew their business. Two came for me and two went for Richard.

We had been expecting it. I wore mail and the mercenaries did not. I was sober and they were drunk. As the two men came towards me I dropped the parchment while drawing dagger and sword. Alfred also stepped next to me with his short sword. His sudden movement meant that one of the men was distracted. I blocked the sword of the other with my sword and tore my dagger across his middle. The other recovered and tried to swing at my unprotected left side. Alfred's sword partially blocked the blow and certainly slowed it down. I was able to stab him in the neck. The blood arced across the room as it sprayed from his neck and the women screamed. Sir Edward helped Ridley to dispose of the two attacking de Gray and my knights slew three others. The rest dropped their weapons.

"Take the weapons from the others and bind them. We will take them for trial at our next assizes."

One of them shouted, "What for? Defending ourselves?"

I bent down to retrieve the document. "While I hold this and serve the wishes of the King then the crime is treason!" They were silenced. "Alfred and Gilles, bind and guard Aimeric of Chartres."

"What for? I did nothing to you. I am not even armed."

"Until the finances and the accounts of the Palatinate are examined by Lord de Gray you will be held. When he is satisfied that all is legal and above board then you will be allowed to leave. I daresay France will be more attractive than Durham."

The last part of my sentence did not seem to bother him but the first part did. He paled. He had been embezzling. I had known that but I now saw the wisdom of King John. He was sending a man who knew how to unravel such secrets.

"Take him away." I was aware of the women who were still huddled together. "You ladies may leave. If you were expecting payment there will be none." Once the mercenaries and Aimeric were taken away we were the only ones in the hall.

Richard de Gray turned to Ridley and Edward, "I am in your debt. They would have killed me but for you!" He sounded shocked at such violence. He saw my look and shook his head, "I am not used to violence. I was training to be a priest," he shook his head, "I have a gift for figures and it has kept me safe until now. Will I be safe here once you are gone?"

"Stockton is not far away but I will not be leaving until I can guarantee your safety. Ridley, have the bodies removed and then stay here to guard our visitors. The rest of us will ascertain the loyalty of the men within Durham's walls."

I went first to the preceptory and the church. The Dean, Archdeacons and the senior clergy were all there as well as the priests. "Sir Thomas, what is the meaning of this? Why are these armed men here?"

"They are to guard you."

"From whom?"

"From those who would wish you harm." I told him of the appointment of a bishop and he looked relieved.

"We are delivered from Aimeric?"

"Delivered? What has he done to you?"

"It is what he has done to God's house. He has cut down the food which we eat. We had no one to whom we could appeal."

"There was me."

He shook his head. "He forbade us to leave. Whenever a messenger came from your castle or whenever the knights of Durham were needed we were confined to the cathedral."

"How long has this been going on?"

"Since William was defeated."

Now I understood. With the threat gone from the north and the interdict in place, it meant he could do as he wished. "Now you will be safe. Lord Richard de Gray will command until the Bishop arrives from Rome. You can trust him but I will send men here once a week to speak with you. If there is a problem then tell me!"

"Aye lord."

"I would have one of your priests bring a Bible with him for I need to speak to the men." The Dean did not question my request and a young priest picked up a heavy Bible and followed me. Leaving the priests, we went to the warrior hall after first visiting the stables. "Dick, fetch Ralph and the other sentries from the walls. Keep watch with Henry and his men until I send for you. The rest of your archers can make certain that none leave here."

Padraig the Wanderer and my men at arms had drawn weapons. As I passed him I cocked an eye, "They questioned our presence, lord. They understand now." I saw one of the garrison with a bloody nose.

I walked to the centre of the room and lowered my arming hood. I laid my sword on the table. "Brother, if you would put the Bible there. You are here merely to observe." I allowed an uncomfortable silence to descend upon the room as we waited for Ralph and the sentries. Dick and Henry accompanied them and then left.

There were twenty-two men in all.

"I am here to tell you that there has been a change in the management of this cathedral and this town. Aimeric of Chartres is now my prisoner. The mercenaries who survived the unwarranted attack on us are also my prisoners." I saw fear and apprehension fill their faces. I waited. "Your fate is in your own hands. You know me and that I am a man of my word. That is a double-edged sword. I can be your friend but if I am your foe then there is no corner of this earth in which you are safe." I paused, "As Bishop Puiset discovered." I had their undivided attention. "Here is your choice: swear on this Bible that you will obey Richard de Gray and me and you can continue to serve here in Durham." I let that sink in. "If you do not swear then I can only assume that you are one of those who should be on trial and you will be arrested. I have a priest here to witness your attestation. The sword is my guarantee that you will adhere to your oath."

All swore as I knew they would.

"You may return to your duties."

I was weary by the time that I returned to the hall. My men had had food warmed up and we all ate at the same table. If Richard and his men were surprised he said nothing. He was still stunned at his brush with death. Edward held up the goblet of wine appreciatively. "I will say this for those villains, they keep a good table and a good cellar. This is as fine a wine as I have enjoyed since Anjou."

Richard de Gray was more concerned with his own safety than the quality of the food. "Are you certain you can trust the men who swore an oath, Earl?"

"They swore on a Bible but my sword was there too. I doubt they will risk my ire."

Weary and with sentries on the walls I slept well. When I woke my good humour left me. Alfred greeted me, "Lord, Aimeric escaped in the night. He was aided by two of the servants. They killed Ralph the gateman."

I cursed myself. I should have made the servants swear too. Because of my lapse, a man was dead. "We must get after them!"

My son shook his head. "You cannot, lord. We did not discover the dead gate man until half an hour since. Sir William then checked on Aimeric and found that he was gone. A blizzard suddenly blew up. The tracks they made have disappeared. They are gone."

I was not certain. My knights had thought it for the best to let me sleep but in my heart, I knew that had I been woken we would have had a chance to catch them. It was too late now. They were long gone. "They might be gone but I will find and hang them. Have the rest of the servants brought here. I will question them personally!"

I was not gentle in my questioning and I terrified the servants. I made them swear on a Bible and then extracted all of the information I could from them. They would have gone to Scotland. One of the servants was a Scot. They would be safe there. When the snows had gone and time allowed I would hunt for men. They would not escape me.

Chapter 7
Fighting for the Scots

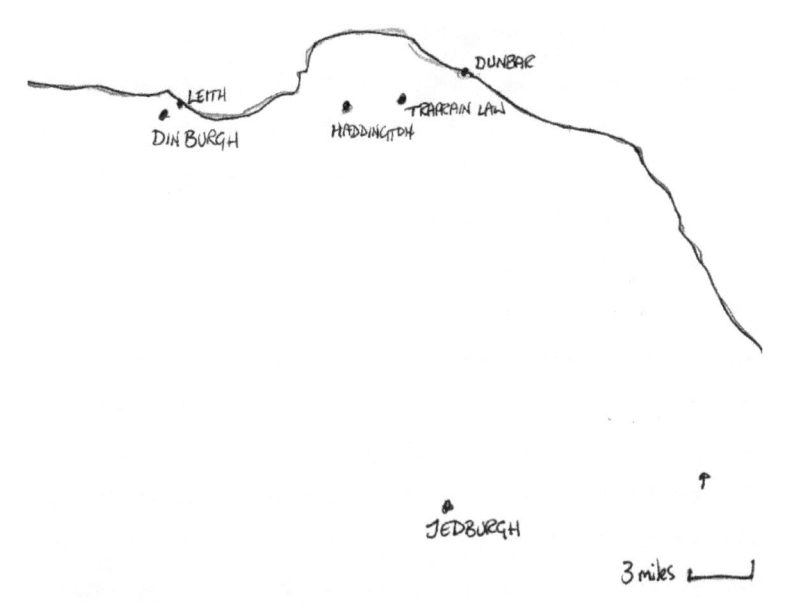

[Map showing: Leith, Dinburgh, Haddington, Traprain Law, Dunbar, Jedburgh. Scale: 3 miles]

We tried the mercenaries fairly. We used a court of my knights and senior men at arms. We listened to their defence but, in the event, there was little to it. The Dean of Durham had been the one to condemn them. He sent a letter which told of their crimes. They included rape and murder. Aimeric had done much which was evil while ruling Durham like a fiefdom. We hanged the eight men we tried. Their bodies were left at the Norton crossroads as a warning to other transgressors. We had never had to hang any of our own people. They were generally law-abiding. The most severe punishment we had imposed had been to walk to Durham cathedral on Sunday to hear the services there. That was a long day's walk. Our locals did not poach. They asked my permission to hunt and I normally granted it. Tam the Hawker had caught poachers but they were not locals and most had been bandits or brigands. I did not have them blinded, as was my right, instead, I had their first and forefingers lopped off their right hand. It marked them as poachers.

I kept my word and either myself or one of my knights visited Durham once a week. It reassured both the clergy and the ever-nervous Richard de Gray. He did not endear himself to any of us. He never thanked us for our visits but regarded it as our duty. He seemed, however, to be good at his job. When I visited at Easter he showed me the squiggles on the wax tablet.

"There, Earl, you can see quite clearly how much Aimeric of Chartres stole!"

I could make neither head nor tail of the squiggles. "Richard, I am a warrior, explain to me where the coin is. I am certain that the King would wish to know that."

He shrugged and waved his arms around, "To speak plainly, Earl, I know not. Aimeric has it. I believe that when he absconded he took the chests with him. The two servants who fled were both scribes. One was the cathedral's reeve."

"Then they must have had horses waiting for them in the town. If not, then how did they get the coin?"

He looked blankly at me, "You are the hunter, lord."

I cursed myself. I should have questioned those who lived close to the town. I sent Ridley the Giant with Alfred to question the folk who lived close to the gate. It did not take long to discover that a man and a woman had left the same night as Aimeric. They had Scottish accents and they had a wagon. I should have trusted my instincts and pursued them immediately. The others had said that the snow would cover the tracks. It would not have covered the tracks of a wagon. Even hours later there would have been indentations in the snow. We could have caught them. They were definitely in Scotland. Aimeric had money. From what Richard had told me it was many pounds of silver and gold. I knew that I would be blamed by King John.

"Is there any news about the new Bishop?"

Shaking his head, he said, "The last news I had from York was a month old and Bishop-elect Poore is still awaiting an audience with the Pope. However, I am confident that we will have news in a month or so."

How can you be so sure?"

He smiled, "The Pope has payments to make too, Earl. It costs money to rule in Rome and the income from the Holy Land is not what it was. King Richard and his crusade was the high-water mark. Since then the Holy Land which is controlled by Christians is shrinking. The Seljuk Turks and the Egyptians are eating into it day by day." He smiled, "I daresay he will be asking for another Crusade soon enough!"

I left him, shaking my head. To him, it was all about coin and income. I had served in the Holy Land. Warriors were dying and Christians were suffering. I headed back to Stockton with the weight of the world upon my shoulders.

A month after Easter and we had some good news. Fótr and Petr were to become fathers. It brightened everyone's lives. My wife and Aunt Ruth were particularly overjoyed for it showed that the two girls who had had to endure such privations had recovered. My aunt's smile became a permanent feature. The illness of the winter was forgotten.

William asked me to ride over to Hartburn. I wondered if it was to ask me to knight Johann. He was the oldest squire that I knew. In the event, it was not. He wished to show me the fields he had cleared. It had been the lair of the wild boar. It had taken some time to completely remove the stumps and then to till goodness back into the soil but he was very proud of his achievement, as was I. As we walked his fields I asked him about Johann.

"Why is he not a knight? He is more than qualified."

"I am afraid he does not wish to be one. He is quite happy to serve me. To be honest, Earl, my eldest son, Robert is training as a squire and I have asked Johann to be my sergeant at arms. He is happy to do so." He looked worried, "Is that acceptable to you, lord?"

I laughed, "We made him your squire and then he became your responsibility. If he is happy and so are you then there is no problem. What about Richard, your younger son?"

"Two squires are always useful, lord."

He was right and I was content.

The contentment lasted until the summer solstice when William Marshal's son, William arrived at my ferry. He had with him just an escort of knights. It was not an army and I wondered what it betokened. I liked the earl's son. He was a good warrior and he spoke plainly. He was a younger version of his father and in a world of deceit that was reassuring.

"It is good to see you, Sir Thomas. How has life treated you since the battles of Welshpool? You saved the battle that day." I told him of Durham. He had a strange look on his face.

"And you, and your father?"

He said, "I will speak in confidence to you for I know that you are a true knight. The King had planned an invasion of Poitou so that he could recover the lost lands. However, when he sent letters to demand service abroad many of the barons, especially those in the north refused. They said that a war in Poitou would require them of more than forty days' service and as they did not own land in Normandy or Anjou the King should use those knights." He shrugged, "According to the letter of the law they were right but, as you can imagine, that did not sit well with the King. He has demanded that those who refused service should repay the debts they owe. If they do not then their manors will become forfeit. King John does not take defeat well."

"He did not ask me."

There was a heavy silence. I could see that he was struggling with an internal dilemma. "The fact is Earl, that he knew you would accept. You are that sort of knight. But he has other plans for you and the knights of Durham." He paused.

"Come, William, I speak plainly, I would ask that you do the same."

He nodded, "King William of Scotland is having trouble with some of his rivals. They are disappointed that he lost the war and had to pay such reparations that Scotland will be crippled. He has asked King John for military aid from England. The King has offered you and the Earl of Chester. I went to Chester first. The Earl is already marching for Carlisle. Alexander, the King's son, is with him. They are meeting with the loyal barons in the west. You are to ride to Jedburgh. There King William awaits you."

I could not believe what I was hearing, "We fight and bleed, for the Scots?"

He sighed, "It is not as simple as that, Sir Thomas. If King William is overthrown and one of the other factions gain power then the treaty of Norham is as good as torn up. That will mean raids along the northern borders."

We were standing in my northeast tower and looking down on my town. It was market day and the town was packed with those who wished to trade. Could I ruin the prosperity it had taken me years to build up? Fighting for the Scots was the logical thing to do. It just went against my nature to fight for our natural enemies.

The Earl Marshal's son sensed my dilemma. "The King has knighted King William's son, Alexander and so long as the two of them are in power then England is safe."

"That is because we defeated him so heavily last time."

"And that was your doing. Think what the effect would be on these would-be rebels if the Earl who captured their King suddenly fights for him. The battles would be won before you took the field."

I shook my head, "Do not insult me by trying to flatter me. I care not for glory. I care about the men I lead into battle. Are you telling me that I will not lose men in this war? This war that I need not fight."

"I apologise, I am so used to the knights who fawn around the King that I grow to think that all are the same. You are right but so am I. You either fight for King William or face the rest of his men when he is overthrown."

"He has no support?"

"Little."

"What happened to it?"

"You destroyed most of his best men in the last battle. They were his oathsworn, they were his best. We both know that it takes time to build up an army of men on whom you can depend." I knew that he was right. We would have to fight the enemies of William of Scotland. "Two things, Sir Thomas, there is coin involved. The King has manors in England. He has promised the revenue from Huntingdon to you and your knights so long as he lives and reigns. That would help you and your knights. He is also happy for you to keep any treasure, horses and ransoms which you might take in battle. All that he wants is security and the time to build up an army."

"And King John wants me to give him forty days?" He nodded. "I will summon my knights. I promise nothing."

"But the King…"

"The King is pushing my patience to the limit. I will do what I must do but only if I have the backing of my knights."

I took William Marshal to his quarters and then sent riders to summon my knights. As I needed Sir Ralph from Northallerton the meeting would have to be the following day. That would give me the night to discuss it with my wife and aunt. My wife knew something was amiss and when William Marshal showed tact by begging for him and his knights to retire early then her fears were confirmed. I allowed Alfred to stay, for he was my squire but the rest were sent away.

I gave them the information and the task. I left nothing out and I gave the reasons both for and against. I could see my wife becoming upset. Aunt Ruth looked less worried.

"Another war, husband? A war which is not of your choosing? You say no! It is madness to fight for an enemy."

Alfred said nothing. I knew he wanted the chance to go to war but he did not wish to upset his mother. Aunt Ruth sipped her wine. "You have no choice, Thomas. You must go."

"Aunt!"

"Listen to me, Margaret, this is an order from King John. He is not a reasonable man. He is not a forgiving man. The de Percy family have lost two manors. Your husband has just two. If they are taken then what do we have left? Secondly, William Marshal is right. If you allow King William to be defeated the hordes of hell will be unleashed. They will flood over the border. Before Thomas came home that was a regular occurrence. He has done what the Warlord did. He has kept this valley safe. He must fight to ensure it continues that way. I think that Thomas should give King William his forty days service for King John and then he has fulfilled his obligations."

Alfred's face showed what he thought. Margaret was too upset to see that my aunt had spoken from the heart.

My knights all knew that something was wrong but I refused to tell them until Sir Ralph had arrived. When he did I gathered them in my hall and told them exactly what I had told my aunt and wife. They came to the same conclusion but it took longer.

Edward summed it up succinctly, "We ride north and kill Scotsmen. We take their treasure and their horses. We do so with the blessing of the King and then he pays us a yearly stipend for the rest of his life. This is a chance not to be missed. Would that all wars promised so much coin before even starting out!"

I gave them three days to muster their forces and I rode to Durham. I summoned the Durham knights. With them, there was less of an option. They would be obeying the King. I did not mention the punishment which the de Percys and other families had suffered. Surprisingly enough they were all happy. David of Stanhope said, "At least we are fighting close to home and the ones we fight are our enemies. There is one condition, Earl, we follow your banner and not King William's"

I nodded. "That goes without saying."

We were at Jedburgh ten days later. We did not bring all of our men at arms and archers. None of us trusted the Scots enough for that. We were expected and, when we crossed the Tweed we were greeted with smiles and not spears. The knight who greeted us and escorted us was an older knight. "I am the Mormaer of Fife, Angus. Your men can camp where they choose. King William has quarters for you and your son." My look must have shown the suspicion in my heart. "You have my word, Earl, that there will no treachery. If you wish to bring two chamberlains then the King will understand."

I nodded, "In that case, I will. Alfred, fetch Ridley the Giant and Padraig the Wanderer."

When the mormaer saw Ridley he smiled, "I hope we have a room big enough to accommodate such a man."

My men at arms and Alfred went to the chamber prepared for us and I was taken to a small room where King William awaited me. He was now old and looked it. "Sit, my lord." I did so and he poured us both some wine. The door was closed behind us. "I thought we ought to talk privately. That way you can express your fears about this directly to me."

"Thank you."

"Here's to a strange alliance." He held up his goblet and we both drank. He laughed, "The last time you were here it was different eh, Earl?"

"It was but we came so often that this was almost like England."

"Aye, your family have ever been the bane of Scotland." There was nothing I could say to that. It was true. "I confess I was surprised with King John's choice of leader. I had hoped he would send some of his knights from further south. There is bad blood between us. You do not want to fight for us." It was a statement and not a question but I answered it anyway.

"When the war was ended it was because we defeated and killed those men who were closest to you. How many survived?"

"A handful."

"And I want to avoid that with my men. It might happen in a war or a battle but I would prefer it to be something I wished to fight for."

"And not me." I nodded. "That is understandable. Look, Earl, there are three enemies here. Dunbar, you have met him, Galloway in the west and, Argyll in the north. All you have to do is defeat Dunbar. He is the most dangerous of the three. My son and Chester can handle Galloway. With those two out of the way then my son and I can deal with Argyll."

"If it were that easy then you would have rid yourself of him before asking for my help."

"Our knights are brave enough but they lack discipline. Your combination of knights, men at arms and archers is irresistible. Our men cannot become that skilled overnight. It will take time. Now that I have had time to think about it I can see that you are the best choice for this quest." He took out a map. "Here are Dunbar's strongholds."

"Where will he be found?"

"Din Burgh. He will be on the rock."

"And that is almost impossible to take without losing many men. Then we will have to tempt him from there."

"How?"

"I do not know yet but give me a few days and I will have a plan."

"The longer you delay the more powerful he becomes. He controls much of the land from his rock. He dominates the river and the trade. I have heard he has hired Norse mercenaries to fight for him."

"I need a delay of only a few days. I am not procrastinating but there will be an additional price."

"More gold?"

"No, information. Last year a couple of Scots with three men, Aimeric of Chartres and some others fled across the Tweed from England. They are being sheltered in Scotland and I would take them back for trial. While I come up with a plan you need to find out their location."

He smiled, "I will do what I can. I can see I am going to learn much from you, Earl"

We drank a jug of wine as I discovered as much as I could about the Lord of Dunbar. I really needed to speak with my knights. I had an idea but they would be able to help me refine it. Edward, in particular, had a cunning mind when he chose and my young knights thought in different ways to me. It was, however, too late to do anything until the morning. We ate in the King's hall. We were surrounded by the last of the King's oathsworn. In their eyes, I saw a mixture of hatred and respect. I hoped that the latter would outweigh their desire for vengeance for the loss of brothers in arms.

The next morning, I went to speak with my knights while the King sent forth his men to seek the information I had requested. My valley knights looked apprehensive as I approached. Sir Edward shook his head, "I like not this, lord. You should be with your men."

"I was safe enough, Edward. Gather around I need your ideas."

I explained to them my initial plan. They saw flaws and weaknesses. We refined it and by mid-morning, we had a plan which, I hoped, would tempt Lord Dunbar and his Scottish rebels from Din Burgh. I sent for David of Wales and he and four of his archers rode north to scout out the land. I returned to King William. For my plan to succeed we needed a spy in the Scottish camp. I had no doubt that there would be at least one. Scots had been coming and going all the morning. I knew that Lord Dunbar knew of the arrival of an English army. He would know that it was a small one and that it was led by me. My banner told him that. I was alone with Alfred and the King when I told him what I needed.

"That is a good plan, Earl, but I can see many flaws and weaknesses, not least the fact that you rely on one of my men betraying us."

I nodded, "King William, I have been fighting enemies for more than half of my life. I can tell you now that the only men I trust completely are those who rode with me from my valley. I am guessing that you felt the same about those who died at Alnwick."

The King nodded, "Aye and you are probably right. It just wounds me to think that there are spies in my army. I will look on each one differently now. I have no news yet of this Aimeric of Chartres."

"You are looking and you will find him. He likes a comfortable lifestyle. He will be noticed."

"What will you do with him when you have him?"

"Take him back to Durham. He will be tried for murder."

The next morning, with my archers still absent, the King held a council of war. His leading lords had been demanding action. Our secret conferences had them all intrigued. They were also more than a little resentful that an English Earl was privy to information that they were not. David of Stanhope and Stephen of Spennymoor accompanied Edward and me to the meeting. King William was getting old. However, none had ruled Scotland for as long as he had and he knew how to command attention.

"Lords, I know that many of you are anxious to rid our land of rebels and traitors. King John has sent us an able commander to help us. The Earl and I have been planning how we can do this. We now have one." Every face looked expectantly at him. "Lord Dunbar, the lord we seek, is in Din Burgh at the moment. To take that rock we would have to bleed ourselves dry. Instead, we strike at his castle at Dunbar. He will have to march from his rock to retake his home."

One of his lords said, "What if he does not come? Din Burgh is a richer manor than Dunbar. He may let us have it."

The King nodded. "He may but he has left his family there." There was surprise on some of the Scottish faces. He laughed, "Just because your King has grey in his beard does not mean that he cannot think anymore. I have men riding the land who tell me what goes on. We are awaiting more men from Hawick." He glanced at me, "When they come then we will leave."

As the lords began talking amongst themselves he came over to me. "Tell me that this is not Alexander of Hawick. If it is then I fear there will be bloodshed in this camp which will end any plans you have of reducing the enemy."

He shook his head. "The privations caused by that vile lord made me appoint another in his place. Sir Malcolm leads fewer men but he is loyal to me and a true knight." He gave me a wry smile, "Of course he may not be enamoured of you, Earl, for he has had to rebuild a hall and a tower. I do not think that the men of Hawick will forget you and your vengeful knights."

My archers returned late on the next day. They looked weary but David smiled for they had been successful. "Your plan should work lord. The old hillfort at Traprain Law has been long abandoned. The wood which was planted as a wall has, in places, taken root." He clutched his cross, "You can feel the ancient people there. It reminded me of places in Wales which once were centres of defiance and defence. The trees which have grown will afford cover."

"Good, now rest. We leave in a day or two." I sought out David of Stanhope and Stephen of Spennymoor. "I know that neither of you are happy to be fighting for the Scots. I suspect that some of your lords will be even more unhappy. We have more knights of Durham this time than came with us to Wales. We know not them all."

"You think there may be some amongst our number with black hearts?"

"Perhaps not amongst the knights but the men at arms? Certainly. Those who followed Aimeric showed us that. For that reason, what I am about to tell you goes no further than the two of you. Once my trap is sprung then it will be too late for any traitors to thwart it." I told them.

Baron Stanhope said, "But that means that you will be bait!"

"Can you think of a better way to winkle Dunbar from out of his rocky perch? We defeated him. We took much gold from him. He will want vengeance. He will come for me but only if he thinks he can do so successfully."

Even as the men of Hawick arrived the King sent for me. "I have news for you, Earl. We have found where Aimeric is hiding." I waited expectantly. He shook his head, "It is not good news. One of Lord Malcolm's men brought it. Aimeric is now with Alexander of Hawick. They are in England."

"England?"

"According to Malcolm Alexander fled there when my Malcolm's men moved in. This Aimeric was in the village and they fled to somewhere called Falstone. It is not far across the border but it is far from the fortresses of England. Elsdon is the nearest manor and it is not a large one."

I nodded, "This makes perfect sense. This Alexander raided and ravaged the area. Thank you, King William. You have fulfilled your part of the bargain. When we have bested Dunbar then I will deal with Alexander and Aimeric once and for all."

As we prepared to march I told my knights what I had learned. Edward nodded, "It is not a surprise that those two would find each other and slip so easily into bed. One has the money and the mind while the other has the warriors. This Aimeric knows the lords of Northumberland and us my lord. He thinks he knows how to defeat us."

"He will learn that he is wrong."

The Scots moved ponderously. Most of their men were on foot and I now saw how we had been able to defeat them so easily. We rode in the van with the King. We represented a small part of his army but the most powerful. We had as many knights as he did. Our men at arms were fewer in number but greater in quality. It was, however, our archers which made the real difference. The men of his levy had hunting bows and there were few of them. His men favoured weapons like the war hammer and Danish axe. Fearsome weapons but they had to be close to an enemy to use them. It gave me hope for it meant that the rebels might be similarly weak.

They would know we were coming and from which direction. The army took up almost a mile of road. My archers were good scouts and they had seen evidence of enemy horsemen watching us. The spies within the Scottish ranks would have already told Lord Dunbar where we were headed. My presence and reputation meant that he would check to see if it was true. When we reached Dunglass we reached the sea and, more importantly, could see the castle of Dunbar. It stood on a high piece of ground and I could see the wooden wall around the town. It could be reduced but I had no intention of losing any of my men to do so. Dunbar was part of the bait to draw out the rebel leader. We had to scotch the snake and take its head.

Our ponderous progress meant that those who were disloyal to the King fled north to take refuge in the castle. I suspected that many of those who stayed might be feigning loyalty. Lord Dunbar was the power in this part of Scotland. Until a hundred and fifty or so years ago it had been part of England. It was the old Kingdom of Northumbria. The links and ties to the Scottish royal family were thin as were the ties to the Normans of England. Traprain Law had once been the seat of power for the Northumbrian earls. By the time we reached the town, it was secured. There were no animals to be found and the walls were manned. Lady Dunbar would have sent to her husband for help. I did not think that alone would be enough. We began to build siege lines around the burgh.

We would have to wait a couple of days to begin the deception. I had told all who were involved what they needed to do but this was something we had never tried before. Who knew if it would succeed? I rode, with Alfred, my banner and my knights as far as the river. I made sure that I was seen. A couple of ships sailed down from Leith which was Din Burgh's port. They would confirm the reports to Lord Dunbar that his enemy was close to hand. By the time the siege works were in place, another two days had passed. We had tried to be predictable. Our archers were used to release ten flights of arrows into the town to thin the defenders on the walls. The first day we slew a dozen but since then we had only managed one or two casualties. It would be wearing for the defenders. They had just returned to the camp when David of Stanhope and Stephen of Spennymoor arrived.

"Earl, we have had enough of this. Either we attack the walls or we go home. We have families who need us and land which needs watching. Already we have given more than twenty days of service by the time we reach home then we will have fulfilled our obligation. What say you? Let us all leave the Scots. This burgh will fall soon enough and with the Lord Dunbar's family for ransom then the rebellion will be over."

"It is not time yet. Give me but a few days more and this will be over."

"I am sorry, Sir Thomas, we would follow you anywhere into battle but sitting around on this windswept headland is not our idea of war."

"You would forfeit the money promised by King William?"

He lowered his voice, "I still do not trust the Scots to honour that agreement. We have lost no men and I will take that. Dead men spend no coins."

I could not dissuade them. The knights and men of the Palatinate headed south back towards Jedburgh and thence Durham. King William was not happy. "I was promised an army by King John and now I have a large conroi. It is not good enough."

I nodded, "I know and we will have to change our plans. That which I had conjured can now not happen. Tomorrow I will take my men on a chevauchée to Haddington."

The King was slightly mollified. "Haddington is well defended and is a prosperous town. My son was born there."

"And it is but twenty miles from Din Burgh. Perhaps a raid there will tempt him from his lair. It is far enough from Dunbar that he will not fear your army."

"It is a risk."

"I have well-mounted men and we can draw him towards you so that you can force a battle. I feel I owe you that. The men of Durham have let me down. I will try to atone for their desertion."

"Very well."

My knights, men at arms and archers were all delighted to be raiding. Sitting around siege lines was no one's idea of warfare. I told them exactly what we would be doing. We left just after dawn. We knew not what awaited us on the road and we wanted clear lines of sight. Once we had passed the high ground of Traprain Law we would be able to see Haddington in the distance and, if it was a clear day, the rock upon which Din Burgh stood. We rode with the archers ahead of us. Cedric Warbow and James rode a mile behind us. When they were certain that we were not being followed they joined David and his archers who rode to Traprain Law. I would raid with just my knights and men at arms. We passed the old hillfort and the road descended towards Haddington.

Without archers, we had to rely on men like Richard Red Leg and Padraig the Wanderer. They had good eyes. Alfred held my banner. It was important that it was seen. When it was spied from Haddington then a rider would, no doubt, head for Din Burgh and report our presence. When we were just a mile from the town the gates slammed shut. That did not worry us. There were isolated farms outside of the walls but the walls themselves were the height of a horse. We could cross them by standing on our horses' backs Five hundred paces from the walls we reined in and my men spread out in a long line.

Edward asked, "Well lord, do we raid the farms or take the walls?"

Before he even had time to answer the decision was taken out of our hands. The gates opened and horsemen poured forth while from the other side of the town came more horsemen. It was Lord Dunbar. Even as I shouted "Fall back! It is a trap!" I counted at least a hundred riders. We had been betrayed. There was a spy in the King's camp. We had a race of eleven miles to reach the safety of our own camp.

Scean was a good horse and probably the best of those who were with me. For that reason, I did not push him. I needed the others to be with me. If we became strung out then those pursuing us would pick us off one by one. Padraig and Richard were at the rear and it was they who warned us that the Scots were closing. There was no panic in Padraig's voice. "Lord, they are two hundred paces from us and they are gaining."

The ride from the camp had weakened our horses. The Scots must have been waiting for us at Haddington with fresh horses. We would not make the camp. I had not expected that we would. So far my plan was working but there were still many things that could go wrong.

I shouted, "We make for Traprain Law. We will make a shield wall. That will be where we will hold them." All that remained of the Bernician stronghold were the ditches and ridges marking where the buildings had stood. There were bushes and trees growing where the palisade had once stood but without gates, they were largely indefensible. Our horses struggled up the slope and that gave me hope that the Scottish horses would also struggle. We made for the wide-area where the gatehouse had once stood. Even as we galloped through, David of Wales and the archers of the Palatinate loosed arrows at the Scottish horsemen who thought they had us trapped. We dismounted and our squires took our horses to the rear. With shields and swords, we made a shield wall in the gap between the trees.

Even though thirty riders lay dead, wounded and dying the Scots still appeared to be without any order or leadership. I saw Lord Dunbar and his banner. They were just behind the front riders and he was urging them on. Perhaps he was not surprised by my archers but the men he might lose would be worth it to kill or capture the Earl of Cleveland.

We had a double row of men but there were just forty of us. Two hundred men were charging us. Our archers could only kill so many. We were lucky that their first rank did not have continuity. They struck us as individuals. Their horses had struggled up the hill and our swords killed horses and men alike.

I heard a voice shout from the Scottish lines, "Dismount. Take them on foot!"

We had some respite as they dismounted and their horses were led away. David and his archers had less success for the men on foot held their shields up. They had just formed up and begun to march towards us when there was the thunder of hooves from our left and David of Stanhope led the knights and men at arms from Durham to charge the right flank of the rebels. They had been waiting by the Luggate Burn and were hidden by a stand of trees. At the same time, a horn sounded from the north as King William led his knights and horsemen to plough into their left flank. Isolated from their horses they could not escape.

"Alfred, sound the charge!" While our archers rained death, I led my knights on a foot charge downhill. The Scots were totally disorganized. They were assailed on all sides. I used my sword to slay three men at arms before the Scots even realised we were attacking down the hill. The knights of the Palatinate had the advantage that they attacked men whose shields were on the opposite side. Their spears found flesh and mail. Men died and the knights drove the enemy towards the centre. Although King William and his knights faced shields some of the men they faced had no stomach for it and that flank began to crumble. Men tried to run away. They merely ran into others.

A mounted knight rode at me with a spear levelled. I waited until he was committed and then I stepped to the shield side of his horse and brought my sword around to hack through his leg. He fell from his mount and his lifeblood pumped away.

Lord Dunbar and his standard-bearer were still mounted. They tried to flee. Their horses were slain by Ridley the Giant and Henry Youngblood and the two fell from their backs. The standard-bearer struggled to his feet. Alfred was on him in an instant. Alfred was lightly armoured and quick. He held his sword at the throat of the standard-bearer. Without a weapon, he had no choice. He dropped the standard. When the standard fell then the rebels surrendered. Their leader was down and they were surrounded,

"Quarter!"

"Mercy!"

"Ransom!"

In that one battle, the rebellion effectively ended. We discovered, later, that the Earl of Chester and young Prince Alexander had won a series of small skirmishes and battles in the west. The Earl of Galloway fled to Ireland.

King William had his helmet in his hand, "Your knights and I must be good actors, Earl. The spy believed our words and reported them to his leader."

"You have the spy?"

He pointed to the dead knight whose leg I had taken. His body was close by my feet, "That is Richard of Falkirk. His brother is in chains at the siege. Robert of Falkirk tried to leave us as we left to spring the trap. When his brother was missing I had him watched." Lord Dunbar was brought to the King. From the way, his right arm hung it was broken. "Dunbar, you are a rebel and a traitor."

Dunbar scowled, "If you are going to kill me then do so out of sight of this English wolf! I have seen enough of him!"

"I may kill you and I may not. Bring them back with us to the siege. We will decide their fate there."

We arrived back at Dunbar just before dusk. With Lord Dunbar in chains, the King went to within bow range of the walls. "Lady Dunbar, the fate of your husband lies in your hands. Surrender or I execute him for treason here and now."

There was silence from the walls.

The King shook his head, "She thinks that I am bluffing. Fetch Sir Richard of Falkirk." The traitor was brought. He had not been well treated. He turned to his bodyguard, a huge warrior with a two-handed sword. "Execute him." Two men held the knight and a third held his hair. The blade came down and severed the head which was then held in the air.

The gates opened and a woman's voice cried, "We surrender. Spare my husband."

Chapter 8
Traitor's fate

We had captured many horses, much mail and weapons. We also had ransoms to collect. It was ten days before we were able to leave. As my men waited for me I went to speak with King William.

"Thank you, Earl, you have saved my kingdom."

I nodded, "And yet this does not make us friends. I think, King William, that despite the Treaty of Norham you and your people still harbour territorial ambitions in England. I will take the revenue you have promised but if war comes then I will fight you as hard as I fought your enemies for you."

"I know and I thank you for your honesty, it is refreshing." He smiled, "When you kill me you will look me in the eyes."

"And that is how it should be between warriors." I pointed to the headless corpse of the traitor which had been left where it had fallen. "A word of advice, King William, choose those you allow close to you a little more carefully. You allowed a pair of them to be close enough to be a knife in the night."

"It has been a harsh lesson to learn!"

We headed south. I sent Fótr and Petr with half of our men at arms directly to Stockton. They would escort the wagons with our share. David of Stanhope sent five knights and their men at arms with his share of the bounty. The remainder then headed for Falstone. I had not heard of it before which suggested it was a small place without a manor. It was at times like this that I needed my grandfather's old scout Masood or Edward's father, Edgar. They were scouts without equal. As it was I had to rely on the knowledge of the men of Durham who had travelled thence.

We rode as far as Norham that first day. It was there that I discovered more about the area. Elsdon had had a lord. He had been killed when the Scots had invaded the last time. So far none of the family, who also had estates further south in England, had occupied it. It was empty. That explained why Alexander and Aimeric had chosen Falstone. The Coquet valley was ripe for picking. They could raid the Tweed as well as the Wear Valley. And as Ranulf of Hexham had discovered to his cost, they could raid the Upper Tyne Valley. When Fótr and Petr left for Stockton they would travel via Hexham and warn their father in law of the potential danger.

The constable of Norham offered me advice. "There are deep forests there and few farms. I know not this place you are seeking but I know others like it here along the border. The Scots are adept at making them into fortresses. You know how hard it is to hunt wild boar in forests?" I nodded. "It is the same hunting Scots. They may not be any good on a battlefield but give them a forest and they are the masters of ambush. This Alexander of Hawick is known to me. He is a cruel man who is little better than a bandit. When you brought him to battle you should have executed him." The constable was a blunt man.

"I can see that now. However, the man is slippery and he escaped me. He will not do so a second time."

"And Aimeric of Chartres; he is also known to me," he shook his head, "I considered riding to Durham to end his miserable life on more than one occasion."

"He robbed you too?"

"Aye, he denied me men at arms and took greater and greater revenue. It was lucky that the Scots did not attack. We would have been hard-pressed to withstand them. Whatever punishment you inflict it will be too kind for him."

As we rode south I discussed with David of Wales what our strategy ought to be. Many knights would have simply ignored the views of what they considered a common man. I was not one of those. Knights were vulnerable in a forest. We could not use a lance or spear and our larger horses were not well suited to the terrain. Archers were better at stalking and moving silently. They too would be somewhat restricted. The trees made accurate archery difficult but they would know how to trap an enemy.

David of Wales gestured backwards with his thumb. "We have more than fifty archers. If we divide them into five groups then they can search the forest for signs of the men we seek. You need to contain them, lord. Once we have found them for you we drive them in on to themselves. Ridley and the men at arms can then act as beaters. You said the constable told you they were as difficult as wild boars to hunt then use those techniques. The knights ride and the rest of us walk. Our net will tighten. The last time we fought this bandit we did so in a straight line. A circle means that he cannot escape."

I nodded, "I do not like you and the men at arms taking the risks."

He laughed, "Lord, each time you go into battle you take more risks than we do. Welshpool saw us almost watching the battle. We do not mind. You pay us well and, more importantly, you respect our views. That is why you have the finest of archers. They choose to serve you."

We had fifty miles to go and we stopped for the night at the high point at the head of the Redes Dale. I gathered all of the men around me. It was a remote spot and no one would overhear us. "I am going to divide us into two tomorrow. Both groups will have about twenty-five miles to travel. The knights of Durham and their men at arms will travel south and west. There is a road that leads to Falstone. You will block that road for that is the escape route back to Scotland. I will lead the rest, including all of the archers. We will take the Otterburn road. It is shorter and means we can use our archers to surround Falstone. I intend to cut them off in the night. When the attack begins I will sound the horn three times. Move slowly, Baron Stanhope. I would not have Alexander and Aimeric escape us again."

"That is unlikely, lord. To get by us they would have to use the forest and that would mean discarding their treasure. I cannot see that happening. Are you sure you will have enough men?"

"I have the archers and they will win this battle for us."

The day turned cloudy, as we left the next day. It was summer but this was England and it was the north. In Durham, de Gray would be discovering that summer did not necessarily mean balmy dry days. The weather could turn autumnal in a heartbeat and then back again. Edward sniffed the air. He had inherited many skills from his father and weather prediction was one of them. "We will have rain before nightfall."

William shook his head, "You are a ray of sunshine are you not, Edward?"

My oldest knight sniffed, "I am just telling you what will happen. Our archers' bowstrings will be affected."

"Aye, Sir Edward, but they will not be using their bows this night. Tonight, they find the enemy and let us know so that we can close with them in the morning. It is good that it will rain for it is more likely to drive the bandits back from their hunting."

Sir Ralph asked, "Is there much around here for them, lord?"

"Within twenty miles there is. The main road crosses from the New Castle to Norham. There are merchants and travellers who use that road. The castles of Northumberland can patrol but only around their manors. The nearest castles to the valley we seek are Alnwick and Morthpath. They are thirty miles from Falstone and Elsdon. They are taking advantage of the abandoned manor. One knight and his men at arms could control this area." I smiled, "Regard this as rat control. We catch the rats and put them out of business. Then I will write to the King and suggest that he orders the lord of Elsdon to do his duty."

Even as I said it I knew that the letter would do little good. The King was unconcerned with the lives of his subjects. His business was power and control. I could see the situation coming to a head sooner rather than later. On which side of the fence would I find myself?

When we reached Bellingham, we found a recently devasted settlement. The bandits had been through there. We found the villagers burying their dead and clearing up. When our banners were recognised we were welcomed. The man who spoke to us, Alan of Bellingham, was one of the few who had survived unscathed. The reason had been that he had been sent to Rothbury to ask for help against the bandits.

He shook his head as he spoke. It was as though he blamed himself for being absent. Had he been there he could have done little. "Lord, for weeks now, since before we harvested our crops we have been plagued with bandits. Animals were taken and those who lived up in the isolated valleys were found dead. We sent to the New Castle for the Sheriff but he said that he was too busy and he did not have men to spare."

I had thought that the leopard had changed his spots but I was wrong. Even though it might incur the wrath of the King I would have to have words with the new Sheriff. I had thought the old one bad enough but it seemed it was the office which corrupted whoever held it.

"When they raided and destroyed Charlton the other men asked me to ride to Rothbury. I returned yesterday and found that I had missed the bandits by moments. They heard my horse and must have thought I was a scout for a larger band. Perhaps I stopped them completely destroying our homes."

"Fear not, Alan. I will rid the land of them."

"But lord, you have so few men. Should we help you?"

"Your work is here making your homes safer. Leave it to warriors who know how to deal with the likes of Alexander of Hawick."

His mouth dropped open, "I thought he was finished!"

"He will be soon!"

We left them to their work and headed to the devastated hamlet of Charlton. The bodies had been buried and it had an empty desolate feel to it. Alan had told us that the hamlet lay just five miles from Falstone. The forest crept around the village. We could spend the night there and eat cold rations. The rain which Edward had promised us came later than he had predicted but he smiled smugly at William. His prediction had come true.

Some of the huts still had a roof and we used those for shelter. David and his archers set off through the forest. The rain would not bother them over much for they had seal skin capes. The men who had served with me in Sweden had discovered them there and they were perfect for keeping men dry. Their bowstrings would be safe in their string purse. They disappeared into the dark like wraiths. We expected them to be in Falstone itself which lay next to the tiny river which bubbled down to Bellingham and beyond. We kept a good watch that night. I shared mine with Edward. He awoke me and I discovered that the rain had stopped.

"All quiet, lord."

"Get some sleep. It is my turn to watch."

It was summer and we knew it would be a short night. I walked to the man at arms watching the horses. He waved. All was well. I checked the other four sentries and saw that they were alert and well. Alfred sidled up to me as I stood looking up the road.

"You should sleep, son."

"You watch."

"I command. When you command remember that."

"Who taught you these things?"

"My father. I was too young to have my grandfather's wisdom. From when I was younger than you he taught me how to be a warrior."

"Yet you only took me to war a year or so back. Why?"

"That was the first war we fought in this land. When we lived in Anjou you had just seen four summers and when we reached England I had much to do at Stockton. I am sorry if you feel that you were neglected."

"No, father, I was not neglected. I just thought that you did not think that I had the potential to be a warrior."

"You have shown me that you have so let us look forward. In a few short years from now, you will win your spurs and become a knight."

Just then I heard a sound and I drew my sword. A low whistle made me sheath it. It was Cedric Warbow.

"I must be slipping, lord. You heard me."

"No matter. Well?"

"We have found them, lord. They are in Falstone. They do not have sentries but this will not be easy. They cannot escape us for our archers have a ring around them but they have women and children as hostages, slaves," he waved a hand down the road and shook his head, sadly, "they are being ill-used by the bandits. David of Wales said that it will not be as simple as we thought."

"Get some food." I turned to look at the east. The sky was beginning to grow a little lighter. "Alfred, go and wake the other knights, not Sir Edward, he needs more sleep."

The treatment of those in Bellingham had made my men angry. That these men had resurfaced and once more devastated poor people meant that they would happily forego sleep. The men ate and the sky showed signs of dawn. I woke Edward. He complained that I had allowed him to sleep. Alfred had saddled our horses but we would walk them through the forest. It was not worth the risk of a fall.

"Have you the horn?"

"Aye father." He knew that the horn would be vital for the knights of the Palatinate would be waiting to hear it.

The men at arms had swords but the knights had spears. The squires, with the exception of Alfred, also had spears. Our spare horses were tethered and, as a greyness filled the sky, we headed through the forest and down the road. Falstone was less than five miles away. We would reach there by dawn. Had they not had captives then we would have risked a night attack but it would have been too easy to hurt innocent people in the darkness. This way we would have the light behind us as we rode in.

Cedric Warbow halted us when we were just five hundred yards from the settlement. It was in darkness but I could smell wood smoke. The light of the dawning sun would help my archers. I could not see them but I knew they were all around. The knights and squires mounted. I raised my spear and mounted my horse. We began to edge forward towards the hall surrounded by huts. Alfred would wait for my spoken command before he sounded the horn. We steadily approached until we were two hundred paces from the houses. The light now showed the doors and the rooves of the houses. It was not a large settlement but there was a hall. The constable of Norham had said that there had been a lord who lived there. That had been some years ago. He might have been another victim of the Scottish raids or perhaps he just died, childless.

Fate intervened when two men staggered from the hall. Their heads were down and they did not see us. They turned and began to make water on the wall of the hall. We could hear the murmur of their voices as they spoke. Steam rose. None of my men had needed a command to halt. Movement might alert the two men. In the end, it was not our movement that told them where we were. It was a pair of doves. Their flapping wings, high in the tree close by us made the two men turn. They saw the birds and then, as they lowered their eyes to see what had disturbed them, they saw us.

"Alarm! We are undone!" Their cry shattered the silence.

Half a dozen arrows thudded into the two men who fell dead.

"Alfred, sound the horn!" Without waiting for the horn to sound I spurred Scean. Ridley and Henry Youngblood were leading my men at arms towards the buildings. They were running in open formation and my knights were able to ride between them. The bandits broke from the buildings. I saw that some had women held before them as human shields. If this had been in the dark then there might have been a problem. As it was my archers sent their arrows to slay the men without harming the captives.

The layout of the hall was similar to the one we had seen at Hawick and suddenly a dozen horses burst out of the far end of the hall. From his size, one of them was Alexander of Hawick. The archers at the far end of the village sent their arrows to hit a couple but the horsemen broke through the thin screen of archers. The knights of Palatinate awaited them.

Leaving my men at arms to deal with the buildings and those who lay within I led my knights and squires after them. Even before we had ridden another forty paces more men burst out from the stable. I recognised one as Aimeric of Chartres. He had two large bags behind him. They had not been secured well and they shifted as his laden horse turned to join the road. He turned in his saddle and he saw me. I pointed my spear at him. He turned and lashed at his horse. He was no warrior. I knew it before but it was obvious now for he struggled to control his horse. It was overloaded and badly laden. The wet road was not a cobbled one and its hooves slipped and slid. The rain had made the forest a difficult place in which to ride and so the fleeing bandits were forced to ride down the road. I was not pushing Scean. I let my horse keep a steady pace.

I was next to the door when two more men burst out. They were surprised to see me so close for Scean was bigger than their mounts and I was mailed. They had no weapons in their hands but their horses forced Scean further to the right allowing Aimeric to gain a length or two on me. I jabbed my spear into the side of one of them and he fell from his horse, taking my spear with him. The other drew and swung his sword at me. Johann, William's sergeant at arms, was on the other side of him and he swung his own sword and it hacked into the bandit's neck.

Scean was able to ride straight again and I was gaining now on Aimeric. I saw him swing his head around to see how close we were. It was a mistake for he lost time in doing so. The ones who had left the hall with him were now paces ahead and he was the last in the line. We were steadily catching him. Ahead of me, I heard the clash of arms as Baron Stanhope led his men into the fleeing bandits. I sheathed my sword. I would not let Aimeric cheat the hangman. I would take him alive.

Ahead of us, I saw swords raised and horses rear. The men of Durham outnumbered the bandits. Aimeric saw the battle and his head went from side to side as he sought a way to enter the forest. He was almost close enough for me to grab for his horse was labouring. I was reaching for him when he turned again. This time he totally panicked when he saw how close I was to him. He jerked his horse's head to the left, away from me. He was trying to enter the forest. The horse's foreleg went into the drainage ditch. I heard the leg snap as it hit the bottom and Aimeric flew from the saddle. His head cracked into the bole of a tree. I reined in and my knights and squires galloped along the road to complete the destruction of Alexander's bandits. The Bishop's nephew was dead. I watched his brains as they slipped down the tree bark. I could see that the fall had been fatal. He had cheated the hangman.

I patted Scean's neck and dismounted. Aimeric's horse had broken its neck. It was still alive but in pain. I took out my dagger and ended the poor beast's misery. Alfred reined in next to me. His eyes stared at the crushed skull of the man who had cheated the King and Durham of so much coin. There was shock on his face. "Alfred, come and take these bags from the horse. They contain the treasure from Durham."

"Aye lord." He had something to do to take his mind from the horrific sight. I had to endure it as I searched his body. He needed to be searched for who knew what he had about his person. There was a seal of office he had taken. I had to lift it from his crushed head. He had two purses attached to his belt. Money was all to Aimeric of Chartres but as I saw Alfred struggle to lift the bags then I knew that it had been his downfall, quite literally. The weight had been too much for his horse and they had been badly packed. Had he just fled with his two purses then he might have lived.

I looked up as I saw the knights of Durham, heading down the road. Their surcoats were bloody and they led horses with bodies upon them. It was Alexander of Hawick and his men. This time we had finished the job we had begun up at Hawick.

"Well done, Baron."

He nodded, "It felt as though this was worthwhile. It was not like fighting knights but it was a job needed doing." He looked down at Aimeric's body. "He was a clever man. I did not like him but he was clever."

"He used his cleverness to the wrong end. Richard de Gray is clever but he uses that cleverness to make money legally. He is not a bandit. I think Aimeric had a bad seed in him. I have seen it in others." As we rode down the road I remembered the Holy Land. There I had seen knights who had gone on Crusade and then seen a way to make money. They were the reason we would never take what once we had held. They were like Alexander of Hawick and Aimeric. They were nobles who had been corrupted by gold.

When we reached the village Ridley the Giant had already built a pyre on which to burn the bodies of the bandits. He had thoughtfully built it so that the wind would take the smell away from the survivors. They were women and children. The men had all been killed and the old disposed of. The women and children were a pitiable sight.

Henry Youngblood came up to me, "Lord, these cannot move yet. They have been ill-treated. We have found some of the treasure the bandits took from other places and the animals they took from Bellingham and Charlton."

I nodded, "Padraig and Richard Red Leg, ride to Bellingham and tell Alan of Bellingham that the bandits are gone but we have captives in need of care."

"Aye lord."

My two men rode off and I dismounted. Alfred reined in. "There is a stable beneath the hall. Feed and water them and then stable them. They deserve the rest."

"Aye lord."

By noon all of the bandits' bodies had been found and there was a pall of black smoke as their bodies were burned. They had not had shrift. They would be burning in hell and that was fitting for men who preyed on the weak. I took off my mail and went to the river to wash. I felt dirty. The new Sheriff had had a responsibility to ensure that bandits and brigands did not harm the people. He had allowed a local warlord to rise. I would have to visit him.

The captives all told a similar tale. The bandits had struck suddenly and ruthlessly in each of their villages and hamlets. The men and the old had been killed and the women and children were taken to be used as slaves. Like Sarah, many of the girls and the children would need to be cared for. As we ate and I considered what to do I remembered a monastery not far from Hexham. The Augustinian monks there would be the best place to send the captives. In time they would return to some sort of life outside of the Abbey but the monks, who had helped Ranulf of Hexham, were good men.

I sat with my knights and Baron Stanhope. "Alfred found some wagons by the stable. Baron, I would have you escort the captives to the Abbot at Hexham. Ask him to take in the captives. Give him this." I handed him a purse from the money we had collected from the bandits. The rest would go to the people of Bellingham. "When you have done that then return the coin we took from Aimeric and the Bishop's seal and give them to Richard de Gray."

He nodded, "And you, lord? Will you return to Stockton?"

I shook my head, "Sir Edward will lead my knights and my archers home. I will take my own men at arms. We need to visit the New Castle."

"Will you not need us with you, lord?"

"No, Sir Edward, I go to counsel the Sheriff not to chastise and punish. If I go alone he may be less intimidated. This will be his last warning."

I took just ten men at arms and we made good time. Flame was sent back to Stockton. We would not need tents. The New Castle was close enough to make in a day and we could then ride back to Stockton in another.

William Stuteville had been Sheriff before. His replacement had been as incompetent and when he had died King John had reappointed Stuteville. Although many knights from the New Castle had been with us at Alnwick when we had captured King William the Sheriff had not been amongst them. I was not certain if that made him a coward or one who preferred the comfortable life within a castle.

My banner was well known and I made sure that Alfred held it high. We were seen from a distance when we headed down the Ponteland road. I wanted the Sheriff to know that I was coming. We rode through the gates and I could not help but contrast the bearing and demeanour of my men and those of the Sheriff's men. Mine looked like warriors. His looked like gaolers.

He was awaiting us in the inner ward. The New Castle had been improved. That had been the work of a good Sheriff, de Vesci.

He gave a slight bow in deference to my title, "This is a surprise, Earl. Does it herald danger?"

I smiled, "No, Sheriff, it reports it!"

He must have sensed that what I was going to say was not for public consumption. "You will stay the night?" I nodded, "Your men can stay in the guardhouse if that is satisfactory."

I said, "Aye for it will be good for your men to brush shoulders with real warriors!" I saw the grins appear on the faces of my men at arms.

The Sheriff had servants show us to a chamber where there was water to freshen our faces. Alfred helped me take off my mail. I left my sword in the room as we descended to the hall. The Sheriff's wife and children were there. She was a shy, mousey woman and after curtsying, she said, "I will leave you and my husband to speak alone, Earl." Had she been the wife of one of my lords then they would have commented about their wife but he seemed to dismiss it as unimportant. It told me much about the Sheriff.

His captain of the guard and squire sat with us at the table as well as his chaplain. A servant poured wine and then left. I did not touch the wine but looked directly at the Sheriff. "You are remiss in your duty, Sheriff." He looked shocked. Before he could protest I went on. "You have had a Scottish Brigand on your borders raiding your land for some time. He recently took up residence close to Bellingham. Twice I have been called upon to deal with the results of his raids. He is now dead but the Earl of Cleveland should not have to travel almost sixty miles to deal with a problem which lies on your doorstep."

He drank wine to give himself thinking time and mine remained untouched. "I thank you, lord, for helping out Durham. I am certain that the King will be pleased. What you do not know is the size of the problems I have with the barons of Northumberland. Many of them are of a rebellious nature. It takes me all of my time to collect taxes from them. The de Percy family are particularly belligerent. I have not enough men to send out to deal with the peripheries of this land."

I nodded, "Then you were told of the incursions?"

He looked at his captain of the guard, "We were told, aye."

I looked at the captain, "How many men do you have in your garrison, Captain?"

He looked uncomfortable to be questioned by a knight who had a reputation such as me.

"Thirty, lord."

"All are mounted." He nodded. "Sheriff, when was the last time you were assaulted here in the New Castle?"

"When the Scots came, lord and you drove them hence."

"And these lords you fear, de Percy and the others, have they ever offered violence towards you?"

"No lord, but they do not pay the taxes they should and they could attack us."

"Yet they have not. Captain, you could have left half your garrison to watch the castle and taken the other half to deal with these bandits."

"Lord, they would have outnumbered us!"

I banged my hand upon the table, "They are bandits and it is your duty to protect the people of this county! Are you saying that their lives are worth less than yours?" I could see in their faces that was exactly what they thought but they could not say that to me. They remained silent, "Sheriff, I have just returned from helping the Scots to fight rebels." I saw the surprise on their faces. "It was on the orders of the King. When I write to him I will tell him of the problems here in the north. If you value your life here in the New Castle then deal with bandits as you should. And as for these so-called rebellious barons then send to me if you feel threatened."

He nodded contritely, "Yes Earl."

Chapter 9
The peaceful year

The wars in Scotland and Wales were ended and they were followed by a short time of peace. It was not a time without turmoil. King John and his barons grew even more estranged. Despite the fact that he had no foreign wars nor domestic insurrection the country was still plagued by unhappy barons and minor disputes not to mention general unhappiness with the King's rule. The relaxation of the interdict should have made things smoother but relations with his church were not good. What alarmed me most was the sinister reappearance of the Templars. Their lands in the east and their holdings there were being taken by the Seljuk Turks. Eymeric, Master of the Knights Templar in England, was increasingly by the King's side. I did not trust the Templars.

However, events further south did not affect us as much and, with Scotland and the bandit problem solved my knights and I could turn our attention to our manors and our families. All of my knights were now fathers. Both Sir Fótr and Sir Peter had children. Sir Peter had a daughter, Margaret, and Fótr a son, Thomas. For Aunt Ruth this was another blessing. She had more young babies who would grow into children and she could help to make them into lords and ladies. Since I had returned from the Holy Land her life had changed immeasurably.

We also had sadness. James Broadsword died. He was old and he died in his bed and not with a sword in his hand. He would have preferred to die in battle for he had ever been a warrior but it was not meant to be. None of us got to say farewell to him. If he had had an illness then he had kept it hidden from all. I would have liked to have told him how much I valued him and that his arrival in La Flèche was a sign that God favoured us for he was a true warrior. The other men at arms were more distraught over his death than any warrior we had lost in combat. It was almost as though he was some sort of lucky charm. Men went to war and returned and James was always there. He knew what to say and he was an ear for those who needed one. His boots would be hard to fill.

We buried him close to the grave of Dick the Archer. It was fitting that they should lie there together with Ralph of Bowness and John of Craven. All had helped to make Stockton what it was and we would not forget them. We would have another name to toast at the remembrance feast. His death made me look at my defences again. Ralph of Appleby was the next oldest warrior. He had suffered wounds. It had not incapacitated him but slowed him down. He was happy to be my castellan and organize my garrison. I walked the walls with him.

"Ralph, this will be your castle to defend. How best should we go about it?"

"In a perfect world we would have a keep but I know King John forbids it. Perhaps two new towers. If we build them over the north gate then an enemy would have to ride around the walls to reach the next gates. There are only the river gate and the main gate. Both of those have a barbican."

We had learned from La Flèche. We had a triangular wall. Inside the buildings were square but three walls meant just three gates. The north wall led to the town. It was a good plan. I nodded my approval.

"Of course, Sir Thomas, it will be expensive."

"We still have the money to spend that we took from the Scots and, until we war again with the Scots, we have the income from Huntingdon. See Geoffrey and order good stone. We might as well have a castle which looks good too."

The only point in having a fortune was to make you safe and secure and your family comfortable. I would invest in the future in Alfred, William, Isabelle, and Rebekah. I would ensure that they did not have to endure what I had, the loss of my land. My two girls were growing too. Rebekah had seen ten summers and Isabelle eight. Time would pass quickly and the young sons of my lords would come courting. I would lose them.

Instead of planning campaigns, my life was split between improving my defences and ensuring that my borders were kept clear of bandits. Alexander of Hawick had been a lesson. Once a bandit had a hold on a land then it was hard to shift them. The general air of rebellion which pervaded every conversation was not good for the stability of my land. If lords could refuse to obey the law then why should not the ordinary farmers? Why should men work and pay taxes when they could steal and not be brought to justice? I was ruthless. Every transgressor was given a fair trial but many were hanged. Others had their fingers lopped. It was draconian but it worked. Soon bandits found other valleys to haunt. Sir Ralph found that many bandits gravitated to his manor and I took my knights and men at arms to scour his land too. After half a year between the Tyne and the Nidd, the land was free from bandits. The rest of the country suffered for Sheriffs were too concerned with collecting taxes and spying on lords to bother hunting down bandits.

Richard de Percy exemplified the unrest and he visited me six months after we had returned from Scotland. He was less friendly than on his first visit.

After politely greeting my wife and aunt who then left us he launched into the purpose of his visit, "Earl, many of those who fought alongside you were disappointed when you rode north and joined the Earl of Chester in supporting the King who ravaged the Tyne Valley. Was it well done?"

"Would you like some wine, Sir Richard?" I would not be hectored in my own castle. To calm myself I poured him a goblet, "The knights I left in France still send me jars of it from my old estates. I think you will find it pleasant." I handed him a goblet. My steely stare belied the gentle words. This was my hall and men spoke politely to me. They did not interrogate me.

He sipped it, "Yes, lord, it is a fine wine but it still does not explain your actions."

"Sir Richard, I do not need to explain my actions to you or any other knight who harbours treachery in his heart. I did what I did to protect your lands! Had I not done so then King William might have been overthrown and Lord Dunbar attacked you instead."

He ignored my explanation. I do not think he even heard it and instead leapt upon one word. "Treachery!"

"You would overthrow the lawful liege of this land."

"You mean the lawful liege who had the rightful king, Arthur, murdered. Some say by his own hand."

"Yet he was anointed. Is there another?" He was silent. "You berated me for fighting for William of Scotland. Had I not done so then he would have lost his crown."

"Good!"

I ignored the interruption, "And in his place would be men who were not bound by the treaty of Norham. Then your lands would have been invaded and attacked by others like Alexander of Hawick. Oh, we would have beaten them. Of that, I have no doubt but what of the lands they ravaged and the people they slew? When the Scots were gone would they be brought back too? We fought those people in Scotland. The land we fought upon was Scottish. I do not trust the Scots. I do not like the Scots but I know them to be my enemies. Do you know your friends? "

He leaned forward, "What do you mean?"

I held up the wine. "When this wine came it also brought a message for me." I did not tell him that I still owned a house in Anjou and that Anna and Jean were, effectively, my spies there. I paid them a stipend and they acted as my agents to buy wine and delicacies we could not buy in England. Each ship brought a report of what they had learned. "The last message spoke of English lords. Fitzwalter among them, who are at King Philip's court. They conspire with the French and are said to be aiding Prince Louis. The French have an invasion fleet. Did you know that?"

I could see that he did not know about the invasion, "Perhaps that would be a good thing. A French invasion might rid us of a bad king."

I laughed, "You are naïve! Do you honestly think that the French would not take advantage of a rebellion to place their own puppet on the throne? Fitzwalter has tenuous claims to the throne. I have fought the Scots many times. I have fought the French more. I know that my loyalty is to England. Can you say the same?"

Percy had a fiery temper. I had insulted him but, at the same time, I had spoken the truth. He shook his head but it was not a convincing action. "I would not see a foreigner rule my country."

"Then you understand me and my purpose. That is why I do what I do and when King John is dead and buried there will be a young King, Henry, who will rule and he will need barons like yourself to guide and mould him."

"Not you?"

I shook my head. "My great grandfather gave his life to that end. My family has done enough for the royal family. I will defend them but this is my home. This is my valley. This is where I will stay." I saw him playing with his wine as he summoned the courage to ask me something. "Spit it out, de Percy. The one thing you know about me is that I do not betray friends and brothers in arms. You can speak in confidence and know that it will go no further than these walls. But do not think to inveigle me with treacherous talk."

"King John has sent letters to knights asking them to serve with him for he intends to invade Normandy and to recover it."

I knew that he had had such an invasion planned almost a year since but had been forced to call it off because of lack of support. "I have had no such letter."

I saw his face. That was the reason for his visit. He wished to know if I would be going to Normandy with the King. He smiled, "Then like those of us who have had the letter and refused service you will be staying in England."

"You refused?"

"Normandy means nothing to us." I nodded. Perhaps he was right. There were too many barons in Normandy who were closely tied to the French. We had lost it and I could not see how it could be returned to us. He hesitated, took a drink of the wine and said, "While the King is in France there will be a secret meeting of those who oppose the King. We will meet in Leicester. I have been asked to invite you. All know you to be a leader who knows how to win battles."

"And you think that I would fight against the King of England?" I shook my head, "Then you do not know my family."

"And if we do choose to fight against King John and his tyranny?"

I said, "I agree, he is a tyrant and he should change. I will support any representation to request him to make such a change but I will not take up arms against him."

"And if he takes up arms against you?"

I finished off my goblet of wine, "Then I will fight him as my great grandfather fought against Stephen of Blois." I put the goblet on the table and smiled, "But I do not think that it will come to that, do you?"

We both knew that there were many lords who would be easier to defeat than me. He nodded, "Then I will tell the others that I have spoken with you, Sir Thomas, and that while you support our desire for freedom, you will not countenance war."

"That is my position."

After he had gone I considered my words. I did not like King John's rule but I had now put myself and my valley in extreme danger. The barons north of the Tyne and south of the Ouse were all in a rebellious mood. The east was against the King. Only in the west did he have any support. He was a foolish King. He had gone to France and he gambled. He was throwing the dice and his kingdom was the wager.

I was honour bound to speak to my knights. I visited each one of them in their hall. I took Alfred and William with me. They needed to know what their father did. The decisions I made would echo into eternity. All of them felt the same as I did. They shared not only my views but my decision. Many would say that we had sold out. We had served King John twice in as many years and we had not endured as much of his ire and malevolence as others. We were still overtaxed but we had not lost land nor had we been fined. Others had. That was why Robert Fitzwalter had fled the land.

My valley settled into an uneasy peace. There was the threat of rebellion and war but we had peace. While our yeomen toiled and the land prospered, every knight, squire, man at arms and archer spent each day preparing for war. Our fletchers made arrows and our smiths made weapons. King William had made good on his promise and the revenue we received paid for the weapons of war.

When the rider brought the news of the defeat of the English army by King Philip of France at Bouvines in northern France I feared the worst. King John had not been defeated. He had recaptured Anjou and beaten Prince Louis. It was his Flemish and north allies who had been defeated. It was the end of John's ambitions. He had to pay a hugely damaging amount of gold and give up Anjou and his claims to the remaining lands in France save Aquitaine. He returned defeated and broken.

Towards the end of the year, the Earl Marshal arrived at my castle. This time he came by ship. He looked even older. Aunt Ruth was quite concerned when she saw him. "Earl, you were not so foolish as to go to war in Normandy, were you?"

He smiled and kissed her hand, "No, dear lady, I am an old warhorse and I stayed in England with Prince Henry."

I ventured, "Perhaps, Earl, had you been in Normandy the King might not have lost."

Shaking his head, he said, "He did not lose. It was Emperor Otto who lost. From what I have heard it was almost an allied victory. King Philip was unhorsed and nearly captured. It was a bloody battle but the French won and the Emperor defeated." He smiled, "If your nephew had been there, lady, and leading the nights, then who knows. No one knows more about leading knights into battle than the Earl of Cleveland."

I saw the pride in my aunt's eyes, "It is a family trait, Earl. I will go and speak to the cook. We should eat something memorable this evening!"

The Earl smiled as my aunt left. "Had she been a man she would have been a fearsome knight!"

I nodded, "You did not come here just to flatter me, my lord. Speak, I beg of you. We live in uncertain times and there are men whose eyes are filled with daggers. My service for England is now viewed as something to be abhorred. If the King were to fall then…"

He sighed, "You are right. Even my son now expresses doubts about King John. I am here, Sir Thomas, to ask you to use your influence amongst the rebels. You have been invited to their meetings. There was one in Leicester I believe?" I said nothing for I had told de Percy that I would be discreet. The Earl chuckled, "Honourable! I like that. Well, no matter. There was a meeting and they decided to appeal to the Pope. The King has also appealed to the Pope. Perhaps he can arbitrate between the two parties. You and I stand in the middle. We stand for England."

"Could you not attend the meetings?"

"I would but I fear I will not be invited. You, on the other hand, will be."

"And you think that I should attend?"

His voice became serious, "You have refused so many times before that one more might result in your name being irrevocably associated with King John and I fear for your family should that day ever dawn."

"But that means you would have me as a spy!"

"No, I would have you as the voice of reason in a camp of hotheads. When they counsel war, you can talk of peace. We need someone amongst the barons who will speak for England. Earl, that will be you."

He stayed for five days. I think it was a relief to be away from the plots and plans of those who sought England and King John harm. He also enjoyed the company of my aunt. They were both relics of the past. They were able to speak of those that they had both known and times which seemed simpler when King Henry and King Richard had ruled. By the time he left, I had decided to do as he asked. I spoke with my knights and it was agreed that when and if I was invited to the next meeting I would attend and Sir William and Sir Edward would accompany me. They had served me the longest and would be with me at the end, should that day come.

When we celebrated Christmas that year I wondered if this would be the last peaceful Christmas we would enjoy. We made the most of it.

Chapter 10
Civil War

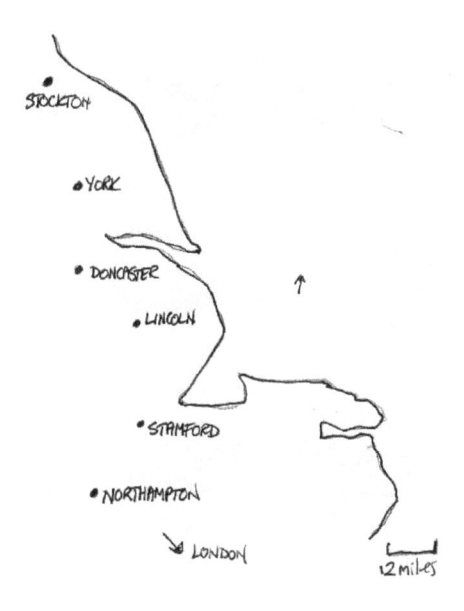

It was a milder winter than we had had of late. The spring flowers came early and the animals bore many more young animals than we had expected. As we were still populating the farms which had been raided by the Scots some years earlier it was a good thing. Many of those we had rescued from Falstone came to us. That was as a result of Ranulf of Hexham. He clung on to his farm, more out of stubbornness than anything else, but he knew from his daughters that life was easier in my valley and certainly safer. Many of the women and their families headed south. They were uncertain of their future save that they thought it would be better than that which they had known in the borderlands. We had many warriors now and they sought families. It was as though this was meant to be. There were weddings and some of my warriors asked to lease small farms from me and Sir William. Their new wives and children could tend the animals and the warriors had somewhere to call home.

That was in direct contrast to the news we were hearing from the rest of the country. The barons were now becoming openly hostile. Merchants who traded with us brought news of dire times ahead. Perhaps they were hoping to drive up prices but we felt somewhat isolated. None of the barons who lived within thirty miles of us were in a rebellious mood. We had been spared many of the land seizures of the rest of the country. Alfred could not understand it.

"Lord, if the barons have had their manors taken then how can they rebel? They will not have the men to support them."

"Simple, son, the barons have great estates. They have not had all of their manors taken. They are still rich but not as rich as they would have been had not the King taken their lands. Some of the others have also taken money from the King. It was a way for him to bribe them. Now he demands the repayment for their disloyalty. This unrest has little to do with rights and more to do with coin."

William was now seven and he followed Alfred around. He was keen to be a squire too but Alfred had counselled him to keep quiet on that subject when my wife was around. "Then there will be no war?"

He was keen for a war as he hoped I would take him with us when that happened. "There may be but we shall try to stay out of it. There is neither right nor wrong in this. If we side with the rebel barons then we are traitors and I would not have that name. If we side with the King then we are supporting a tyrant. We will fight, but only if England is threatened."

We also had bad news from Durham. John de Gray had been appointed as Bishop of Durham rather than Richard Poore but he died on his way north from Canterbury. His nephew left Durham for his family estates in the south. I could not blame him but it was typical of him that he did so the moment he heard the news. My knights still made a weekly visit to Durham; they joked about it and called it St. Cuthbert's pilgrimage. When I heard that de Gray had left I went with my men at arms, Alfred, and William to speak with the Dean.

I had got to know the Dean well over the last couple of years. He trusted me. Shaking his head, he said, "It seems the office of Bishop is a parlous one. We live in troubled times, lord."

"We do. I can still be called upon for help with secular and military matters but religion is not something I know much about."

"Now that the interdict has been removed then we can appoint priests. The Archbishop of Canterbury, Stephen Langton, has sanctioned all of my requests up to now and Richard de Gray has left us on financially solid ground. He was not a particularly pleasant man but he knew his business."

"You know where I am if you need me."

He nodded. Lowering his voice, he said, "I do not like to talk of such matters but I feel I can trust you, lord, and can confide in you."

"Of course."

"Some of the barons of Northumberland have tried to suborn the knights of Durham to the rebel cause. So far none have joined for they are loyal to you but I thought that you should know."

I had expected something of the sort and so I nodded. "I will ride to Stanhope and thence to Prudhoe. I will speak to de Percy."

Baron Stanhope confirmed for me that he had been visited by not only by Richard de Percy but also Eustace de Vesci. "Lord, I am unhappy with King John's rule but until you indicate that you will side with the rebels then the knights of the Palatinate will adhere to your standard and that of England."

"Thank you for your loyalty. This seems to me to be a storm which must be endured and like all storms, it will pass."

"Aye, lord, but what will be the consequences?"

He was right and I rode in silence to Prudhoe. The castle had now passed to the Percy family but I remembered those days when it had held out not once but twice against the Scots. That was in the days of my grandfather and the Warlord. It was a symbol of northern defiance against the Scots. Now it seemed it would be a symbol of defiance against the English King.

I found that Richard de Percy was in residence as was Eustace de Vesci. Since King John had ordered the demolition of

Alnwick and Barnard castles de Vesci had no stronghold to call his own. I was admitted to the Great Hall. De Percy was effusive in his welcome but de Vesci was more guarded.

"Sir Thomas! Does this mean that you have decided to join our cause?"

"No Sir Richard, I come to warn you against rousing the knights of Durham to fight their lawful king."

Baron de Vesci waved a derisory hand, "You were only given control over those knights to defeat the Scots and they are now humbled."

"Yes, my lord, and the ones who drove them hence were mainly my knights. You squatted like a toad behind your walls and did not stir yourself." His face darkened. "If you wish to dispute that then I am more than happy to give you satisfaction."

The challenge had been issued. I saw de Vesci wondering if he could risk facing a warrior who had fought more battles than the rest of the rebels combined. De Percy ended the tension, "My lords, there is no need for such confrontation or threat. We are all friends and your arrival is timely. We have decided that you are right. We need not a military solution but a legal one. The barons are holding a meeting in Northampton in May. You said that you would participate in such a meeting. This seems a perfect opportunity for you to show that are a man of integrity."

"I do not need to meet with belligerent barons to do that, lord. My deeds speak for me but I will attend with two of my knights. I do not promise to agree with what is spoken but I will listen and if I agree with your plan of action then I will support you but if this is a meeting of traitors then I will oppose you."

They both nodded but de Vesci could not resist adding a barbed comment, "It is obvious that you have not fallen foul of King John as I did. My castle was destroyed."

I turned to him, "My castle was destroyed and the grave of my grandmother desecrated. Get your facts straight before you insult me, my lord. The next insult will not be suffered so lightly. Heed my warning!"

As we headed south William, in particular, could not contain himself. "Would you have fought him, father?"

"I knew it would not come to that but had he not backed down then I would. I will not be a traitor and I will not have my family honour impugned."

"And what now, father?"

"We go to Northampton, Alfred."

"And do we come too?"

I smiled for Alfred included his younger brother. "I am uncertain. That depends upon your mother. We will see but it is a couple of months away. Let us see."

I could tell that tensions were brewing for the visitors who passed across our ferry brought news of increasingly fractious relations between what was being called the royalist supporters and the rebels. People were taking sides. I chose my men at arms who would accompany us carefully. I wanted reliable and experienced men. We would be mixing with the men at arms of other lords and some of them would seek confrontation. I would try to avoid that situation.

My wife was concerned and unhappy that William might be coming with us. I tried to calm her fears. "My love, there will be neither violence nor war. I go to talk. If there is any hint of danger then we will return. I go because I was asked to do so by William Marshal and I feel that I should attend. I go so that civil war may be avoided."

She nodded, "You swear that William will be safe?"

"I do but know you that soon he will be old enough to train as a squire. Alfred is close to beginning his training as a knight. Your chicks are growing. They will fly the nest."

She nodded, "I know but I would hang onto them for as long as possible."

I planned our route carefully. I wished to see what support the King had while travelling south. I would avoid those places which had declared for Fitzwalter. I would ride to York first and speak with the new Archbishop. From there I would ride to Doncaster. The land around that part of England was King John's. Peveril Castle and others were nearby and they were his heartland. Lincoln was still a royal castle and Stamford was the manor of William Marshal. I was aware that my youngest son would be with me and I wanted him safe.

It took six days to reach Northampton. By which time I had a better idea of the mood of the country. The royal castles were all preparing for war. Visitors were viewed with suspicion. As we neared Northampton then there was more evidence of rebellion. Men openly cursed King John. I saw why Northampton had been chosen.

When we reached it, I was astounded by the banners which greeted me. Many had fought for King John when he had had an empire. Now they sought to bring down his kingdom. We camped apart from the other barons. Edward and William had brought good men at arms too and we had a secure boundary to our horses and to our camp. I rode with my two knights and our squires to the castle. We were admitted but it was grudgingly. The barons were becoming more belligerent. It seemed to me that I was too late. The conversation was openly about war.

I almost turned around to leave and return home when Richard de Percy saw me. He greeted me like an old friend, "You came! That is what many of us hoped."

"This was a mistake. I have heard talk of civil war."

He waved a hand as though shooing away an annoying fly. "And that is all it is, talk. The King will have to see reason. With you behind us then I am certain he will accede to our peaceful demands."

He was persuasive but I was still unhappy. "I will listen. Do not try to put words in my mouth. I will not have my name used. If I choose to speak then I will do so without worrying about what I say. If Eustace de Vesci is typical of the men who are gathered then I fear blood will be shed... by me!"

"He was wrong and he knows it." He took me to one side. "Robert de Fitzwalter arrives tomorrow. He arrived in the country not long ago. He is to speak to us on the morrow. He has news from France and Rome."

I was glad to have the excuse to leave the rebellious camp. We headed into the town. It was as we were in a tavern that I met William Marshal's son William. I was surprised by his presence. "Do not be, lord. My father sent me as he sent you. His name is tied too much to the royal family. We, on the other hand, are not. The King and my father hope that our voices of reason will prevent bloodshed and rebellion."

I looked at him, "But, like me, you do not think so."

He nodded, "They are gone too far to come back."

"Where is your father?"

William Marshal grinned, "He is a cunning old bird. He is with young Prince Henry. He will keep him safe. The King might be unpopular but the eight-year-old is not yet tainted. We can trust to the Earl Marshal's judgement."

We saw and spoke with other moderate barons and they joined us. Some had come as we had to inject the voice of reason. Others had come because they did not wish to be left out in the cold. There were few of us. Alfred and William were the ones who enjoyed the experience the most. To them, this was a game. They had not heard all of the stories of the first civil war between Matilda and Stephen. My grandfather's accounts had been graphic. Large parts of the land had been a wasteland as a result of wars. Baron had turned on baron. Enemies had come across borders. I knew that would happen again. I began to regret coming. If civil war broke out then the treaty of Norham would be ignored. King William might not come south, after all, he was now old, but his son, Alexander might. There were other Scots who sought vengeance. My place was on the border.

When I voiced my concerns, Edward was the voice of reason, "We are here now, lord. One more day cannot make much difference. Even if there is a civil war it will not happen overnight. It takes two to make a war. We do not yet know what the demands will be nor what the King will respond. You are looking on this mug of ale as half empty. Who knows, it may be half full."

I did not think it would but I agreed. The hall was packed when we arrived. Our squires were forced to stay outside with the men at arms and our horses. Ridley the Giant would keep a close watch on them.

When Robert Fitzwalter arrived, he was acclaimed as though he was King already. He had been at the court of Philip for some time. His sudden arrival in England was no coincidence. There was collusion and there was planning. I had feared the Scots. If the French invaded then it would be even worse. They had put two large tables together so that they formed a platform on which the leaders could stand. The ones who sought power, the leaders, stood behind Fitzwalter, they were showing solidarity. I recognised them all. All were powerful men: Saer de Quincy, Earl of Winchester, Richard de Clare, Earl of Hertford, Geoffrey de Mandeville, Earl of Essex and Gloucester, Eustace de Vesci, Richard de Percy, John de Lacy, Constable of Chester, William d'Aubigny, and William de Mowbray. Whatever came out of Fitzwalter's mouth would be what all of them thought. I would not trust de Percy again. I saw now that I was here to blacken my name and to force me to be associated with the rebels. I tried to leave but the press of men behind me was too great. I would have to listen. If there was treason then I would be guilty of treason by association. I took comfort from the fact that William Marshal's son stood with me.

The leading rebel spoke, "You have all come here because you are sick of the tyranny that now rules this land. John Lackland is a murderer. He slew Prince Arthur, the rightful king with his own hands. He abducted and raped my daughter, Matilda. He has stolen land and exiled lords. He is not behaving as a King of England should. His powers need curbing. We have sent to the Pope to ask him to arbitrate. He has not yet responded and we have waited long enough."

Everyone cheered. I saw de Vesci and de Percy exchange looks. They were looks of triumph. Neither wanted conciliation. They wanted war. I had been duped.

Just then the men on the platform parted and, like a magician, performing a conjuring trick, Robert Fitzwalter held an arm out and Stephen Langton, the Archbishop of Canterbury appeared. "The archbishop has been advising those of us who care for this land in which we live. He has made certain that our demands are reasonable. We will send them to the King and demand that he either accepts our demands or we take his throne from him."

The Archbishop nodded. This was the final nail in the King's coffin. He now had the clergy against him. The Archbishop gave legitimacy to this rebellion.

"To ensure that what we do is legal I want every baron here to renounce his feudal ties to this corrupt king."

Barons shouted, "Aye!" There were almost hysterical. I looked at the two barons who were next to Edward. They had wild eyes. I had seen it before in men who then recklessly charged overwhelming numbers of enemy warriors.

"We have an army here. I will lead half of it to London! Let us take London. I will invite allies to come and help us in this war against the tyrant!" There were more cheers. "Eustace de Vesci will lead a quarter of our army north and they will take Lincoln. The Earl of Gloucester will lead the rest to take Exeter. The King is at Windsor and he will be cut off! He will have to accede to our demands! Our strength and solidarity will prevent bloodshed and bring about a peaceful solution." The mob roared their approval.

I had heard enough. I pushed my way out. Edward and William helped me to force my way to the door. Edward punched the sentry who tried to stop us leaving. Behind us, I heard shouts. Our departure had been spotted.

"Mount! We ride for Lincoln!" We had chosen our men at arms well and they were mounted before we even reached the horses.

Sir Edward shouted, "We will be the rear guard. Ride, Sir Thomas."

Barons were pouring from the hall. They were trying to stop us but most had not brought their horses. We had a chance. I prayed that the gate would be open. I spurred Scean. I hoped that Alfred and William were close behind. I risked a glance as we thundered through Northampton's narrow streets. They were there and Ridley and Henry Youngblood were behind them. Even as we approached the gates I saw the sentries closing them.

I shouted, "Open them, in the name of the King!" They hesitated a moment before they realised that their orders were to stop any escaping. The pause allowed me to pull my sword and sweep it into the side of the sentry to my right. Sir William took the other and we were out. We had completed the journey south from Lincoln in two days. We would do the return to Lincoln in one. Instead of heading east to Stamford we headed north for Grantham. It would save many miles and the lord of Grantham was not a rebel.

We had men following us. We were not fools. We knew that to ride the seventy miles to Lincoln we would have to conserve our horse's strength. We halted in Grantham. I did not risk bringing harm to the lord of the manor there, Baron Aubigny, instead, we stopped in the town square and used the water trough. One of Edward's men, James of Thorpe had been watching the road. He galloped in. "Lord, the men of de Vesci are pursuing us. They are half a mile down the road."

I made an instant decision, "Ridley and Henry, take all of the squires to Lincoln. Tell the constable that she will soon be under attack." I saw the question on his face and I remembered my wife's words. "Save my sons!"

He nodded, "Aye lord! They will be safe with me."

"No, father!"

"Alfred, obey!"

"Aye lord."

I donned my helmet and drew my sword as Ridley and Henry led the squires north. "We will block the road and when they ride up we will force them to slow down!"

Edward shook his head, "You make life interesting, lord!"

I shrugged, "The horses need the rest and my backside aches."

We stood in a line where the road turned. Those pursuing us would not see us until they turned the corner. They were in for a shock! We heard their hooves as they thundered. I did not know how many men there were. It did not matter. They would not have weapons ready. They were hunting us and until they cornered us they would concentrate on catching us. I was in the middle with Sir Edward and Sir William beside me. They were reassuring figures. We had fought together for so long that I felt I knew their thoughts!

As the first horse came around the end house Padraig the Wanderer swung his sword. It connected with the side of the skull of the leading horse. His blade bit into its head and struck its brain. The horse fell and as it slid across the cobbled street, taking out two of the following horses. My men at arms leapt over the dying horse to slay the three men at arms who followed and fell. A man at arms appeared before me and he made his horse rear. Many men would be frightened by such an action. I lunged beneath the flailing hooves, relying on my mail and helmet to protect me. My sword drove deep into the animal's chest. The rider fell backwards pulling his horse with him. The rest of my warriors all struck either horse or men.

Magna Carta

"Back to the horses, we have done enough!"
The narrow streets of Grantham were blocked by dead and dying horses. None could pass quickly. We mounted and headed up the road. I knew that the castellan of Lincoln castle, although a woman was a supporter of the royal family. She was my best hope. Nicola de la Haie had been married to a brave knight, Gerard de Camville. He had been a friend of Henry the second and his widow had dedicated her life to his memory. If we could close the gates then we could thwart de Vesci and de Percy's attempts to take this royal castle.

The short and bloody skirmish had bought Ridley and my squires the time to get well ahead of us. We rode steadily north. I rode next to Edward and William. "Civil war, lord, it is our worst fear."

"You never know, Edward, the King may accede to their demands. We know that he has fewer men at his side. I have never seen so many banners before. It was as though it was a coronation."

William had lost his home in Anjou, La Lude. I could hear the apprehension in his voice as he asked, "But lord, where does that leave us? We did not join the rebels. If they win then we are on the wrong side."

"No William, the words are not *'the wrong side'*. It may be the losing side but we did what was right. De Percy and de Vesci said that the meeting in Northampton was to talk to the King. Patently that was not so. As far as I can tell no one has asked him to deal with their grievances. Who knows he may do so."

"I do not think so, lord; the die is cast. If they take London then they will do so with swords. That is insurrection. That is civil war."

Edward was right and I wondered, as we rode the last few miles to Lincoln, just what King Philip had had to do with this. He was a cunning and ambitious king. Fitzwalter had taken refuge at his court. It seemed to me that the baron had deliberately inflamed the barons to make their rash promise. The use of the Archbishop had been a master stroke. It gave their cause the apparent backing of the church. William was incorrect. We had not chosen the wrong side. We had chosen the right side. We had chosen England for it was clear to me now that King

Philip had created this war. That could only mean one thing. The French were coming. We would have something we had not seen for a hundred and fifty years; an invasion of England!

We rode into Lincoln and then the gates were slammed shut. As we passed through the town we were not greeted by those who cheered and welcomed us but by scowls. The castle was the King's but the town belonged to the rebels. It was but a short way from the town gates to the castle and once we were inside the gates were slammed securely shut. This was a royal castle., My great grandfather and the Countess of Chester had helped to hold it against King Stephen and his army. My great grandfather had captured King Stephen after the battle. But for the disastrous rout of Winchester that would have ended the civil war t much earlier. As I slipped from my horse I could not help sensing that I was meant to come here and walk in the Warlord's footsteps.

Nicola de la Haie reminded me of my aunt. Although a little younger she had the steely stare of a warrior in a woman's body. "Your son has told me of the events in Northampton. Fitzwalter shall not have my castle. We will defend it to the last." She smiled, "I confess that we might have struggled to do so for there are but four knights here but with your retinues we shall watch them batter their blades against our stout walls."

Edward pointed behind him, "My lady, I do not think that the burghers of Lincoln will stop the rebels. From what we saw as we rode through, they are more likely to open the gates and welcome them."

She looked at me and I nodded, "It was scowls and not smiles which we saw as we rode through the streets, my lady."

"They are ungrateful for all that I have done for them!" She sighed and sat down. She waved a servant over, "Wine for these lords and see that their men and animals are housed."

"Yes, my lady."

"Within these walls there is naught but loyalty. Outside?" She shook her head. "The rebels have been filling the ordinary folk of this land with nonsense. They have promised them that which they cannot deliver. We all know that the King has made mistakes but the rebels have said that once the King meets their demands then they will pay less tax and have more freedom. We all know that will never happen for these lords who are rebelling are doing so to get more coin and more power. The ordinary people would be worse off under such a regime." The wine came and the servant left.

I nodded, "You are right, lady. These are empty promises. I have spoken with some of these lords and while they smile and speak well I can now see that they are deceitful. They serve their own ends and worse."

"Worse lord?" I now had the attention of all of the knights in the room as well as Lady Nichola.

"Yes William, King Philip's fingers are all over this move. This civil war is just the beginning. I believe that the French will come."

Lady Nichola fingered her cross, "My husband is well out of this. I thought when he died it was too early. Now I see that he is the one who is better off."

I put my hand upon hers. "My lady, we will endure."

She smiled, "Of course we will. If Robert Fitzwalter thinks that his bandits can take Lincoln then they have an old lady to contend with!"

She was a mighty woman. I was lucky that it was she who held the castle. That evening the captain of her guard, Robert of Lincoln, took me around the walls. They were well made. "My grandfather served here, lord, alongside the Warlord. I am honoured that his great-grandson is here with us and the hero of Arsuf to boot."

I laughed, "Arsuf was many years ago."

"Aye lord, we all have grey hairs to show for what we have learned." He pointed to the mighty Lucy Tower. "That was built in the wake of the first civil war lord. The keep is a strong one but we have the advantage of a keep on our walls which the enemy will have to force. The rabble of Lincoln might join with our attackers but the narrow streets preclude the use of mighty siege engines. They would have to use ladders and I have not seen a ladder big enough to scale the Lucy Tower."

As we walked I saw that they had embrasures. If I had had my archers with me then we could have easily held the castle. As it was we would be stretched to the limit. The weak point was the town gate. Unlike my castle there was no barbican. It was a gate with a second one behind but if one gate fell then there were neither murder holes nor traps to stop the second one being breached. All that it would do would be to allow the defenders to meet the attackers once they broke through.

"Have we enough water and pig fat?"

He nodded, "Aye lord. We can reach the River Witham from the north wall and haul water up in buckets." He pointed to the huge metal cauldrons which hung from tripods on the two towers which flanked the gate. "These were put in after the last battle of Lincoln. There is stone beneath so that we can heat the pig fat here."

I nodded. That was sensible. Most castles had a wooden walkway. A fire would have been impossible while carrying boiling fat up to the fighting platform was risky. This way the fat could be heated and then brought to the walls to finish off the boiling. "And how many in the garrison?"

He looked down. "The four knights of her ladyship have twenty men at arms and we have a further twenty." My face showed the disappointment I felt. "I know, lord. You have brought more men than we had in the garrison." He made the sign of the cross. "God has sent you!"

Lady Nichola was taking no chances. The gates were kept barred and a close watch on the town. When we awoke there was an eerie silence in the town. We did not know it but the men of the north, led by de Vesci and de Percy had arrived and they were formulating their plan. There were plenty of supplies for us in the castle and we ate well for I feared it would be a long day. When young William appeared next to me in his short hauberk I felt guilty. I had promised his mother that he would be safe for we would be just talking. I had been wrong. The previous night when my youngest son had fallen asleep, through exhaustion, I had made Alfred promise to watch his younger brother. I could not afford to worry about my son when I had a castle to defend. A momentary lapse in concentration could cost me more than my son's life.

A herald sounded a horn. I was already on the fighting platform over the town gate. Lady Nichola made her way to join me. She was sixty-six years old and yet she moved well. She joined me as De Vesci and de Percy rode up. It was de Vesci who spoke. "The council of barons have sent us to demand that you surrender this castle. We promise that will those within will be allowed to leave unharmed."

Edward, standing next to me, snorted, "Aye, save us who would be ambushed as we headed north."

"Peace, let the snake speak, Edward, and then we can scotch him!"

He laughed, "Aye, lord, sorry lord."

Lady Nichola spoke, "This is the castle of King John. A month since he asked me to hold the castle for him in lieu of my dead husband. If King John asks me to relinquish this royal castle then I will do so. Until then you are committing treason by threatening the loyal subjects of the rightful King of England."

De Vesci's face became angry as did his words, "Lady, I cannot guarantee your safety! We will attack and your castle will fall!"

She laughed, "Do you think I have lived these sixty odd years to be afraid of a cockerel like you? I have the great grandson of the Warlord by my side. Do your worst, de Vesci!"

He raised his fist, "So be it! I gave you fair warning!"

Ridley said, "And if David of Wales was here, lord then these two traitors would be already plucked from their horses."

"We cannot touch them for they came in peace."

"It did not sound like that, lord. In the tavern when a man threatens you punch him first! I am sorry but the way you lords fight has too many rules!"

Lady Nichola laughed, "I like your giant and his sentiments. I will get out of your way, Sir Thomas. I will have the pig fat heated. They are in for a shock, I think!"

I waved over Johann, "Take the squires and man the Lucy Tower. I am not certain that they will attack there but if they do we need you to defend it. The two most vulnerable places are the tower and the gate."

I was not certain that Johann believed me but so long as the squires did then I was happy. They would be safe there. I was confident that they would come to no harm but the walls of a castle being attacked was not the place for squires. The fighting would be brutal. If we had to use pig fat then the smell of burning hair and flesh would give young William nightmares for months to come.

Once they had left us I organised the men. We had seven knights in total and I spread those out amongst the men at arms and the men of the garrison. I did not bother with either a shield or a helmet. The battlements would protect us from the crossbows the men of de Vesci and de Percy used. I needed good hearing and a clear sight of the foe. We had to hurt them so much in their first attack that they would break off and retire. Both the barons would be keen to get to London. They were ambitious men and the power lay around Fitzwalter. They would seek to be close to him. If they managed to overthrow the King then they wanted to be on hand to be given the best manors. I did not think it would come to that but the two barons would.

I heard a great deal of noise from the cathedral. William looked at me quizzically. "It is the two barons. They are engaging in a little rabble rousing. If they can get the burghers of Lincoln to fight their battle for them then they will lose fewer men." I nodded to the cauldrons. "Better light those and get the cauldrons hot."

Sure enough, a short while later a mob ran at the walls. They had ladders and improvised weapons. Behind them came the men who wore the liveries of de Vesci and de Percy. I lowered my sword and the ten archers from the garrison sent their arrows into the air. They were not as good as my men but the mob who ran at us had no protection and each time an arrow struck it found flesh. The crossbows the enemy used hit the embrasures or the crenulations. None found a warrior. That was de Vesci's mistake. He was trying to use ordinary men to force the walls. I relied on warriors. We were outnumbered but they had to ascend a ladder and try to fight one handed.

Despite the casualties suffered by the burghers as they attacked some still reached the walls and they raised the ladders. That was the reason the barons had sent them. Their men could ascend the ladders and fight. The burghers had just carried them for the barons.

I heard a voice from behind me as the first men began to climb the eight ladders they had placed against the walls. "Pig fat coming up, lord, ware behind!" The servants laboured up holding the cauldrons with the steaming pig fat. I stepped away for if it splashed it would burn.

Magna Carta

I went to the gate and peered along the wall. Robert of Lincoln had been correct. They made no attempt to take the Lucy Tower. I saw that Johann had managed to find some bows and javelins. The squires were using their elevated position to send their missiles at the flank of those attacking. It would not win the battle but it would weaken the resolve of the attackers. I saw men with axes, protected by shields run at the gate. The gates were studded with metal so that it would blunt the axes they used. It would add to the time it took to break down the gates.

"Edward, take charge of the pig fat. When it is ready then it will be your decision when to use it."

"Aye, lord!"

I peered over the wall again. The men ascending were half way up. More than half of those climbing wore mail. The ones who did not were being struck by the arrows and javelins of our men.

"Stand by to repel our enemies! The cry is 'The Fair Lady of Lincoln.'"

The cry, 'The Fair Lady of Lincoln', was taken up and rippled down the wall. When the squires in the Lucy Tower shouted it then it almost became an echo.

The ladder which was closest to me was too far below me for me to dislodge it. The men who ascended would use the crenulations to pull themselves up. The first man who came thrust his spear up blindly. I was back from the edge but I feigned a cry as though he had struck me. If he was any kind of warrior then he would know that he had not. I pulled back my sword and waited for his hand as he used it to pull himself up and place a foot on the crenulation. I rammed my sword into his middle. He could not help himself. He tried to move away and stepped out into fresh air. My sword blow was not fatal but the crack as his body hit the cobbles was. I peered over the edge and saw that the next man was only half way up. I suspect the falling warrior had taken another with him. I glanced to the rear of the attackers and saw that the two barons were with their knights and standard bearers safely away from the fighting.

I watched Sir William sweep his sword sideways. He had risked the crossbows for he had had to lean out but when he did he managed to hit the man at arms on the side of the head. As he fell he clutched at the ladder and he pulled it and the two men climbing. It fell towards the next ladder and that was knocked to the ground. The men on the third ladder jumped before they were hit.

At that moment I heard Sir Edward shout, "Let go!" The two cauldrons of boiling pig fat emptied over the side of the gatehouse. There were thirty men crowded below. Pig fat burns on contact and, even worse, it insinuates itself through any crack and crease it can find. A man cannot rid himself of it. To make matters worse Edward had had two of his men light brands which they threw down on the mass of screaming men. The pig fat ignited then all those who were not already dead ran back towards the town. Some were on fire. Panic ensued as burning men ran blindly into buildings and their comrades. The attack ended almost instantly. With three ladders gone and the attack on the gatehouse ended the rest ran back to the town gate. They had had enough.

It was not a time for cheering. A few of the men who had been burned were saved by their friends who smothered the flames. The rest died. Some writhed and twitched, blackened bodies, for a long time. The smell of burning flesh, hair and clothes filled the air. I watched as the two barons turned and led their surviving men south. The siege had been brief and it was over. We had won.

Chapter 11
Magna Carta

We cleared the bodies from around the castle and my men and I went through the town. Fearful of reprisals the people of Lincoln wisely stayed indoors. We found more bodies close to the gate. Men had, somehow, managed to hang on to life until it became too much and they died. The removal and the burial of the bodies was not pleasant. To make certain that the rebels had gone I led my men the next day to ride the countryside. We found no sign of them. They had gone to London.

That evening Nichola de la Haie asked the question that was on everyone's mind, "What happens now, Earl? Will you take your men home or will you try to find the King and join him?"

I had to confess that I did not know the answer. I had too few men to make a difference to the forces available to the King but if I left then it would be like handing over power to the rebels. On the other hand, I might be needed at home. Would the Scots take advantage of my absence and the unrest in England to launch an attack? I did not like this. I preferred to know what was going on.

Alfred was the one who came up with a sensible suggestion. "Lord, send two of your men at arms to Windsor. The King will be there. If he is besieged then they can return here and if not then we will have a better idea of what we face."

He was right, "Then we will do so. I am afraid, my lady, that we will have to impose upon you for some time longer."

She waved a hand, "Nonsense it is good to have you and your men for company. I will send Robert of Lincoln into the town. I will fine the townsfolk for attacking our walls. It will replenish my larder!"

The choice of men was easy. In the absence of archers, it would be Padraig the Wanderer and Richard Red Leg. They were both clever, resourceful and lucky. I never discounted luck! I gave them a spare horse each and they set off with clear instructions. They wore my surcoats and had my sign on their shields. They would be recognised. As a precaution, until they reached Windsor, they would keep them covered. They would only need them to gain access to the castle of the King. We waited.

It was not the worst castle in which to wait. Lady Nichola had lived there for most of her life and had made it comfortable. She was also pleasant company. She enjoyed having my young men talk to her of their families. Each evening she kept us all engaged with her tales of life in the castle. She was hereditary constable and that was unusual for a woman. I told my knights the story of Maud, Countess of Chester, who had sneaked my great grandfather into the castle and they had held it for the Empress.

During the day we patrolled the streets and I kept a watch on the road to the north. It proved a good decision. Two days after my men had left we intercepted two of de Percy's men. Henry Youngblood captured them without having to injure them and they were brought to the castle to be questioned. They knew of me but it was the presence of Ridley and Edward which loosened their tongues. They were happy to talk. They were not on some secret mission. Their task was to relay the news to the north that London and Exeter were now in the barons' hands. The King, it seemed, was willing to talk and the two men had been told that the King would accede to all of their demands. I did not believe so but I could see why Richard de Percy would want that news spread around his manors. They also said that many more barons had joined the rebellion. I believed that for they had witnessed it with their own eyes and they named the knights who had joined. All else was guesswork. We put them in the gaol. I told them that they would be set free but only when my men were returned. I would not throw away two men who might be used to bargain for captured prisoners.

At the beginning of June, my men returned. I had begun to worry but they seemed surprised, "We were in no danger, lord. The Earl Marshal saw us and not the King. He was pleased that you held Lincoln. He confided in us that there may yet be war. The King has offered to have the Pope arbitrate the dispute but the barons refused. The Archbishop of Canterbury offered to organise peace talks."

I slapped one fist into the palm of the other, "The King does not know he cannot be trusted! Damn such churchmen. They should stay out of politics!"

"The Earl knows, lord, and he said he was giving the Archbishop enough rope to hang himself. The King and the barons are meeting seven days from now at a place called Runnymede. It is half way between Windsor and the rebel camp at Staines."

"Thank you." I turned to the Constable and my knights. "And so now we wait. In seven days we will know the outcome."

As a gesture of goodwill, I sent our two prisoners back to their lord. I told them not to go north but south. I wanted the other rebels in the north to be kept in the dark. I sent Henry Youngblood and William of Lincoln back to Stockton with young William. He was not happy until I told him that I needed someone to deliver the news of the meeting back to my home. The letter which he took would be disseminated amongst my knights. We needed to prepare for war.

That night, as we ate in the hall, one of the knights of Lincoln, Sir Eustace, asked, "Prepare for war, lord, why? There is a charter of peace. They are making an accord. That is what your men said."

"The accord has been drawn up by one of the rebels, the Archbishop. I now see what the Earl Marshal meant. When the King realises that he has been duped he may well repudiate the accord. Until we receive word that peace is here we prepare for the worst."

William Marshal's son, William reached us at the end of June. His words sounded hopeful but not his demeanour. "There is peace, my lord. My father sent me to tell you that. Both sides have signed an accord. There will be a council of twenty-five barons and churchmen who will ensure that the King keeps to the agreement. The barons have all renewed their oaths to the King."

This did not sound like King John to me, "This council, what power does it have?"

"If there is a transgression and the twenty-five councillors feel that it breaches the treaty then the King has forty days to remedy the transgression. If he fails to do so then the King's castles may be seized."

"I cannot see him agreeing to this!"

"He has done, lord."

"And who are these councillors?"

He took a parchment from his saddlebag and handed it to me. "These are the twenty-five."

I unrolled it and read them. I recognised the Earl's hand.

Richard de Clare, Earl of Hertford
William de Forz, Earl of Albemarle
Geoffrey de Mandeville, Earl of Essex and Gloucester
Saer de Quincy, Earl of Winchester
Henry de Bohun, Earl of Hereford
Roger Bigod, Earl of Norfolk and Suffolk
Robert de Vere, Earl of Oxford
William Marshal junior
Robert Fitzwalter, baron of Little Dunmow
Gilbert de Clare, heir to the earldom of Hertford
Eustace de Vesci, Lord of Alnwick Castle
Hugh Bigod, heir to the Earldoms of Norfolk and Suffolk
William de Mowbray, Lord of Axholme Castle
William Hardell, Mayor of the City of London
William de Lanvallei, Lord of Walkern
Robert de Ros, Baron of Helmsley
John de Lacy, Constable of Chester and Lord of Pontefract Castle
Richard de Percy
John FitzRobert de Clavering, Lord of Warkworth Castle
William Malet
Geoffrey de Saye
Roger de Montbegon, Lord of Hornby Castle, Lancashire
William of Huntingfield, Sheriff of Norfolk and Suffolk

Richard de Montfichet
William d'Aubigny, Lord of Belvoir

"But apart from you, these are all the rebels we saw in Northampton."

"Quite so, lord. I think they had me join the council so that they could make a pretence of being fair. I will be outvoted. At the first transgression, they will order the King to remedy it and he will not. When they try to seize his castles, there will be war."

"There will be war before that! And what of Prince Henry?"

"Safe with my father. He begs you to ride north to your castles and to defend against foreign enemies."

"Scotland?"

"And France! My father intercepted a letter sent from Fitzwalter to Prince Louis."

"Tell your father I thank him."

Taking our leave of the constable we rode north. We had a peace which was not a peace. Both sides would look for an opportunity to tear up this charter. William had given me a copy of it. It was a long document and would take some reading. I had to prepare for a war first.

We headed north but I was a dull companion. There were too many things for me to think and worry about. From the list of counsellors I had seen I knew that I was surrounded. The Earl of Chester had not signed but he lived on the other side of the country. He was still a staunch royalist. There was no Bishop of Durham and so I could order those barons to follow me but the rest? All were rebels. The land around Derbyshire and Lincoln was safe but south of the Thames and east of the Roman road were rebel country. With a few exceptions, the west was loyal. The most worrying aspect was that there would be no one to oppose Prince Louis should he invade England. He would not even need to invade. He would be invited by his friend, Robert Fitzwalter. Unlike my great grandfather I could do nothing about the south. I did not have the Earl of Gloucester as an ally. I would do that which I knew I could do. I would make Stockton and my valley safe.

As we left York I wondered about William Marshal, the earl's son. Why had he been included in the signatories? True he had ridden north to speak to me but why had the other barons included him? His father I would trust. The son I would view with suspicion. My valley was now an island surrounded by powerful barons with strong castles. I would not be able to fight an aggressive war, it would have to be defensive. By the time I crossed the Tees then I knew what I had to do.

I saw the relief on my wife's face when I arrived back. I had made the mistake of not ordering William to be economical with the truth in his description of the siege. I had had much on my mind. He would have told her of the burning bodies and the slaughter. It would have brought it home to her how parlous my life was.

"We have peace?"

I shook my head, "They have signed an accord. There is a charter but all that it does is buy both sides time. War is coming. I am sorry, my love, I cannot prevent it."

She held me tight to her, "And I know that no man could do more. You kept our sons safe and for that I am grateful."

I held her at arm's length, "That promise may not hold good for the future." I slipped my arm around her shoulders and walked her into the hall. I told her my assessment of the situation. "We have a peace but it is not real peace. Both sides will look to break the charter. I will not do so but others will. I will convene a meeting here of the knights of the valley and those knights of the Palatinate on whom I can rely. For once I am grateful that there is no Bishop. I still have King John's mandate to command the Palatinate barons. I need you, my love, to be my link with Stockton. The people must all pull together. I need the burghers and their families to be behind me. I will speak with Father Abelard and explain the situation to him. We will have to sail stormy waters but I honestly believe that we can emerge intact."

"Since you have been away I have spoken with your aunt at length and she has told me many stories about your family. They steered this valley through more difficult times than we have had to endure. Your great grandfather did it alone. You are not alone. You have me!"

My wife's words gave me hope.

Magna Carta

The next day I saw Alan the Horse Master, "We need as many horses as we can get. War is coming. Now that we have peace the prices will be low. Buy and breed as many as you can. I care not if they are palfrey, sumpter or rouncy. When war comes we will need to be mobile."

"Aye lord, you can rely on me."

I summoned the iron workers and smiths to my hall. I had a bag of coins for each of them ready on the table. "For the next six months, I wish you to work for me. I need swords, spear heads, arrow heads, helmets and mail. When you have earned this purse of coins come and see me for there will be more."

Old John asked, "Is war coming, lord?"

"I will not lie to you for that is not my way. It is coming but it will pass and we will be stronger. My family is not leaving this time!"

Next, I saw Geoffrey, my steward. "We need great quantities of food and supplies. It must be preserved. I know that we had a good crop and plentiful animals this year. Buy any surplus you can. If you can buy from the markets north of the Tyne so much the better."

Geoffrey was a wise man. He smiled, "If we buy their animals then they cannot eat them. I will do so, lord, for the treasury is in a healthy position. The money from Huntingdon was more than welcome."

"You cannot rely on that. We have had this year's?"

"Aye lord."

"Good then use that!"

I sent riders to Durham and to my knights. I held a meeting on St Swithins' day. I hoped it was not prophetic. My wife arranged a feast but she made certain that Tam the Hawker had hunted. We would not eat our domestic animals until we needed to. She also bought as much fish and shellfish as she could. She understood our dilemma.

I had said nothing to any of my knights but William and Edward had not been sworn to secrecy. They knew the problem. The six Durham barons also had an idea of the issue. I did not mince my words. I spoke plainly. "War is coming. It may be in a month or a year, I know not for I have not the second sight but war will descend upon us. If we are to survive then we must stand together. If it comes from the north, and the Scots, then Durham needs to tell me so that we can meet them beyond our borders. If it is the men of de Percy, de Vesci and de Clavering then, again, I need to know. If it is from the south then Ralph of Northallerton will bring us word."

David of Stanhope asked, "And the west?"

"Chester and Lancashire stand with the King. However, I do fear for Carlisle. We can do little about that."

Sir Ralph asked, "Can we win this war?"

"A more important question is can we afford to lose it?"

None were downhearted about the odds we faced. Everyone had a castle which could be defended or, like Sir William and his family, they were close enough to Stockton to seek shelter there. Sir Ralph and Sir Peter were the most isolated but York stood for the King. There was no Archbishop there but the High Sheriff, William de Duston, was King John's man. The rebel barons hated him. He had to stand with the King. We had more horses than any other knights in the north. Our men at arms and archers were all mounted. I was confident that we could reach danger quicker than any and, more importantly, extricate ourselves equally quickly.

One day, as Alfred and I rode with men at arms and archers along the Roman Road which led west, he asked, "Why do we need to ride to war, father? We have a strong castle and any enemy would die trying to take it." The short siege of Lincoln had shown my son the benefit of high walls, strong towers and a good gatehouse. We had all three of them.

"Some of our allies in the Palatinate do not have such strong castles. Durham itself is the exception. We might be needed to help the ones who have small castles to escape to Durham. However, I do not think that is where we will need our horses. It is the Scots I fear. We do not want them tearing out the heart of England. Remember Alexander of Hawick and multiply it tenfold. We have to be mobile to contain the Scots. They are numerous but they have few horses. Our battles and reparations have ensured that. When they come south we need to use our horsemen to deter them.

The three months of the uneasy peace were a godsend. We heard that the war had resumed when one of the Earl Marshal's

Magna Carta

knights, Robert Fitz Clare, rode into my castle with just ten men accompanying him. I could see that he had ridden hard. His horse looked exhausted. He had barely slid from his horse when he burst out with his news. "Earl, there is war! The King has marched on Rochester and he fights the barons there. The Earl Marshal has sent those knights he can trust to warn his loyal barons to fight his enemies." He shook his head. "Between Northampton and York, it is rebel land. The King has London ringed but there are many enemies. He is driving north to retake the rebel castles. The Pope has sided with King John. The rebels and their priests have been excommunicated for forcing the King to sign the charter. It is no longer valid. I was told to tell you that the Scots have sided with the rebels. The treaty of Norham is null and void."

"I expected that. And now what? Where do you go next?"

"How stands Durham?"

"The Palatinate is with us and you need not ride north. I will use one of my messengers."

"Then I will ride to Carlisle. Another left to take them the news but it will be easier and safer for me to head south to the Earl of Chester."

He stayed the night and we learned that every royal castle was now a stronghold. The rebels did not have the siege equipment to take them. King John had learned something from the first civil war. Then the castles like Wallingford which had held out the longest had saved England from King Stephen. As he and his men left it felt like being the last one at a feast. The room seemed emptier. We were alone. De Percy and de Vesci would send their men south and I would be the target. If they took Stockton then King John would have to battle across the Tees.

It was September. Our crops were harvested and our animals ready for the autumn cull. I sent orders out to begin it. Any spare animals would be brought in to be protected within castle and manor walls. The last thing we needed was to leave food for our enemies. I rode to Durham. I went with half of my garrison for I knew not the state of the land. In the event I was pleasantly surprised. The barons of Durham had all remained loyal to me. The Dean of Durham had heeded my instructions and the castle was well prepared for a siege. I had asked for the captain of the guard, Thomas of Trimdon, to be made Constable until a new Bishop was appointed. The Dean was a good man but he was no warrior. Thomas was. The burghers of Durham and the garrison in particular were grateful to me for what I had done. They would defend Durham as though it was mine.

The bad news that Carlisle had fallen was waiting for me when I reached Stockton. Two of Fitz Clare's men brought the news. "Our lord barely made it out of Carlisle safely. He rode south with four men and he sent Tom and me with two others here to warn you."

"The others?"

"Dead, lord. We will have to serve you until our lord returns. He went to the Earl of Chester. He will bring the Scots to book."

"Find Ridley the Giant and tell him that you join our numbers until order is restored to England."

The news left us exposed. Barnard Castle had pro Scottish sympathies. The lord there, Balliol, would side with the Scots. There were no other castles west of us. Raby was a Durham castle to the north but it was Stockton that controlled the Tees. The manor of Piercebridge no longer existed. When King John had ordered the destruction of Stockton, he had taken the manor of Piercebridge for himself. Its lord had died with my father at Arsuf. Now the King's chickens were coming home to roost. The Scots could head south and ravage Yorkshire. I sent two archers to warn Sir Ralph. He was close enough to Piercebridge to contest the crossing.

It was November when one of David of Stanhope's men rode in. "Lord, the baron said to warn you that Baron de Clavering is heading south towards you with an army. We fought them close by the bridge over the Tyne but we were outnumbered and we lost. We retired in good order. They brought many banners. Eight knights fell and our lord was wounded. He said he was sorry that he had failed you."

"He has not failed me. Where is he now?"

"Our barons retired to their castles. We are well stocked for a siege and already the ground hardens. The rebels will not eat well! The fields are empty of animals."

"Then return to your castle and tell the baron to remain hopeful. The Earl Marshal will not leave us without succour. I will dispute this land with de Clavering."

He left us on a fresh horse to return north and I sent for my knights and their men. Wulfestun, Norton, Elton and Hartburn were not strong enough to hold out against an army. My townsfolk were already warned and prepared. Our town now had two strong gates and a stone wall. King John might have prevented me from building a keep but he did not bar me from making my town as strong as it could be. While we awaited my knights' families I sent Mordaf and Gruffyd north to watch for the rebels of the north.

I would use our mounted men to meet them and, hopefully, slow them down. I did not want them joining with the Scots. Once again, my son William wished to come with me. This time I had a more logical reason to refuse. "Your horse is not large enough and you would slow us down. When you are big enough to ride a palfrey then you may come."

That was an answer he could understand. My knights and their families began to arrive. They had left a token force to guard their halls but most of their archers and men at arms were with me. We had so many that we had to use the common for their horses and their camp. With just ten knights I knew that our banners would be outnumbered but we had more than a hundred and fifty men at arms and almost as many archers. The feast that night was more of a council of war.

"We will meet them north of Thorpe at Far Layton." There was a ridge of high ground there with the forests of Brierly which rolled towards Wulfestun to the east and the stream filled woods of Whitton to the west. Between them was open fields of, perhaps two hundred paces. We would have the slope with us and they would have to attack uphill.

Sir Edward nodded, "It is a good place to fight and if we have to fall back then we are not far from Stockton."

"We will have to fall back. There were many banners. Our best hope is to slow them down and then let them break upon our walls. When Alfred sounds four blasts on the horn we fall back, in good order, to Stockton." Good order meant that our archers would leapfrog behind us. Half would ride to the next ambush point while the other half slowed them down with arrows. That was the advantage of mounted archers. I wondered why others had not thought of this.

"But what if they do not come that way, lord?"

I smiled, "Fótr, the road was put there by the Romans for a purpose. It is the shortest route from the north to the south. They could head further west and cross the river at Piercebridge or even risk fording at Hurworth. Both strategies suit us for we could attack them as they crossed. Sir Ralph and Sir Peter will be waiting south of the river for them."

Sir William was close to his people. "If there is a siege, lord, will not our people suffer?"

"If we have to fall back then you will send riders to your folk and they can come to Stockton. The walls there are manned. I do not think that the men of the north will have siege engines. This is not a chevauchée. This is a battle to rid the land of us the enemies of the rebellion."

Sir Edward shook his head, "There is an irony here, lord. You and I fled this land because of King John and his tyranny and yet here we are fighting for him."

"We fight not for the King but for England and his son. Henry is raw clay to be moulded. We fight one battle at a time."

The next morning, we headed north to travel the four and a half miles to Far Layton. We were at the farm of Summerville when my two scouts rode in. "Lord, the men of de Clavering are camped at Bishop Middleham. They have ravaged and destroyed the Bishop's hall. They are heading south. They will be close to Sedgefield soon."

They had travelled faster than I had thought. "David of Wales, take all of the archers and line the ridge. If they approach before we arrive then slow them down."

"Aye lord."

"Mordaf, how many men were there?"

"We counted fifty banners. They had, perhaps a hundred men at arms, twenty archers and sixty crossbows. The bulk of their men were the levy. They had a thousand of them."

"Rejoin David of Wales. We ride. Let us hope their levy slows them down!"

We had just a mile and a half to travel. We reached the ridge and there was no sign of the rebels. David had divided the archers into two groups and they were hidden on the flanks and the fields which abutted the road.

"Henry Youngblood, I want forty men at arms dismounted. They will be in two groups and protect the archers. Ridley, the rest of the men at arms will form up with the knights. We will have two ranks. Squires, you will be the third rank with spare spears." Knowing that we would be fighting a battle I had brought Flame. I needed a warhorse. I dismounted and watched the road from the north.

When they finally came, it was without scouts. They were confident. They had defeated one army. Mine, they knew, would be smaller. All those visits by Baron de Percy had been spying expeditions. He knew my numbers exactly. He would pay for his treachery sometime. I had a long memory and as Hugh de Puiset had discovered I did not forgive.

Once we were spotted the host halted and a conference took place. De Clavering knew our numbers. He might expect some of the levy to be with us but as they knew the way I fought they would expect them to be behind me. They would have to respect my archers. I wondered what strategy they would employ to neutralize them. As they formed up I saw that they had chosen to match my archers with their crossbows, archers and levy. We had a chance. I would back my archers against any crossbowmen and our elevation gave my more skilful archers a longer range. They would be attacking us with a hundred and fifty horsemen. We would be outnumbered. We had to hit them so hard that they recoiled. That would allow us to fall back and for our archers to aid us.

There was no talk and no preliminaries. Once they had formed their three lines a horn sounded and they began to move up the road towards the ridge. There were a couple of areas of dead ground but my archers were experienced. Our arrows fell upon their archers and crossbowmen before the rebels were in range. Men fell. I turned my attention to the horsemen for David and his archers would deal with the flanks. The rebels were four hundred paces from us. I shouted, "Forward!" and we began to walk down the slope. The rebels were still cantering. The energy was being sapped from their horses' legs. When we were one hundred paces apart and the rebels were galloping I shouted, "Charge!"

We were together in solid lines. We were stirrup to stirrup. I had intended charging the standard of John FitzRobert de Clavering but he had not led the attack. I could see that he was with his squires at the bottom of the slope. When we were fifty paces apart I lowered my spear. Some of the knights who charged us had lances and they had held them for longer than we had. I saw the ends of many of them dipping toward the ground.

The knight I chose to hit was desperately trying to control his weary horse and raise his lance when my spear struck him in the right shoulder. His lance brushed my side. He tumbled from his horse. His body fell from my spear and I was able to ram it at the surprised knight who was following. He had an open helmet and my spear entered his skull below his nose. It was a mortal blow. The man at arms who followed was a veteran. He would not be caught out. He had a spear and I saw him pull his arm back. I used Flame's power, speed and my control to suddenly switch to the man at arms' left. His spear struck fresh air and my spear shattered on his shield. Flame leaned into his horse and the combination of my blow and Flame's strength sent the rider and man at arms crashing to the ground. Mayhem ensued as the horses following fouled themselves on the horse and rider. I spurred Flame and hit a rider who had been labouring up the slope. He grasped the shaft of my spear as it entered his gut and tore it from my hands.

There was no one between me and John FitzRobert de Clavering, Lord of Warkworth. "Alfred, with me!" Drawing my sword, I galloped towards the baron. There were no warriors between me and him, there were just servants. They ran at my approach. On the flanks, the levy had been halted by my archers and were wavering. My knights and men at arms were engaged in a bloody mêlée behind upon the road. The battle hung in the balance. I shifted the balance. The baron had two squires and two men at arms with him. Only a madman would risk charging five men with just two.

The Lord of Warkworth did not see two men charging at him. He saw the standard with the gryphon. He saw the man who had

Magna Carta

captured King William and defied a king. He saw me and he chose to flee. His two men at arms rode to face me as the baron, his standard and his squire fled. I was travelling so quickly that I had little time to think. As the man at arms spear smashed into my shield my sword hacked across his chest and bit through to the bone. The baron had a twenty-pace lead on me and Flame had charged for almost half a mile. I would not catch him. I turned to see Alfred ram my standard into the face of the other man at arms. As the man at arms reeled I turned and brought my sword across his back. His arms flew in the air and his back arced. Mortally wounded he tumbled from the saddle.

The levy had seen their lord leave and they fled. As they ran my archers cut them down. Their knights and men at arms saw the flight on their flanks and they fled. At least those who could disengage fled. The rest yielded. They had been beaten and when a leader left you then it was time to surrender.

I took off my helmet and sheathed my sword. Clasping Alfred's arm I said, "Thank you, my son. That was bravely done!" There would be no recall. There would be no need for an orderly fall back. The rebels had counted on a quick victory such as the one against Durham and they had failed.

Chapter 12
The King comes North

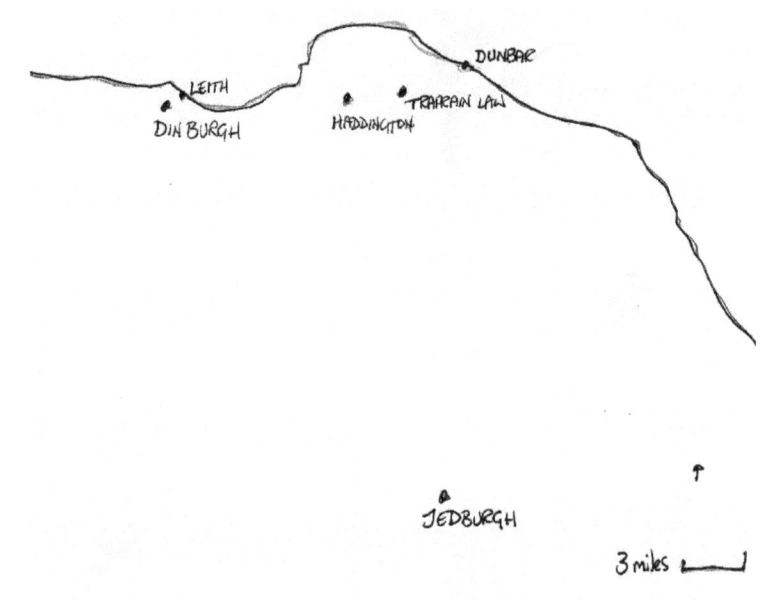

We had six captured knights. Twenty men at arms had surrendered. They did so because of my reputation as a fair man. King John would have had their hands lopped off for defying him. We sent our wounded and our dead back to Stockton while my archers mounted their horses and rode after the fleeing rebels to ensure that they did return home. Sir Fótr was the most seriously wounded of my knights. He had a badly gashed calf. Father Abelard was with us and he used fire to seal the wound. It would be an ugly scar but none save Maud would see it. He returned to Norton along with his wounded.

Sir Edward pointed at the captured banners. "No de Vesci nor de Percy."

"They seek power. They are both looking for more than that which lies in the north. They will cling to Fitzwalter like leeches until they gain some estate in the south. We fight for England and they fight for what they can get out of it. I read the charter. It does little for the common man nor the ordinary lord. It serves to enhance the position of the twenty-five counsellors. Our position remains the same. We have gained little but we have lost nothing. My hope lies in the future King of England."

It was dark by the time we returned home. Maud had gone back to her husband. The threat was gone and my knights could safely return to their halls. Poor William was the unhappiest in my hall. While the rest rejoiced in the lack of casualties and the removal of the threat he was annoyed that he had missed what others were calling an easy battle. It had not been easy. It had hung in the balance. The enemy had been badly led. If de Clavering had been at the fore with his men they might have prosecuted their attack and overcome us. My reckless charge could have been halted. Five to two might have ended the threat of Stockton but my reputation was as big as my horse and men feared me.

A week later news arrived from Sir Ralph that they had met and defeated a force of men heading south from Barnard Castle. They had three knights to ransom. The knights we had captured had been ransomed within three days. News had reached their families that King John was coming. If he had the power then they might lose their estates and their lives. I had no doubt that Sir Ralph would also be paid quickly.

At the end of November news reached us that the Earl of Chester had retaken Carlisle and defeated a rag tag Scottish army. King William and his son were at Din Burgh where they were building up a larger army. He had learned that the English were hard to defeat; even when they were led by a bad king. Riders came from the Earl Marshal to keep us informed of the progress of the royal army. I learned that Prince Louis had sent knights to help Fitzwalter and I began to fear that the French would, while the King was in the north, invade in greater numbers. We did not relax our vigilance nor did we stop preparing for war.

After the knights had been ransomed I gathered the captured men at arms. They had been treated fairly since the battle but had been kept under guard. None had tried to escape. My own men at arms and archers had spoken with them. Some knew each other from the campaigns against the Scots. I gathered them all in my outer bailey. I had Father Abelard with me. We had had a seasonal change in the weather. The first heavy frost had coated the castle in a white hoar shimmering cloak of ice.

"You were all captured because your leaders left you. Your leaders were rebels. That does not make you rebels. You were following your lords. Your lords are not here and so I ask you a question. Who will swear that they are not a rebel and will support King John and his son Henry? If you refuse you will not be punished. At least not by me. Every man has the right to choose who he follows."

"And if we choose to reject rebellion then what will happen to us?" The solitary voice belonged to a sergeant who wore the livery of de Percy.

I pointed to the gate, "Then you can leave and head south. There are barons who seek good warriors. I know you, Roger of Hauxley. You are a good warrior. A lord would be lucky to have you in his retinue. Your poor judgement in choosing de Percy should not be held against you."

I saw him smile and men laughed.

He nodded, "Lord, you are right. Suppose a man chose to follow you; what then?"

"A fair point." I pointed to Ridley the Giant. "There is my captain. He is the one who chooses his shield brothers. You swear an oath to me but it is Ridley the Giant who commands my men at arms. Should any of you wish to follow my banner then when you have sworn speak with him. His word is final." I saw Ridley nod.

In the end, it was not surprising that all chose to swear and all but five asked to join my retinue. The five who did not join us left my castle and crossed the river. I suspected that they would become brigands or bandits. Ridley told me, later on, that those five would have been rejected by him anyway. Their lord had died and he had not been from the north. His manor had been close to Norwich. I was relieved that we had no prisoners for when King John arrived he would not be in a merciful mood.

By Christmas, the King was at Nottingham. Although the south east was held by the rebels and the French were pouring men into England the King was capturing castle after castle. I was kept informed, not by the King but William Marshal. He knew that I was the key to holding the north. I did not relax my vigilance. Just because we had defeated the rebels of the north and the Scots did not mean that all was well. King William and his army were still poised. I wondered why he had not come south. All that I could think of was that he was waiting for the rebels to begin another attack. It was then I remembered our campaign against his own rebels. The King of Scotland lacked confidence. This offensive was his son's idea. The old lion had passed his best years and it was the young cub we needed to watch.

January brought two things, snow and the King. He did not stay with me. I was not offended. After all he had tried to eradicate Stockton Castle before now. He did call to thank me for my defence of Lincoln and the defeat of the rebels. It was hardly gracious but we did not like each other. He carried on to Durham. He was a careful man. He had brought his wagons with the crown jewels and the regalia of state. He feared for his position. The Earl Marshal and Prince Henry did stay with us much to the delight of my wife and Aunt Ruth. Prince Henry was as yet untainted by his father's action. Both made a great fuss of him as did my daughters Rebekah and Isabelle.

It allowed Sir William, Sir Edward and the Earl, along with myself to speak openly about the war. "We have to defeat the Scots, I know that but I like not the fact that the French and the rebels have a free hand in the south. Our royal castles are holding out but support for the rebels grow."

I nodded, "They are like predators gathering around the carcass of a wounded beast. They each seek the largest portion. That is why de Percy and de Vesci are in the south."

The Earl nodded, "Even my son is being seduced by the rebels."

I was shocked, "William?"

"He is being courted for he is one of the twenty-five councillors. I do not like the company he keeps but I can do little about it." He gestured with his thumb. The Prince is my hope. Fitzwalter will invite Prince Louis over."

Sir William said, "Why?"

"To make him King of England."

The news shocked us all into silence. It was unthinkable but I knew that it could happen.

"Then we will keep fighting until we have an English King on the throne once more."

"And that is why we need you and your men when we go to Scotland. You have defeated the Scots more times than any man since the days of the Warlord. King John needs you at his side."

"Yet he would not stay here and was grudging in his praise of my men."

"Is that why you do this, Thomas? So that men will sing your praises? I thought better of you."

"Do not insult me, Earl Marshal. The King needs my help and yet he is too proud to ask me for it properly."

"It is not the King who needs your help; it is England."

I could not argue with him. I sent word to my knights that we would be riding north, again. We would muster at Durham at the end of January. Once more we would fight the Scots but, unless they suddenly came south, we would be fighting on their soil. We would be fighting on the same ground where I had helped the Scots. This time it would be to our advantage!

As we headed towards Norham and the Tweed I wondered if King William would try to stop us at Berwick. King John was moving quickly. We had no siege engines and winter was not the time when you could build them easily. As the Earl who had fought here more often than not, I was sent for as we approached Norham.

The King was not in the van but he was close enough to be aware of any problems. "Earl, should we be worried about Berwick?"

"No, Majesty, we merely pass it. The Constable of Norham can watch it. So long as we hold Norham then Berwick is a good castle with a pleasant view."

He gestured to the Earl of Salisbury, William Longespée, "My brother here does not think we should leave a bastion barring our route home."

"With due respect, my lord, it will not be a problem. King William's men are of such poor quality that he asked His Majesty to use our men to put down a rebellion. The problem might come if he decides to sit on the rock that is Din Burgh. He would take some shifting and, in my view, not worth the effort."

Magna Carta

William Longespée asked, "Then if you do not think it is worth the effort of taking then what should we do?"

"Defeat the Scots as soon as we can and get back to the real war with the rebels."

King John laughed, "You know, Earl, I may have misjudged you. You do have a sharp mind. How do we defeat them if they hide in their fortress?"

"Leith, Haddington, Dunbar, all of the places which surround Din Burgh are valuable to the Scots. Traprain Law is still seen as a special place. While the main army surrounds the rock the rest raid and capture the treasure that the Scots hold. He will either sue for peace or he will have to come forth and defeat us. If his son is with him then he will attack."

We saw Norham in the distance. King John said, "I like that plan but we can make it better. You and the knights of the Palatinate are all mounted. Leave on the morrow and raid those places you mentioned. King William might come to attack you."

"This sounds, Your Majesty, like the last time we faced the Scots. As I recall the main army arrived late."

He scowled, "Just when I think that I might like you then you say something like that. If the Scots come to attack you then draw them back to the main army." I nodded, "You can do this?"

"I can do it," he nodded, "for England!"

There was only room for the King and his entourage in the castle. That suited me for I needed to speak with my knights. I spoke quietly for there were many around us I neither knew nor trusted. My knights, my captains and the men of Durham were trusted. "Tomorrow we teach King William a lesson. He used us once to save his crown and his throne. He owed it to us, if no one else, to keep to the treaty. We will punish him for his treachery. This is a chevauchée. We are here to raid and take as much as we can from the Scots. We want him to fight us so that King John can defeat him and then we can go home. It is twenty odd miles to Dunbar. David of Wales you and your men will ride to cut the town off from the west. We will take the castle."

David of Stanhope laughed, "Just like that?"

"They will not have repaired the damage we did last time and they will fear our banners. We ride up and, if their gates are closed then we demand they open them. From there we go to

Haddington. It is a rich town and that too has few defences. If those attacks do not draw the Scots to battle then when we burn Leith and all the ships they might."

It was a bold plan but I knew a little more about my foe now and I deemed it the right one. When we woke it was to a sky which was black and a ground which was white. Snow had fallen. We were lucky. The coast road was relatively clear and so we rode as quickly as we could while the weather held. With our white cloaks wrapped around us, my knights and men at arms were almost invisible. Just before we reached Broxburn the snow, which had been falling intermittently, suddenly blew up into a blizzard. We had had them in Sweden. There they called them white night. I was lucky. In the fore were all the men who had served with me in Sweden. The snow was inconvenient and that was all. We pushed on. As we neared the castle, in the later afternoon, I saw that the blizzard had been sent by God. The gates were still open. We had not been seen.

"Come let us ride before they close them." It was almost madness but we galloped through the blizzard. We were seen but it was only as we rattled across the drawbridge and by then it was too late. We galloped through the town towards the castle proper. I saw men trying to close the gates. I was riding Scean and my horse seemed to have wings. Sir Edward and I forced open the gates with our horses. Two of the sentries foolishly tried to stop us and they paid with their lives.

I shouted, "I am Thomas Earl of Cleveland and this castle is now mine. If you resist then you die! Throw down your weapons if you wish to live!"

The snow deadened the sound of the metal swords being hurled to the ground. We had taken Dunbar without the loss of a man. I sent for my archers. There was little point in them enduring a night in the blizzard when there was a castle with chambers and hot food! King William had taken over the castle as his own and there was only a constable and his garrison. He and the captain of the guard cowered in the Great Hall as we swept in. I had sent David of Stanhope and his men to organize the food. I needed to speak with the constable quickly before he could gather his wits.

"I want the treasure brought here, now!"

"Treasure, lord?"

"This is a royal burgh. King William will have coin and crowns here. Fetch them." There was a slight hesitation. "Constable, you have surrendered to me and thus far just two men have died. Do not anger me. Your King has betrayed me and broken his word. I lost men fighting for him. I would have reparation. If there is no treasure then the garrison will be slaughtered and before I leave I will burn the castle and the town to the ground."

"I will fetch it, lord."

"Sir William, go with him and watch for tricks. The Scots, it seems, cannot be trusted to speak the truth or to keep their word!"

The King had left much treasure in the castle. He had not expected our attack and the snow had been unforeseen. It was a good start.

We awoke to a world of white to the west. We knew the way to Haddington and the terrain. I sent a rider to King John to inform him of our position. I would have no qualms about pulling back if the Scots attacked in force. I would not be the sacrificial lamb again. Even with the snow the ten miles would not take long and we knew that we had destroyed Haddington's defences. The King had not taken it as a royal burgh and so it would have been left the way it was. This time our attack would have archers. Without the benefit of a blizzard we were unable to approach unseen and we were spotted. They closed the gates. My archers formed a double line two hundred paces from the walls and fifty of our men at arms dismounted while the rest waited with the knights. There was another gate and the Scots would be sending a rider to their king. That was what we wanted. This was a chevauchée to draw the spider out. The archers began to methodically clear the walls while the fifty men at arms, ten of them armed with axes, marched resolutely forward. The garrison and burghers of Haddington had not expected this attack. It was the middle of winter and warriors did not make war in winter. They were not ready. The arrows they had were hunting arrows and they fell woefully short. Even when they struck the phalanx of men at arms they could not penetrate the shields, helmets and hauberks. I led the column of horsemen closer. We were six men wide. That was just enough to break through the gate when my men destroyed it.

The sound of the axes must have been like the crack of doom for one of the men we had sent to watch the road to Din Burgh galloped back, "Lord, they are fleeing."

"Sir Edward, take our knights and men at arms. Stop them taking anything of value. That is our payment for this work!"

"Aye lord."

When the gates were rent asunder we galloped through them. A few had stayed but they were not up for the fight. They cowered and awaited my judgement.

I pointed east, "Take the clothes on your back and leave. Your faithless King has betrayed me. Go and tell him that the Earl of Cleveland comes for him!" I knew that it was overly dramatic but when the story was retold it would be exaggerated even more. Either the King would yield or he would fight. He would not squat in his fortress. Once again, our men ate and drank well. We slept under cover. I smiled for I knew that King John and his army would be sleeping in tents. He had thought that he had given us the harder task. So far it was not. Sir Edward and my men brought back wagons and horses with the treasure of Haddington. It was a rich burgh and we had done well from a painless raid. I sent the wagons back to Stockton with ten men at arms to guard them. It would be enough.

The next day we left. As we headed towards the sea we left a black column of smoke rising in the air. The burned town would tell all the punishment for treachery. Perhaps they would think we headed for Din Burgh. It mattered not. The snow was lighter closer to the estuary and the going much easier. When we reached the sea the icy wind from the east chilled us to the bone but the sight of the masts of the ships in Leith harbour warmed us up. It lay just a few miles to the north of Din Burgh. We could see the battlements as we approached. That meant they could see us. I sent David of Stanhope with ten knights, twenty men at arms and twenty archers to cut the road to Din Burgh. This time it was to give us a warning if King William and his men sallied forth. I did not think that they would.

Apart from a couple of wooden towers they had little to defend the port. It was so close to Din Burgh that, perhaps, they

Magna Carta

thought that they did not need it. We proved that they did. We galloped in like Viking raiders from times past. Their two towers were set alight. I did not even have to draw sword. The soldiers who were there had been the remnants of a healthier garrison. The rest had gone to Din Burgh to fight for the King. Most of them surrendered. As with Dunbar and Haddington we sent the people of Leith to Din Burgh. They would have hundreds more mouths to feed. He would have to fight King John. We collected even more wagons this time. The ships were emptied of cargo and the warehouses stripped of all that they contained. Then we burned the ships. Some of the captains were French and others were Danes. They complained that they were not Scottish.

Sir Edward was not sympathetic, "Then think carefully before you trade with them in the future."

We headed south. We had done exactly what we had been asked. This time I had twenty men at arms and ten archers guard the wagons for there were far more of them. We would share our booty with the men of Durham. None pursued us. The castle lay to our right and had they chosen they could have attacked us. I do not think that they were ready. From what I had learned of King William he did not think quickly.

Riders from King John met us at Dalkeith, "Earl, the King is a mile down the road. He asks that you hold this town for him!"

I looked at Sir Edward who shook his head, "Do we have to do everything for this King?"

I nodded, "Apparently." Turning to the messengers I said, "Very well." As they rode off I said, "Look at it this way, Edward, we will have the better rooms in Dalkeith and our treasure is well on the way to Stockton. We have been paid well for very, very little work."

He nodded, "I know but it still annoys me."

I laughed, "I am certain that King John will lose sleep over that!"

By the time the King arrived we had two cows we had found roasting. We had left the best hall for the King but the rest of our men and knights would be warm within buildings. Those who had marched with King John would be camping, again. The King, of course, was given the choicest cuts of meat but my men had already taken our food before the other lords came for their share. So far, we had borne the dangers and we deserved the rewards. The fact that we had barely had to draw a blade was down to luck and the skill of my men.

I was summoned to the council of war. I sat next to the Earl Marshal and young Prince Henry. The throne that would be his was now a wager in a great game. I took it as a good sign that he attended. The King was still eating when I entered. The Earl Marshal said, "You have justified the high opinion men hold of you. If the King does not seem effusive in his praise then do not be offended. It is his way and he has much to think on. If nothing else this offensive has shown that he is a king and one who knows how to fight."

I nodded, "We have done all that we can. I think that there will be a council of war this night on the rock and that they will have a harder debate than we do. We have driven many extra mouths within their walls. They need to feed them and the ships in Leith which held supplies are now burned. He either surrenders or fights."

"You know him better than any. What do you think he will do?"

I was suddenly aware that the room, crowded though it was, had grown silent over the last few moments and every eye, especially the King's, was on me. "The King is old and he is weary. He has lost confidence in himself. Alnwick was a bitter blow for him and he lost those warriors who were close to him. If he was alone then he would surrender." I saw nods. "But he is not alone. His son is with him. Alexander seeks to flex his muscles. He will be persuading his father to attack us tomorrow. Our advance has met little opposition. His army is within the castle and to the east."

King John leaned forward and pointed the rib he had been gnawing at me, "You know this? Or is this a guess?"

"A guess, Majesty, but one based on the facts. We have not seen any evidence of men to the south and the east. If they are not to the west of the castle then they will surrender for they have not enough room on the rock for the refugees and an army big enough to face us."

He nodded and chewed. He tossed the bone to the waiting dogs and wiped his hands on a napkin. "Tomorrow we array for battle. We have the men at arms and archers on the two flanks and our knights in the centre. We will demand that the Scots surrender. Perhaps they have no army and they hoped that the weather would deter us. Tomorrow we shall see."

The Earl Marshal turned to me and said, "I believe you are right, Thomas. There are not enough stables in the castle for all of his knights. Where are their horses? I will ensure that we keep a good watch to the west."

The blizzard which had helped us some days earlier was finished and the clear skies made it an uncomfortable night for those forced to camp. We used furniture to keep a fire going all night. We awoke to a painfully bright blue sky. Breath seemed to freeze before our eyes. The men who had camped out were wrapped in cloaks and clothes that they had found. Half of the army looked like vagabonds. Alfred brought Flame. In the last couple of years, he had grown both physically, he was almost as tall as me, and as a squire. He was now confident. He no longer had to ask what was needed and he knew my preferences. He brought Flame for, if we fought, then this would be a day for warhorses. One of King John's household knights, Eustace de Merville came to tell us that I had been assigned the right flank. The knights of Durham and I would be next to my men at arms and archers. As we waited I watched the heralds and priests ride to the gates of Din Burgh and speak with the garrison.

They were there for some time. I turned to Edward, "This delay is deliberate. I hope that the Earl Marshal keeps a good watch to the west."

The priests and heralds rode back. A short while later the gates opened and the army which had been within the castle rode forth. I saw that the walls were lined behind them. They were not warriors. They were the burghers of the towns we had taken and the men of Din Burgh. They were there to give the illusion of numbers. I saw King William but not Prince Alexander. The King had less than fifty knights and just two hundred men at arms, half were mounted. Even as King John began to give orders I heard shouts from our left flank and the thunder of hooves on frosted snow. I could not see but Prince Alexander and the rest of the Scots were attacking from the west.

King John must have been listening to me the previous night for Sir Eustace galloped up, "Earl, the King asks you to swing around your horsemen, archers and men at arms. Attack King William!"

I nodded. David of Wales and Ridley, who led the men to my right were mounted. Their men, although dismounted were within walking distance of our mounts. I said, "Alfred, tell Ridley and David to mount their men. They are to follow us."

"Aye lord."

The Scots were just half a mile from us and showed no sign of advancing. They were staying close to the walls of Din Burgh so that the men on the fighting platform could use their slings and bows to defend them. King William was the bait.

I raised my spear, "Knights wheel left!" I pulled Flame's head around.

The knights to my left walked their horses backwards while those to my right advanced. By the time we were in three ranks obliquely facing the Scots, Alfred had returned. As he tucked in behind me I saw that King John had turned the whole of the rest of the army to face the charging Scottish knights led by Prince Alexander. He was exposing his right flank to the men led by King William. He was trusting me to protect him. If I had harboured any rebellious thoughts then that would have been the time when I would have shown them.

"Forward!"

We moved at the walk. Until my men at arms and archers mounted then the eighty of us who moved forward would be isolated but we had to fix King William's attention on us. As we moved I saw him give a command so that they also turned to face us. There would be two battles this day: a king against an earl and a prince against a king.

I spurred Flame to the canter. I knew King William now. I had fought against him and for him. He was now in his seventies. He had lost confidence. Worse, each time I had fought him I had defeated him. I knew that he would not risk charging me even though he had more knights than I did. He would stay as close to his walls as he could. I counted on his archers having just hunting arrows and that the cold would make the crossbows difficult to use. We would take casualties until David of Wales

Magna Carta

could dismount my archers and clear their walls. It was a risk. Knowing or, rather, believing, that the Scots would not counter charge us made it easier for me to gauge when to unleash my horses and charge. At the canter we could keep a straight and unbroken line. Once we galloped then the line might become uneven. I chose to wait until the last moment to charge.

I could hear the clash of arms to the west but that was not my battle. You fought the one before you and hoped that your brothers in arms did as well as you. When we were fifty paces away from the waiting Scottish knights I lowered my spear and shouted, "Cuthbert's knights! Charge!" As I spurred Flame he leapt and Sir William and Sir Edward were hard-pressed to stay with me. I was slightly ahead of them.

I saw a household knight. He had William's golden lion on his shield. I pulled back my arm as the Scottish knights belatedly tried to charge us. It was an erratic response as some seem fixed while others, like the knight I faced, chose honour and glory and charged. He was a brave knight. He had a helmet that covered his face and he held his shield close to his chest. I was using my knees to control Flame. My horse knew how to charge and to fight. My foe had a lance and, as he thrust it at me I punched with my shield and my spear at the same time. His lance shattered on my shield. My spear drove into his left shoulder. The shaft broke leaving the spear head and a hand span of ash sticking from his arm.

Flame was snapping and biting at the Scottish horses. I could not have slowed my war horse down even had I wanted to. I held my shield before me as I drew my sword. Another lance smacked into my shield and I reeled a little. Drawing my sword helped to balance me and I swung it, instinctively, at the knight whose lance lunged at my side. He hit me and the wooden tip broke mail and went into my side. My wild sweep with my sword connected with his head and he fell.

We had broken their main line. I saw men at arms on foot race back to protect the King and his royal standard. When arrows flew over my head then I knew that David and his archers were close to hand. That also meant that Ridley the Giant was leading the finest men at arms in the land to my aid. We were no longer alone and I rode at King William.

Magna Carta

Before men became Christian they believed that dying with a sword in their hand guaranteed them a place in the afterlife. King William was old. Perhaps he thought to do the same. He charged at me with his sword raised. As he galloped towards me I turned my sword so that I would strike him with the flat of my blade. I would not kill a king. Even as I pulled back my arm I saw his sword drop and he slid from his horse. No arrow protruded from him and he looked to be without a wound. As he fell to the ground his men at arms gathered around him.

Raising my helmet, I shouted, "Your King is hurt! Yield for I am the Earl of Cleveland you know what my archers can do!"

His standard-bearer threw down the standard and said, "The King is dead, lord! We yield."

To the west the battle raged and Prince Alexander did not know that he was King. I turned to Ridley, "Take the King's standard to King John. Tell him that the Scottish King is dead!"

The news must have reached Prince Alexander before my man at arms could reach King John or perhaps he was already beaten. He surrendered and the battle was over. We had won and Scotland had a new King.

Chapter 13
French Invasion

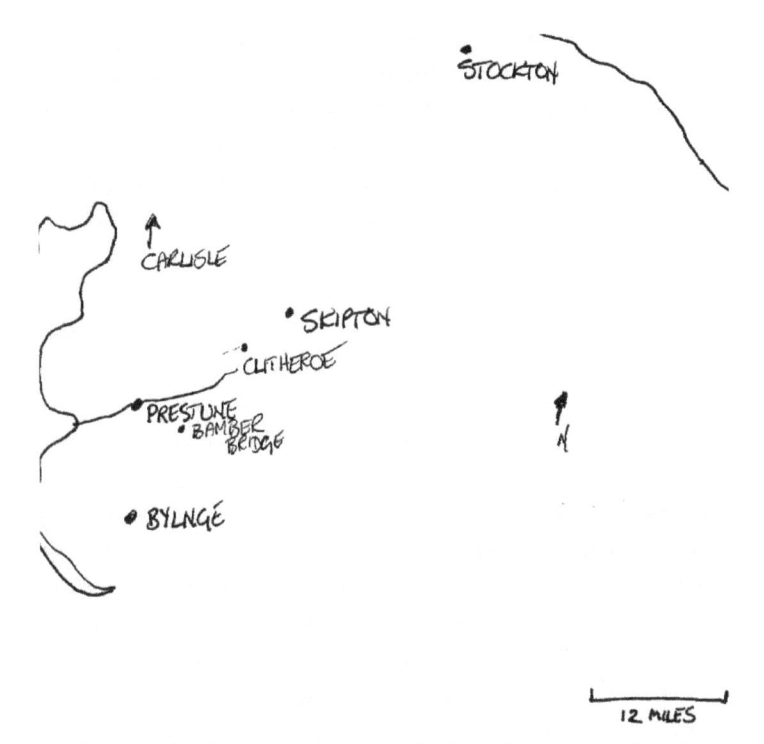

[Hand-drawn map showing Stockton, Carlisle, Skipton, Clitheroe, Preston, Bamber Bridge, and Bylnge, with scale of 12 miles]

Father Abelard saw to my wound. If we had not had healers with us then the wound might have become poisoned. As it was I would merely have discomfort as I rode home.

The King was pleased with our actions and he allowed the knights of Durham and myself to go home directly. Edward was cynical enough to believe that the King did this so that the reparations he extracted from the Scots would not be shared with us. I did not mind. Our chevauchée had yielded more than the coin the King would take from the Scots. The journey home was not a pleasant one. January was a harsh month and, when we reached my castle, I vowed that I would not stir again until the new grass was grown. My wound had ached all the way home. The King was also heading south. He had done what he intended. The north was now free of rebels. There were isolated areas such as Scarborough. He would deal with them but they would be slight detours on his progress south. He would reach his heartland by March.

The treasure we had taken was divided equitably between every knight. I did not take more than my fair share. If truth be told I did not need it even though I had now lost the revenue of Huntingdon. It did not go to his son, King Alexander. King John had revoked the gift and it became a royal manor. Some knight would reap the benefit. I had had two years of Huntingdon's fief. I was happy.

Alfred was now a young man. He was almost fourteen and he had been to war. That made a boy into a man. William, my youngest child, looked up to his big brother. He was everything William aspired to be. The story of his heroics in the Scottish campaign just made him more determined to become a squire. He was just eight and he would have some time to go. We could now talk around the table for although William was young he could understand weightier matters. For my daughters what was said around the table was important for it might affect their chances of a good marriage.

"Will the King win, Thomas?"

"I do not know, aunt. I confess that his behaviour in Scotland impressed me. He was decisive and bold. We could, if there had been no trouble further south, have conquered the whole of Scotland."

"But the rebels still hold London and the south."

I nodded, "And the rebels are drawing more and more support. Perhaps they hope for a new king, I know not."

My wife said, "Young Henry?"

"No, my love, Louis of France. When I spoke to the Earl Marshal that was his fear. Many of the barons have more ties to France and Normandy than to England."

Alfred sipped the watered wine I had poured for him, "And we stay here?"

He was astute. "We need to stay here until we are ordered south. The King knows that my presence will deter the Scots. King Alexander is not bound by the treaty of Norham. I know that we hurt the Scots but give them time and they will recover. The French may bolster them with gold. They have done so before. However, you are right, my son. We may have to go south; not to save the King but to save the country. Alan the horse master has secured us enough horses that we could reach Lincoln in two days. We can afford to wait until summoned."

We had not taken the new men at arms to war with us. I had thought it best to leave them in the castle so that my garrison could get to know them. The reports were favourable. The men had fitted in well. I gave them a surcoat each and a shield. With the new horses we had both captured and bought we were able to give them good mounts. I could now leave Ridley and Henry to train them and teach them to fight our way. They would need to know the signals we used. As we employed mounted archers they had to work with David of Wales and his men. Close cooperation was vital.

The snow had gone by March although the ground had failed to warm up. The new grass and animals would be delayed. I had heard that the King had left Northampton and was headed to East Anglia. If that was the case then there would be no war for a while. Once he had retaken London then there might be and I needed to put in place plans to stop the rebels. I rode with Alfred, William and ten men at arms to visit with Sir Ralph at Northallerton. We rode, huddled beneath cloaks for the wind came from the east and was bitingly cold. The small castle at Northallerton was a welcome refuge. As luck would have it Petr and his wife and daughter were visiting and so I could kill two birds with one stone.

I had kept them informed of our success as they had with their own. As I sat before a roaring fire drinking mulled ale we each filled in the details of our battles. We had both lost men and we mourned their loss.

"And now, Earl?"

"I wish I knew. Everything is finely balanced now. The King has regained some of the lands he lost but the rebels still draw men to their cause. The Earl Marshal has taken young Henry to Gloucester. We do not want the King and the heir in close proximity."

"But that means the King is without his two best advisers, you and the Earl Marshal."

"He has his half-brother, Longespée, he is competent."

"But we need a leader with proven experience to advise the King. I am competent, lord, but I would not dream of advising the King."

"You are more than competent. You did well at Piercebridge."

He laughed, "Sir Peter and I just used the techniques you taught us and they worked. Our archers thinned out the enemy and then we struck with horsemen. If they had not worked then we would have been stuck."

"You will learn. I fear that this civil war may go on for some years. Hopefully not as long as the other one but this one will not end any time soon. Both sides still think that they can win." They both nodded. "If the French invade then the King will need every loyal knight and baron to stand with him. I will be leading all of my men south. How stand your castles? Would your families be safe with you away?"

They looked at each other and Sir Ralph nodded. "Something else we learned from you lord was to hire men when you did not need them. We have invested the money we took from ransoms and our captives in more men at arms, good weapons and strong defences."

Sir Ralph took me on a tour of his manor. There were no natural features such as I enjoyed. If an enemy came it would be the fabric of his castle and the mettle of his men which would determine the outcome. "And your neighbours?"

He shook his head, "They are mainly rebels who would side with de Percy and his men. De Percy lost Topcliffe and that is a rich manor. Many of his neighbours fear that they could lose theirs."

"Are you threatened?"

He laughed, "With you as my sponsor? They are terrified of you and your men. You are close enough to be here within a few hours and my castle could hold out against a large army for days. So long as you are safe then so are we."

By the time I returned home, a few days later the icy winds had gone and we had balmy warm weather. Such was the climate of the north. It was hard to predict. It meant that farmers took advantage of the sun to sow crops. Ewes which had been waiting to give birth did so in great numbers. Although I was not directly

Magna Carta

involved in any of those events it drew my attention away from weightier matters.

Towards the end of April, I received a missive from the Earl Marshal. He was in Gloucester with the Prince and, as such, further away from the major events around the south east. It was, however, good news. The King had managed to wrest control of London from the rebels. Even more importantly the Pope had finally given his judgement on the charter. I showed the most important section of the letter I had received to Aunt Ruth and my wife:

He declared the charter to be 'not only shameful and demeaning but also illegal and unjust' since King John had been 'forced to accept' it, and accordingly the charter was 'null, and void of all validity forever'; under threat of excommunication, the King was not to observe the charter, nor the barons try to enforce it.

The rebels were now, clearly in the wrong. I had read the charter, or a copy of it, at least. I could not see what the Pope found so offensive. It was Aunt Ruth who pointed out that the salient point was that King John had been forced to sign it. It seemed the rebellion might soon be over. With the King in control of London and with the Pope's support, the rebels would wither and die. All of the preparations for war would now not be needed. The weapons and horses would not be wasted. We might not have a civil war to fight but when King Alexander grew in confidence then he would come south again.

In May I knew that my hopes of an end to the baronial conflict would be dashed. Prince Louis had been invited to England and he landed on the Isle of Thanet. The messenger who brought us the news told me that the King had fled to Winchester. Prince Louis and the rebels held London again. A second rider arrived just two days after the first to tell us that Prince Louis had been proclaimed King of England by the rebels. This was a disaster. I had sent riders out to my knights, including the Palatinate as soon as I heard of the rebels retaking London. I was just glad that William Marshal had the young Prince Henry safe in Gloucester. The west was still loyal, in the main, to King John. As I waited for those knights whose manors were in the Palatinate to arrive and the one or two other loyal barons of the north, I sat with Sir

Edward and Sir William to try to decide what we ought to do. There was no easy solution.

"We could march south and help King John."

I nodded, "Aye William, but where will he be? The last I heard he had divided his army into five so that he could control more of the land he stills holds. The Earl of Salisbury has one, his steward, Sir Falkes de Breauté a second. I know not the leaders of the others but I do not know where the King will be. The last I heard he was in Winchester. That is a long way from here. We could waste time travelling the country trying to find him."

"Lincoln will be crucial, father. We should go there. We are still close enough to home to return if there is a problem and just a couple of days march from London."

Sir Edward nodded, "Your son is right, lord. The Constable will resist all efforts to shift her."

"You are right. That is as far south as we dare risk going and any army heading north would have to pass through Lincoln. The Lady de la Haie will not relinquish the castle easily. When the other knights arrive, we will head south."

In the event the Scots pre-empted any decision I might make. They took Carlisle. It was Robert Fitz Clare who brought the news. He arrived in the afternoon following the arrival of my Durham knights. His arrival threw my plans into disarray. After he gave me the bad news he said, "I sent a rider to the Earl of Chester but you are better placed to intercept them."

"Intercept them? Do they not consolidate their gains?"

He smiled, "No lord. The young King is set on going to London. There he will offer his support and army to the French Prince. They will leave a small garrison at Carlisle. Even now I expect that they will be heading south and using the plains of Lancashire. With the Pennines as your barrier, he will feel safe from your wrath."

"And none other can stop them?"

"There is a castle at Skipton but there are many roads which they can take to avoid it. Once they are in the plain of Lancashire then they can flood the land."

"I take it they are largely on foot?"

"I believe, my lord, that you took most of their horses."

Magna Carta

I was thinking even as he was speaking. By using my ferry, we could cut across country. Ripon was still loyal to the King; Sir Ralph had told me that. From there we could take the narrow road which headed to Clitheroe. If they were avoiding Skipton then they would either come east and we would dissect their path or they would head further west and go towards Prestune. The castle at Prestune would bar their crossing of the Ribble and that meant we had a chance. Our horses would mean we might be there before them.

"Alfred, fetch David of Wales." I turned to William as my squire ran off, "William, go and tell Geoffrey that we have guests this night. Tomorrow we ride."

Despite my wife's best efforts, the talk around the table was about war. Everyone knew what the proclamation and the invasion of the Scots meant. It was the first civil war again. Then, London had proclaimed Stephen to be king and the Scots had taken advantage and invaded Yorkshire. It had been my great grandfather and Archbishop Thurston who had defeated them. If I failed to stop the Scots then all of my family's work might be in vain. I had to succeed. I had sent David and twenty archers to find and watch the Scots. My archers rode the fastest of horses and could both scout and remain hidden. When I had fought for the Scots I had seen little evidence of the use of scouts.

David of Stanhope asked the question which was on everyone's mind. "The Scots are a problem but not as great a problem as the rebels. Can the King defeat them?"

It was an unspoken question because none wished the answer. Was he strong enough and, if we lost, what would our punishment be? Were we all risking our manors and our families?

I answered the question. "If we stand firm then I believe that we can defeat the rebels. The question beneath your words is harder to answer. I know not what will happen if Prince Louis is King of this land. I know that I am no friend of theirs." I shrugged, "I have been forced to be an exile before now. I have been a sword for hire." I smiled. "There are benefits. That is how I met my wife and how Sir Fótr came to serve me. If I had to leave this land then it would not be the end of the world. It would just be the end of the world that I know and love. England is worth fighting for. Our enemies had best fear us for we are the best that this land has to offer."

On that message, my men retired for we would be up early. We would make forced marches using the many new horses we had obtained. We would cross the land at the speed of the wind. King Alexander was in for a shock.

We reached Ripon just before dark. I used the common land to graze our horses and we bought barley and oats for them. Our horses would be the way we would defeat the Scots. We had to look after them. We would catch the Scots.

I had not heard from my archers. That was not a surprise. They would not return until they had news. We left the next morning to begin the climb over the mountains. The road we used was not Roman and it twisted and turned. There were sheer drops to the side and we did not move as quickly as I might have hoped. I sent Cedric Warbow and two other archers to search for David of Wales. I was becoming anxious. We reached Skipton and the lord there had seen no sign of either my archers or the Scots. We still had some hours before sunset and rather than staying in the castle we pushed on towards Clitheroe.

The manor there was small but there were fields where we could camp. Many of the Durham knights were becoming despondent about the lack of news. I still had confidence in my archers. We had just lit the fires when Cedric Warbow rode in alone. "We have found them, lord. They have crossed the Ribble and are camped at Bamber Bridge which is a few miles upstream of Prestune and on the south bank. David of Wales has men watching them. He said, lord, that he has men looking for somewhere further south where you can ambush them."

"He is a good man."

Robert Fitz Clare asked, "Is it not a risk to anticipate where they will go?"

"I would not wish to keep chasing them. That just exhausts our mounts. If we can cut across their line of march we meet them sooner."

Cedric explained the best route for us to take. "David of Wales will keep us informed as to their movements and the best ambush site."

Magna Carta

We left well before dawn and headed down the Douglass valley. It was not easy going for the roads here were little better than tracks. This was not the fertile plain. This was an area of high ground crisscrossed by becks and brooks. Mordaf ap Tomas found us. "Lord, there is a hill north of Newton le Willows. It is called Bylnge locally. There is a ridge that overlooks the road the Scots will pass. They cannot avoid it. David of Wales thinks that it will be the best place to attack."

Robert Fitz Clare said, "An archer decides where we fight?"

Sir Edward laughed, "He is a better commander than many I have met. If he chooses this place then it will suit us."

My archer turned to return to his captain. He did not follow the road, as we did, he took off over the fields and up the hill sides. Once we crossed the last hill we saw before us the flat plain which stretched west to the sea. There, to the south west, was a single ride with a conical shaped hill. David had been right. It was perfect. As we headed towards it I wondered why no one had thought to build a castle here and then I realised that it should not have needed one. Carlisle and Lancaster blocked an enemy from the north while Chester guarded the south and west. So long as we were ahead of the Scots then we had a chance.

I saw that the archers were there already. We headed south and west to approach the hill and the ridge from the south. We would be hidden from view. The ridge ran obliquely across the landscape. We could use the dead ground behind it to mask our numbers. The sudden sight of my men rising like wraiths from the ridge might surprise the Scots enough for them to ignore our paltry numbers. Cedric had already told me that they outnumbered us by more than five to one. This would not be a charge of heavy horsemen. This would be a defensive battle which would make them bleed their resolve away.

Dick One Arrow greeted me, "The captain and the two Tomas boys are watching them. They are a few miles up the road. You have made good time, lord."

"We rode hard, Dick. Dismount. Today we fight on foot. Tether the horses on the lower slopes. Feed and water the animals. Knights, gather below the crest." I slung my shield over my back and carried my helmet as Alfred led Scean away to join Flame and the other horses. He would return with my spear. The conical hill at the top of the ridge was a distinctive feature. It was not particularly large but it could be seen from miles. That was what we needed. We needed to be seen and arrest the progress of the Scots. The ridge itself sloped gently but the hill itself looked almost man made. It reminded me of a larger version of the Bishop's old castle at Bishopton. I saw that John the Archer and James were on the hill itself. They were not wearing my surcoat. When they scouted they used brown cloaks and the two were almost invisible.

John slid down and came towards me without exposing himself on the skyline. "I see them, lord." He pointed to the south west. "The road passes within a few hundred paces of this ridge and heads towards a small village called Birchley. We scouted it out and there is neither lord nor hall there. The only folk we found was a farmer and his family. We told them that the Scots were coming and they fled to Ashton. They have family there."

"Is there a lord there, at Ashton?"

He frowned, "I think that there must be from what he said but I do not know for certain."

This was the domain of the Earl of Chester and he would know. I waved over Padraigh the Wanderer, "Ride south and east. There should be a hall there. Tell the lord that the Earl of Cleveland needs him and his men to face the Scots here on this hill of Bylnge."

"Aye lord."

I followed John and bellied up to the ridge. My surcoat would stand out like a banner if I walked. I saw the snake that was the column of Scots as they marched down the narrow, twisting road. It was not Roman and it adhered to the fields. It explained their slow progress. Once they reached the lands south of Chester they would be on a Roman road. The Earl Marshal was there with the young prince. If the Scots knew of his presence then a slight deviation could make all of the Earl Marshal's plans irrelevant. We had to stop them.

I slid down the slope. Ridley and Will son of Robin were there with my knights. "I will be on the top of that hill with my standard. The rest of you will form three lines below the ridge line. There will be knights, men at arms and archers. I will stand with my banner and my squire. I wish them to see me. When Alfred sounds the horn then you walk to the ridge. The archers will stand on the top protected by the men at arms and knights."

David of Stanhope asked, "And if they do not choose to attack?"

I smiled, Then King Alexander will show that he is a fool. The road is within our archers' range and our horsemen could fall upon his baggage. I think he will attack." While they arrayed themselves in their lines and I awaited Alfred I waved over Robert Fitz Clare. "The Earl of Chester should be close, should he not?"

"It is a longer journey from Carlisle to Chester than I had to reach Stockton. His knights are in the castles which border Wales. He will have mustered and he will be coming but his men are not all mounted."

"Then we fight alone." He nodded. "Was your banner seen by the Scots at Carlisle?"

"Aye lord."

Then you and your squire can be with me on the hilltop. Let us see if we can confuse them."

He went for his squire and banner. Alfred arrived with my banner and two spears. "Come, let us see what sort of view the top of this slope affords." The steep hill was hard to climb. The ridge itself had been gentle. The Scots would be able to use their horses to charge us. The hill itself would be an obstacle. Horses could not climb it. That would be the place for a last stand; if it came to that. The wind was from the north east and we had some protection when we reached the top. The wind made it feel cooler. I saw the Scots. They were now less than two miles away and I saw a knot of riders heading for the ridge. That would be David of Wales and my scouts. "Do not unfurl your banner until Sir Robert arrives."

"Aye lord." He pointed at the Scots. "They have many banners."

"This is the first time their King has led his men into England. He will have brought all of the knights we did not slay."

Sir Robert and his squire huffed and puffed their way to the top, "That is a prodigious climb, lord."

I nodded, "And yet it is but fifty or so paces higher than the ridge. It will serve." I waited until the Scots were a mile away. I could see the Lion Standard which his father had used. We would be visible but not a worry. "Now squires, let fly your banners." The wind from the north east made them flutter square above our heads. They would know now that the Earl of Cleveland, the bane of the Scots was here. I had not killed King William. It was age that had taken him but his son would hold me responsible. That alone would draw him to me. He would know that I would not come alone but he would not know where my men lay nor how many of them there were. I watched David of Wales lead my archers behind the ridge to join the other archers. He would lead them now. I looked to my left and right. Hidden from the Scots were my three lines of warriors. With under a hundred knights, two hundred men at arms and fewer than a hundred and fifty archers we alone were not enough to defeat the Scots. We were enough to deter them. We had half a day to weary them until night fell.

William of Lincoln ran up the slope, "Lord Geoffrey of Asheton has arrived he has twenty men at arms and twenty of his yeomen."

"Good. His yeoman can watch the horses. It will release men to fight and he can join Sir Edward." It was little that he brought but the ten men who would have had to guard the baggage and the horses could now fight. They might make all the difference.

I saw that we had been seen for the Scots stopped. A few riders, light horsemen on ponies, detached themselves and headed closer. They would be looking for the rest of my men. I had more than enough time to order them to rise to the top of the ridge. The more uncertainty in the young king's mind the better. They rode to within four hundred paces of us. There were eight of them and I wondered if they were considering charging at me. If they did then they would find the slope too steep even for their hardy ponies. I still held my helmet and my arming cap was hanging down. My face was well known. Once I had been identified they turned and rode back to the main army. There was another discussion when they arrived and then the Scots arrayed. Their knights would lead. I saw that their King would be with them but he left a third of his army with the baggage. They formed a circle around it. I smiled. My reputation for cunning was well known. The Scots approached in four lines of men two hundred paces wide. The leading line was made up of knights. The gentle slope was no obstacle. The land had never been tilled and animals had grazed it to make an easy turf on which to ride.

The young king had learned how to use his men. They did not come recklessly at us. They were steady and kept a tight line. When they were five hundred paces from us I shouted, "Alfred, the horn!"

The horn sounded and there was the slightest hesitation from the Scots. Our horns normally presaged disaster. Were my men coming around their flanks? The banners of my knights rising like a bright and colourful wave over the ridge was the first sight they had of my men. The banners were followed by knights and then men at arms. The archers would be hidden behind my two ranks. We moved down from the summit of the small hill to join Sir Edward and Sir David who would flank us. The Scottish King waved his sword and they moved forward again. Even when they charged the gentle slope would take the edge from their speed. The knights and men at arms who stood in two lines presented a forest of spears. That was what the Scots would see and they would deem it to be assailable.

When they were three hundred paces from us I shouted, "They are in range, David!"

Their arrows already nocked my captain of archers shouted, "Draw!" They could not see to aim but they would lay down a shower of arrows which would be the length of our line. Any within that area would risk death or a wound. He waited a heartbeat to allow them to come closer and then shouted, "Release!" Even as the arrows rose he shouted, "Draw!"

The Scots did not see the arrows which were sent high in the air. They were in the process of lowering their spears and watching the ground to ensure that they did not trip or fall. When the arrows struck, as they closed to two hundred paces from us, there was a mixture of cracks as arrows hit metal and wood and screams from men and horses as some arrows found flesh. The horses suffered the most. Some fell. Others tumbled, stumbled and veered; as they did so they brought down other horses and riders. The second and third flights added to the confusion and mayhem. The continuous line of knights was now broken and uneven. Before they managed to come into contact with us another twenty horses and riders joined the twenty who had already fallen. Some knights were struggling to their feet and they broke up the lines which were following.

"Brace!" I angled my spear up and put my foot against the shaft. Behind me Ridley the Giant's long arms held his spear so that it was an arm's length beyond my shield. The slope, the arrows, the dead and dying horses as well as the wall of steel tipped ash meant that the horses of the Scots would not charge home. They baulked and they stopped. Two spears struck my shield but one of the knights' horses, already pierced by my spear, was struck in the throat by Ridley's jabbing spear. The knight fell to land at Sir Edward's feet. Unable to move his spear he swung his leg and kicked the man under the chin. He fell backwards. The Scottish horses were now the problem for they were panicking and King Alexander, just twenty paces from me shouted, "Sound fall back!" The horn sounded and knights began to disengage. I saw that the King had arrows in his shield and in his saddle. His helmet showed a dent where he had been struck too.

Some did not obey the King's orders. They were angry and they jabbed and hacked at our line of knights. They did not heed the command and they fell. As the knights rode down the hill my archers continued to rain death upon them. They descended quicker than they had attacked.

David of Wales shouted, "Hold! Archers retrieve arrows!"

We broke ranks to allow the archers to race down the hill and recover the arrows which were unbroken. As they did so they despatched any knights who were beyond help. They fetched back four who were wounded. They would be held by Sir Geoffrey's men with the horses.

Sir Edward walked down to recover the sword and purse of the knight whose neck he had broken and Sir Robert asked, "What will they do now, Lord?"

"If I led them I would make camp and then send men in the night to surround us and make a night attack. They will not do that. King Alexander wants glory. He now knows our numbers. They will come on foot. With shields held aloft and before them

Magna Carta

then our archers will not kill as many. When they have to negotiate the dead knights and horses we will kill more but he will rely on sheer numbers to overcome us. Remember King Alexander hopes to gain Northumberland from this!"

Our squires brought water and we watched and waited. There would be another couple of hours before dusk. These would be long days. It was still a couple of weeks before the longest day. We had not yet finished our work but we had made a good start.

As I had expected they formed lines of men on foot and this time they would come as one mighty block. They were using fewer men for they now needed horse holders. The King, I saw, stayed mounted with his household knights and they watched. Perhaps the arrows had suggested that he might die an inglorious death. Crucially he had fifty knights with him. That was fifty fewer knights for us to face.

I shouted, "We hold them. Night will soon fall and we are well placed here."

Men began banging their shields and chanting. "Warlord! Warlord! Warlord!" It was mainly my men but it spread. When you were attacking such things prey on your mind. You begin to worry. What the Scots should have done was chant the King's name in response but they did not. They advanced.

"Now David!"

This time I waited until they were two hundred paces from us. David would be able to send his arrows almost vertically. The wind from the north east would ensure that they came nowhere near us but with a vertical angle they might strike men who held their shields before them. There were many men advancing without mail. Only the front ranks wore mail and the rest would have to endure David's arrows. As I had Ridley the Giant behind me I hefted my spear up. I only liked using my spear from horseback. I pulled back and waited. When the Scots were twenty paces from us and with men behind the front two ranks dying they could wait no longer and they charged at us. When a man runs he cannot help but use his arms to gain speed. Their shields did not protect them. I hurled my spear at the chest of the knight with the four yellow stars on a blue background. Even as it tore into him I drew my sword.

The spears of the Scots rattled and cracked on our shields. Once the spears had struck then they were useless as weapons. I found myself face to face with a red bearded knight. He had a helmet with a nasal and aventail. He roared at me but the spear shaft would do me no harm. My sword was above me and the press of men was too great to swing it and so I began to saw it back and forth across the mail links of his ventail. I pushed with shield. Ridley the Giant and Henry Youngblood, not to mention Alfred, stood behind me and they would not be shifted. My sword had a good edge and as the blade rasped against the mail I saw the links break. It was then he realised what I was doing. He could do little about it as the men behind him were pushing into his back. His spear and his shield were trapped against my men. He should have dropped his spear and tried to draw his dagger. He did not. I saw panic in his eyes as my sword broke through the mail and began to tear through his gambeson. Designed to absorb blows it would not stop a sword. When my edge caught his neck, the blood did not seep and ooze, it spurted and it arced. Sir Robert took advantage for the blood sprayed into the eyes of the knight he was fighting and Sir Robert's sword gutted him.

All along my line men were dying on both sides but the greater casualties were on the Scottish side for they were fighting uphill. Our swords could crash down on heads. They might not penetrate the helmet but they could knock a man out. The dying knight before me meant that I had room to swing. Ridley the Giant's spear still protected me. Our lines were looser and he was able to thrust next to me. Soon he would join me as we spread out to compensate for the fallen knights. Father Abelard and our priests would be pulling the wounded from the line to tend to them.

The energy sapping slope was taking it out of the men who faced us. As I rammed my sword above the shield and into the shoulder of a knight I realised that there were just men at arms before me. That gave me hope. The knights were the leaders and if they fell we might weaken the resolve of the rest. The King still had enough knights with him to prevent a victory but we did not have to win. We had to make him return home, that was all.

The man at arms I faced wore a leather jerkin studded with metal blades. The edge of my sword was not as sharp as it might have been. The mail of the red bearded knight had dulled it. I had to use the point. The man at arms jabbed at me with his sword and I blocked the blow. Expecting a sweep, he was surprised and shocked when my sword darted in to take his right eye. The nasal on his helmet prevented penetration to his brain but he was hurt and he screamed and spat at me. As Ridley stabbed a man at arms trying to slice off my right arm, he stepped next to me. The movement distracted the half-blinded man at arms and the tip of my sword entered his throat.

Ridley had had to be defensive while he stood behind me. He was now freed from that role. He hurled his spear into the mass of men behind their front rank and picked up the war hammer that one of the Scottish knights had dropped. A warhammer is a fearsome weapon especially when wielded by a warrior of Ridley's size. The men behind him moved as he swung it all the way from behind him. The beak smashed through the helmet of the man at arms and into his skull. He would have died instantly. Henry Youngblood joined his comrade. With those two on one side of me and Sir Edward on the other we were an irresistible force. We began to drive the Scots down the hill. On the flanks our battle was not going as well but, in the centre, we were winning.

Suddenly I heard a Scottish horn. It sounded three times. The men before us hesitated and in that instant fifteen died for we did not hesitate. Then the Scots began to stream down the hill. As they disappeared before us David's archers slew even more of them. I wondered what had made the Scottish King call off his attack. We were not winning. I saw him and his knights turn. The baggage was already heading north. Sir Robert shouted, "Look lord, it is the Earl of Chester!"

Looking to my left I saw the Earl of Chester leading two hundred knights. They would not catch the King and his knights for the men streaming down the slope would all slow down the Earl's men. They would, however, destroy his army! I raised my sword, "Charge!" Thus released, my men poured down the hill!

It was darkness that saved the Scots. It became too dark to hunt them. Our blades were blunt and we were weary. The Earl of Chester, Ranulf de Blondeville reined in, "I am sorry we took so long, Sir Thomas, but it appears we were just in time."

Sir Edward snorted, "We were ready to attack them anyway, my lord, but your help was timely!"

Ranulf de Blondeville laughed, "I meant no insult, Sir Edward. Once my men told me that the Earl of Cleveland blocked the progress of the Scots then I was confident we would win."

The next day we headed north. The baggage had yielded much treasure. The Scottish King was bringing gifts for Prince Louis. We found their dead littering the road north. We stopped following them at Bamber Bridge for there they headed north east to cross the Ribble. We took the shorter route through Prestune. In that way we got ahead of them. They were forced to head due north. They would not be able to hole up in Carlisle. The Earl and I had decided that our priority was not the King of Scotland but the castle at Carlisle. We had so many men that our sheer numbers made the garrison that Alexander had left, flee. Our border fortress was once more in English hands and Ranulf de Blondeville left a strong garrison to deter the Scots from repeating their attack.

Chapter 14
The King is dead!

It was July by the time we reached Stockton. We had hunted isolated bands of Scots who had gathered along the border. The last thing we needed would be bands of bandits and brigands in our heartland. I had left Ranulf de Blondeville to collect the ransoms from the knights we had captured. I was anxious to discover what had been happening further south. We now had two kings. Only one was legitimate in my eyes for Louis had not been crowned nor had he been anointed. Those summer months before the harvest were a strange time for us. The rest of the country fought amongst themselves but, thanks to the men of the Tees Valley the north was at peace. De Clavering had fled south to join his rebel friends and the rest of the barons in the north feared that I would punish them if they rebelled. We collected in our harvest even though most of the country did not. I did not relax my vigilance. I had the knights of Durham ride beyond the Roman wall into the land of the rebel barons. They ensured that no spark of rebellion was ignited.

In September I received a message from William Marshal. He wished to meet with me in Lincoln. Although he did not specify that I bring men, I thought it foolish to risk riding abroad without knights. I would not, however, empty my land. I took Sir Edward and Sir William with me. We left most of their men at arms in their manors and my men at arms and archers acted as my escort. I would trust to the knights I left at home and my strong walls to defend my family.

William came to me the night before we left. "Why cannot I come, father? Is there danger and that is why?"

He was becoming more perceptive. He had heard me tell my wife that the meeting was just that, a chance for the Earl to inform me of the state of the land. If that was true then William could safely come with me.

"William, we live in dangerous times. I believe that all of the men I take will come back safely with me but if you are there? Who will watch over you? It cannot be me for I lead. Alfred watches over me."

"I need no wet nurse."

"True but you cannot fight a warrior and that is what it might come to. Each day you are growing. Alfred tells me that you are better with a sword and shield than many boys your age. You can ride." I saw his face light up with the praise from his big brother. "Yet you still cannot ride a palfrey and you cannot fight. That is why I leave you here. There may be danger. It is not for you, it is for the men who would have to watch over you. If they are watching over you then they cannot fight." That argument seemed to work.

We left in the second week of September. We took no war horses but we did take spare palfreys and extra weapons. We stayed with Sir Ralph and I told him of our news. He had grown in stature since taking over Northallerton. Younger knights deferred to him and the older lords of the manor recognised, in him and Sir Peter, warriors who could defend the land. When time allowed I would speak with the new Archbishop and seek a post for Sir Ralph which would allow him to have official backing as a leader.

The further south that we travelled the more we felt threatened. Once we had left the land which owed fealty to York then we passed through an area of baronial influence and loyalist strongholds. We stayed in the latter. We reached Lincoln before the Earl Marshal. Nicola de la Haie was pleased to see us. There had been other attempts to take her castle. Some had been by force while others had been legal challenges to the rule of a female constable. She had endured both and survived but she was no longer young.

"And the folk of Lincoln?"

"They side with the barons. They have been promised so much and yet I know it cannot be delivered. I run a benevolent manor. The poor are fed and housed. My taxes are lenient and my punishments are far from harsh. Some seem to think that they just need to live in my manor and all will be provided. The barons make it seem as though they need not work."

I nodded, "I know. I am lucky to be living in Stockton. After the manor was taken from my family they had many years of hardship. When I returned they appreciated what my family had done and now we have those who move to live within our lands."

She smiled, "I have but a few years left to me. It shall not worry me if I am unpopular. I know that what I do is right." She patted Alfred's hand, "And this one will break girls' hearts soon." He blushed and that made her laugh, "Oh it is good to see a young man who can still blush. Too many of the ones I see are worldly wise. What is wrong with innocence?"

To divert the attention away from himself my son asked, "And do you have children, my lady?"

"Aye, I have a son, Richard and two daughters, Matilda and Nichola. I never see any of them nor my granddaughter, Idonea." She looked earnestly at Alfred, "When you marry do not neglect your mother! She will miss you. Your father will be busy making war somewhere but your mother will need you and your children around her."

He knew that already. Aunt Ruth's joy in her surrogate grandchildren was clear evidence of that.

William Marshal arrived with a remarkably small escort. There were just twenty men in the livery of the Earl and ten warriors who looked like Swabians to me. He had brought young Prince Henry with him. I wondered at that for it was a risk to bring the heir through enemy lines. There was also a papal representative with them. The Earl introduced him, "This is Cardinal Guala Bicchieri, the papal legate to England. He is proving to be of great help. This is the Earl of Cleveland and his son and this fine lady is the Constable of Lincoln, Lady Nichola de la Haie."

He bowed and gave his hand for her to kiss. "The Holy Father is keen that rightful rule is established. We cannot have lords commanding kings. He is most unhappy that Prince Louis has taken it upon himself to invade England to be proclaimed king. His father, King Philip is also unhappy."

I looked at the Earl, "I would have thought that he would be delighted."

The Earl shook his head, "You do not understand the game of thrones. If Philip's son rules England then he also rules Aquitaine. He would have a claim to Normandy and Anjou. King

Philip worries that his son would have more power. Perhaps, his father fears, he would take France from him."

The Cardinal nodded, "And he does not like this growth of baronial power. If it happens here then why not in France? Kings have a divine right to rule. The barons are upsetting that natural balance."

I wondered why I had been summoned. I knew, from past experience, that there was little point in expecting the Earl Marshal to tell me before he was ready. For once, Alfred remained silent for he knew that he was amongst the great and the good. I had often told him to listen in such company. That way he would learn how to behave when he became a knight. I noticed that Prince Henry also followed that axiom. He was almost ten and he must have known that he was in the most dangerous of positions. My son sat next to him while we ate. I saw them talking but I knew not what about for I was seated next to the Earl Marshal.

The Cardinal and the Earl waited until the meal was almost over before they spoke. The Earl Marshal did the talking but I noticed that Cardinal Guala Bicchieri nodded agreement throughout.

"Firstly, the cardinal here has ruled that as the baron's revolt is a crime against God then the King's war becomes Holy Crusade." I knew that was a momentous decision. King John had been excommunicated a few years ago. He must have paid a king's ransom to have made the Pope switch sides so completely. "However, there are places in England where the church opposes us. York is one such." I did not know that. I knew that Langton had been appointed Archbishop but that the Pope had rejected his appointment. "King John and Pope Innocent have agreed that Walter de la Gray will be the next archbishop." I waited, there was more to come. "The canons of York deem him to be too ill-educated and have appointed Simon Langton the brother of the Archbishop of Canterbury instead."

Now it became clear. The canons of York were siding with the barons. "And the Archbishop of Canterbury drew up the charter."

Cardinal Bicchieri said, "And he has been excommunicated for doing so!"

Magna Carta

"We need you to escort the Archbishop to York and see that he is able to take office."

I nodded, "Of course. Where is the Archbishop?"

"That is the problem. He is in Winchester. Between here and there wait the men who support Fitzwalter and the French forces. We have asked him to come to Gloucester. We need you to come back with us and escort him."

"Why did you not ask me to meet you in Gloucester?"

"Cardinal Guala Bicchieri goes to London to inform those churchmen there that they are excommunicated."

He smiled, "Archbishop de la Gray may not be safe but as Cardinal I am. Besides I have some guards with me. They are Swabians. I will be safe enough."

That night, before I retired, I wrote a letter to my wife. We would be away longer than I expected and I did not want her to worry. Sir Edward and Sir William did the same., We did not tell our wives where we were headed nor of our mission but our letters would reassure them. I sent two archers back to Stockton and asked them to return to Lincoln when they were done. The Cardinal left at the same time as we did. We shared the road briefly. I saw now that the Earl had risked much with such a small escort. I asked him why as we headed for Newark.

"I felt safe so long as I had the Cardinal with me. None would risk harming a representative of the Pope."

"Then you should have asked me to bring more men. I brought a small escort. This is not the escort for the heir to the throne."

Prince Henry said, "My father lives, Earl. I am just a pawn at the moment. I have to reach the other side of the chess board before I become a threat to another."

He was bright boy. "Prince Henry, my great grandfather watched over your namesake, Henry FitzEmpress. You are more than a pawn. I am sure that the Earl has told you that the kingdom is balanced on a precipice. The last time an army crossed the channel it conquered this land and that was without rebels trying to help the invader."

I saw him taking that information in. The Earl Marshal said, "You are right, Sir Thomas, but now that we have the Pope behind us I am sure that King John will prevail."

I could not argue with that but I was not convinced. Excommunication had not caused King John too many problems. Having begun to speak with us Prince Henry chatted all the way to Gloucester. He had rarely travelled outside of his father's castles and was interested in the north. Alfred told him of our campaigns against King William. They got on well. I did not know it then but this would become a deep friendship. We reached Devizes at the end of September and I was relieved for we could have been attacked any time and we would not have had the protection of the Cardinal. My archers had to ride far ahead and far behind to make certain that we were neither ambushed nor followed. Prince Henry was impressed by them.

I knew from my grandfather that my great grandfather had often fought in the castles around this land. Devizes was not a big castle but it looked easy to defend and I wondered if my great grandfather had stayed here. I seemed to be walking in his footsteps. As we waited for the Archbishop I fretted and I worried. I was as far from my home as it was possible to get. Although I trusted my knights I knew that events were not going the King's way. The south of the country and the north were supporting the barons. The fact that my men held the Tees and the Earl of Chester the land to the west neutralized the baron's influence. King John was in the land around Essex and with winter almost upon us his army was enduring awful conditions.

As we waited I asked William Marshal something which had been on my mind since the invasion. "What of the Fair Maid of Brittany? Does she not have a claim to the throne?"

The old Earl shook his head, "You are like a dog with a bone. You know not when to leave something alone. Arthur and his sister were not meant to rule. The Maid has spent too long away from the world to be able to rule. Young Henry has seen more in his short life than she has."

"That does not make it right, Earl. She has been locked away for more than ten years; longer than Prince Henry has been alive."

"Can we do anything about it?"

I looked at him and knew that he was right. "You and I are knights, Earl. One of our oaths was to protect the weak and the innocent. The Fair Maid qualifies on both counts and I do not

Magna Carta

think that either of us could look her in the face and say that we had protected her as we should."

"You are right but what we have both done has been for England and that is worth more than the life of any individual." I did not agree with him but I found it hard to muster arguments against him.

Walter de la Gray arrived in the third week of October. He was accompanied by Pierre des Roches, Bishop of Winchester. He was as dynamic a churchman as I had ever met. He knew all that was going on and told us in detail of the gains and losses of the campaigns. I was just pleased that my charge had come. I did not relish a journey across England in the heart of winter.

Walter de la Gray was not enthusiastic about the journey and his new appointment. "I think, Earl Marshal, that I would prefer to wait until the King has defeated the rebels and the land is safer."

William Marshal laughed, "That day may be a long time coming, Archbishop. You are in the safest hands in England. The Earl of Cleveland will get you safely to your See. That I promise you."

The Archbishop was a fussy man and he prevaricated for three days. In those three days, our world changed completely. Cardinal Guala Bicchieri and his Swabians arrived, along with William Longespée and some of King John's leaders, with the news that King John had been struck down by dysentery in Kings Lynn. To compound the problem when crossing the Wash, he had lost his baggage including the crown jewels. The dysentery had proved fatal. The King was dead!

"On his deathbed, the King asked that you, Earl Marshal ensure that his son is crowned King of England."

We all looked at Prince Henry. Earl Marshal bowed, "The King is dead, long live the King."

We all dropped to our knees and acknowledged the nine-year-old as King of England. Pierre des Roches said, urgently, "We cannot delay. We must have him crowned before Prince Louis discovers that the King is dead."

Walter de la Gray said, "But that is impossible. There are no crown jewels and the barons hold London."

Pierre des Roches said, "Nonsense! We can go to Gloucester Abbey. We have more than enough churchmen here! We even have a cardinal to see that all is done well and with two such earls I think that we will be safe!"

William Marshal nodded, "Sir Thomas, get your men organized. The Earl of Salisbury's men will be tired. We need fresh men who are alert to guard the King."

I was still stunned by the news and grateful that I had something to do. Edward and William would both be happy for they had become bored as well as worrying about their families. They were with Ridley, David of Wales and Henry Youngblood. That would save time.

"King John is dead. We have to escort Prince Henry to Gloucester Abbey where he is to be crowned."

Sir Edward was the first to react, "There was a time when I would have cheered that the tyrant was dead. Now I may mourn for it leaves England with a nine-year-old to rule."

"Let us worry about then when he has been anointed. Until he is crowned and anointed it is increasingly likely that Prince Louis will be our liege lord!"

We chose our best horses. It took time to don mail and helmets but, even so, we were ready before the churchmen. "David of Wales, send a dozen of your archers to the abbey. It should be safe but it won't hurt to be certain."

It was a mad dash through a gloomy late October day as we headed towards the abbey. The Earl Marshal had found a golden necklace amongst Queen Isabella's jewels and it was improvised into a crown. My knights, men and myself were used to guard the Abbey. It would be too small for us all to attend. I did not mind. The protection of the new King was far more important than for me to be a witness.

Sir Edward said as we waited at the Abbey doors, "And now we go home, lord?"

"And now we take de la Gray to York and hope that we can cow the deans into acceptance of the Pope, and the King's command." Young Henry's life was changing beyond recognition. He had been a passenger riding behind the Earl Marshal. Now he would be the centre of all. There were thirteen councillors who would be responsible for seeing that he attained his kingdom but it would be the sixty-nine-year-old Earl Marshal who would have to steer his ship through the treacherous waters of this rebellion.

There was no time for celebration and once we were at Devizes, and while my men prepared for our departure I was invited to the council. Ranulf de Blondeville was now rewarded for his constant support of King John. Along with the Earl Marshal he was given the responsibility of guiding the young King.

It was, however, William Marshal who took the lead, "We need to gather all of our army together." He turned to me, "I am afraid that we will need the Earl of Chester and his men to swell our depleted ranks. It falls to you, Sir Thomas, to ensure that the north is safe. The war will be fought here in the south but if we lose the north then we lose the war. Secure the Archbishop in his town and then rally the knights of the north behind King Henry."

De la Gray said, "Perhaps I should stay here close to the King and give him my support."

The Cardinal snapped, "Archbishop, your duty is to York. There you can help the Earl of Cleveland and his men save England! We churchmen can do our part but I am afraid it will be warriors who will bleed and die for King Henry."

The Earl Marshal nodded his thanks. He turned to me, "The Earl of Chester and I will keep you informed and if we need you then I know that you will hasten to our side."

"Of course. My family is ever mindful of its obligations to the royal family."

He smiled, "You are of the Warlord's blood. You fill his boots and armour well."

The Cardinal turned to King Henry, the third to bear that name, "Your majesty, I would suggest that you herein pledge to go on Crusade."

William Longespée said, "But he is a child!"

The Cardinal smiled, "I did not say he would go on crusade just that he says he will do. The Holy Father will give him his support against Louis."

"I thought he already had it."

"No, Sir Thomas, his father had it. However, I am sure that if King Henry commits to a crusade some time in the future then Pope Innocent will throw the weight of the Church behind him."

King Henry looked at the Earl Marshal who nodded, "Then when I am able I will go on crusade."

Once we had established an overall plan I went to join my men who were awaiting the arrival of the Archbishop. I told my knights of the decisions which had been taken. Sir Edward shook his head, "So we guard the whole of the north and when those in the south need us we ride to their aid! They do not expect much of you, lord."

I nodded, "You, above all people, know that this is not a course you choose. When my great grandfather saved King Henry in that forest in Maine he placed our feet on a path the direction of which we have no say. We just follow whither it wends and we do our best. That is all that God can expect."

Just before the Archbishop joined us King Henry, with the two bodyguards appointed by the Earl Marshal emerged. "Sir Thomas, before you go I wished to tell you that I am grateful for all that you have done and all that you will do. It is not a little thing. If I ever regain my kingdom then know that you will be rewarded."

I bowed, "Thank you, King Henry, but know that a truly loyal subject does not do this for gain, he does so because of his King and country. Beware those who serve you for gain."

"I will and I have much to learn."

"The Earl Marshal is wise and can be trusted. Listen to him."

"I will."

Alfred suddenly dropped to his knee, "King Henry, my great great grandfather helped your grandsire, Henry FitzEmpress attain the throne and keep it. I swear that I will be your man and when I become a knight I will stand behind you against all enemies."

The King smiled and looked like a boy again. The frown and serious expression disappeared, "And for that, Alfred, I am grateful. Since we met at Lincoln I have come to know you. When you are knighted then you will become as great a knight as your father. I will not forget." He waved an arm around my men, "I will not forget any of you. That I swear!"

Magna Carta

Peter des Roches and the cardinal had listened to Walter de la Gray bleating about his safety and they provided him with twenty men at arms to act as guards. I do not think that William of Wallingford was happy to be given the whining priest to protect, he would rather have been fighting for his king, but he was a loyal man and he did as he was ordered. As we galloped north I spoke with him. He would be crucial. His presence meant I could stay the briefest of time in York. The north called me.

Sir Edward rode next to me. As we had passed through the towns and villages we heard of the unrest which was now spreading. Some of the lords who had opposed John now supported Henry but, equally, there were others who felt that England needed a stronger King and not a child. They had also changed sides. Such a climate meant that loyalty was hard to discern. All that I knew was that I could rely on my knights and those of the Palatinate. We moved at the pace of the Archbishop and his priests. I sent Padraig the Wanderer and Richard Red Leg to ride to Northallerton. I needed Sir Ralph to meet us at York. I had been working out how to ensure that the Archbishop was safe while still holding on to the north. Sir Ralph would be the key. With William of Wallingford guarding the Archbishop himself, Sir Ralph could keep the land free from rebels.

It took three days to reach York. That was a day longer than I had hoped. Who knew what mischief was brewing in the north? We swept through the Micklegate like a conquering army. I had sent a dozen archers ahead to secure the gates. The deans of York might be belligerent but they were not military men. David of Wales and his archers ensured that the Micklegate was open and we rode directly to York Minster. The deans and the priests were within and when the doors were hurled open light flooded in.

I bellowed, "York, I give you your new Archbishop, William de la Gray. King Henry and the Pope have given him their support. The Earl of Cleveland expects all men of God to respect those wishes!" My words echoed around the vaulted church. They seemed to roll on and on. I stood aside and the Archbishop and his priests, somewhat nervously walked towards the altar. We did not have swords drawn and we wore no helmets but the men at arms led by William of Wallingford and my knights were enough of a threat to impress the deans. They dropped to their knees as he walked between them.

One of them, a grey-haired and frail-looking priest, after looking in my direction, said, "Welcome Archbishop, The See of York welcomes you."

With that, all belligerence disappeared. The deans knew me from the time of Geoffrey Plantagenet. They knew that I guarded them against the Scots. Had the Earl Marshal told me of the problem earlier I could have ridden to York and spoken to the deans. I would have eliminated any dissent. I suppose that we were meant to go to Lincoln and for Alfred and Henry to become friends.

Sir Ralph arrived the day after we did. With William of Wallingford and the Archbishop, the four of us discussed the problem.

"Sir Ralph here has the men who can keep your lands safe. You, Archbishop, need to summon the knights of the manors of York. You must make him the leader of your knights. William de Harcourt, the former Sheriff has fled. I suggest that you make Sir Ralph High Sheriff. He need not live here in York. In fact, it will be better if he is without your walls. William of Wallingford can guard you within."

I think that Walter de la Gray realised that until King Henry was secure on the throne then his survival depended upon me. I was the law north of Lincoln and Chester. He agreed. I wasted no time on departures. We had to leave for the north. Sir Ralph, now High Sheriff came to the stable with me.

"Earl, are you sure that I can do this? It is not that long ago that I was your squire."

"And you have grown since then. Ralph, you will be a just Sheriff for there is not an ignoble bone in your body. Your family suffered at the hands of a corrupt sheriff and a tyrannical king. I hope that we have a good king but you can be a just and incorruptible High Sheriff."

He nodded, "I will not let you down, Earl!"

"I have known that since we first met in Maine!"

We rode for Stockton as though we were being chased by the devil. It was winter but that would not stop those who wished mischief. Our only advantage was that, I hoped, we were closer

Magna Carta

to the north than either de Vesci or de Percy. De Clavering had been easily dealt with. I had fought alongside the other two barons and they knew their business. King Henry had confirmed that I was his representative in the north. As he was in his minority it did not mean as much as it might but it gave me authority and I would use it.

When we reached my river and I saw the standard still flying then I was relieved. That had been my fear over the last few miles that, with a smaller garrison some disaster had struck. Sir Edward and Sir William went directly to their halls. They would be riding north soon enough although I had decided to use my other lords first.

Rumour only had reached my family. My wife asked, "We heard that the King is dead and that Louis is now our king. Is that true?" My wife knew the danger in that. I was an implacable foe of King Philip and his son would bear a grudge against me. We had had to flee two countries. It would be beyond the pale to have to flee my homeland again!

"No, my love. We were there when Henry was crowned King. Louis is still a threat but he has no validity to his claim. Fear not!"

My men knew that they would be needed again and they, like me, made the most of their time in Stockton. I could only afford a short time to my family. As we ate, a cosy affair with just the seven of us, I told them all what had happened. All were now old enough to understand the world beyond Stockton's walls.

Rebekah was on the cusp of womanhood. If there had been no war then she would have been preparing to win a knight to be her husband. There were many young knights without wives and the daughter of the Earl of Cleveland was a rich prize. "And if King Henry loses and Prince Louis wins?"

My son was sixteen now and a man. He had eaten and spoken with the great and the good. He smiled at his sister, "Then we will lose everything. Our fortunes are tied to King Henry. We have to ensure that we do win."

Rebekah had expected a softer, more hopeful answer but my son was grown. He would not tell an untruth no matter how painful.

I patted her hand, "There is a long way to go, daughter. We have yet to fight a battle. I trust in Englishmen to see that we are better off with an English King, no matter how young, than a Frenchman foisted upon us by greedy barons."

Aunt Ruth smiled, "The Warlord would be proud of you. And you go to war again soon?"

"I have been charged with bringing the north in line. In two days I will ride north and visit all of the castles north of the Tyne. That is where rebellion and disorder fester. Before the embers become a fire, I will impose my authority. King Henry has made me lord of the north!"

It sounded easier than it was but I had a strategy. I had already humbled de Clavering. I would visit Warkworth first. Perhaps the sight of the knights of Durham and my men might make him either change his allegiance or realise the futility of fighting me. I would pick off my enemies piecemeal and leave de Vesci and De Percy for the end. If I could isolate those two then the rest would have to bow to my will and, ultimately, that of the King.

We left in the middle of November. Edward and William had insisted upon accompanying me. I also took William. He had grown while I had been away and Alan the horse master had worked with him. He could now ride a palfrey. He was a good rider. Aunt Ruth had worked on my wife and she allowed William to come. I had no choice really. He had met the criteria I had laid down. I had to keep my word. He had a good hauberk and a helmet with a nasal. He was given a short sword by his two, bigger sisters but Alfred and I were determined that he would not need to use it.

We rode to Durham. There was no Bishop there yet although Cardinal Bicchieri had one in mind, Richard de Marisco. With the need to secure the throne for Henry then the appointment of a new Bishop was irrelevant especially as I had the backing of the deans, canons and knights. I had sent messages asking the knights to gather at Durham and they did not let me down. We gathered in the cathedral where, as the King's representative I went through the formality of asking them to swear allegiance to the new King. None declined. I then led them, through a grey, drizzle filled day, to cross the Tyne at Hexham. At each manor we passed, where there was a knight or baron who had not sworn

Magna Carta

allegiance I stopped and asked them to do so. I knew the ones who would cause a problem for, as we progressed north I found some lords of the manor absent. That way they did not need to swear an oath and yet they thought they had avoided my wrath. There were eight such lords before we reached Warkworth.

Forty years ago, it had been a wooden castle which was so feeble that it had not been defended when William of Scotland invaded. John de Clavering's father had improved the castle but the work was still ongoing. Its position meant that it was vulnerable to a siege. The river ran along two sides of the castle and village with the sea close by. There were two narrow necks of land which could be used by an attacking army. The baron had not bothered yet with a town wall. I intended to divide my army in two and cut off the baron from his town. He could use ships to supply his castle but intended to stop that. Warkworth harbour was a mile from the castle. I could stop ships sailing up the river. We reached Warkworth at the end of December. To the west we could see snow covered hills but the coast was slightly warmer and the salt air stopped snow forming. The ground was, however, hard. That made the digging of ditches hard. I sent David of Stanhope with fifty knights to seal off the north end of the town and we approached through Hauxley and the little village of Amble.

Despite our slow and steady approach, we appeared to have caught the Baron by surprise. The villagers, mindful of what had happened when the Scots had attacked and massacred many of the inhabitants, fled into the castle. Like the chevauchée against the Scots this merely added to the mouths they would have to feed. We, on the other hand, managed to collect the animals they had left in the fields. We would have enough food for a month, at least. Baron Stanhope's men occupied the houses of Warkworth and we used those of Amble and Warkworth harbour. That way we could guard the river mouth and the gate without risking our men. We were careful to use what we could. In lieu of ditches my men hewed down the baron's trees and embedded them as stakes. I did not think that they would sortie but I did not know that for certain. This way I was prepared.

When the stakes were in place and we had a defensible camp, I rode with Sir William and Alfred to speak with the baron. Sir

Edward had ridden south to speak with the lords of the manors who lived south of us. It would also give us an indication of any danger which might come from that direction. The Sheriff of Newcastle had been silent. It was typical of the man that he waited to see who would emerge successfully from this civil war.

We took Father Abelard with us. We had the banner of the Palatinate with us. It showed those inside that we had the backing of the church. I knew that we had to win the hearts and minds of the ordinary folk as well as the knights and men at arms. We stopped a hundred paces short of the ditch. That was close enough to speak with the baron. I knew he would have to be summoned from his hall on the north side of the castle and I did not mind waiting. It gave me the chance to look at the improvements that had been made. The gatehouse had two towers and there was a large tower close to the river. If we had to attack then crossbows and bows on the top could wreak havoc with us. The drawbridge over the ditch could be raised but, at the moment it was down. I wondered at that.

The baron arrived. He shouted, "I wondered when you would get here, Earl. Those knights you thought to coerce have joined me here. If you wish me to support a nine-year-old king then I fear you are wasting your time."

"You would rather follow a French King?" He did not answer. "King Henry and the Council of regents have empowered me to give you the choice of swearing an oath of fealty to King Henry or suffering the consequences if you do not."

"And what would they be?"

I paused so that my words would have the greatest effect. "Excommunication." His silence was eloquent. "I have brought Father Abelard with me so that he can attest to the truth of what I say." Father Abelard nodded.

"I do not believe you. Why would the Pope do that? He excommunicated Henry's father for many years."

"And now Cardinal Bicchieri is a supporter of King Henry who has promised to go on Holy Crusade!"

"I would say you lie but this sounds like a plan of yours. You are ever cunning. It makes no difference to me. I do not believe you."

"Then I suggest that you speak with your people for some of them may not relish the removal of God's grace. They know, as does all of England, that I never lie. I will return in two days, Baron. If you need me earlier you will find me feasting on Warkworth beef."

As we turned Sir William laughed, "Each time I ride with you, Sir Thomas, I learn something new. A clever barb about the cattle right at the end; I could almost hear the hunger pangs already."

Father Abelard said, "The baron is being unfair to his people if he does not tell them of the Pope's decision. A man's soul is more precious than either land or gold."

"You are right, Father Abelard but de Clavering seeks power and coin. That is why he rebels. Men's souls do not worry him."

That evening Sir Edward and my men returned with more animals and blunted swords. "Trouble?"

"Sir Geoffrey of Ulgham and his men objected when we took their animals."

"You told them of the excommunication?"

"Aye, lord. We did as you said. We asked the baron to choose the King or Prince Louis. He said he could not support a boy." We took the animals and he and his men tried to take them back." Three of his men died before he withdrew."

"Tomorrow I will send David and his archers further south. We need to know if our enemies move upon us. I cannot believe that de Vesci and de Percy will sit behind their walls while we ride through their land."

"It could be that they fear you."

I shook my head. "That may be true of de Clavering but not the other two. They have too high an opinion of themselves."

My decision was one of the wisest that I ever took. Before noon David rode in, "Lord, there is an army heading from Morthpath. I saw the banners of your enemies. They are coming to relieve the siege."

We did not have long. "Alfred, ride around the castle. Tell Baron Stanhope that I need his knights and most of his men at arms. He should leave enough men to prevent the enemy sortieing. You should be able to find a ford upstream. It is vital that they join us."

"Aye lord."

"William, find Ridley and bring him here. Sir Edward, have the knights prepare for battle." As they left I turned to David of Wales. "We will use the ridge and Gloster Hill to meet them. We anchor one flank in the village and tempt them to ride betwixt the ridge and the river. Have your archers on that flank."

He smiled, "The ground there is boggy and muddy, lord. It will be a death trap."

The hill was the highest point for miles around. I had used the potential of such a hill at Bylnge and although this was a pimple in comparison, it would serve. Our stakes now faced the wrong direction but, as they protected the village they would help deter an outflanking movement. When William and Ridley arrived, I explained what I needed. Ridley the Giant was calmness personified. "Consider it done, lord."

William helped me to dress for war. "Today William, you will take over from Alfred and you will carry my standard. It is a hard task."

"I know, Alfred has been instructing me. I need my shield and I cannot use a sword. My skills as a horseman will be sorely tested."

"Good and you must stay behind me for I will instruct you to signal with the banner."

"I will."

A bedraggled Alfred led the knights and men at arms of Durham to join me. We had to array them quickly for one of David's archers rode in to say that the enemy were at Hauxley. The would be upon us soon. I mounted Flame and rode to the hill's peak so that I could see my men. We had interspersed knights and men at arms. We only had enough for a double line. Some archers made a third rank but the bulk of our bow men were on our right flank where I was leaving a sufficient gap on the other side of the small farm, to tempt them to try to flank us.

Magna Carta

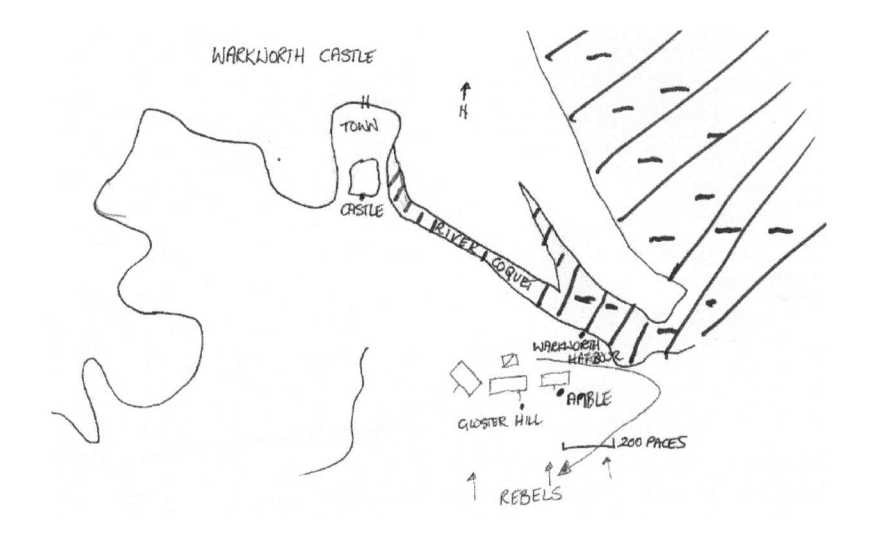

This time there would be no preamble. The rebel barons would form lines of battle and charge. Even as they began to move into position I saw that they outnumbered us but, once again, it was in men on foot and not knights. Had we not ensured that many rebels had switched sides then we might have faced overwhelming numbers. This was why they came. I was eating in to their support. I needed to be removed. If they had planned this well then de Clavering would sortie behind us once we were engaged. I had Father Abelard and the servants watching north.

When the rebels deployed before us I saw that they had strengthened their left. They were going to try to flank us up the narrow beck. David and his archers would thin their ranks as they attempted to join up with the forces in the castle. Whoever was leading the rebels, and I suspected it was de Percy, thought that they had me trapped against the sea, the river and the castle.

The enemy horns sounded. "Stand to!" Our men at arms and knights were on the slope. They had a curved double line behind which the archers stood. I had just twenty knights and squires with me. We were the only reserve but as most of the knights were my own household knights I was confident that we could deal with any break in our line. The ground was still frozen hard except for the ground twenty paces in front of my men at arms and knights. That had been softened and churned up as we had moved over it. The whole rebel line came as one. Their crossbows and archers were before their knights, men at arms and levy.

The forty archers who were behind my lines let loose their arrows. David and the bulk of my bowmen waited. The forty arrows struck the advancing men. They did not look to see the results of their work, they kept loosing arrow after arrow. We had plenty of arrows and the fact that just one in five found flesh was expensive. They were being thinned and they had not even reached the muddy ground. When they were fifty paces from my men at arms a horn sounded and the rebel knights charged. When they hit the muddy ground, it was as though they had struck ice for their horses could not keep their footing. As horses slipped then men were hit. When their line struck ours, there was the sound of spears shattering. On slightly higher ground our spears hit faces and helmets while the men of Northumberland struck shields. The cries and shouts told me that men had been hurt.

On our right the heavier press of men had already begun to flow around Henry Youngblood and the men at arms of Stanhope and Spennymoor. David of Wales shouted, "Draw!" I was close enough to hear the creak of yew as the bows were pulled back. When he shouted, "Release!" it was as though a hundred birds had taken flight at once. I turned my attention back to the centre. Our men were holding while on our left the rebels were making no headway at all. Sir Fótr and the knights of Durham were like rocks. Their spears were broken and now they were hewing heads with their swords. They were fighting men at arms and Sir Fótr and the knights who followed him were winning. When I looked to the right I saw that de Percy, who led that attack had pushed my men at arms back but, in his wake, he left a muddy field littered with bodies.

I saw an opportunity. "William, stay here with the standard. Knights, dismount!" If my knights were confused by my command they said nothing. We had been visible on our horses and now we disappeared for the fighting warriors obscured us. I waved my spear and led the knights and their squires towards the river and the sea. As we dropped down Gloster Hill towards Amble I said, "Mount!"

Magna Carta

Once mounted we rode around the houses and huts which made up Amble. I did not form a line. Instead, I just shouted, "Charge!"

With spears levelled we burst out from behind the buildings and behind the men at arms. There were just forty of us but our approach had been as silent as men creeping at night. It was only when we galloped that they knew we were there. As I speared a man at arms in the side there was a wail which rippled west. Our archers were now causing greater casualties. I stabbed another man at arms and then spied Eustace de Vesci. I spurred Flame and he responded immediately. The rebel baron had to turn his horse and disengage from Sir Richard of Fissebourne. Two men at arms tried to intercept me but arrows from the archers on the hill hit them in the back. I pulled back my arm and rammed it at de Vesci. He was a strong man. My spear smashed into his shield and then the head embedded itself in his shoulder. Still he kept his saddle. Spurring his horse and with blood pouring from his wound he and his squire galloped across my front. I was alone and by the time I had drawn my sword he was gone. I had to fight off two of his men at arms and it might have ended badly had not Alfred, now with a spear instead of a standard appeared and speared one, allowing me to hack into the arm of the other. I heard de Percy's horn and the rebels fell back. We had won.

We could not give pursuit. We had been hard pressed and most of my men were dismounted. Instead our line surged forward and those that did not surrender were butchered. We had no ransom for the knights fled and left just the dead. We saw to our wounded and then David of Wales sent archers to follow the rebels. I wanted to know where they were going.

As we ate, around our campfires David of Stanhope asked, "Why do you not speak with de Clavering? He might surrender."

"Oh he will surrender but I want you and your knights to return to the town. I will give him a night to wonder and to worry. When I make my demands then he will surrender."

William was full of the battle. It was the first time he had carried the banner. Although he had not joined his brother in the charge he had been instrumental in fixing the enemy's attention on our banner. I had not had to risk him. I praised him and saw him grow. "And you did well, Alfred. Those men at arms might have done for me. I made the cardinal error of charging too far."

"I was with you, lord, and you would have beaten those two. I just did that which I was supposed to do. I watched your back."

The next morning, we returned to the gate. I did not give de Clavering the chance to speak. "Your plan failed! You were the bait and de Vesci and de Percy thought to trap me against this castle. That is why you did not raise the drawbridge! Had you had more courage then you might have obeyed your orders and sallied forth but you did not and now you have lost. Surrender and swear allegiance or suffer the consequences."

"Consequences?"

"You have more mouths in the castle than you can feed. Who will starve and who will die? People have long memories. Last night there were voices in your castle speaking of excommunication and a punishment from God." The guilty look he gave to the priest next to him confirmed what I had conjectured. "We are happy to sit here until disease and famine are rife. When you are struck with the pestilence then you will beg us to help you and we will not. You surrender now and bend the knee or you will all die. Men, women, children and the old!"

I saw his men at arms looking at each other. The baron was considering his options and he had few. He nodded, "We surrender and I will swear an oath to King Henry!"

Chapter 15
The Battle of Lincoln

We spent twenty days in the north. De Vesci and de Percy locked themselves in their castles. We left them alone. They were finished as a fighting force. We reached our homes at the end of January. We had little ransom and treasure to show but what we did have was a peaceful north and the end of the rebel threat. Of course, I knew that if the Earl Marshal lost in the south then Prince Louis would come north and reignite the flames of rebellion. But I had done my duty.

There were letters waiting for me when I reached my home. Sir Ralph had defeated Robert de Ros the Baron of Helmsley and he had forced the rebel knight to swear an oath. It meant there were no major barons left to defy King Henry in the north. The campaign had cost us men and, being fought in winter, had diminished our horses. But we had won! For the next two months we worked to become a fighting force again. I learned from the Earl Marshal that despite his best efforts Prince Louis had failed to take Dover Castle. A siege of three months had not succeeded and he had withdrawn.

Alfred began to prepare to become a knight. All the work he had done with Petr now helped him. I told him that he would have to wait until William could function as a true squire and not just a standard bearer.

"There is no rush, father. I am still learning but I would be a knight for I saw, at Warkworth, that you need more men like Sir Edward and Sir William. The knights who were your squires fight better than any others. One day William will follow me and become a knight too."

I nodded, "And you need to look around for someone who can become your squire. Candidates are not as common as you might think."

Another missive arrived in April. Prince Louis had returned to the siege of Dover while his other leaders and the rebels tried to push out from London. The Earl Marshal might have been old but he was showing that he had lost neither his fighting spirit nor his skill. I began to believe that there was hope.

As the new grass appeared and our animals had their young, my eldest daughter, Rebekah became a woman. Unlike my sons who knew that when they became a man, they would bear arms and become a warrior or some might choose to be a priest, for a woman there was little choice. Rebekah had no suitors and that, along with her changed state, mean that she and her mother were like jousting knights. The land might have been at peace but not so my hall. There were arguments and rows which disturbed all. That was why my Aunt Ruth was a godsend. She had lived alone for most of her life. Her husband, Sir Ralph of Gainford had been slain by the Scots. When Rebekah began to complain and moan it was Aunt Ruth who dealt with her. Rebekah and my wife clashed too often. My aunt had a way of diverting aggression and making Rebekah think about her life.

However, after she had calmed her down for the fourth time in as many days, Aunt Ruth said, "You need a celebration."

"Celebration? We have little to celebrate, Aunt Ruth."

She laughed, "Half empty, Thomas! Of course, you do. You have your life to celebrate. You lost all and were abandoned by your King yet look at you now! You are one of the five or six most influential barons in the land. From what Alfred has told me the King holds you in equal esteem with the Earl Marshal! High praise indeed but I do not speak of a celebration now. This needs to be planned. Rebekah needs something to anticipate. She needs a stage on which she can be seen. This summer she will see fourteen summers. King Henry' mother had been married for two years when she was that age. You plan for Alfred to be knighted?" I nodded. "Then choose a date and make it into something worthy, a feast, a festival. Make it special so that knights and their families will come. Rebekah can help to plan it. It will make her work so that she is too tired to be argumentative. Midsummer's Day! This would be a propitious time."

I was not convinced but, after speaking with my wife, who thought it a wonderful idea, I mentioned it next to Alfred. "If you think I am ready, father, then so be it. I would prefer to wait a year or two."

I liked the honesty of his answer but it did not help me. However, when I confided in him the real reason he changed completely. "I will do it for my sister. I am glad that I was not born a woman. I would hate to sit at home while others went to war."

Rebekah was delighted! Peace reigned in my land and in my home. While Rebekah and her mother planned a feast I sat with Geoffrey, my steward and Alfred and we planned a war. The latest letter from the south had told us that Prince Louis had left the siege of Dover and was leading an army north. They were already at Northampton. Geoffrey had already gathered the supplies we would need. We had spare spears and the local fletchers had been making arrows since the battle of Warkworth.

Alfred said, "But the Earl has not yet sent for us. Why is that, father?"

"He has armies to hand. There are more men now than he once had. He must keep pressure on the army besieging Dover and watch Prince Louis. He does not yet know where he needs us. We are the surprise. All will think that we are staying in the north. They will not expect us. Can you imagine the effect of our banner on a battlefield? However, if we leave too soon then they can plan for us. We will receive a command but it will come by rider and we will need to leave within hours of the message. That is why we sit here and Geoffrey looks at his lists and his wax tablets."

My steward smiled, "It is another lesson for you, Master Alfred, on your road to winning the spurs. From what I have seen being a knight is only partially about going to war. Your father has to know how to fight the peace too!" He rose. "I will go and see the tanner. It would not do for baldrics to break at the wrong time."

When he had gone Alfred asked, "You know who you will take?"

"I do. I intend to leave the knights of Durham here. I will leave Sir William in my stead. He needs to spend more time with his wife." His lady had been ill during his last absence. As his sons were with him on campaign she had had to endure it with just her daughters. William had felt guilty. "The rest I will take and Sir Ralph and Sir Peter. From the letters I have had from de la Gray the County of York is stable now."

"And William?"

"Will come. He has grown and when we knight you he will need to be ready. Your mother understands. The fact that you survived so well gives her hope."

It was the first week in May when Robert Fitz Clare and his escort galloped in. He threw himself from his saddle, "Lord Prince Louis has taken the town of Lincoln. The castle is besieged and the Earl Marshal needs you and your men!"

I had been ready for the call and my riders rode out immediately to summon my knights. We would meet south of the river at Yarm. Sir Ralph and Sir Peter would meet us close to Catterick. To Sir Robert it seemed as though I was some sort of magician. "Not so but I have planned for this since we returned from Warkworth. I take it the Earl is marching in secret to Lincoln?"

"He is! How did you know?"

"He is a complete commander. Surprise is everything. Prince Louis will think that he is in the west, or the south. I am guessing that we meet north of Lincoln."

"Aye, lord! Stowe! Do you have second sight?"

"No, but it is what I would do. I am afraid that we will be leaving here by the third hour of the night. We have to do the journey in less than two days. By leaving in the hours of darkness we can steal a march. The rebels will have spies close by watching for my departure. I will leave my standard flying and we will simply slip across my river. No matter what, within a day or so they will know that we have gone but by then we will be at Lincoln and then it will not matter."

We slipped across the Tees silently on the ferry. There were no trumpets, there were no thundering horses. We went like thieves in the night. There were men waiting for us at Yarm. The old castle was long gone. It had been made of wood and had been one of Prince John's first vindictive acts after Stockton had been destroyed. By the time dawn broke we were approaching Northallerton. Unlike my castle this one was a hive of activity. I saw lights in the windows and men were up and about.

"I have food for your men, Sir Thomas. I know that the horses will need a little rest. I have ten Yorkshire knights." He saw my face fall and smiled, "I have left twice that number to watch this

Magna Carta

land. This county and the See are safe and the gateway to the Tees is secure!"

With just Sir William absent this was a reunion of the knights who had fought for me in Anjou and Normandy. The men who had rescued the Fair Maid of Brittany were reunited. Here Ralph was not Sheriff of York he was Ralph the earnest squire. Less youthful but still the same. After the horses had been fed and watered, when the men had eaten hot bread and freshly cooked ham we left. This time we did not ride through York. We rode due south. I had said that we might take two days but as we ate up the miles and passed the Roman markers which had stood for a thousand years I began to hope that we might make Stow by the time darkness fell. We changed horses every ten miles. We drank the water from the troughs in the towns and villages through which we passed and left them dry. We ate as we rode but we moved at the fastest pace I had ever known.

My mind was filled with the coming battle. The Earl Marshal would not risk the young King unless he thought that we could win. That alone was the reason for my haste. As soon as Prince Louis and Fitzwalter knew that the young King was close to Lincoln then the siege would become irrelevant and they would try to end the war by capturing the King. We had sworn to protect the King and we would do so.

I knew that William was finding the journey hard. Alfred and I had ridden as far many times before but for him this was new and I saw the pain and discomfort on his face each time we stopped. We had brought Alan the horse master with us and he offered advice to my son each time we changed horses. William would remember this, his first campaign, for the rest of his life.

We reached Stow just after dark. We had travelled almost fifty miles in one day since we had left Northallerton. One of my ancestors had once walked from London to Stamford Bridge to fight the Vikings and had done so in less than seven so I did not feel as elated as some of those with whom we rode. As we saw the camp fires Sir Robert said, "A remarkable feat, Earl. I would not have believed we could have done what we did in such a short time."

"I lead good men, Sir Robert."

He nodded. "I envy you. The Earl Ranulf has good men too but they cannot compare with these."

Stow was little more than a church surrounded by houses. Less than ten miles from Lincoln it meant we would be attacking from the opposite side of Lincoln to the French and rebels who were in the town side. The Earl was seated outside the church. There was a fire burning and I saw the Earl of Chester and William Longespée with him as well as the young King. Henry was kitted out in a mail hauberk but I doubted that the Earl Marshal would allow him to get close to the fighting. When he saw me the Earl Marshal stood, "You must have ridden Pegasus to reach here so quickly, Earl!"

I nodded, "I thought it urgent. We left at night so that our enemy would not know I had gone until it was too late."

"Aye well, your arrival is timely. The enemy warriors are led by the Comte de Perche."

"Prince Louis is not with them?"

"He has returned to the siege of Dover. It is another reason why I have chosen to make this the place where we begin to drive the invader hence. Fitzwalter and the leaders of the revolt are here at the siege. Our scouts have stopped the French and the rebels from determining our true numbers. Like you and your battle most of the men arrived secretly. He thinks this force is led by the Earl of Chester alone. You know this castle better than most for you and I were here recently. I have told these my plan what would you do?"

It was a test. "The east and west gates to the castle have barbicans and they will be hard to take. I am guessing that de Perche is attacking from the south. The north gate to the town is not the strongest. I would attack the north gate with archers and then force it with stout men."

I saw Ranulf de Blondeville laugh, "The same plan, to the last detail as the Earl Marshal conjured."

"Good. We will need your archers, Sir Thomas. They are the best." He pointed to his right. "Falkes de Breauté and his crossbows will support you. Your horses have had a hard ride. The rest of us will be mounted. Could you and your knights take the gate with an attack on foot?"

"Aye, Earl, I have great faith in my men at arms and knights. When do we attack?"

"We leave while it is still dark. When dawn breaks I would have us at Lincoln's north gate."

"Then I had best speak with my men."

"There is food."

"Thank you, Ranulf, but I will speak with my men first."

As I expected David of Wales and his archers were unhappy about having to fight alongside Falkes de Breauté's crossbows. "Look at it this way, David, we know that they will not force the gate but you and your archers will."

"Aye lord. We are all on the same side, I suppose!"

"Ridley, we need men with axes to be at the fore. We force the gate and hold it. That will allow the Earl Marshal and the rest of the army to enter Lincoln. The French have miscalculated. If they knew there was an army here they should have come to stop us. The Lady of Lincoln will not yield her walls and once we are in the town then, no matter how many men they have, we will succeed."

Alfred and William had secured me some food. As I ate I told them what they would be doing. "Alfred you will be behind me tomorrow. Your task is to watch my back. William, you will watch the horses. A siege and the fighting there is not the place for someone who has little experience of such things."

For once William accepted his fate. He already knew that King Henry would be left, under guard, with the horses. I knew that he saw himself protecting the King should danger arrive. I knew that would not happen. If the King was threatened then we would have lost the battle and the Earl Marshal and myself would be dead!

We reached the outskirts of Lincoln by dawn. We were spotted. There were too many of us. We could not remain hidden. The French and the rebels did not rouse themselves to chase us hence. My knights, archers and men at arms dismounted. The Earl Marshal, the knights and the other mounted men waited on the road. Behind them were the foot soldiers. I raised my sword and, along with Falkes de Breauté, marched towards the town walls. The knights and men at arms walked in front of the archers and crossbowmen. We held our shields before us. Arrows and bolts thudded into them. We stopped two hundred paces from the town wall. There was no ditch and no drawbridge. I heard David of Wales order our archers to draw. Crossbows clicked. When the order was given to release I thought a cloud had passed overhead. Some bolts and arrows struck the stone walls and the wooden gate but most struck flesh.

I was not wearing my helmet. I had left that with William. An arming cap would suffice. I shouted, "Forward, men of Cleveland! For God and King Henry!"

With a roar we ran forward. Neither arrow nor bolt stopped us. We reached the gate and held our shields above us. The hammer and crack of axes on wood soon filled the air. I heard French voices within the town shouting. It mattered not. We had made the gates without losing a single man. Ridley and Henry had relays of men at arms wielding the axes and it did not take long to break them. We burst in through the gates.

I shouted, "David, take your archers to the fighting platform. Rain death on the siege lines."

"Aye lord."

"Falkes de Breauté, take your crossbows to the rooftops!"

As the archers and the crossbows ran to their positions we stood aside to allow the horsemen led by the Earl Marshal to gallop in. The siege lines were less than half a mile away but none responded to our attack. Perhaps they thought it was just a force of raiders. Had they attacked us then who knows what the result might have been but they did not and our knights and mounted men at arms poured through the gates.

Raising my sword, I led my men through the narrow streets. This way the Earl Marshal could use the wider road. His horses would find it hard to move along these narrow ways. This was the perfect place for my men to fight. Each one was a complete warrior. As we ran, French soldiers ran to meet us. Dotted amongst them I saw the surcoats of rebel barons. What I did not see were leaders. In the narrow streets it was hard to swing a sword. I held mine low with my shield before me. I turned the first French man at arms' sword with my shield and brought my sword up under his shield and through his leather jerkin. He fell to the ground. I barely broke my stride. It felt good fighting

Magna Carta

without a helmet. There was a risk of injury but the increased vision and hearing compensated for that.

Men were falling before us and we reached the siege lines before the horsemen. Our archers and crossbowmen were sending arrows and bolts into the midst of those who had been attacking the walls. This was not a battle on an open field where a man saw the enemies immediately before him. The buildings of the town and the castle were a barrier all around us. The men who had been besieging Lincoln were armed and many were mailed. This would be a long and bloody battle. I heard the horsemen, led by the old Earl Marshal as they thundered into the town. Even with buildings shielding us I still felt their hooves as they made the ground shake.

Edward and Ralph flanked me and they were flanked, in turn by Sir Peter and Sir Fótr. Behind me came our squires and my men at arms. We would fear no foe. We were fighting Frenchmen. They were less familiar with my livery. They soon came to recognise and fear it.

A French knight wielding a mace led a handful of French knights towards us. Perhaps I would regret not wearing my helmet. A blow from a mace might not be fatal to a knight wearing a helmet but an arming cap was something else. It was a mace which was as long as my sword. As he swung I timed the block and the angle of my shield to perfection. If I had met it square on then I would have risked breaking my arm. I allowed the mace to slide down the side of my shield, the weight pulled his arm down, exposing his middle. I swung my sword. He could not match my parry for the sword hit across his shield. I put my weight behind it and he reeled backwards. Stepping on to my right foot I brought my sword over arm. He was unbalanced and he struggled to completely block my blow. The end of my sword hit his helmet. It stunned him and he fell a little further backwards. As I stepped and lunged forward I exposed myself to an attack from the side. A man at arms lunged at my unprotected right side with a spear. I would have been a dead man had it struck. Alfred brought his own sword down to shatter the spear in two and then he backhanded his sword across the throat of the man at arms. As the French knight tried to recover I punched him in the face with my shield and he toppled over the body of a crossbow man slain by one of my archers. Before he could cry for mercy I stabbed him in the chest. He had good mail and I had to lean on my sword to shatter the links and pierce his heart.

We were now within the siege works around the north gate of the castle. The French and the rebels must have thought, when they saw my knights, that I had made some sort of suicidal attack with a handful of men. It was the sort of reckless action for which I was famed. All knew of my affection for the Lady of Lincoln. They did not retreat and that would have been the wisest option. They fought and they came for me.

The battle soon degenerated into small battles between handfuls of knights and men at arms. The barons and the knights sought me. I became slightly isolated. I had Ridley and Alfred with me. The rest of my household knights had been pulled to the side defending me from those attacks. We were close to their catapults and rams. I saw Robert Fitzwalter and his son, Robert, leaving the siege lines to come for me. They did not come alone. They had with them four men at arms. If they could eliminate me then they might dream that the attack would fizzle out. Ridley stood on my right with his axe and Alfred on my left.

The younger Fitzwalter saw my squire and in him recognised an easy target. He swung his sword contemptuously at my son's head. Alfred had sparred with Ridley the Giant. When my captain of men at arms' blow hit you then it was like a ram hitting a gate. Alfred had endured many such blows. His arms were like knotted oaks and he took the blow easily. He traded blows and swung his own sword diagonally downwards. Ridley had taught him the stroke. Robert Fitzwalter fell backwards and cracked his head on the wheel of a ram. He lay still. The elder Fitzwalter came at me. He brought with him a man at arms for support. I smashed my shield into the face to the leader of the rebel barons and I blocked the man at arms' sword. Hooking my right leg behind his left I suddenly pushed and he toppled backwards. This was not a place of honour and as Fitzwalter swung his sword at my shield I skewered the man at arms in his neck. Fitzwalter's blow was weak.

Ridley faced two men but he was Ridley the Giant. He had long arms and he used them to good effect. He held his shield before him and then swung his axe diagonally. It smashed through the side of the man at arms head and drove the dead body into the man next to him. As he reeled Ridley used his axe as an extension of his fist. The man at arms was unconscious before he hit the ground.

As the last man at arms stepped over the prone form of the younger Fitzwalter I swung my sword at the shield of the leader of the rebels. He was no warrior and he barely blocked it. He fell. I had my sword at his throat. "I would dearly love to kill you but honour demands that I ask if you will surrender."

He dropped his sword, "I yield."

The last man at arms tried to ram his sword into Alfred's middle. My son spun around and the rebel's sword struck fresh air. Alfred's sword cut through to his spine.

Around us the fighting had ceased or, at least, we had an oasis of peace. This was not a battlefield which could be seen from one place. I had no idea if we were winning or losing. I knew that here, at the castle's north gate, we had won. David and his archers had continued to rain arrows on the French and the rebels. Nicola de la Haie had her men do the same. My knights and men at arms had prevailed. Both rebels and French surrendered.

A voice from the roof called out, "Sir Thomas, the enemy are fleeing towards the south gate. We cannot see them."

Cupping my hands, I shouted, "Make your way around the fighting platform and harass them."

"Aye lord."

Sir Fótr had a slight wound. "Sir Fótr, stay here with your squire and your men at arms. Guard these prisoners!"

I raised my sword, "Come, knights of Cleveland, our work here is not yet done!"

We hurried from the smaller streets to the large open area which marked the main thoroughfare of Lincoln. I saw the Comte de Perche and his French knights. They had formed a shield wall between the castle walls and the town walls. Even as we arrived I heard the Earl Marshal shout, "Comte, you have lost. The siege is lifted and all that remains if you continue to fight is death. There is no dishonour in surrender."

"There is for me, Earl Marshal, for I will have let down my Prince. Do your worst."

The Earl Marshal was too old for such combat. He wearily backed his horse away and said, "Finish it, Earl."

He meant the Earl of Chester who was at his side but my men and I began to hack and slash at the French who stood with their doomed leader. Comte de Perche was a good warrior. Ranulf de Blondeville had made the mistake of attacking while mounted. The Comte swung his sword as the man at arms at his side lunged with a spear. The sword hacked into the side of the head of the Earl's warhorse and the spear eviscerated it. As the animal fell it threw the Earl from the saddle. He lay in an inert heap. The man at arms ran to get at him. I swung my sword into the side of the knight I was fighting and, as he fell, used his body to spring at the man at arms. I landed clumsily but knocked him to the ground. As I slowly rose the Comte swung his sword at me. Alfred raced between us. It was a powerful blow but it hit Alfred's shield and he was knocked to the ground. As Ridley ended the life of the man at arms I lunged at the Comte. This was personal now. He had almost killed Alfred and there would be no quarter.

I would not underestimate this man. Prince Louis had left him to command the siege for a reason. He knew his business. He had an open face helmet and I saw him sneer. "You fled France for you feared my master. You think that you have the skill, mercenary, to defeat a knight of France."

"Comte, you are like all Frenchmen. You have a higher opinion of yourself and your nation than you merit. I will cut you down to size."

His honour impugned he punched at me with his shield as he lunged with his sword. I emulated my son. I stepped back and spun. The Comte stumbled and Ridley laughed, "He is clumsy too, lord."

The Comte spun himself before I could strike a blow. His sword clattered against my shield. I used my foot and rammed it against his left knee. The knee bent backwards. It made my men cheer even more. They loved tricks like that. I had hurt him. His knee was damaged and his pride was hurt. As he swung his sword I blocked it with my shield and stepped close to him. Neither of us could use our swords but he had a helmet with a nasal and I had an arming cap. He brought his head back to butt me. Hooking my left leg behind his right I leaned to the side so that his head hit my shoulder and then I pushed. He fell backwards and my right arm was freed. I brought my sword down diagonally across his neck. The blow was so powerful that it almost severed his head.

His death and that of his men marked the end of all rebel resistance. It became a rout. The Earl of Chester's men rode to avenge the hurts their lord had suffered. William Marshal rode over to me, "Sir Thomas, I see in you the spirit of your grandfather, the Warlord. The King is in your debt."

That evening we gathered in the Great Hall. The King wished to thank the Lady of Lincoln for her valiant defence. Outside the town was being cleared of the enemy and the townsfolk, for colluding with the enemy were being pillaged. None tried to stop our men. The burghers of Lincoln had made their choice and it had been a bad one.

After the King had praised Nicola de la Haie he said, "Sir Thomas, your son, this day, showed great courage not once but three or four times. Just as you were knighted at Arsuf so your son Alfred should be knighted now." He reached for his sword, "I would be honoured to do it."

The Earl Marshal smiled, "You are not yet a knight yourself, Your Majesty, but I will do the honours."

Alfred stepped forward, "Without showing disrespect, Your Majesty, Earl Marshal, I would wait." Everyone looked in shock at his words. He was refusing to be knighted. "I can think of no greater honour but I have promised my sister that I will be knighted in Stockton on Midsummer's day and my father will dub me and give me my spurs. I would wait."

The King smiled and the Earl Marshal nodded, "Like your father, you will be a true knight and King Henry is lucky to have you as a friend. So be it!"

Epilogue

The Battle of Lincoln ended, effectively, the Baron's War. With the leaders now prisoners Prince Louis returned to France for more men. Eustace the Monk brought ships across from France with the necessary reinforcements. The French ships were defeated by Hubert de Burgh in the Battle of Dover. The Earl Marshal, in one of his last acts negotiated a peace. In return for ten thousand crowns Prince Louis relinquished all claims to the English crown. King Henry was safe. His crown was secured and the rebellion was over.

With the reparations from Fitzwalter and the other knights, we were rich. King Henry confirmed Sir Ralph as Sheriff of York and I was given the title, Defender of the King. Once an outlaw, hunted and persecuted by King John, his son had now made me the First Knight in the land.

What made me the proudest was when I was able to knight my son. All of my knights and the knights of the Palatinate attended. My aunt and my wife nodded approvingly as young knights queued up to speak to Rebekah and Isabella. All of the work they had put into the feast had not been in vain.

My son had shown knightly virtues when he had not needed to. I had raised both of my sons well. With the rebellion over and the Scots cowed, I hoped for years of peace. Perhaps Alfred and Rebekah would find partners to wed and my legacy would live on. I had been told that I was the embodiment of the Warlord and I owed it to him to see that his line continued on into the future.

As the young folk danced before my wife I sat with Aunt Ruth. She had her arm linked in mine, "Thomas, if you were my own son I could not be prouder. What you have achieved is quite remarkable. You have behaved honourably and you have saved the crown. I have spoken with Ridley and your men. They are in no doubt where the praise should go. Yet you have not made capital of it and you behave modestly. That is how a true knight should be. Sir William saw those attributes in you all those years ago when you returned from the Holy Land. Many men might have changed but you are the same and, my nephew, you are my grandfather, father and brother in one. Enjoy this night for this is your night as much as Alfred's"

As one of the young knights of the Palatinate, Geoffrey Fitzurse, danced with Rebekah I caught my wife's eye. She smiled at me and blew a kiss. My son's gesture had been worthwhile and I was content. My land was safe, my country was whole again and my family had come to no harm. What more could a knight ask?

The End

Glossary

Bylnge -Billinge, near Wigan
Chevauchée- a raid by mounted men
Fusil - A lozenge shape on a shield
Garth- a garth was a farm. Not to be confused with the name Garth
Groat- English coin worth four silver pennies
Luciaria-Lucerne (Switzerland)
Mêlée- a medieval fight between knights
Nissa- Nice (Provence)
Reeve- An official who ran a manor for a lord
Rote- An English version of a lyre (also called a crowd or crwth)
Vair- a heraldic term
Wrecsam- Wrexham
Wulfestun- Wolviston (Durham)

Historical Notes

This series of books follows the fortunes of the family of the Earl of Cleveland begun in the Anarchy. As with that series the characters in this book are, largely, fictional, but the events are all historically accurate. For those who have read the earlier books in the series the new information begins with the section:
Timeline of the novel.
Templars
No matter where they were based the Knights Templars followed a strict routine:

- Night- Matins sleep until dawn
- 6 am Rise- Prime and then mass
- 9 am Terce
- 12 Noon Sext
- 3 pm Nones, Vespers for the dead, Vigil for the dead

There were set times to speak with their squires and see to their horses.
Prince Arthur
Arthur was born in 1187, the son of Constance of Brittany and Geoffrey II of Brittany, who died before he was born. As an infant, Arthur was second in line to the succession of his grandfather King Henry II, after his uncle Richard. King Henry died when Arthur was 2 years old, and Richard I became the new king in his place.
Margam annals
William des Roches
In May 1199, King Philip of France met with William des Roches at Le Mans and together they attacked the border fortress of Ballon, the fortress was surrendered by Geoffrey de Brûlon, the castellan, but not before being demolished. A quarrel ensued between King Philip and William over the lordship of the site. William was adamant that Ballon belonged rightfully to Duke Arthur, while King Philip wished to retain it as his own.
In June 1199, King John of England launched a massive attack into Northern Maine from Argentan. On 13 September he was successful in repulsing King Philip from the fortress of

Lavardin which protected the route from Le Mans to Tours. Arthur's supporters were forced to come to terms with John, and William met with the English king at Bourg-le-Roi, a fortress of the pro-John viscounts of Beaumont-en-Maine on or about 18 September. John convinced William that Arthur of Brittany was being used solely as a tool of Capetian strategy and managed to convince him to switch sides. With this, John promised him the seneschalship of Anjou. During the night, John's incumbent seneschal, Viscount Aimery, took Arthur and Constance and fled the court. They fled first to Angers, then to the court of King Philip. King John officially designated William seneschal of Anjou in December 1199 and entered Angers triumphantly on 24 June 1200.

Courtesy of Wikipedia

Treaty of Le Goulet

The Treaty of Le Goulet was signed by the kings John of England and Philip II of France in May 1200 and meant to settle once and for all the claims the Norman kings of England had as Norman dukes on French lands, including, at least for a time, Brittany. Under the terms of the treaty, Philip recognised John as King of England as the heir of his brother Richard I and thus formally abandoned any support for Arthur. John, meanwhile, recognised Philip as the suzerain of continental possessions of the Angevin Empire.

The treaty also included territorial concessions by John to Philip. The Vexin (except for Les Andelys, where Château Gaillard, vital to the defence of the region, was located) and the Évrécin in Normandy, as well as Issoudun, Graçay, and the fief of André de Chauvigny in Berry were to be removed from Angevin suzerainty and put directly into that of France.

The Duchy of Aquitaine was not included in the treaty. It was still held by John as heir to his still-living mother, Eleanor. The treaty was sealed with a marriage alliance between the Angevin and Capetian dynasties. John's niece Blanche, daughter of his sister Leonora and Alfonso VIII of Castile, married Philip's eldest son, Louis VIII of France (to be eventually known as Louis the Lion). The marriage alliance only assured a strong regent for the minority of Louis IX of France. Philip declared John deposed from his fiefs for failure to obey a summons in

1202 and war broke out again. Philip moved quickly to seize John's lands in Normandy, strengthening the French throne in the process.

Eleanor Fair Maid of Brittany

I did not know the story of Eleanor until I began researching this book. Hers is a sad story. Eventually King John captured her and imprisoned her in a castle: although the exact location is uncertain. Some said Corfe and then Bristol. When King John died his heir, Henry III continued to have her incarcerated. Her burial and her final resting place are unknown. There is a story there.

Fall of Normandy

Prince Arthur was in Falaise and, after he was moved to Rouen he was, reputedly, killed by his uncle. That action and the ill treatment of prisoners drove William des Roches into the French camp. Between 1202 and 1204 Normandy, Brittany, Anjou and Maine were all lost. Most of Poitou also fell and only the wine rich region of Aquitaine remained in King John's hands. He never gave up on Normandy and spent the next ten years trying to retake it. He even built a fleet to defend the seaways to Bordeaux.

He might have succeeded but he had a poor relationship with the barons. They cost him Normandy and, as events turned out, almost cost him England.

King William and Scotland

King John invaded Scotland and forced William to sign the Treaty of Norham, which gave John control of William's daughters and required a payment of £10,000. This effectively crippled William's power north of the border, and by 1212 John had to intervene militarily to support the Scottish king against his internal rivals. John made no efforts to reinvigorate the Treaty of Falaise, though, and both William and Alexander in turn remained independent kings, supported by, but not owing fealty to, John. I gave King William an extra year of life. He died in 1214 at the age of 71. I chose to have him lead his army against King John in one last battle. I think William the Lion deserved that end.

Rote

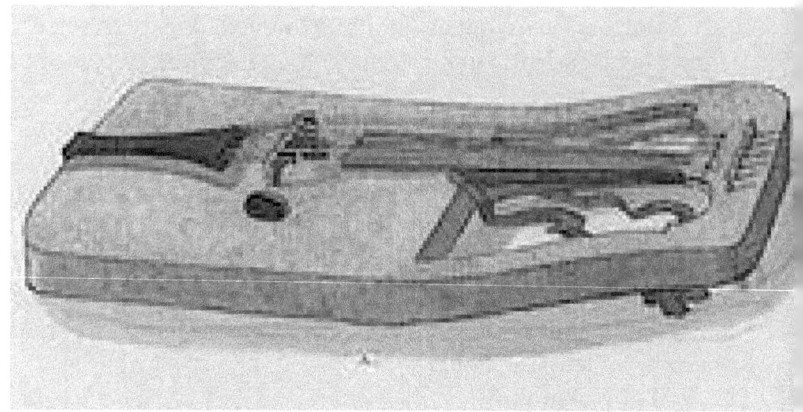

Timeline of the novel

The events which form the basis of the story all happened. I have changed some of the participants to suit my story. Below is a timeline showing the major events of the period.

1209- King John invades Scotland and imposes draconian punishments. The King is excommunicated

1210- King John goes to Ireland

1211- King John goes to war with Wales.

1212- King William asks for help from King John to fight the rebels in his land.

1213 -King John pays a fine to the Pope and his excommunication is lifted

1214- King John invades Normandy. Defeated at the Battle of Bouvines

1215 -Rebel barons gather in southern England. Confront the King who is forced to sign the Magna Carta. King Llewelyn attacks the west of England

1216 -Prince Louis invades southern England. King Alexander of Scotland takes Carlisle. Civil War. Prince Louis goes back to France and there is a stalemate. King John died on the night of 18/19 October, probably of dysentery although there were rumours of poisoned plums!

Counsellors named in Magna Carta

- Stephen Langton, Archbishop of Canterbury, and Cardinal
- Henry de Loundres, Archbishop of Dublin

Magna Carta

- William of Sainte-Mère-Église, Bishop of London
- Peter des Roches, Bishop of Winchester
- Jocelin of Wells, Bishop of Bath and Glastonbury
- Hugh of Wells, Bishop of Lincoln
- Walter de Gray, Bishop of Worcester
- William de Cornhill, Bishop of Coventry
- Benedict of Sausetun, Bishop of Rochester
- Pandulf Verraccio, subdeacon and papal legate to England
- Eymeric, Master of the Knights Templar in England
- William Marshal, Earl of Pembroke
- William Longespée, Earl of Salisbury
- William de Warenne, Earl of Surrey
- William d'Aubigny, Earl of Arundel
- Alan of Galloway, Constable of Scotland
- Warin FitzGerold
- Peter FitzHerbert
- Hubert de Burgh, Seneschal of Poitou
- Hugh de Neville
- Matthew FitzHerbert
- Thomas Basset
- Alan Basset
- Philip d'Aubigny
- Robert of Ropsley
- John Marshal
- John FitzHugh

Nicola de la Haie
Born about 1150, she was one of three daughters and coheiresses of Richard de la Haie, a major Lincolnshire landowner whose family had founded the Premonstratensian house of Barlings Priory, and his wife Matilda, daughter of William Vernon. Her paternal grandfather Robert de la Haie, of Halnaker in Sussex, had in 1115 been granted the posts of hereditary constable of Lincoln Castle and hereditary sheriff of Lincolnshire. When her father died in 1169 she inherited these

two posts, which in practice were filled by her two husbands in succession.

When King Henry II died in 1189, she and her second husband Gerard de Camville travelled to Barfleur in Normandy to obtain a charter confirming her rights from the new king Richard I. Richard then went off to the Holy Land on the Third Crusade, leaving authority in England in the hands of William de Longchamp. In 1191 Longchamp removed Camville from the shrievalty and the castellancy, ordering him to hand over the castle.

When this was refused, Longchamp ordered an armed assault on the castle, while Camville stayed with Prince John at Nottingham. Nicola held out against a month-long siege by a force of 30 knights, 20 mounted men-at-arms and 300 infantry, together with 40 sappers who attacked the walls of the castle. Having failed to take the castle, Longchamp reached a compromise with Camville and restored him to his two posts, but then had him excommunicated. When King Richard returned from crusade and captivity in 1194, he removed Camville from both posts.

Things improved when King Richard was succeeded by his brother John. Though a difficult man who fell out with most people, both Nicola and her husband remained loyal to him and were fortunate in maintaining a cordial relationship. In 1199 he restored the castle and the shrievalty to Camville, who held them until he died shortly before January 1215. Nicola then held both posts and, when John came to Lincoln in 1216, she is reported to have gone out to meet him with the keys of the castle in her hand, saying that as she was now a very old widow she was unable to continue in office any longer. He replied: "My dear Nicola, I want you to hold on to the castle as you have so far until I decide otherwise." He also confirmed her right to the shrievalty.

Lincoln Castle then came under attack by the rebels against John, led by the French prince Louis. While besieged there, Nicola was visited by Peter des Roches, the influential bishop of Winchester, who knew a secret way in and assured her that loyal forces would soon attack the besiegers. Her sturdy defence kept the castle intact until May 1217, when the Second Battle of

Lincoln resulted in the defeat of the rebels and their French allies.

Nicola then had to face a new threat, this time from William II Longespée, son of the Earl of Salisbury and husband of her granddaughter Idonea, who tried to evict her. In 1226, when she must have been over 70 years old, she retired from the castle to her estate at Swaton, where she died on 20 November 1230.

Magna Carta

I have reproduced the first two paragraphs to give you a flavour of the language. If you wish more then follow the hyperlink below.

http://www.britannia.com/history/docs/magna2.html

John, by the grace of God King of England, Lord of Ireland, Duke of Normandy and Aquitaine, and Count of Anjou, to his archbishops, bishops, abbots, earls, barons, justices, foresters, sheriffs, stewards, servants, and to all his officials and loyal subjects, greeting.

Know that before God, for the health of our soul and those of our ancestors and heirs, to the honour of God, the exaltation of the holy Church, and the better ordering of our kingdom, at the advice of our reverend fathers Stephen, archbishop of Canterbury, primate of all England, and cardinal of the holy Roman Church, Henry archbishop of Dublin, William bishop of London, Peter bishop of Winchester, Jocelin bishop of Bath and Glastonbury, Hugh bishop of Lincoln, Walter Bishop of Worcester, William bishop of Coventry, Benedict bishop of Rochester, Master Pandulf subdeacon and member of the papal household, Brother Aymeric master of the Knights of the Temple in England, William Marshal, earl of Pembroke, William earl of Salisbury, William earl of Warren, William earl of Arundel, Alan de Galloway constable of Scotland, Warin Fitz Gerald, Peter Fitz Herbert, Hubert de Burgh seneschal of Poitou, Hugh de Neville, Matthew Fitz Herbert, Thomas Basset, Alan Basset, Philip Daubeny, Robert de Roppeley, John Marshal, John Fitz Hugh, and other loyal subjects:

1. First, that we have granted to God, and by this present charter have confirmed for us and our heirs in perpetuity,

that the English Church shall be free, and shall have its rights undiminished, and its liberties unimpaired. That we wish this so to be observed, appears from the fact that of our own free will, before the outbreak of the present dispute between us and our barons, we granted and confirmed by charter the freedom of the Church's elections - a right reckoned to be of the greatest necessity and importance to it - and caused this to be confirmed by Pope Innocent III. This freedom we shall observe ourselves, and desire to be observed in good faith by our heirs in perpetuity. We have also granted to all free men of our realm, for us and our heirs for ever, all the liberties written out below, to have and to keep for them and their heirs, of us and our heirs:

When Henry became King, the charter was reissued without this contentions clause:

(61) SINCE WE HAVE GRANTED ALL THESE THINGS for God, for the better ordering of our kingdom, and to allay the discord that has arisen between us and our barons, and since we desire that they shall be enjoyed in their entirety, with lasting strength, for ever, we give and grant to the barons the following security:

The barons shall elect twenty-five of their number to keep, and cause to be observed with all their might, the peace and liberties granted and confirmed to them by this charter.

If we, our chief justice, our officials, or any of our servants offend in any respect against any man or transgress any of the articles of the peace or of this security, and the offence is made known to four of the said twenty-five barons, they shall come to us - or in our absence from the kingdom to the chief justice - to declare it and claim immediate redress. If we, or in our absence abroad the chief justice, make no redress within forty days, reckoning from the day on which the offence was declared to us or to him, the four barons shall refer the matter to the rest of the twenty-five barons, who may distrain upon and assail us in every way possible, with the support of the whole community of the land, by seizing our castles, lands, possessions, or anything else saving only our own person and those of the queen and our children, until they have secured such redress as they have determined upon. Having secured the redress, they may then resume their normal obedience to us.

Any man who so desires may take an oath to obey the commands of the twenty-five barons for the achievement of these ends, and to join with them in assailing us to the utmost of his power. We give public and free permission to take this oath to any man who so desires, and at no time will we prohibit any man from taking it. Indeed, we will compel any of our subjects who are unwilling to take it to swear it at our command.

If one of the twenty-five barons dies or leaves the country or is prevented in any other way from discharging his duties, the rest of them shall choose another baron in his place, at their discretion, who shall be duly sworn in as they were.

In the event of disagreement among the twenty-five barons on any matter referred to them for decision, the verdict of the majority present shall have the same validity as a unanimous verdict of the whole twenty-five, whether these were all present or some of those summoned were unwilling or unable to appear.

The twenty-five barons shall swear to obey all the above articles faithfully and shall cause them to be obeyed by others to the best of their power.

We will not seek to procure from anyone, either by our own efforts or those of a third party, anything by which any part of these concessions or liberties might be revoked or diminished. Should such a thing be procured, it shall be null and void and we will at no time make use of it, either ourselves or through a third party.

Fact and Fiction

All of the major events happened. King William did ask King John for help against his rebels. The Lady of Lincoln held out twice against rebels. The Cardinal was a real person and it was largely due to his influence that William Marshal was able to have King Henry crowned. There was no crown and he had to improvise a crown from a necklace. Much is made of Magna Carta but it must be remembered that the men who formulated it cared not a jot for the ordinary people. They just wanted more power! Knights like William Marshal and Sir Thomas were rare. De Vesci and de Percy were more common knights.

A copy of the 1864 Ordnance Survey map of Warkworth. I doubt that it would have changed much from 1217. From Amble to Warkworth is less than a mile. The fictitious battle would have taken place between Amble and New Barns.

For the English maps, I have used the original Ordnance survey maps. (See above for an example). Produced by the army in the 19th century they show England before modern developments and, in most cases, are pre-industrial revolution. They are now reproduced by Cassini and they are a useful tool for a historian.

I also discovered a good website http://orbis.stanford.edu/. This allows a reader to plot any two places in the Roman world and if you input the mode of transport you wish to use and the time of year it will calculate how long it would take you to travel the route. I have used it for all of my books up to the eighteenth century as the transportation system was roughly the same. The Romans would have been quicker!

Books used in the research:
The Crusades-David Nicholle
Crusader Castles in the Holy Land 1097-1192- David Nicolle
The Normans- David Nicolle
Norman Knight AD 950-1204- Christopher Gravett
The Norman Conquest of the North- William A Kappelle
The Knight in History- Francis Gies
The Norman Achievement- Richard F Cassady
Knights- Constance Brittain Bouchard
Knight Templar 1120-1312 -Helen Nicholson

Magna Carta

Feudal England: Historical Studies on the Eleventh and Twelfth Centuries- J. H. Round
English Medieval Knight 1200-1300
The Scandinavian Baltic Crusades 1100-1500

Griff Hosker
May 2018

Other books by Griff Hosker

If you enjoyed reading this book, then why not read another one by the author?

Ancient History

The Sword of Cartimandua Series
(Germania and Britannia 50 A.D. – 128 A.D.)
Ulpius Felix- Roman Warrior (prequel)
The Sword of Cartimandua
The Horse Warriors
Invasion Caledonia
Roman Retreat
Revolt of the Red Witch
Druid's Gold
Trajan's Hunters
The Last Frontier
Hero of Rome
Roman Hawk
Roman Treachery
Roman Wall
Roman Courage

The Wolf Warrior series
(Britain in the late 6th Century)
Saxon Dawn
Saxon Revenge
Saxon England
Saxon Blood
Saxon Slayer
Saxon Slaughter
Saxon Bane
Saxon Fall: Rise of the Warlord
Saxon Throne
Saxon Sword

Magna Carta

Medieval History

The Dragon Heart Series
Viking Slave
Viking Warrior
Viking Jarl
Viking Kingdom
Viking Wolf
Viking War
Viking Sword
Viking Wrath
Viking Raid
Viking Legend
Viking Vengeance
Viking Dragon
Viking Treasure
Viking Enemy
Viking Witch
Viking Blood
Viking Weregeld
Viking Storm
Viking Warband
Viking Shadow
Viking Legacy
Viking Clan
Viking Bravery

The Norman Genesis Series
Hrolf the Viking
Horseman
The Battle for a Home
Revenge of the Franks
The Land of the Northmen
Ragnvald Hrolfsson
Brothers in Blood
Lord of Rouen
Drekar in the Seine
Duke of Normandy
The Duke and the King

Magna Carta

Danelaw
(England and Denmark in the 11th Century)
Dragon Sword
Oathsword
Bloodsword

New World Series
Blood on the Blade
Across the Seas
The Savage Wilderness
The Bear and the Wolf
Erik The Navigator
Erik's Clan

The Vengeance Trail

The Reconquista Chronicles
Castilian Knight
El Campeador
The Lord of Valencia

The Aelfraed Series
(Britain and Byzantium 1050 A.D. - 1085 A.D.)
Housecarl
Outlaw
Varangian

The Anarchy Series England 1120-1180
English Knight
Knight of the Empress
Northern Knight
Baron of the North
Earl
King Henry's Champion
The King is Dead
Warlord of the North
Enemy at the Gate

Magna Carta

The Fallen Crown
Warlord's War
Kingmaker
Henry II
Crusader
The Welsh Marches
Irish War
Poisonous Plots
The Princes' Revolt
Earl Marshal
The Perfect Knight

**Border Knight
1182-1300**
Sword for Hire
Return of the Knight
Baron's War
Magna Carta
Welsh Wars
Henry III
The Bloody Border
Baron's Crusade
Sentinel of the North
War in the West
Debt of Honour
The Blood of the Warlord
The Fettered King

**Sir John Hawkwood Series
France and Italy 1339- 1387**
Crécy: The Age of the Archer
Man At Arms
The White Company
Leader of Men

Lord Edward's Archer
Lord Edward's Archer
King in Waiting
An Archer's Crusade

Magna Carta

Targets of Treachery
The Great Cause

**Struggle for a Crown
1360- 1485**
Blood on the Crown
To Murder a King
The Throne
King Henry IV
The Road to Agincourt
St Crispin's Day
The Battle for France
The Last Knight
Queen's Knight

Tales from the Sword I
(Short stories from the Medieval period)

**Tudor Warrior series
England and Scotland in the late 14th and early 15th century**
Tudor Warrior
Tudor Spy

**Conquistador
England and America in the 16th Century**
Conquistador

Modern History

The Napoleonic Horseman Series
Chasseur à Cheval
Napoleon's Guard
British Light Dragoon
Soldier Spy
1808: The Road to Coruña
Talavera
The Lines of Torres Vedras
Bloody Badajoz

Magna Carta

The Road to France
Waterloo

The Lucky Jack American Civil War series
Rebel Raiders
Confederate Rangers
The Road to Gettysburg

Soldier of the Queen series
Soldier of the Queen

The British Ace Series
1914
1915 Fokker Scourge
1916 Angels over the Somme
1917 Eagles Fall
1918 We will remember them
From Arctic Snow to Desert Sand
Wings over Persia

Combined Operations series
1940-1945
Commando
Raider
Behind Enemy Lines
Dieppe
Toehold in Europe
Sword Beach
Breakout
The Battle for Antwerp
King Tiger
Beyond the Rhine
Korea
Korean Winter

Tales from the Sword II
(Short stories from the Modern period)

Other Books

Magna Carta

Great Granny's Ghost (Aimed at 9-14-year-old young people)

For more information on all of the books then please visit the author's website at www.griffhosker.com where there is a link to contact him or visit his Facebook page: GriffHosker at Sword Books

Milton Keynes UK
Ingram Content Group UK Ltd.
UKHW031951111224
3581UKWH00010B/345